Praise for the Grille

"Masterful misdirection coup... ... ...
beat, Linda Reilly has grilled up a winner for sure!"
— J. C. Eaton, author of the Sophie Kimball
Mysteries, the Wine Trail Mysteries, and the
Marcie Rayner Mysteries, for *Up to No Gouda*

"A well-crafted and fun start to a new series! Carly and her
crew serve mouthwatering grilled cheese sandwiches while
solving crime in a quaint Vermont town. Plenty of twists and
turns to keep you turning the pages and guessing the killer
to the very end."
— Tina Kashian, author of the Kebab Kitchen
Mysteries, for *Up to No Gouda*

"A delightful and determined heroine, idyllic small town,
and buffet of worthy suspects make this hearty whodunnit
an enticing start to a decidedly delectable new series! This
sandwich-centric cozy will leave readers drooling for more!"
— Bree Baker, author of the Seaside Café
Mysteries, for *Up to No Gouda*

Also in the
Grilled Cheese Mystery Series

Up to No Gouda

NO
PARM
NO
FOUL

A Grilled Cheese Mystery

LINDA REILLY

Poisoned Pen
PRESS

Published by Poisoned Pen Press, an imprint of Sourcebooks
P.O. Box 4410, Naperville, Illinois 60567-4410
(630) 961-3900
sourcebooks.com

Printed and bound in the United States of America.
KP 10 9 8 7 6 5 4 3 2 1

This book is for health care workers everywhere.

CHAPTER ONE

GRANT ROBINSON SWEPT THROUGH THE FRONT DOOR OF Carly's Grilled Cheese Eatery and scooted behind the counter. "It's over, Carly. I finally did it. I gave my notice at the sub shop."

The grilled cheese Carly Hale was flipping did a slight wobble. Grant, the twenty-year-old food aficionado who'd been Carly's part-time grill cook since she first opened, also worked part time at Sub-a-Dub-Sub, a sandwich shop located across the town square. Or rather, he *had* worked there.

Carly shifted the grilled cheese back onto her spatula, then placed it, butter side down, on the grill. "Wow, you really went through with it. What did Mr. Menard say? Was he upset?"

"Upset? From the steam coming out of his ears, I'd say he was like a water heater about to burst."

Using her spatula, Carly slid the Sweddar Weather—a grilled Swiss and cheddar on marble rye—onto her cutting board. She sliced it in half, transferred it to a plate, and added chips and pickles to the dish, along with a cup of tomato soup. The heady aroma of melted cheese and butter-grilled bread never failed to delight her. It was the primary reason she'd returned to her hometown of Balsam Dell, Vermont, and opened her grilled cheese eatery. She'd taken over the space where a failing, decades-old ice cream parlor had finally gone belly up.

The other factor that prompted her return to her hometown was the death of her husband two years earlier. To escape the memories and start a new life for herself, she came home, as she thought of it, and opened her dream business. Sharing her favorite comfort food and earning a living from it was the best of both worlds.

Carly glanced around the dining room. At a bit past 2:00, only one booth was taken. Its sole occupant was Steve Perlman, a fortysomething man sporting rimless eyeglasses, a paperback book in front of him. Mr. P., as Carly referred to him, had been one of her high school teachers. Physics, her least favorite subject, she recalled with a shudder. But he'd been an earnest young man then, passionate about science as well as a good teacher. When he spotted Grant, he waved. Grant returned the gesture with a big smile.

Carly had opened her eatery earlier in the year, and though summer had brought in visitors galore, it was autumn that was proving to be her busiest season. While leaf-peepers descended on the town in droves, it was the high school that was turning out to be her best source of customers. The kids, and even some teachers, had been invading her restaurant daily after the last bell rang. They scarfed down grilled cheese sandwiches and cheesy dippers with gusto while they droned on about the disgusting food in the school cafeteria.

"Why don't you tell me all about it later," Carly told Grant. "Right now, you can give me a break before the hungry hordes come in, okay? Suzanne had to leave early for a meeting with Josh's teacher."

Suzanne Rivers was Carly's other server. With a son in fourth grade, Suzanne normally worked from 11:00 a.m. to 3:00 p.m. so she could be home for Josh after school. Lately she'd been putting in some extra hours to help Carly get through the midday rush. It helped that Josh had signed up for a few after-school programs, so on most days it worked out perfectly.

"Say no more." Grant hustled through the swinging door that led into the kitchen. He returned moments later wearing a crisp apron and vinyl gloves.

Carly delivered the sandwich plate to her sole customer. "There you go, Mr. P., and sorry for the holdup. Need a coffee warm-up?"

"I'd love one." He picked up a sandwich half and aimed it toward his mouth. "And Carly, please stop calling me Mr. P. It's been a long time since you were in my physics class. 'Steve' will do just fine."

"Force of habit," Carly said with a smile. She returned and refilled his mug. "By the way, how did you manage to beat the kids here today? School doesn't get out till two-thirty."

Steve swallowed a bite of his sandwich. "I had a doctor appointment, so I took the afternoon off." He winked at her. "Good excuse, right? Plus, it gave me a chance to pick up a few sci-fi books from the library. I read at least three a week."

"Ah. Got it." She smiled as if to assure him his secret was safe with her.

Carly went back behind the counter. Grant looked dismayed as he wiped down the grill.

Carly knew him so well. She was sure he felt both guilt and relief at having ditched his job at the sub shop. The owner's lackadaisical approach to food hygiene had, apparently, finally pushed him over the edge. Although Grant had only recently turned twenty, he was more mature than most thirty-year-olds and had a passion for all things culinary. He was also a gifted cellist, but to his musical parents' dismay, he was determined to become a chef.

With Grant's help, Carly had added some inspired new sandwiches to their grilled cheese menu, including their most recent offering—Brie-ng on the Apples, Granny. The new autumn sandwich was made by grilling creamy Brie, thin-sliced Granny Smith apples, and cherry relish between slices of raisin bread. After its debut in early September, it quickly became an eatery favorite.

Grant had also helped her design their entry in the town's annual Halloween Scary-Licious Smorgasbord competition, which was only two days away. *Yikes.* Aside from supplying light sticks to kids for trick-or-treat night, it was Balsam Dell's only concession to Halloween.

It would be Carly's first time participating in the event, and she was feeling more excited as the day approached. The competition, sponsored by the town's recreation department, was held every year on the Saturday before Halloween. Tables were set up on the town green, and local restaurants gave out samples of their creepy culinary creations. Attendees voted—one vote per ticket. After all votes were tallied, the winner was awarded a $500 cash prize, along with the coveted plaque engraved with the restaurant's name. Carly had already chosen a spot for the plaque, should it be awarded to her eatery.

"Carly, we're probably gonna be mobbed soon, so I'll tell you what happened real quick." Grant winced, then spoke in a low voice. "Mr. Menard is blaming you for my quitting.

He thinks you put me up to squealing on him to the board of health."

"But…but…I would never do that! I would never try to influence you." She tried to keep her tone quiet, but she knew she'd hit a few high notes. Still, she was both aghast and furious at the man's accusations.

"I told him that. I defended you to the moon, but he kept ranting right over me." Grant shook his head. He looked worried. "At one point I got scared his heart would give out. He takes medication for it, even though he's only in his forties. His face got bright red, and he stumbled backward. His daughter, Holly, made him sit down and take a pill of some sort. She said he has angina."

"I'm sorry to hear that," Carly said. "I hope he's getting the proper care for it. But it doesn't give him the right to attack my character."

"It's weird," Grant said, looking puzzled. "He was blaming you more than he was me. Almost like…like he had a vendetta against you."

"I'm sure he was only lashing out," Carly said. "No doubt he's bummed about losing you right before the Halloween competition, but he has his daughter to help him. Once he calms down, he'll see that you had every right to give your notice and to tip off the board of health. Maybe it'll inspire him to clean up his act, right?"

Grant looked unsure. "Yeah, maybe."

"Hey, now that you're here, do you mind if I pop into the kitchen for a few? I need to make a call about my Halloween costume. I'm having it specially made for Saturday!"

"Take your time. I'll handle things here." He gave her a half-hearted smile.

Carly headed into her commercial kitchen. She fixed herself a quick cup of tea with one of the pumpkin spice teabags she'd bought earlier in the week. Though coffee was her normal comfort drink of choice, the Halloween season seemed to inspire cravings for anything pumpkin-spice-flavored.

She sat with her mug at the pine desk beneath the window that overlooked the small parking lot behind the eatery. Only four months earlier, she'd found a body out there. With her help, the murderer had been caught. Nonetheless, she hoped never to go through anything like that again. Pushing away the memory, she grabbed her cell phone and tapped a saved number.

"Miranda Busey. Can I help you?" came a squeaky, tired-sounding voice.

She sounded so young. Carly could hardly believe Miranda was a student who was taking design classes in college. "Hi, Miranda, it's Carly Hale. I'm just checking on my costume. Can I pick it up tonight?"

Carly and the man she'd been seeing, local electrician Ari Mitchell, were attending the Scary-Licious Smorgasbord competition dressed as Morticia and Gomez Addams. Ari's costume was finished, but Carly's required a slinky, lacy stretch of fabric over a full-length, gauzy black dress.

A long silence followed. "Miranda?" Carly prodded.

Miranda groaned. "Carly, I am so, *so* sorry. I was putting the zipper in the back of the lace overlay when my hand slipped and I tore the whole thing. I was so exhausted. I was practically seeing double. I was up almost all last night, sewing."

Carly's stomach dropped. She'd been counting on being

Morticia to Ari's Gomez. With his dark eyes and neatly trimmed mustache, he fit the part perfectly—and much more handsomely than any Gomez she'd ever seen.

"It...it can't be fixed?" Carly swallowed.

"Unfortunately, no. I had to send away for that lace fabric. Even if I had more of it, I'm jammed up the wazoo with more jobs to finish. I guess I took on more than I could handle."

"Can I wear the dress without the lace?"

"Only if you want the entire world to see your underwear." Miranda hesitated. "There's one thing I can offer, but I'm not sure you'll like it. I made a darling lady vampire costume for a customer who changed her mind. It's kind of a pale gray, with a filmy cape that extends out like bat wings. I think it'll fit you, and it's super pretty. Wanna try it?"

Carly was positive she didn't want the entire world to see her underwear. "Sure. I'll stop by after work and try it on."

Disappointed, Carly gulped the rest of her tea and returned to the dining room. As if a magic door had opened, in the short time she'd been gone nearly every booth had filled. The high school contingent had arrived.

A sudden burst of gratitude filled her.

With every passing week, her restaurant was gaining popularity. Only recently, an informal newspaper poll voted it one of the "coziest eateries" in southern Vermont. She had to admit, she agreed. With its exposed, pale brick walls, aqua vinyl booths, and chrome-edged counter lined with stools, it was exactly the way she'd hoped it would look when she first imagined the concept. In every booth, a vintage tomato soup can filled with faux flowers of the season graced the table. October's flowers were orange and yellow mums.

If she won the competition, it would add another feather

to her culinary cap, so to speak. With luck, that would trans-
late to an increase in business. It would be a perfect way to
usher in the start of the holiday season.

Ferris Menard had won the competition the past three
years in a row, according to Grant. It made Carly even more
determined to emerge as this year's winner.

At one of the rear booths, a former middle school class-
mate of Carly's—Stanley Henderson—sat with books and
notebooks spread over the table. These days he was preparing for the Realtor's exam and enjoyed reviewing his study
notes while he scarfed down a sandwich and a cola. His current job as a guidance counselor at the high school was no
longer "floating his boat," as he'd put it. He wanted to make
his own hours and be his own boss, not to mention earn
some serious commissions selling homes.

When he caught Carly's glance, he gave her a wide, pleasant wave. "Hi, Stan," she mouthed, then went behind the
counter.

In the booth behind Stan's, Evelyn Fitch, a retired English
teacher, sat with a book of crossword puzzles and a pink notepad. Carly had never had her as a teacher—she'd retired about
ten years too early. Now somewhere in her eighties, Ms. Fitch
spent at least three afternoons a week enjoying a late lunch of
a Vermont Classic—sharp cheddar on country white bread—
while she pored over a puzzle. "It's both my lunch and dinner,"
she'd told Carly one day, "which is why I always come here
midafternoon." Carly suspected it was more a case of the
lonely Ms. Fitch enjoying being around loads of people, but
she'd told her, "Good plan," and let it go at that.

Carly's heart skipped when she saw Ari seated on one of
the stools. She went over and leaned toward him. "Hey."

"Hey yourself." His smile warmed her, and she felt her cheeks grow pink. She gave him the bad news about the Morticia costume.

Ari reached over and squeezed her wrist. "Don't worry. It'll be fine," he soothed. "Actually, I'm sort of anxious, now, to see you in that lady vampire dress." His deep voice and stark gaze made her heart leap skyward again.

Carly grinned, and in the next moment the door to the restaurant swung open, hard. Ferris Menard stormed in, his blond brush cut gelled into porcupine quills, his face a scary shade of red. "Carly Hale," he boomed. He looked around, spotted her, and strode over to the counter. "Yeah, you. I heard about your little sabotage ploy. Well, it won't work—do you hear me?"

As if someone had turned off a switch, the dining room instantly quieted. Stunned by the verbal assault, Carly took a step backward. Grant, who had the protective instincts of a mother grizzly, moved to stand in front of her. "Mr. Menard," he said quietly, "what are you doing here?"

"My beef isn't with you, Grant. I know she put you up to it!"

"But—"

Carly shifted around Grant to face the man. "Ferris," she said tightly, "I will thank you to behave courteously in my establishment. Otherwise, you need to leave. Is that clear?"

"Oh, yeah? Well, I'll thank *you* to stop trying to ruin me." His small blue eyes blazed with fury. "I got a little visit from the health inspector this afternoon, but you already knew that, didn't you, *Miss Hale*. Unfortunately for you, I run a clean, sanitary operation. Oh sure, I got cited for one dumb thing, but it was ridiculously minor. As for this place"—his lip curled as his gaze flickered around the dining room—"suffice it to say, you wouldn't know an aged cheddar from a bale of hay. You're a fraud, and I'm going to prove it."

In the next instant, Stanley Henderson shot out of his booth and strode toward Menard, one fist curled at his side. Steve Perlman was right at his heels, and between the two of them, they blocked Menard's view of Carly.

With a shake of his head, Ari slid quietly off his stool. He went over to Menard and took him firmly by the arm, propelling him toward the door. "Time for you to go, Ferris."

Feigning bravado, Menard stumbled sideways a step, trying unsuccessfully to extract himself from Ari's grip. "Let go of me," he hissed. Spittle formed on his lips, and he swiped at it with his free hand.

"Wait a minute, Ari." Carly circled around all of them and moved to stand directly in front of Menard. "Ferris, I did nothing to sabotage you, as you put it. But if you ever come in here and accuse me again, you can expect a visit from Chief Holloway. Is that clear?" She turned to her would-be protectors. "Stanley, all of you, go back to your seats. I appreciate your help, but I can handle this myself. Besides, Ferris is leaving now. Aren't you, Ferris?"

The rage in Menard's expression was so dense it could have been sliced up and served on a buttered biscuit. Stan flinched, and Steve took a step backward.

Menard wrenched his arm away from Ari, who was edging him closer to the door. Then, with a shake of his fist, he stalked outside into the crisp October day.

CHAPTER TWO

"It was so embarrassing," Carly groaned to her bestie, Gina Tomasso. "First Ferris verbally attacking me, and then Stanley and Mr. P.—Steve—jumping out of their seats to come to my rescue, like I was some damsel in distress. I swear, if they'd had pitchforks and torches, they'd have chased Ferris into the street, like the villagers who went after the Frankenstein monster."

Carly was seated at Gina's kitchen table in the apartment upstairs from her restaurant. She'd stopped in after closing time to give her friend the lowdown on the day's events. Glancing around, she saw that Gina's digs were really shaping up. Though she'd moved in only five weeks earlier, Gina was filling it with every 1960s artifact she could find. Gina's mom, who'd died when she was nine, had loved the décor of that decade. Carly suspected that her friend was subconsciously choosing furnishings that would've pleased her.

Gina chuckled. "Well, at least they had your back, right? Gotta give them credit for that."

"They did," Carly admitted, "and I felt bad afterward for scolding them. I apologized later to both of them, and also to Ari and Grant, but they waved it off. Truth be told, I was relieved when Ari escorted Ferris to the door."

"It just infuriates me," Gina said darkly, "to think that

Menard barged in like that and caused a scene in front of all your customers. Personally, I'd have wanted to sock him in the snout."

"I draw the line at fisticuffs," Carly said dryly, "but don't think I wasn't tempted. Now, though, I'm almost dreading the competition on Saturday."

"Why? You didn't do anything wrong."

"I know, but now it feels like there's a dark cloud hanging over me in the shape of an angry Ferris Menard." With a slight shiver, Carly plucked a handful of candy corn from Gina's candy dish and funneled them into her mouth. "You should've heard the sarcasm in his voice when he called me *Miss Hale*. I couldn't tell if he was being intentionally formal or if he doesn't approve of a woman keeping her maiden name after marriage."

Gina waved a dismissive hand. "Probably the first one, but don't let him intimidate you. Every year, Ferris Menard enters the same thing in the competition, with only a slight variation. I'm *so* over his sub sandwiches shaped like reptiles or zombies."

Carly had heard about Ferris's triumphs. His sub shop was known for its special blend of dressing, created by Menard himself. It was used on all the cold subs they served.

Carly's own entry was going to be eye-catching, delicious, and tangy to the third power, as Grant had put it. In addition to the scrumptious grilled cheese he'd designed, he'd also created two dipping sauces—a ghoul green and a bloodred—both of which would be presented in hollowed out pumpkins.

Gina set her jaw and tucked a dark brown curl behind her ear. "If I were you, I'd just let Menard stew in his own juices.

Or rather," she snickered, "in his own oil and vinegar dressing, which he thinks is so special. Anyway, just cross the jerk off your list of worries."

"I know you're right, Gina. It's just—"

"It's just that men are pros at making women feel guilty," Gina interrupted tartly. "You remember my ex-husband?"

Oh, Carly surely did. It was his body she'd found in her parking lot at the beginning of the summer.

In fact, it was only after the discovery of Lyle's body that Carly's defunct friendship with Gina had been reignited. In high school, the girls had been almost inseparable—until a huge misunderstanding over Lyle's pursuit of Gina had severed their friendship. Gina had married Lyle straight out of high school but divorced him three years later. By then Carly was living with her husband, Daniel, in northern Vermont—a good two-hour plus ride from Balsam Dell. Neither woman had attempted to contact the other, a mistake they now both regretted.

These days, having resolved their conflict, their friendship was stronger than ever.

"Well, that was one of Lyle's specialties," Gina went on. "That and cheating. Are you sure you don't want a cup of coffee?"

"No, thanks. I have to stop by Miranda's and try on the vampire costume. Plus, I have a dog at home who doesn't tolerate tardiness." She grinned at the thought of Havarti, her sweet little Morkie, rushing to the door to greet her. Half Yorkie and half Maltese, he was perky and funny and perpetually ready to shower everyone he encountered with kisses.

"I thought Becca took him outside during the day?"

Becca Avery, an army veteran, was the live-in caretaker

for Carly's landlady, Joyce Katso. The pair lived in the apartment downstairs from Carly in Joyce's two-family home.

"She does, but Havarti has a sense of timing like you wouldn't believe. If I'm ten minutes later than usual, he does a circular dance around my feet and barks at my shoes."

Gina giggled. "I love that dog."

Carly glanced at the tangerine-colored Lucite clock on Gina's wall. "Hey, I've really gotta run." She hoisted her pumpkin-themed tote bag—a gift from Ari—onto her shoulder and rose. As she did, a folded slip of pink paper fell out of an outer pocket. Smiling, she picked it up and handed it to Gina. "Look at the note that adorable Evelyn Fitch left in her booth this afternoon after she paid her bill."

Gina unfolded the paper and read: "'Carly's food is tempting and tasty. Always stuffed with melted cheese. Remnants of cheddar sizzle and brown. Leaving a flavor so unimaginably fine. You'll return again for more.'" Gina's face softened. "Aw, it reads kind of like a poem, doesn't it?" She raised a dramatic hand to her heart. "Ode to Carly's Grilled Cheese." She grinned and tucked the note back into Carly's bag. "You really do have a loyal posse of customers."

"On a different subject, are you seeing Zach tonight?" Carly asked her in a teasing voice.

Gina and Zach Bartlett had been an item for about four months. His job as an account manager for a national delivery service kept him on the road a lot, but he and Gina managed to see each other every chance they got. So far, they seemed to be nuts about each other.

A fierce blush colored Gina's round cheeks. "Can't. I've

got a custom order for shower invitations that has me burning the midnight oil."

Gina owned a shop aptly dubbed What a Card—a gorgeous card shop located opposite the town green in the next block. Having mastered the technique of quilling, Gina was constantly filling demands for her custom-made cards—especially shower and wedding invitations. Carly worried that sometimes she took on too much work, but Gina never complained, even when she had grueling deadlines.

"So anyway, tomorrow night," Gina explained, "Zach and I are gonna see some new scary movie. I hope I don't scream as loud as I did at the last one. I felt like a total wuss."

"Not to worry. I'm sure Zach'll save you from any zombies."

"Are you kidding? He screamed louder than I did."

Carly laughed. "Later!" She waved and bounded down the stairs and outside to car.

~

The vampire dress fit Carly to a tee. And, she had to admit, added a touch of sex appeal without her having to work for it. The pale-gray satin hugged her form without being overly snug. When she extended her arms upward, the filmy cape swept around her like shimmering bat wings.

To help her celebrate her first year entering the competition, Ari had bought her a pair of sterling silver spiderweb earrings. More whimsical than creepy, they would work just as well for a lady vampire as they would for Morticia. The fact that they were a gift from Ari made them that much more special.

Carly carefully removed the dress and slipped it over a hanger. She hung it in her closet—away from Havarti's curious black nose and prying paws. A pleasant little zing of electricity went through her.

Which is appropriate, she thought with a tiny smile. Something told her that Ari, her very own electrician, was also going to feel a zing when her saw her.

Carly's thoughts drifted to her first husband, Daniel Brownell, who'd died in a tragic accident in January of the previous year. Daniel'd been working as a lineman for the power company and Carly as the restaurant manager at a historic inn. Exhausted after returning home from an eighteen-hour shift repairing downed lines, Daniel had made a fateful decision—to deliver firewood to a family in desperate need. Over Carly's pleas to wait until morning, he'd loaded his pickup, promised to return soon, and drove off into the snowstorm.

That was the last time Carly saw him. His truck, overburdened with logs, had skidded off an ice-covered bridge and tumbled down an embankment.

After months of moving robotically through her daily tasks, including her job at the Ivory Swan Inn, she made the decision to return to her hometown. A prime commercial space in the heart of the quaint downtown had become available, and it was time, she'd decided, to invest in her longtime dream of opening a grilled cheese eatery.

As for Ari, the fact that he was kind and caring and infinitely patient added several checkmarks to his "plus" column. If Ari had any serious faults, they hadn't yet bubbled to the surface.

Carly had just fed Havarti his evening meal of kibble when her cell rang.

"Hey, Mom!"

"What's this I hear about Ferris Menard harassing you this afternoon?"

"Wow, not even a 'hello' first?"

Rhonda Hale Clark and her hubby, Gary, had made Carly's life complete when they left Florida at the end of the summer and moved back to Vermont—permanently. The bugs, the occasional stray alligator, and the ceaseless air conditioning had finally gotten to Rhonda. When she announced to Gary they were moving back home, he'd smiled and replied, "Anything you say, dear."

"I'm sorry, honey." Rhonda puffed out a breath. "But I saw blood red when I heard from Evelyn Fitch's daughter what happened today! She volunteers with me at the library, you know. By the way, she told me how much her mom loves eating at your place."

"Evelyn's one of my favorites." With her free hand, Carly removed a bottle of apple cider from her fridge. "She wrote me a darling note today."

"That's lovely, but do you want me to have a word with Ferris? I'm pretty handy at putting the fear of eternal damnation into people."

"As Norah and I well know," Carly said wryly. Norah was Carly's older sister by two years, and they'd both experienced the force of their mom's scare tactics. "Honestly, don't worry about it, Mom. I'm not giving it a second thought. Really."

"Harrumph! That's a fib and you know it."

After several minutes of cajoling, Carly managed to soothe her mom's nerves. She was taking a sip of the sweet, delicious cider when she heard the rumble of a noisy car engine outside in her driveway.

Carly hurried over to her front window, Havarti trotting at her heels. She peered out into the dark. In the driveway, Becca Avery's massive vintage Lincoln hunkered like a primitive beast to the right of Carly's green Corolla. Behind Carly's vehicle, a smallish car idled loudly. Maybe Becca and Joyce had ordered takeout, Carly thought, and the delivery person had a defective muffler.

Carly watched for another minute or so. When no one came out of the house, she slipped on her jacket, then headed down the stairs and out the front door.

The night air was cold and crisp, redolent of decaying leaves and chimney smoke. She'd barely reached the bottom step when the porch light snapped on. Seconds later a car door slammed, and the noisy vehicle backed out of the driveway with a roar. Then it turned and barreled toward the center of town at a seriously fast clip.

Flashlight in hand, Becca hurried up beside Carly. An army veteran, she was always on high alert to anything happening in the neighborhood.

"Who was that?" Becca asked her, scanning the area with the beam from her flashlight.

"I don't have a clue. I thought maybe someone was delivering takeout to you and Joyce." Carly rubbed her arms and shivered.

Becca shook her head. "We had takeout last night. Whoever that was, they should invest in a new muffler," she said tartly. She took in a long, deep breath, then jogged over to the back of Carly's vehicle. Carly followed her.

"I knew I smelled paint. Look at this," Becca said, aiming her beam at Carly's trunk.

"Oh!" Carly gasped.

The image of a grinning skull gleamed with fresh, sparkly white paint. Tiny curlicues around the hollowed-out eyes suggested the skull was supposed to be female. At the bottom of the image, the paint had dribbled off. The artist probably panicked when the porch light went on and fled before he, or she, got caught.

Carly's heart hammered her rib cage. Who would do something like this?

The name dropped into her head without a second's hesitation. *Ferris Menard*. Did he even know where she lived?

Probably. Since her return a year earlier, she'd learned that nothing much stayed private. Balsam Dell was a small, close-knit community. Most everyone in town knew Carly rented the top floor of Joyce Katso's home. And since the house had been in the Katso family since the early 1900s, Joyce was somewhat of a local fixture.

"You need to report this, Carly." Becca's expression was somber.

"Do you really think so? What if it was just a prank?" she offered weakly. "Halloween *is* only four days away."

"Maybe, but—" Becca shook her head and slung an arm loosely around Carly's shoulder. "But it's better to be safe than sorry, right?" Her words were heavy with meaning. Becca was no doubt remembering Carly's near fatal encounter with a killer four months earlier.

"You're right," Carly agreed with a sigh.

Becca called the police from her cell, then took a few pictures of the graffiti. She texted the pics to Carly, and a few minutes later a patrol car swung in. The officer took statements from both women and promised to file a report. He didn't offer much in the way of hope that they'd nab the vandal. The loud engine was probably the best clue, so he advised them to keep their ears peeled for any such vehicles. Before he left, he snapped a photo of the offending image with his phone. "Looks like water-based paint," he said before he left. "It should come right off with some nail polish remover, or maybe even soap and water since it hasn't dried yet."

After Carly thanked Becca for her help, she bade her good night. Then she fetched a pail of soapy water and made quick work of eradicating the gruesome image.

She'd purposely stopped herself from telling Becca about the confrontation with Ferris in her restaurant that afternoon. Why drag anyone else into her pool of worries? Taking care of Joyce, who was challenged with MS, and studying to earn a degree as a licensed nursing assistant, kept Becca busy enough.

After securely locking her apartment door, Carly swept Havarti into her arms. "Well," she told him wearily, "I don't think much more could happen today, do you?" Havarti licked her nose in response.

When her cell rang, she set Havarti on the sofa. She smiled at the name on the screen. "Hey, Suzanne, what's up?"

"Oh, Carly, I hate to tell you this. I fell and sprained my ankle this afternoon when I was helping Jake put up a curtain rod in the bathroom. The doctor said I need to stay off it for a week!"

Carly flopped onto the sofa next to Havarti, squelching the urge to scream. After offering Suzanne healing hugs and instructing her to take proper care of herself, she disconnected the call.

First Ferris's verbal attack, then the graffiti painted on her car, and now Suzanne's accident.

If the universe was trying to mess with her head, it was doing one heck of a good job.

CHAPTER THREE

CARLY HAD AWAKENED TO A PERFECT SATURDAY MORN-
ing—at least as far as the Scary-Licious Smorgasbord was
concerned. Clear blue skies and wispy clouds heralded a dry,
sunny autumn day.

The competition would begin at 11:00 and end at 3:00.
That gave the judges sufficient time to tally the votes and
announce the winner before dark, which was slipping in earlier every day.

Halloween season was, by far, Carly's favorite time of
year. For her, it was a surefire "treat" before the days grew
shorter and colder. She was anxious to see all the costumes
people would be wearing. Her own costume was hanging
in the coat closet. As soon as she and Grant were ready to
set up on the green, she'd slip into the restroom and put
it on.

Grant had agreed to meet her at the restaurant at 8:00
a.m. sharp to help prepare for the event. Judging from
past years, he'd estimated they'd need about two hundred
fifty of the mini sandwiches they'd be grilling throughout the competition. Not only would each one be made
with pumpkin bread—it would also be pumpkin-shaped.
Carly's mom had donated one of the cookie cutters from
her vast collection.

"This bread is fantastic," Grant said. "There's only a touch of pumpkin, so it's not sweet and it doesn't overpower the cheese. And the pale-gold color is perfect."

Sara Hardy, the bread baker who supplied all the artisan breads for Carly's eatery, had created the pumpkin bread recipe especially for her.

"I'm really going to miss my mom," Carly said with a sigh, glancing at her mom's cookie cutter as she removed Grant's homemade dips from the commercial fridge. "Gary's favorite niece is getting married this afternoon, so it's not like she can skip the wedding."

"Lousy timing, but I'm sure they'll enjoy the wedding. I wonder how Suzanne is doing," he said, feeding chunks of extra sharp orange cheddar into a shredder. They'd decided to use shredded cheese, not only for ease of preparation but for faster melting. "Is she taking pain medication for her ankle?"

"Only ibuprofen." Carly set two hollowed-out pumpkins on the worktable in the kitchen. Grant had carved faces in each—one scary and one smiley. He'd prepared a guacamole dip for the scary pumpkin and a spicy marinara for the smiley one. "Her ankle's not so much painful as it is annoying. She has to wear one of those clunky orthopedic boots."

"Oh boy. She must hate that."

"She's not a happy camper, as they say."

Over the summer, Suzanne had reunited with her almost ex-husband, and their marriage was on a path to healing. Recently, they'd rented a house that they hoped eventually to buy.

Carly set a glass bowl in each of the pumpkins. "I'm thinking we should keep the reserves of our dipping sauces in our fridge. When we start to get low, one of us can run across the street for more. Gina said she and Zach can act as gofers."

"Cool. Is she home right now?"

"I haven't seen her this morning. I think she stayed at Zach's last night. I meant to ask you, Grant. Did you help Ferris Menard last year when he entered his sub sandwiches in the competition?"

"Yeah." Grant made a face. "Even though he won, it was a nightmare getting ready for it. That whole week we were prepping for it, he was constantly screaming orders at me and Holly—that's his daughter. Made us both crazy."

"Any idea what he's making this year?"

"He's doing another version of the dragon bites he did last year. Only this time he's using wraps instead of sub rolls. And, of course, his *famous* dressing." Grant's words held a touch of sarcasm.

"You don't think they'll be good?"

"It's not that. Mr. Menard's been acting *really* weird for the last few weeks. On a good day he's like a grenade ready to explode, but lately it's been different. Something's definitely bugging him. Even his daughter's been tiptoeing around him."

Carly wondered if that explained Ferris's outburst on Thursday. "Do you regret quitting?"

"No way. Don't even think that, Carly. I'm *so* glad I'm out of there."

When the preparations were done, Carly headed into the restroom first to don her costume.

Grant grinned when he saw Lady Dracula emerge. "My gosh, you look so cool, Carly. You even drew bite marks on your neck!"

She'd also brushed baby powder over her face and neck

to simulate an "undead" look. On one side of her neck, she'd drawn two "bloody" holes with lip liner, and she'd outlined her lips in black.

"Thanks. I like it too." She especially loved the spiderweb earrings Ari had bought for her.

When it was Grant's turn to change, Carly gasped. Atop his short dreads he'd attached a curly black wig that trailed down his back, a la Prince. Over a ruffled white shirt, he wore a long purple coat, with black leather pants and boots completing the look.

"You look amazing," Carly squealed. "Straight out of *Purple Rain*!"

By the time they packed up their food and supplies and reached their assigned spot on the town green, Ari had already set up their table. *Reliable and efficient*, Carly thought. *Another checkmark in the plus column.*

He'd also set up the large portable griddle they'd be using. When he saw Carly approaching, his eyes danced. "Bless my soul, you are the prettiest vampire I've ever seen." He came over and squeezed her in a firm hug, holding her for a beat longer than usual. Then he planted a featherlight kiss on her powdered cheek.

"Thank you, Ari," she said, hoping the flush in her cheeks wouldn't bleed through the baby powder. She took a step back and stared at him. "And you—you switched costumes! How did you find a vampire getup so fast?"

"It's actually only a cape with a turned-up collar. The black pants are mine. I called three costume places until I finally lucked out. One of them still had a few vampire capes in stock." He grinned, and his brown-eyed gaze burned into hers. "Now you and I are an authentic undead couple."

Something in his tone made Carly's insides go all squiggly. She was impressed that he'd taken time from his busy schedule to hunt down a costume that would complement hers.

That "plus" column just keeps growing...

By 11:00, the town green was bustling with goblins, ghosts, princesses, and wizards. Thirteen local restaurant owners were participating in the competition. The tables were set up in neat rows on the green. A large placard attached to the front of each one advertised the name of the eatery, along with its assigned number. Carly's number was 12—the month of her mom's birthday. She hoped it would bring her good luck.

Gina showed up with Zach shortly after 11:00. Dressed as plain M&M's and peanut M&M's, they bustled around Carly and Grant's table, taking turns with Ari at cleaning up used plates, emptying trash, and replenishing supplies.

"These things are like, ridiculous," Gina gushed, rescuing a blob of gooey orange cheddar from her cheesy, pumpkin-shaped sandwich. "I'd better not eat any more or you'll run out."

Carly smiled at her friend and slid another grilled cheese onto an orange paper plate. The line at her table ebbed and flowed, but she and Grant managed to keep up with the demand without any serious backups.

"This is *so* much more fun than last year," Grant said, piling shredded cheese onto a row of cutouts.

He was so focused on his task that he didn't notice the young, full-figured woman with blond sausage curls waving at him from a few feet away. Over a frilly, long-sleeved white blouse, she wore a flouncy blue jumper. Her feet were clad in black leather patents so shiny they gleamed in the sunlight. She sidled in closer to Carly's table. "Hey, Grant."

Grant looked up. "Oh, hi, Holly," he said with a polite smile.

Holly. So this was Ferris's daughter.

Avoiding eye contact with Carly, the young woman stared hungrily at the offerings on their table.

A tiny hobgoblin of suspicion slithered into Carly's brain. Was the woman spying for her dad? Or did she genuinely come over only to say hello to Grant?

Seeing Holly's glum expression, Carly instantly felt bad. "Would you like to try one?" She slid a cheesy sandwich onto a paper plate.

With a nod, Holly accepted the treat, then snagged a condiment cup filled with "guts" dip—aka guacamole—from a tray. Carly had set out the cups so that people wouldn't be tempted to dip their sandwiches into the condiment-filled pumpkins.

Holly's blue eyes widened after the first bite. "This is awesome." She swallowed another huge bite, then turned and shot a quick, worried look behind her. "Grant, I have to go. If you want to come back, Dad says all is forgiven, okay?"

Grant looked pained. "Holly, I can't." He turned his attention back to the grill. "I-I have to work now. Sorry."

Holly's face fell. Clutching the meager remains of her cheesy pumpkin, she dashed off into the throng.

So that was her mission, Carly thought with annoyance. *To lure Grant back into the fold.*

They continued grilling and serving, and Carly was pleased to see a few of her regulars stroll over to her table. Evelyn Fitch came by and introduced her daughter, Lydia, an attractive brunette who was a younger version of her mom. Both women sported cat ears, and they each taste-tested a cheesy grilled pumpkin. "The best so far!" Evelyn pronounced, with a resounding thumbs-up.

Carly leaned toward Evelyn and said quietly, "Thank you for the note you left. I loved it."

Evelyn beamed and ambled off with her arm looped through her daughter's. Moments later, Stan Henderson, dressed as a roguish pirate, waved at Carly as he approached her table. "Whoa. I knew you'd have the best treats!" His eager smile faltered a bit when Ari came up behind Carly. "Hey, Ari, how's it going?"

"Great, Stan. Enjoying the festivities?"

"Aw, you bet. This is one of my favorite days of the year. Can I cheat and have two?"

"Not a problem," Carly said, handing him a plate.

Accepting his double order, Stan looked like a kid who'd just been given carte blanche to plunder a candy store. He swallowed a huge bite, his eyes closed in apparent bliss. When he opened them again his smile was wide, his hazel-eyed gaze locked on Carly. "These are going to win, Carly. Hands down."

"I hope so, Stan. Keep your fingers crossed for me."

Moments after Stan walked away, Carly spotted Don Frasco. Don was the sole owner of the *Balsam Dell Weekly*, a free paper that published more ads than news. He'd earned some recognition early in the summer for his role in putting away a local crime ring. He sported an auburn goatee that matched his eyes and an old-style fedora with a large "Press Pass" pinned to it.

"Hey," he said, snapping a photo of her and Grant. "Nice spread. Too bad I hate cheese."

Too bad indeed, Carly thought dryly as he moved on. One thing about Don, he was blunt with his opinions.

Carly was pleased when Suzanne's husband and son came by to sample her offerings. She greeted them warmly and handed each a sandwich.

"Mom is like, so bummed that she couldn't make it here," Josh mumbled over a mouthful of melted cheese.

"How's she doing today?" Carly asked them.

"Better, but she's cursing herself for being a klutz. Her words, not mine," he added quickly. "She's worried about how you guys'll be able to handle the restaurant without her."

"Not that we won't miss her, but we'll be fine," Carly assured him. "Tell her to stop worrying and stay off her ankle. "

In truth, it was going to be a challenge for her and Grant to do everything without Suzanne. Carly was half tempted to contact a temp agency to see if they could send in a ringer for a few days.

By 2:30, things had quieted down. The noise level had dropped from a jumbled cacophony to a low drone. Either everyone had eaten their fill, or the chilly air was sending them inside to warm up. Carly noticed a short line at the ballot box, where participants were dropping in their votes.

Like most of the other restaurateurs who participated in the competition, Carly had closed her eatery for the entire day. Once the winner was announced, they'd pack up their table and return any perishables to the restaurant, after which everyone could go home. She and Ari had a quiet evening planned—Chinese food at her apartment, followed by a classic horror movie. And, with any luck, they'd be popping open the bottle of champagne she'd stashed in the fridge to celebrate her eatery's win.

Grant had packed up the remaining supplies—they'd brought more than they needed—and he and Ari began lugging them back to the eatery. Carly was getting antsy for the judges to tally the votes and announce this year's winner. Each person who paid for a ticket was entitled to one vote. Votes were deposited in a tamper-proof box and would be counted promptly at 3:00 p.m.

Carly was also itching to know how Ferris Menard's dragon bites looked and tasted. For obvious reasons, she didn't dare go within twenty feet of his table. And he no doubt knew that Gina and Carly were best buds.

Hmmm…

Gina came over and whispered to Carly, "I'm taking a quick bathroom break. Need anything before I go?"

"No, but is Zach up for a little spying? I want to see what Menard is giving out."

Gina grinned. "Say no more."

Ten minutes later, a triumphant Zach strolled casually back to Carly's table carrying a greasy white paper plate. "Got one." Taking her and Gina aside, he lifted a napkin off his plate. "Way too oily, and wraps don't really slay me. But the cold cuts are good, sliced thin the way I like them, and this one's packed with mozzarella. The edible eyeballs"—he shrugged—"nothing special. Anyone can hollow out an olive to make an eyeball."

Without tasting it, Carly had to agree. The visual was nothing to write home about, and in her mind, a greasy plate was far from appetizing. "What about the salad dressing?" she pressed.

"Again, it's good, but I wouldn't give it a ringing endorsement."

"Which is interesting," Gina pointed out. "Because I heard that Menard's soon-to-be-ex-wife started bottling the stuff and selling it under her own brand. Supposedly, she tweaked the formula to make it spicier. And...get this. She made a deal to sell the modified recipe to a boutique spice company. For some pretty serious bucks too."

"Really?" Carly marveled at friend's never-ending supply of local intel. "Gina, where do you hear this stuff?"

"Same place as usual. My aunt Lil at the Happy Clipper."

Carly smiled as she mulled over this latest bit of news. A hair washer at the local beauty salon, Gina's elderly, lavender-haired aunt collected more tidbits of information than an FBI bugging device. "I can't imagine that Ferris is too thrilled about *that* development."

"According to Portia, he's furious over it. Portia's his almost-ex," Gina explained. "I think—uh oh." She swallowed. "Speak of the devil. And I do mean that literally."

A man wearing red devil's horns came barreling in Carly's direction. Ferris Menard's face, nearly the same shade of scarlet as his long, flowing cape, was contorted with anger.

"Why you little witch," he said ferociously. "Sending your minion"—he aimed a thumb at Zach—"to steal my food so you could analyze it? You are the lowest of the low, you know that?" He used a few expletives that sent Carly reeling.

Zach moved in closer to Menard. "First of all," he said, his voice deceivingly soft, "no one *stole* your food. I sampled your dragon bites as part of the competition. I paid for my ticket and I'm entitled to one vote, which means I get to taste the entries. And second, you can keep your foul language to yourself. Got it?"

Carly stared at Zach. When had the mild-mannered account manager grown fangs?

"It's all right, Zach," Carly said evenly, refusing to be baited. "He knows full well he sent his daughter over to spy on me too."

"The reason my daughter came over here," he sniped, "was to say hi to Grant. That's *it*. And she only ate one of those leaky pumpkin things to be polite."

Leaky pumpkin things? Like the one she practically inhaled?

In the next instant, Ari and Grant came up behind the women. Ari's dark brown eyes blazed, and his smile was anything but cordial. "I see you're overstepping your bounds again, Ferris. Do you need an escort back to your table?"

Menard glared at Ari but didn't respond.

Carly took a step closer to her nemesis. Flashing him the sincerest smile she could muster, she said, "The votes will be counted soon, Ferris. If you win, I will personally come over and congratulate you. If I happen to win, I'd like you to do the same for me. Deal?" She held out one hand as a gesture of goodwill.

He glared at her proffered hand as if it were a dead rat. Then he told her to go to a hot place, turned on his heel, and stomped back over to his table.

~

By 3:10, the crowd was buzzing with anticipation. Gina frowned up at the makeshift podium where the town's recreation director, Teresa Gray, was deep in conversation with a bespectacled young man. "I wonder what's taking so long," Gina groused to Carly. "By now they've usually announced the winner."

"Patience," Carly teased her friend.

The mic squeaked. Everyone's eyes went to the podium. Ms. Gray, her expression oddly blank, spoke in an even tone. "Good afternoon, everyone. I would first like to extend a huge *thank you* to everyone who participated in this year's Halloween competition—not only the chefs but those of you who purchased tickets and voted. We saw some wonderful offerings and tasted some mighty delicious treats this year, didn't we?" She paused for a brief clapping of hands and a handful of cheers. "Best of all, we raised over one thousand dollars, five hundred of which will be awarded to the winner. The remainder will be gifted to local food banks. As for this year's winner—"

Grant grinned over at Carly with crossed fingers.

"We have counted the votes. *Twice*," Ms. Gray emphasized. "Unfortunately, due to a mix-up, we are not yet ready to announce the winner."

"*What?*" Gina blurted.

A nervous hum went through the crowd. "Whaddya mean, mix-up?" someone squawked.

Carly caught Ari's worried look and said, "Has this ever happened before?"

"Not since I've been attending."

Ms. Gray fingered the mic nervously. "We hope to have an announcement by later this evening. Please check our Facebook event page for updates. Thank you." She turned and scurried away as if she'd spotted a mouse.

Grumbles and moans rose from all the people who'd

gathered to hear the winner's name. Carly didn't know how to process what had just happened. Her first year entering the competition and they'd encountered a glitch.

Don Frasco came up next to Ari and Carly, his eyes glittering. "Don't say where you heard it," he said, "but the reason they can't announce the winner is that someone stuffed the ballot box with illegal votes."

Carly's mouth opened but nothing came out. Though she knew it sounded crazy, she couldn't help wondering if her first entry into the competition had brought bad luck to the entire town.

CHAPTER FOUR

"MY FIRST COMPETITION, AND IT WAS RIGGED," CARLY groaned to Ari. She slipped a tiny bit of chicken, *sans* the fried coating, to the little dog gazing up at her with pleading brown eyes.

They were at Carly's apartment, picking at the remains of their Chinese food feast. Carly had changed out of her vampire costume into a fuzzy-knit, pumpkin-colored sweater and black jeans. Ari had removed his Dracula cape and stashed it in the back of his pickup.

In keeping with their usual practice of cost sharing, it'd been Ari's turn to treat, and they'd gone with the crab rangoon, the sweet and sour chicken, the vegetable lo mein, and the pork fried rice. Carly added a bottle of chilled sauvignon blanc, which she'd been saving for just such an evening. In spite of the delicious meal, not to mention the charming company, she felt decidedly out of sorts.

Ari gave her a sympathetic look. "I know it's disappointing, honey, but eventually they'll straighten it out. Once they do, I'm willing to bet they'll find out that you won." He gave her a smile clearly meant to be encouraging, but Carly's heart felt heavy.

An hour earlier, she'd gotten a call from the recreation director further explaining the situation. During the counting of the votes, they'd discovered the number of votes removed from the ballot box had exceeded, by a total of twelve, the number of tickets sold. At this stage, it was impossible to determine which were the illegal votes, but they were determined to resolve the mystery. Those twelve votes had pushed Sub-a-Dub-Sub into the winner's category, but it was unclear if those were the phony votes. The cheater, whoever it was, had used a photocopier to reproduce the original ballot and print out additional ones. Unfortunately, it had been easy to do. The original votes had been printed on plain white paper.

"Ms. Gray said they don't have any idea who did this," Carly had told Ari. "Not yet, anyway. They're going to start an investigation. She's confident they'll figure out who the culprit is, but I'm not so sure."

Ari reached over and wrapped his hand around hers. "The organizers have always done a great job, Carly. I'd be willing to bet it won't take them long to figure out who tried to cheat. Someone must have seen the fraudster copy that ballot. Maybe in the library or in a local office somewhere. Who knows? Menard himself might have a copier in his restaurant."

Carly made a scrunched-up face, then gave up a reluctant smile. "I know. I'm being a whiny baby, aren't it?"

"Not in the least. You have every right to be ticked off." He leaned over and kissed her nose, then delivered their empty plates to the sink.

"Ms. Gray said they're going to examine every vote to see if they can figure out which are the bogus ones."

Together they cleaned up the rest of the dishes and put the leftovers in the fridge. After finishing off the wine, they shared a humongous, mummy-shaped frosted sugar cookie from Sissy's Bakery. In keeping with the theme, they curled up together on Carly's sofa and watched the 1959 version of *The Mummy*. Havarti, acting as canine chaperone, nestled between them. Despite rolling their eyes at the cornier parts of the movie, they agreed it had undeniable vintage appeal.

After they watched the highlights of the eleven o'clock news, Ari wrapped Carly in a massive hug and bade her good night. "I had a wonderful day and a terrific evening," he told her huskily. "But you're super tired. I can see it in those beautiful green eyes."

Carly smiled at him and stroked his cheek with the back of her fingers. "I can't deny that. It's been a day, hasn't it? Thanks for everything, Ari."

"No thanks are needed. I'll call you in the morning, okay? Maybe by then we'll have some answers."

Carly leaned into him for another long kiss, then reluctantly closed the door, locking it behind him.

She was trying mightily to take Ari's advice and trust in the process, but it wasn't easy. The idea that someone would attempt to skew the results of the competition still felt like a sliver of wood wedged under her thumbnail.

Was Menard involved?

It was hard to believe he wasn't.

"Things will look brighter in the morning," she told Havarti over a huge yawn. Only half believing it, she lifted him into her arms and squeezed him to her chest.

The dog gave her a quizzical look, then licked her cheek.

"Don't worry," she said. "Regardless of how it turns out, it won't affect your lifestyle. You'll still get everything your little canine heart desires."

~

The jingle of her cell phone jerked Carly out of a half sleep. Rolling to one side, she peered over Havarti's furry head and glanced at her bedside clock.

6:56 a.m.

Who in the name of galloping goldfish was calling her on a Sunday at this unforgiving hour?

She fumbled for the phone and blinked at it through filmy eyes. Rhonda Hale Clark's smiling visage beamed at her from the screen. Carly swiped open the call. "M-Mom?"

"He's dead," Rhonda bleated through the phone. "Ferris Menard is dead!"

Carly jerked upright. The sudden jolt sent Havarti scurrying off the bed. "What do you mean, he's dead? You mean dead as in, he didn't really win the competition?"

"I mean dead as in, he's never going to wake up again."

Carly sucked in a gasp. A lump landed in her gut like a block of lead.

"I'm heading over to your apartment now with breakfast. Norah's coming too. And you'd better get dressed. Chief Holloway will be right on my tail if he doesn't get there first."

"Wait a minute. What does Chief Holloway have to do with—" Before Carly could complete her question, her mom disconnected.

Ferris must have died from a heart attack, Carly reasoned. Hadn't Grant mentioned that he was on ticker medication?

Throwing on a pair of jeans and a warm sweatshirt, Carly hurried into the bathroom and scrubbed her face. After turning up the heat a notch, she headed into the kitchen. Havarti was wagging his tail as he danced around his food bowl, but first things first. She clipped on his leash, put on a warm jacket, and escorted him outside into the yard for a bathroom visit.

The early morning air was chilly, damp with a slight mist. Her head spun with questions: Was Ferris really dead? Had his heart given out? Or had her mom gotten hold of some bad information?

Back in the kitchen, she poured kibble into Havarti's dish and replenished his water. At the sound of footsteps clomping up her stairs, she raced to her door. Luckily, she now had a peephole that allowed her to check out visitors. Ari had installed it over the summer after her encounter with a killer.

She aimed an eyeball into the opening. "Thank goodness," Carly breathed, letting her mom and Norah in.

Rhonda Hale Clark, her brunette hair pulled back neatly from her face and secured with a decorative black comb, looked as crisp as ever at barely 7:00 in the morning. "Good morning, dear." Rhonda deposited a pink bakery box into Carly's hands. "Take these and set them out on a plate, would you please? Norah, bring the coffee into the kitchen."

A few strands of Norah's usually perfect blond hair stuck out haphazardly as she rolled her eyes, threw Carly an air kiss, and shuffled into the kitchen with a yawn. In her hands she carried a cardboard holder with four covered cups tucked into the cutouts.

Four cups?

"Mom, what's going on?" They followed the trail of caffeine into the kitchen. "Is Ferris Menard really dead?"

Norah grimaced. "He'd better be, for Mom to get me up at this hour."

"Norah!" Carly's mom scolded. "That's a terrible thing to say."

Carly wanted to scream. "Will someone please fill me—" A knock at the door interrupted her. "Oh, for the love of daffodils in December, who's here now?" She went over to the door and pulled it open. "Oh, hi Chief."

Police Chief Fred Holloway removed his hat, displaying a head full of thick gray hair. "Good morning, Carly. May I come in?"

The chief was a longtime family friend. His wife, before she passed, had been in Rhonda's book club, and his daughter, Doctor Anne, was Havarti's veterinarian.

"Sure, why not?" She sighed. "My mom and sister are already here. I think they brought you a coffee."

"That's thoughtful of them. I called your mom first so I wouldn't have to alarm you with an early morning call."

Which made not an ounce of sense. Any early morning call would alarm her, regardless of the caller. She wondered if he'd wanted her mom there to help soften the bad news about Ferris. "Chief, I need to know what happened."

They sat around Carly's table, each with a cup of steaming coffee. Only Norah, not a fan of breakfast, passed on the pink box full of donuts.

After fortifying himself with a long gulp of black coffee, the chief sighed. He reached down to pet Havarti, who was vigorously sniffing his knees. "I'm sorry to confirm that Ferris Menard is dead. His daughter found him this morning in the restaurant. He was on the floor, face up, clearly not breathing."

Carly shivered. "Oh, no, that's terrible news. Sadly,

though, it doesn't surprise me. Grant told me Ferris was on heart medication. He obviously had cardiac issues."

The chief nodded slowly, but then his jaw hardened. "Which doesn't, I'm afraid, account for the steak knife that was found jabbed into his chest."

The chunk of cinnamon cruller Carly had just swallowed stopped in its tracks. She managed to choke it back with a slug of coffee, but it still felt lodged in her throat. She looked at everyone in horror. "Mom, did you know about this before you got here?"

"I did," Rhonda said quietly. "But I wanted Fred to be the one to tell you."

"Chief," Carly said with a gulp, "are you saying Ferris was murdered?"

"As best we can piece it together, it looks that way. Turns out Menard was taking medication for angina. His pill bottle, the one with his nitroglycerin tabs, was found on the floor, sitting upright, but out of his reach. One of the investigators has a working theory. He thinks that during his scuffle with the killer, Menard suffered an attack of angina and tried to get to his medication. The killer taunted him by setting it just out of his reach and waited until he…*expired* to stick the knife in his chest. It's only a theory, and at this stage we're far from proving it. There was one other critical finding, but we're not releasing that information."

"But why would the killer stab him if he was already dead?" Carly asked him.

"Again," the chief said wearily, "it's only an early theory, but the investigator believes the steak knife was added post-mortem, for effect. There was very little blood around the point of insertion."

Post-mortem. Point of insertion.

Carly felt her head swim. She pushed away her cruller and took a long, slow sip of her coffee. Havarti, who always sensed her moods, reached up to her with both paws. She lifted him into her lap and pulled him close. "Do the police know what time this all happened? I mean, shouldn't the sub shop have been closed?"

"It *was* closed." The chief released a breath. "Like you, Ferris had closed for the duration of the competition, but he apparently decided to open afterward to take advantage of the usual Saturday night influx. On Saturdays he closes at nine, but his daughter explained that he often worked long after closing time. He'd roast meats for the next day, get them set up for the sub sandwiches, do some general cleanup." His face reddened. "She said Grant used to do a lot of that for him, but now Menard was having to pick up the slack."

Carly groaned. "Chief, Ferris thought I encouraged Grant to quit, but it's not true. Grant did that on his own."

"I believe you." Holloway took another sip of his coffee. "I've gotta hand it to Menard, though. Hostile personality aside, he was a hard worker. Anyway, his daughter said that he always locked up when he left, of course, but while he was still there, anyone could have slipped in through the back door from the alleyway."

An icy chill washed through Carly. She wrapped her arms around Havarti and cupped her elbows with her hands. "How's Menard's daughter doing? Finding her dad like that must have been a horrible shock."

"She was in rough shape when we got there, crying so hard she could barely talk. She calmed down after a while.

She kept wanting to throw herself at her dad's…body, but obviously we couldn't let her near him."

Rhonda flicked a worried gaze at her daughter. "There's one more thing, honey. Tell her, Fred."

Holloway nodded. "Let me backtrack a little. From the way the place looked when we got there, we believe Menard was probably in the dining area when the intruder came in and confronted him. Bags of chips were scattered on the floor. A cardboard display of candy bars had been tipped over, so there was probably a scuffle. Also, according to the daughter, Menard had a row of plastic Halloween figurines lined up along the top edge of the counter, above the chips rack. You know—a ghost, a zombie, things like that. He puts them out every year during the season. With the exception of one, they were all found on the floor."

"What about the other one?"

After a long pause, Holloway said, "The other one was found under Menard's body. One of the investigators has a theory. Since it was too small to use as a defensive weapon, he's thinking Menard probably grabbed it at some point during the tussle, that he might have chosen that particular one intentionally."

"You mean, like he might have been trying to get a message across?"

"Exactly."

"So, which figurine was under Menard?"

"I'll get to that in a minute. Right now, I need to speak to you privately for a moment. Can you see me to the door?"

"Um, sure," Carly said, still half in shock.

Holloway drained his coffee cup and rose from his chair. "Rhonda, thanks for rounding up the troops, so to speak.

Everything we discussed here is confidential, so please be sure it stays in this room."

"Of course, Fred," Rhonda assured him. Her worried expression broke Carly's heart.

Setting Havarti gently on the floor, Carly accompanied the chief to the door. From his expression, she suspected she wasn't going to like what he had to say.

Holloway rolled his hat in his hands. "Carly, I want to make something clear. My visit here this morning was strictly a courtesy. I wouldn't have asked your mom and Norah to join us if it wasn't. But after this, the state police will take the lead on the investigation, so you'll be required to come down for an interview with one of the detectives."

An interview? An interrogation, you mean.

A cold lump landed in Carly's chest. Unfortunately, she knew the drill. "I understand, Chief."

Holloway lowered his voice. "But first I need to ask you something. It's personal, but it's extremely important. Were you with Ari Mitchell last night?"

The question took Carly by surprise. She felt a quick flush of heat color her cheeks. Was he trying to find out if Ari spent the night with her?

"Yes, Ari was here with me last evening. We had Chinese food, and then we watched an old horror movie and a bit of the news. We were both really tired, not to mention bummed by the news about the phony votes in the competition. I'm sure you heard about that. Anyway, Ari left well before midnight. Around eleven fifteen, I'd say."

"I heard about the voting. At this point we don't know if the competition has any bearing on Menard's death, but I seriously doubt it. Right now, it's minor in the scheme of things."

Carly agreed. Nothing about the competition had been worth killing for. At this point, she didn't care if they ever figured out who the real winner was. Menard's unexpected death had cast a dark shadow over all of it.

"So, Ari didn't return after he left?" the chief prodded.

Sneaky question, Carly thought, a little irked by the implication. "No, he didn't return. I'd have told you if he had."

"When he left, was he wearing the costume he had on at the competition yesterday?"

"You mean the vampire cape?" Carly frowned. "No, he took it off and stashed it in his pickup before we ate dinner. Why does that matter?"

Instead of answering the question, the chief rubbed a hand over his eyes. "Ari is at the police station now, being interviewed by one of the state police detectives. Carly, when I said you'd be required to come in for an interview, I'm afraid I meant right now. I need to bring you in for questioning. Your mom and Rhonda have already agreed to stay here with Havarti."

Carly felt her knees wobble, and she grabbed the doorknob for support. "You're serious?"

The chief looked at the hat in his hands and then at Carly. "I'm afraid so."

That all-too-familiar feeling of dread gripped Carly by the throat. She'd felt that same numb horror after Gina's ex was found murdered in her parking lot. She'd been questioned in connection with that murder too.

"So much for this being a courtesy visit," she said stiffly. "Before we leave, I'll ask you again. Which figurine was found under Menard's body?"

After a long hesitation, Holloway said, "The vampire. The figurine under Menard's body was Count Dracula himself."

CHAPTER FIVE

By the time a patrol car dropped off Carly in her driveway, it was nearly 2:00 p.m. A damp chill had crept into the air—the kind that seeps into the bones and settles there. The sun remained tucked behind a cluster of gray clouds as if it were afraid to face her mood.

At the station, she'd been questioned by two detectives—one acting as the good cop while the other played the bad one. After all the decades of crime shows on TV, did they really think that routine fooled anyone?

It hadn't been too hard to figure out what they'd wanted from her. Question after tricky question about Ari's demeanor the night before—not to mention his where-abouts. They'd wanted her to implicate him in the murder of Ferris Menard.

"I'm back," Carly called out wearily, after stepping inside her apartment. Havarti rushed over and jumped up excitedly, bouncing off her knees like a soccer ball. If she'd had the energy, she'd have lifted him into her arms, but she felt as if she'd been threaded through a clothes wringer and hung out to dry.

Rhonda hugged her daughter so hard that Carly had to gasp for breath. She pushed back a lock of Carly's chestnut-colored hair. "Oh honey, I was so worried. Was it awful?"

Worse than awful. "Not really. Mostly it was a lot of

repeat questions." She raised her chin toward the kitchen. "Something smells delicious."

"Well, you eat so many grilled cheese sandwiches, I decided you needed a home-cooked meal for a change."

Carly smiled. "A *mom*-cooked meal, you mean."

Rhonda shrugged. "Same difference. Pasta and meatballs, salad, and rolls. Gary picked up the supplies at the market for me and dropped them off. By the way, he's sorry he can't be here for dinner. He already had plans to watch football with his old college buds this afternoon, the ones that are still around anyway. He'll probably come home stuffed to the gills with pizza, nachos, and other assorted junk food. Some diet for a doctor."

Gary Clark was a retired dermatologist. He'd married Carly's mom seven years earlier, and the two had proven a perfect fit for one another. Nevertheless, he needed his "space" every so often, as did Carly's mom.

"That's okay. Male bonding and all that." Carly closed her eyes and inhaled. The aroma of her mom's cooking would normally have her swooning. Unfortunately, her appetite was in a holding pattern, waiting for permission to land. She hoped it would make a fast comeback so she could enjoy the fruits of her mom's culinary labors.

"You made all my favorites," she said, squeezing her mom's shoulder. "Did Norah leave?"

Rhonda's lips twisted as she hung Carly's jacket in the hall closet. "That new boyfriend of hers came and got her. He didn't even come upstairs. He waited for her in the car. I guess they had some sort of gig to attend at his father's house," she huffed. "If you ask me, a man his age who still dresses like a clown has a couple of bolts loose."

For some reason, Carly's mom had taken an odd dislike to Norah's latest beau. Rhonda had been so accustomed to the "bags of wind" and "pretty boys," as she'd referred to Norah's past boyfriends, that the attractive, soft-spoken man with the exquisite manners had thrown her completely off kilter. The fact that he'd been dressed in an elaborate clown costume when Rhonda met him hadn't added to his allure.

"I think we should give him a break," Carly said. "You only met him in person once, and he told you he'd just come from work."

"Then why won't Norah tell us what he *does* for work?" Rhonda huffed. "Is she ashamed of it?"

Carly had no answer for that. She only knew she didn't want to make any judgments until she'd learned more about the man.

"Maybe that was only a side job," Carly suggested. "Maybe he's a...surgeon or something."

Rhonda ignored her.

"Mom?" Carly raised her voice slightly. "Did you hear what I said? Maybe the clown thing is only a side gig."

Rhonda rolled her eyes at the ceiling. "Whatever. Since it's just the two of us, what time do you want to eat?" She slid a glance over at Carly. "Although, you could always invite Ari to join us."

Carly had been texting Ari since she left the police station. So far, she'd gotten no response. The patrolman who'd driven her home had been clueless when she'd asked him about Ari's whereabouts. Had he been detained by the detectives? She wondered if he'd been forced to turn over his cell phone, in which case he'd be incommunicado.

"I'm not sure where he is," Carly admitted. "I'm worried

about him, Mom. I wish he'd never changed his mind and worn that darn vampire cape to the competition. He was trying to match my costume, so we could be a vampire couple." Her voice hitched, and she pushed back tears.

Rhonda slid her arms around her daughter and gently shook her. "He'll contact you as soon as he can, honey. Ari's as dependable as the sunrise."

When Carly's phone jangled, her heart jumped. Relief flooded her when she saw Ari's face pop up. "Ari? Are you okay?"

"I'm fine," he said calmly. "I knew you'd be worried, so I called as soon as I could. Is it okay if I stop over?"

"It sure is. Mom's here, and she made a terrific meal. She was hoping you'd join us."

"Say no more."

Five minutes later, Ari's pickup pulled into the driveway and parked behind Carly's Corolla. She hadn't planned to cry. That wasn't her style. But when he got out of his vehicle, she couldn't help herself. She ran into his open arms, and he pulled her into a fierce hug. She felt bad sobbing on his flannel shirt, but she knew he didn't mind.

Before they headed inside, she rubbed away her tears with her fingers—not that her mom would be fooled. "Mom, that visitor you inquired about is here," she trilled, trying to sound playful.

Rhonda beamed at the sight of Ari. "Excellent! Now we have a full house."

Over a delicious meal of angel-hair pasta, tangy meatballs, crisp salad, and Parmesan rolls, Ari gave the women a recap of his day. "The worst part was trying to explain to the police how my vampire cape went missing." He looked baffled as he helped himself to a third scoop of salad. "I know I stuck it in a brown bag and dropped it in the back of the pickup. But when I got home last night, it was gone."

"Didn't you find that odd?" Rhonda asked him, cutting a meatball in half with her fork.

"Sort of, but I never expected it to get stolen. The way the wind was blowing last night, I figured the bag might have been swept out of the back of my truck and carried off to who-knows-where. I was going to look around for it this morning, but the police got to me first."

Carly jabbed a cucumber round with her fork. "How do things stand now? With you and the police, I mean."

"I'm not sure I know," Ari said. "One of them asked me if I had plans to travel this week. I assured them I did not, although I'll be working on that project in Pownal again tomorrow and probably Tuesday. It's coming along well, but the electrical installations are a bear. Bottom line, I think what the police were really saying was, *Don't leave town.*"

"I suspect you're right." Carly popped the cucumber into her mouth.

"Plus," he added with a wry chuckle, "I think I left my work boots at the construction site on Friday. I thought I'd tossed them in the back of my pickup, but they're not there so they must still be in Pownal. I want to get them before someone else decides to claim them."

Carly rolled several strands of spaghetti around her fork. "People would actually steal someone else's work boots?"

"Unfortunately, it's happened," Ari said, helping himself to another meatball. "The steel-toed boots like the ones I wear are pricey."

"Why did you take them off?" Carly asked him.

"I do that sometimes when I'm working at a site with a lot of dirt and sawdust flying all around. After I'm through for the day, I put my sneakers back on and toss the dusty work boots in the back of my truck so I can clean them up when I get home. They're not in my pickup, though, so I must've left them at the site. Is it okay to give Havarti has a teeny-tiny piece of meatball?"

Carly couldn't help smiling. "Technically he shouldn't eat people food, but I guess a speck won't hurt."

Winking at the dog, Ari cut a small chunk of meatball from his plate and carried it over to Havarti's dish. "There. That's your people treat for the day. Your mom will give you some doggie treats later."

Goes out of his way for animals, Carly thought, adding another checkmark to Ari's "plus" column.

"Ari, do you remember who else was dressed like a vampire at the competition?" Carly asked him after he sat down again. "I never got a chance to mosey around the other tables."

"Gotta be honest, I didn't do much moseying either." Ari wrapped angel hair around his fork. "But Don Frasco was taking pictures. Maybe we should ask him. You know how he loves playing detective."

"Good point. I'll text him as soon as we finish eating."

When their meal was over, Carly insisted on cleaning up the table and doing the dishes while Ari sat with Rhonda in the living room. On occasion she'd sneak a peek at the pair, sitting on Carly's lilac-patterned sofa and speaking in low tones. The easy rapport between them was heartwarming to observe—another huge checkmark in Ari's favor. In an odd way, Carly suspected her mom liked Ari more than she'd ever liked Carly's deceased husband, Daniel. Daniel was bigger, louder, and more opinionated than Ari, but inside he was a squishy marshmallow who'd do anything to help someone in need. Nonetheless, it had always seemed to Carly that her mom had viewed him as a grizzly bear in human clothing.

Carly wiped her hands dry on a dish towel, then retrieved her cell phone from where she left it on the hallway table and dropped onto the sofa next to Ari. "I'm stuffed, but if anyone wants spumoni let me know."

"Maybe later," Rhonda said. "Don't forget to text Don Frasco."

"Doing it right now." Carly sent off a quick text to the reporter, asking if he'd seen anyone else in a vampire costume at the competition. Most likely the person who'd stolen Ari's cape was the culprit who'd attacked Ferris, but she wanted to be sure the theft of the cape hadn't simply been a coincidence.

Less than a minute later, she got a response: Only one other vampire that I saw. Can I come over?

Suppressing a groan, Carly texted back: Sure.

"I guess we're having company," she announced.

~

Don arrived twenty minutes later, looking as thin as ever in a brown sweater and beige corduroy trousers. His auburn hair had been tousled with a touch of gel—in a stylish way, Carly noticed. After greeting everyone politely, he plopped onto the rocking chair opposite the sofa.

As the sole writer/editor of the *Balsam Dell Weekly*, Don loved chasing down a hot story. Unfortunately for him, their quiet town offered him few opportunities. Stumbling onto a crime ring back in June had been the highlight of his career.

When Carly was a teenager, Don's mom had asked her to babysit him one day. The experience left an indelible mark on her, and not in a good way. He was the most over-active, vocal kid she'd ever met. When she tried to make him a grilled cheese for lunch, he'd screamed his lungs out. *Not a fan of cheese* was an understatement. Carly was grateful that his mom had never called her again. One dose of that babysitting gig was good for a lifetime.

Remembering Don's favorite beverage, Carly brought him a root beer.

"Thanks." He gulped back a mouthful. "So, Ari, word has it you were questioned by the state police this morning."

Carly sat down beside Ari. "That's quite an opening," she pointed out, "considering you're supposed to be here to tell us who else was dressed a vampire yesterday."

Don squirmed in his chair. "Don't worry. I'll get to that. But remember, I'm a reporter. It's my job to report the news."

"True," Carly conceded, "but I don't want us getting side-tracked from my original question. Why don't you tell us who you saw wearing a vampire costume?"

He blew out a breath. "Do you know Tyler Huling? He works at Quayle's Hardware."

Ari was already nodding. "I know Tyler. He tends the checkout counter. I buy a lot of my supplies there."

"Okay, well, Tyler was wearing a pretty snazzy looking vampire outfit yesterday, right down to the fangs."

Carly smiled slyly at Don. "And I'll just bet you have a picture of him, don't you?"

"I have pictures of a lot of people," Don said evasively.

"I'm doing a whole spread about the competition in this week's edition. Of course, we still don't know who won…" He let his words dangle, then lifted his gaze to meet Carly's.

In Carly's mind, Ferris's death had far overshadowed the voting debacle. Now, though, she wondered if the incidents were connected. Did the phony votes play a role in someone attacking Ferris in his restaurant?

"Don," Carly said, her patience waning, "do you have a picture of Tyler in his vampire costume?"

He pulled his cell phone from his pants pocket, tapped it a few times, and handed it to her. "I transferred the pictures I took yesterday from my camera to my phone. Start there."

Holding the phone to one side so Ari could view the pics with her, she swiped slowly through them.

"That's Tyler," Ari said a few photos into the group.

Don had snagged the photo of Tyler as he was taking a bite from his sandwich. Tyler obviously noticed he was being photographed, as he made a point of flashing his vampire fangs, along with a big scary grin.

"I remember him, now," Carly said, recalling the young man with longish black hair sporting one silver earring. "He waited on me the day I bought my air conditioner. Isn't that one of Ferris's dragon bites he's eating?"

"Yeah, he'd just come from Sub-a-Dub-Sub's table when I took his pic."

Carly peered more closely at the photo, and her breath caught. "Isn't that Ferris's daughter standing next to him?"

"Yup," Don said. "I think Holly sort of *likes* Tyler, if you get my meaning, but I'm not sure if they're actually dating. Tyler's the kind of guy who's hard to read."

"Sounds like you know Holly," Carly said.

"Her mom was a friend of my grandmother's," Don explained. "I always remembered Holly because when I was fourteen, we were both coerced into taking ballroom dancing lessons at the community center. It was excruciating. Even though she's younger than me, we ended up being friends. I always thought she was a good kid."

Carly added that little morsel of gossip to the list of mental notes she was making, then continued viewing the pictures. So far, the only vampire she'd seen had been Tyler.

"Okay, it's my turn to collect information," Don said. "Ari, why don't you start by telling me how you ended up at the police station this morning. I'll interject with questions, if I have any."

"First," Ari said, "how did you know I was at the police station this morning? It wasn't even eight o'clock. Seems a bit early for you to be out on a Sunday morning."

"Gimme a break," Don said testily. "I'm a reporter; I work seven days a week. On Sundays I go to Sissy's Bakery early to get fresh-baked cinnamon rolls. Otherwise they run out. On my way home I saw a ton of state cop cars in front of the police station, so I knew something big must've gone down."

Ari fixed Don with a brown-eyed stare. "Before we go any further, we need to agree on something. Everything we discuss here this afternoon stays with the four of us, at least for now."

Don pursed his lips. "Agreed," he said. "For now."

"Good. It's pretty simple. I got a call from Chief Holloway early this morning asking me to come into the station."

"Did he tell you why?"

"Not until I got there."

"What did he tell you?"

"He told me that Menard's daughter found him in his restaurant early this morning, deceased."

"Did he tell you they suspected he was murdered?"

"Not at that point. Don, I'm not going to reveal any of the details I discussed with the detectives. I'm sure you know that they withhold certain facts from the public. If I blab them, it might compromise their case."

"I already know about the vampire figurine," Don said with a touch of smugness. "And about the steak knife in Menard's heart."

"Really?" Ari said. "And how, pray tell, do you know that?"

"Actually, Holly told me. When I saw all those staties parked at the police station, I grabbed my camera and headed into the building. I spotted you walking down the hallway with one of the cops. That sure piqued my curiosity. But I really lucked out when I saw Holly coming out of the restroom. She looked awful, poor kid. Her eyes were puffed out like golf balls. So anyway, when I asked her what was going down, she blurted out everything. How she discovered her dad's body at the sub shop early this morning, about the steak knife, the vampire figurine—the whole kit and kaboodle. It was like she couldn't stop talking. Then her stepmom came up behind her, told her that was enough, and took her firmly by the arm. They bolted out of there before I could ask her anything else."

"Do you know Holly's stepmom?" Carly asked him.

"Only by sight. Her name's Portia, that's about all I know."

Rhonda suddenly sat up straight on the sofa. "I know Portia. She comes into the library quite often. I haven't known her long, since I only moved back to town a short while ago. But I've chatted with her a few times."

"What's she like?" Carly asked.

"She seems intelligent, personable—a real go-getter in business, I hear."

A sudden memory popped into Carly's head. What had Gina said at the competition yesterday? Something about Portia tweaking Menard's salad dressing recipe and selling it to a boutique spice company?

"We're getting off track here," Don said crossly. "Ari, you haven't told me why the police wanted to talk to you, specifically." And then, as if light had suddenly dawned, his eyes glittered. "It was the costume, wasn't it? You wore a vampire costume yesterday at the competition."

"I wore a cape, but I have no reason to believe that's why I was interviewed."

"No reason except sheer logic." He looked sharply at Carly. "That's why you texted me this morning asking me who else was wearing a Dracula outfit, isn't it?"

"It is," Carly said. "I thought that much was obvious."

"Did you have to turn over your vampire getup to them?" Don asked Ari.

"No, I did not."

Don looked confused. "That seems weird. I'd have thought they'd want to test it for—" He stopped abruptly. "Of course, the killer didn't necessarily wear the costume when he entered the sub shop."

Carly knew Ari was withholding the fact that his vampire cape had gone missing.

"Wait a minute." Don swerved his gaze over to Carly. "Weren't you wearing a *lady* vampire costume yesterday?"

"I was," Carly said, irritated now. "I'm actually surprised there weren't more vampires. Doesn't anyone like Dracula anymore?"

Don shook his head. "Vampires are old hat. These days people are into zombies, witches, dinosaurs, that sort of thing. And the kids love the Harry Potter characters."

Ari had taken Don's phone from Carly, and now he pointed to one of the photos. "Aw, look at this one," he said to her. "It's you, serving up a grilled cheese to Evelyn Fitch. You both look so happy."

I was happy, Carly thought gloomily. *And that was barely a day ago. How could everything turn so upside down in less than twenty-four hours?*

CHAPTER SIX

After Don left, Carly called the town's recreation director.

"I'm sorry, Ms. Hale." Ms. Gray sounded deeply apologetic. "I should have called you sooner, but I haven't been able to get off the phone. As you can imagine, the discovery of Ferris Menard's...*body*, as it were, has taken priority over everything today."

"Certainly. I understand," Carly said, not wanting to appear unsympathetic.

They'd moved from the living room to the kitchen, where Rhonda was doling out scoops of spumoni while Ari put on a pot of coffee. Havarti was doing his usual fine job of supervising the work.

"What happened to Ferris Menard," Carly went on, "is a terrible tragedy, and I'm very sad for his family. But if the voting had anything to do with his death, I feel it's my duty to find out what happened. Please, Ms. Gray, for my own benefit, how did you determine which votes were the phony ones?"

After a long pause, during which it sounded as if Ms. Gray had gulped down a bite of food, she said, "Two volunteers and I sat up quite late last evening. We examined each vote— there was a total of one hundred ninety-three—under a strong light. What we discovered is that twelve of them had been printed on different paper. It was white paper, but not the bright white that the official votes had been printed on. All of those twelve votes," she went on grimly, "were in favor of Sub-a-Dub-Sub."

So, someone had tried to rig the voting in Ferris Menard's favor.

"But there had to be a master sheet that they were printed from, right? How did the forger get his—or her—hands on it?"

Ms. Gray hesitated. "There is a master sheet, but it's in my computer in a protected file. No one except myself had access to it." Her voice softened. "Ms. Hale, I know this was your first time entering the competition, but please know that this kind of thing has never happened before. We *will* get to the bottom of it, I assure you. Whoever was behind this had to be extremely naïve to think we wouldn't notice the extra votes. I predict it won't be long before the culprit tips their hand. Or we tip it for them," she added with a chuckle.

"Thank you." Sensing that the woman was anxious to end the call, Carly quickly added, "One last question. How many blank votes were on a printed page?"

"Six," the administrator said, "on a standard, letter-sized page." She paused. "Um, Ms. Hale, due to the unfortunate events of this morning, we are keeping this information under wraps for now. It wouldn't be fair to the family to cast aspersions on Mr. Menard's character. Especially since we don't know who was responsible for the attempt to skew the votes."

"I agree, and I promise it won't go any further." *Except to my mom and Ari.*

Carly thanked her for the update and disconnected. She related Ms. Gray's explanation to her mom and Ari, emphasizing that it needed to stay between them and not be repeated to anyone.

Rhonda focused at a spot on the wall, her eyes taking on a faraway look as she made typing motions with her fingers.

"Mom?" Carly finally said.

Rhonda turned sharply and looked at her. "Sorry, I was just thinking," she said. "If someone was a really good typist, like I am, I'll bet they could whip up a sheet of blank votes in no time. If I recall, they used a standard font. Nothing fancy."

"I didn't think of that." Carly stirred a few drops of milk into her coffee. "But you're right. Type it once, then cut and paste it five more times until you have six on a page. From there they'd have to either print it out or copy it."

In her former life, when she and Daniel were married, Carly had worked as a restaurant manager at the historic Ivory Swan Inn. Using a word processing program to create ever-changing menu templates had been a large part of her job.

"Which means," Rhonda mused, "whoever did it had access to a computer and a printer, or a copy machine."

Ari looked thoughtful. "Each participant had to pay for a ticket before they were given a blank vote. But once they had that vote in hand, it wouldn't have been too hard to find a place to duplicate it. A copy machine would've been all they needed."

"Were any tickets sold in advance?" Carly asked him.

"No, it doesn't work like that. No one can buy a ticket until eleven o'clock Saturday morning, the official start of the event." Ari took a small sip of his coffee.

Carly felt her heart sink like a stone. Whoever created the phony blank votes, they did it sometime between 11:00 a.m. and 3:00 p.m.

"Twelve fake votes," she said, "all in favor of the man who picked a fight with me at the competition—in front of a lot of people. I even accused him of sending his daughter over to spy on me."

Rhonda pushed away her empty spumoni bowl and rested her elbows on the table. "I don't like this, Carly." She reached over and squeezed her daughter's wrist. "If the police determine that Ferris fudged the votes, I'm afraid they'll decide that either you or Ari had motive for murder."

Motive for murder.

Surely no one would believe that, would they? Who would kill over a food competition? It wasn't as if the winner stood to make a fortune from it.

But even as Carly thought it through, she couldn't discount the possibility. The police could believe anything they wanted, couldn't they? In their line of work, they'd seen people commit murder for far less.

Carly had already been entangled in solving one murder. It was an experience she never wanted to repeat.

But if the authorities deemed that Ferris's death was intentional, she might be headed down the same path again.

~

For the first time in her thirty-two years, Carly was dreading Halloween. This year it fell on a Monday, the beginning of her work week.

As she'd done on Sunday—the day Ferris's body was

found—she skipped her usual early morning walk with Havarti. Instead, she led him outside to her landlady's fenced-in yard so he could take care of business. The little guy looked crestfallen at having to go back inside the apartment afterward. Carly vowed to make it up to him the next morning with a proper long walk.

Despite her mood, it couldn't have been a more perfect Halloween morning. Captured by the breeze, fallen leaves blew swiftly across front lawns, swirling in the brisk wind. Jack-o-lanterns grinned from porch steps in anticipation of greeting hordes of trick-or-treaters. In front of the used bookstore, A Fitting End, a skeleton loitered against a faux gravestone, his bony fingers beckoning all who dared to enter.

It was almost 8:30 a.m. when Carly parked behind her restaurant and entered through the back door. She flipped on all the lights, then pushed through the swinging door into the kitchen, stowing her tote in the pine desk beneath the window.

Carly's mornings were typically spent preparing for the onslaught of customers, which would begin promptly at 11:00. Chopping onions and celery for the tuna, slicing tomatoes and cheese, sizzling up bacon for sandwiches. Cleaning the bathroom. *Ugh.* At least she'd gotten it down to a science. Armed with rubber gloves, she could scrub everything and make it shine in under four minutes.

First things first. She hung her jacket in the kitchen closet, then returned to the dining room and put on a pot of coffee. Most mornings, Ari joined her before the restaurant opened for a golden-grilled biscuit stuffed with warm cheddar and bacon. Today she was on her own, since Ari was off in Pownal. They'd agreed to keep in touch during the day if any news came through about Ferris's demise.

Once the coffee was ready, Carly poured herself a cup. After a few soothing sips, she replenished the plastic pumpkin next to the cash register with her last bag of miniature candies. She decided to skip her morning biscuit and get straight to work.

She glanced at the wall over the coffee station. A beautifully framed sign with the words *Human Beans Need Coffee Beans* reminded her that she hadn't talked to Gina in two days. When Gina first moved into the apartment above the eatery, she'd made the sign for Carly as a gift, using the quilling technique she'd mastered. While tiny scrolls of paper spelled out the words, the whimsical coffee cup was made from real coffee beans.

A little after 9:00, Suzanne called. "How are you feeling? How's your ankle?" Carly asked her.

"Never mind my ankle. How are you guys doing? I heard about Ferris Menard."

Carly stifled a groan. "I know. It's awful, isn't it? His poor daughter must be devastated."

"Jake told me Menard confronted you at the competition on Saturday."

"Oh no. He saw that?"

Suzanne sighed into the phone. "I guess a lot of people did."

Great. More witnesses to tell the police about my blowup with Ferris.

"You didn't answer my question about your ankle," Carly reminded her.

"Well, it's stuck in a boot that feels like sandpaper glued

over particle board, and I'm ready to go nuts. Can I come in and work?" she whined. "I can't wait tables, but I can sit on a stool in the kitchen and help with prep work. *Pleeeease.*"

In truth, having Suzanne there would be a relief. Carly was sure there would be enough for her to do—including helping Grant make his signature tomato soup—without putting weight on her foot.

"Of course you can, if you promise not to overtax your ankle. But how are you going to get here?"

"All taken care of. Jake's going to drop me off right in front."

That decided, Carly went over to unlock the front door for Suzanne's anticipated arrival. Grant was standing outside, his hand raised to knock. She'd momentarily forgotten that he worked full time now, thanks to quitting Sub-a-Dub-Sub.

"Hey," he said, stepping inside. His normally cheery expression was absent.

"Hey yourself. How are you doing this morning?"

Averting his eyes, he shook his head. "Not great. When I heard about Mr. M's death yesterday, it hit me sort of hard. He might not have been the most congenial guy, but he was always respectful to me."

"I know, and I'm so sorry," Carly said.

"Plus the police asked me to come in for an interview yesterday. My folks are, like, furious, Carly. They want me to quit this job." He blew out an exasperated breath.

Carly slid onto one of the stools and faced him. "They're worried about you. They have every right to be. I'm so sorry."

"Yeah, plus they've been pressuring me to sign up for the next semester at the college. If I apply now and get accepted, I can join one of the string ensembles right away and start classes next semester."

Carly had learned quite by accident over the summer that Grant was a gifted classical cellist. Not only had he been playing since he was a child; his mom and dad were both music professors at the college. Both parents were adamant that Grant was wasting his talent pursuing a career as a chef—hence their refusal to contribute to his culinary school education.

Grant's voice lowered. "They think what happened to Ferris was a sign. A sign that I'm following the wrong path by working in the food industry."

The door opened and Suzanne came in, one foot encased in a huge black boot. "Good grief, I'm so happy to see you both."

Carly and Grant rushed over to help her. "Yeah, well it's good to see you too, lady." Carly smiled and took her by one arm.

"I thought you had to stay off your ankle!" Grant took her other arm firmly but gently, and they walked her over to the counter. Suzanne lowered herself gingerly onto one of the stools, setting her oversized boot on the foot ledge.

"Whew. Made it this far."

Carly and Grant exchanged glances. "Suzanne, are you sure you want to work today? Why don't you stay home for a few days and rest that ankle instead?"

"No!" She held up a hand. "I'm okay, as long as I keep this ball and chain on. But I desperately need coffee."

Grant went behind the counter and slid a mug of java over to her, then topped off Carly's and poured one for himself.

Suzanne pushed a strand of her dark blond hair behind one ear, then took a long, slow sip from her mug. "Listen you two, I want to know what you've heard. There's all sorts of rumors going around about what happened to Menard, and I'm not sure what to believe." She set her mug on the counter.

Carly related everything she knew about Menard's death. She was careful to omit what Ms. Gray had confided about the phony votes.

"I was interviewed by the police too," Grant told her. "What Carly said is pretty much what I know."

Suzanne's eyes creased. She swallowed another slug of coffee. "Yeah, well, I heard something else. You can't say where you heard it though, or Jake could get in trouble."

Carly's ears perked. She looked at Grant, and they nodded simultaneously.

"Jake bowls with one of the Balsam Dell cops, and they've sort of gotten to be buddies. This cop overheard two of the state police detectives talking yesterday. They were saying that a partial footprint was found on Menard's chest. You know, as if someone stood on him."

"S-stood on him?" Carly felt her own chest sink into her rib cage as a picture formed in her mind.

The attacker standing on Ferris's chest. Ferris, gasping for breath as he struggled to reach his heart meds…

Is that how it happened? Or was she letting her imagination run rampant?

"It was only a partial print, not much to work with," Suzanne added. "Could've been a man's or a woman's." With two big gulps she finished off her coffee. "Remember, guys, you can't repeat that to anyone."

Grant nodded absently, a look of horror on his young face. "Standing on his chest? That's truly diabolical. I mean, I know Mr. Menard could be hot-tempered and testy, but he was always fair to me. Regardless of what everyone thinks, the man had a good side." His eyes watered, and Carly's heart broke for him. "If I'd known all this stuff was going to happen, I would've waited to give my notice."

Carly reached over and squeezed Grant's arm. "I know, and I'm so sorry you have to listen to all this."

An awkward hush fell over them. As if by silent consent, they immediately went to work. With Carly's help, Suzanne hoisted herself onto a stool at the worktable in the kitchen. Grant set her up with onions to slice and ripe Roma tomatoes to chop for the soup. Carly went about her usual tasks, but Grant insisted on doing the bathroom.

By 10:30, the eatery was sparkling clean and ready to open for business. Waves of tomato soup wafting from the kitchen infused the dining room with a tantalizing aroma.

Carly's initial plan had been to extend the delicious offerings from her stint at Saturday's competition into the last day of October. Given the grim circumstances though, she'd decided against it. She felt it would seem insensitive and didn't want to offend customers.

"Listen, Grant, with everything that's happened, I don't want to serve anymore cheesy pumpkins. Out of respect for, you know, what happened to Ferris." She swallowed back a lump.

Grant breathed out a sigh of relief. "Good decision. Why don't we use the rest of the pumpkin bread to make our cheesy dippers? If we use muenster cheese, we can call them *muenster* fingers." His dark brown eyes lit up at the idea.

Carly smiled. "I like that. Let's make it a plan." She squeezed Grant's arm to show her support. "Hey, I'd better unlock the back door for the compost people. I know you haven't been around here mornings, but I've asked the company if they could do their pickup and delivery before customers get here. So far they've been very obliging."

"Is it Balsam Dell Compost? That's who Mr. Menard uses. I mean, *used*," he added quietly.

"It is."

A ping in Grant's pocket signaled a text message. Carly noticed he'd gotten several since he'd arrived. "Aren't you going to check it?"

He shook his head. "I know who it's from."

Moments later, there was a sharp rap at the back door. Without waiting for it to open, a thin man wheeling two compost containers on a dolly stepped inside the dining room. Garbed in a green uniform with the words *Balsam Dell Compost* embroidered on one shirt pocket and *Chip* on the other, he lifted his wraparound sunglasses from his face and propped them under his cap. "Morning," he mumbled to Carly.

"Good morning." Carly held open the swinging door into the kitchen for him. He made fast work of unloading two block-shaped containers and sliding the existing ones onto the dolly. Task completed, he pulled off a glove and removed an electronic device from the dolly's handle. Carly couldn't help noticing the man's milky white skin, so pale it resembled paper.

"There you go," Carly said, signing the device. "Would you like a bottle of water to take with you?"

Without smiling, he said, "Um, no, thank you, ma'am. I'm good. See you Thursday."

On his way out, the man's gaze landed on Grant. He shot him a quick wave before rolling his dolly out through the back entrance.

After he left, Carly realized Grant was staring at the door. His expression was so tense she thought his face might crack. "Grant? Is something wrong?"

"That man, Chip Foster," Grant nearly had to choke out the words.

"What about him?"

"He was Mr. Menard's compost guy too. The first time he came into the sub shop, I noticed Mr. Menard was polite to him, but not overly so. But here's the thing. After Chip left that first time, Mr. Menard smirked and clapped me on the shoulder and said, 'Well, how about that, Grant? Drac is back.'"

CHAPTER SEVEN

DRAC IS BACK.

The words reverberated in Carly's head.

A glance at the clock signaled that it was nearly time to open. She and Grant went behind the counter to prepare for the first customers of the day, assuming they'd have any. Five months earlier, when a body had been found in the parking lot, business had suffered—if only for a short time.

"Do you know why he called him Drac?" Carly heard the tremor in her voice as she opened the compact fridge under the counter to check the supply of condiments.

With a shake of his head, Grant placed two metal spatulas on the cutting board next to the grill. "He never told me. At the time, I wondered if it had something to do with his pale-white skin. I think the man has a condition of some kind. He's always covered up like he can't—"

They locked gazes. "Like he can't be exposed to sunlight," Carly finished.

The impact of that hit them both.

"I think," Carly said, "that this casts a whole new light, to coin a phrase, on Ferris's death. What do you know about Chip?"

"Not very much." Grant furrowed his brow. "He started working for the compost place a few months ago. He never smiles. I don't think he likes his job. I heard him tell Mr. Menard one day that he got laid off from his job at an office supply warehouse, but the way he said it was weird. He said he was trying to find another inside job so he could quit the compost place."

An inside job, Carly thought. *Not the criminal kind, but the kind of job you can perform indoors. That had to be what he meant.*

A pang of sympathy for the man gripped Carly. But what if he was a murderer? What if he'd killed Ferris Menard?

"Do you have any idea how old he is?"

"I'm not sure. I'd guess somewhere in his forties."

Ferris had been about the same age, Carly thought. Did the two have a past? "Grant, I need to find out more about Chip Foster."

Grant made a pleading motion with his hands. "Carly, I can tell from that look on your face you're already thinking of investigating. Please, *please*, I'm begging you in advance, do not do anything dangerous. Remember what happened last time?"

As if she could forget. Her confrontation with a killer had left a permanent scar on her psyche.

"I'm only going to ask a few questions," she said lightly. "And I'll do it in broad daylight."

Grant rolled his eyes. "Yeah, because murderers only come out after dark," he said dryly.

The unintended meaning behind his statement grabbed them both at the same time.

"If you believe in vampire lore, which I don't," Carly said, "then you know that vampires can only appear after sundown. They can't survive in sunlight." She felt her own face drain of color.

"Carly, please stop all this talk of vampires. Mr. Menard's death had nothing to do with a vampire. A real human caused his death." Grant's voice shook, and Carly instantly felt bad.

"I'm sorry. I didn't mean it that way," she told Grant. "My mouth got ahead of my brain."

"And I'm sorry I snapped. I—"

The front door inched open, and two elderly, white-haired women toddled in. Carly smiled and breathed out a grateful sigh. The sight of the ninetysomething twin sisters—Maybelle and Estelle—gave her heart a huge lift. And their timing couldn't have been more perfect for defusing the sudden tension between her and Grant.

Carly escorted them over to their favorite booth. She was surprised to see them at the eatery on a Monday, since the twins ate there faithfully on Tuesdays and Fridays. Carly could practically set her watch by them.

Grant came over and flashed his gorgeous smile at them. "Great to see you, ladies. I know you prefer tea, but would you like to try our fresh apple cider today? It's straight from a local orchard and spiced to perfection."

The twins nodded in unison. One of them—Maybelle?—touched Grant's wrist and winked at him. "That sounds delightful. Thank you, dear."

Carly smiled at the sweet flirtation. These ladies were gems, for sure.

She left Grant to prepare their lunches and headed into the kitchen to check on Suzanne. She found her perched on a stool in front of the stove, stirring Grant's first batch of tomato soup. From her expression, it was obvious she was in pain. "I might take a break soon, Carly. I think I need to put my foot up and take some ibuprofen."

Hands propped on her hips, Carly shook her head. "I had a feeling you were trying to do too much, too soon." She fetched two ibuprofen for her friend, then offered to drive her home.

"You don't have time to drive me home," Suzanne protested. "Jake can pick me up. On Mondays he takes an early lunch." She set down her stirring spoon. "I feel awful leaving you guys in the lurch."

"I know you feel bad not being here for us, but it's more important that you follow doctor's orders," Carly told her. "We'll make do, I promise. A week from now, the world will still be spinning on its axis."

Arrangements with Jake made, Carly hugged Suzanne. For all her joking, she had to admit she was worried about her and Grant's workload over the next week or so—or however long it would take for Suzanne's ankle to feel better.

"Carly," Suzanne said, "I hate to add one more burden, but we could really use another cutting board and one of those heavy bowls with a pouring spout. The tomatoes were spilling over the top when I was dumping them into the pot."

Carly blew out a breath. Both items had been on her "to buy" list, but October had turned into a wildly busy month and she'd let it slip.

"I know. The last few weeks, I got so wrapped up in the competition that I let some things slide. I promise to give them priority."

"I know I picked a rotten time to mention it. It's just that—" Suzanne lifted her head at the sound of a horn beeping outside. "Oops, that's Jake."

Holding on to Carly's arm, Suzanne shuffled outside to

the parking lot. With Jake's help, Carly got her friend safely ensconced onto the front seat of his car. The pair waved as they drove off.

After putting on a fresh apron, Carly returned to the dining room. Two booths were already occupied, and three regulars sat at the counter. She was pleased to see Evelyn Fitch in one of the booths, her pink pad open on the table, her usual crossword booklet nowhere in sight.

Behind the counter, Grant looked a tad panic-stricken. "Can you start taking orders, Carly? I've got the three counter orders, so just the tables for now."

"You got it."

She took orders from the two couples seated in one of the booths, then headed straight for Evelyn. "It's great to see you," Carly greeted the senior. "You're so early today! And looking lovely in that pink scarf."

The retired schoolteacher's porcelain cheeks flushed nearly the same color as her notepad. "Thank you. I've been feeling restless ever since I heard about—" She shook her head and pursed her lips. "Anyway, I wanted to be sure you were all okay, so I decided to eat early today."

"We're fine," Carly assured her, touched by her kindness. "Suzanne is home nursing a sprained ankle, so Grant and I are holding down the fort."

"I'm glad you and Grant are okay, but I feel bad for Suzanne. I hope her ankle heals quickly. I'm going to order your Sweddar Weather today. No chips, but I'd love some extra pickles."

"You got it, Evelyn. Shall I bring your coffee?"

Evelyn chuckled. "Does a cat like tuna?" She touched Carly's wrist. "By the way, I was up last night till after midnight finishing that wonderful book you recommended—the one about the woman who rescues animals?"

Carly grinned. "I'm glad you enjoyed it. Did you cry at the end, like I did?"

"I did," Evelyn said, "but they were tears of joy. When I get home, I'm going to start on the next one in the series." She fluttered her hands. "Oh, listen to me, keeping you here with my babbling when you're so busy."

"I always enjoy our chats," Carly assured her. "I'll put your order in."

By 11:30, people began streaming in. Carly saw several faces she didn't recognize, but she was always happy to have new customers. Any worries she'd had over Ferris's death being a turnoff were soundly kicked to the curb.

By 12:45, Carly and Grant were both frazzled. In addition to that, Carly was sure something was bothering Grant. On one order he'd added bacon to the sandwich when the customer ordered it plain. The bacon had been a welcome bonus to the man, but it wasn't like Grant to get an order wrong.

She was pondering that when she spied the face of a welcome visitor strolling in through the front door.

"Mom!" Carly ran over and gave her a brief hug.

"Hi, honey." Her hair tucked neatly into a bun at the nape of her neck, Rhonda's sharp gaze flitted over the dining room. "I had a feeling you'd be slammed without Suzanne today, so I'm here to help." She lifted one foot to display her favorite padded shoes, the ones made entirely from recycled ocean trash. "See? I even wore my comfy shoes. I'm ready to rock."

Carly didn't know whether to rejoice or panic. "Mom, I am thrilled that you want to help, but are you sure? It gets crazy busy in here."

Rhonda gave her that sweet, all-knowing mom smile. "Carly, did I not make you a grilled cheese every day when you were growing up?" she reminded.

Yes, but you didn't have to serve thirty or so people at a time.

"Today's my day off at the library," Rhonda insisted, "so I'm ready to roll up my sleeves. So, what it'll it be? I can work the grill, or I can wait tables."

Carly looked over at Grant, who hadn't even noticed Rhonda come in. "I'll take over for Grant and give him a break. You can take orders and deliver them, okay?"

Rhonda gave her daughter a thumbs-up. "You got it."

After giving her mom an order pad and a few quick pointers, Carly fetched an apron for her and set her loose in the dining room. She had the sinking sensation she was releasing a gazelle into a pride of starving lions.

Insisting to Grant that he take a break, Carly took over for him at the grill. He looked relieved and apprehensive at the same time. Carly couldn't help wondering if the text messages he'd been pointedly ignoring all day were the cause of his obvious distress.

For the first fifteen minutes or so, things progressed smoothly. Until Carly realized she wasn't getting enough orders to match the number of hungry customers awaiting service in the booths.

When she dared to glance up from the grill, she spotted her mom chatting amiably with Evelyn Fitch. Evelyn noticed Carly staring at them and waved, then poked Rhonda's arm. Rhonda whirled and returned to Carly with a handful of orders.

"Mom," Carly said, perusing the slips, "did Remy Gatto ask for gluten-free bread?" The slip didn't say so, but Carly knew he'd switched to the gluten-less version for dietary reasons.

Her mom didn't respond.

"Mom?" Carly said, a bit louder. She repeated her question.

"Oh." Rhonda's smile faded. "He might've said GF, but I guess I didn't hear him. I'll be more aware next time. Oh, and Evelyn wanted to be sure you got this." She handed her daughter a pink sheet of paper folded in half twice. "Pink slip!" she chuckled, then flounced off to deliver sandwiches to a booth packed with customers.

Pink slip. With an inward groan, Carly shoved the paper into her pocket. Her mom was clearly embracing her temporary gig as server.

Unfortunately, it was Rhonda who'd be getting the pink slip. Carly was going to have to fire her mom as soon as Grant returned.

~

"I didn't know being a server was such a hard job, even with comfortable shoes." Rhonda groaned as she sat at Carly's pine desk in the kitchen, rubbing one foot with her hands. The tremor in her voice made Carly's heart hurt. "I'm sorry, honey. I messed up everything, didn't I?"

"No, you didn't," Carly told her. "You pitched in and did the best you could. At least Grant was able to take a break. Plus, the customers loved you. Didn't you get great tips?" *Pity tips, but tips nonetheless.*

Rhonda waved off the compliment. "I didn't want tips. I'm giving them to the animal shelter. I just wanted to help you."

"I know, but we'll be fine the rest of the day. You helped us get through the lunch crunch, and that's a biggie."

Grant had returned after a forty-minute hiatus and immediately taken control of the grill. With Rhonda still acting as server, Carly had managed a ten-minute lunch break. She wanted to sneak over to the hardware store to chat with Tyler Huling, if he was working. Not only was Tyler the other vampire at the competition on Saturday, but according to Don, he was also friendly with Ferris's daughter, Holly. If he could shed any light on what happened to Ferris, Carly needed to know.

"Before I forget," Rhonda said, piercing her daughter's thoughts, "Gary and I would like to treat you and Ari to dinner one night this week. Can you squeeze us in? Any night but Wednesday."

Carly pretended to mull the offer, then she smiled at her mom. "Actually, I'd love that, and I'm sure Ari would too. Let me run it by him first, okay? Shall we aim for Thursday?"

"Let's go for it," Rhonda said, grunting as she slid her shoe back onto her foot.

After hugging her mom and waving goodbye at her through the front window, Carly set about tidying up the empty booths and delivering dishes to the kitchen.

By 2:00, the eatery had quieted down. Carly asked Grant if she could sneak off to do a quick errand. She promised it wouldn't take long.

"You're the boss," he said with a shrug. "Just don't go looking for killers." He'd said it with a touch of humor in his tone, but Carly knew he was half serious.

Luckily, Suzanne had unwittingly given her the perfect excuse to leave for a half hour or so.

Five minutes later, she was swinging her Corolla into the lot behind Quayle's Hardware.

Back in the early 1900s, the footprint of the hardware store sat on the site of an ancient barn—part of a small farm that had once housed chickens and goats. After the farmer's death—he'd passed without heirs—the barn sat sagging and empty for well over a decade. The property was eventually taken for unpaid taxes and sold to young Lorenzo Quayle, an enterprising gent with a keen sense of business. Lorenzo subdivided the farmland and sold off the back section, keeping the barn and a good-sized chunk of land for himself. He razed the barn and rebuilt it in the image of the original, adding a weather vane graced by a copper quail at the top.

These days, with Lorenzo's grandson at the helm, Quayle's Hardware carried nearly everything the big box stores did. To Carly's delight, that included a well-stocked row of kitchen supplies.

Keeping her fingers crossed that she'd find Tyler working the checkout, Carly headed inside. Near the entrance, a display of eco-friendly logs caught her eye. It reminded her of all the chilly nights she and Daniel had spent curled in front of the fireplace in their chalet-style home.

With a soft sigh, Carly pushed aside the memory. She glanced over at the checkout and saw Tyler at the cash register. He was ringing up an order for a man in overalls who, it appeared, was buying a lifetime supply of flashlights and batteries.

Carly grabbed a shopping cart and wheeled it toward the aisle of kitchen supplies. Minutes later, she'd added an oversized maple cutting board, along with two large ceramic bowls with pouring spouts, to her cart. Although she was tempted to browse further, Carly cut her shopping short. She didn't want to leave Grant alone in the eatery any longer than necessary. Besides, she hadn't really gone there to shop. What she needed was a chat with Tyler.

She waited until Tyler was finished with his current customer, then wheeled her cart up to the checkout. "Good afternoon," she said in a cheery voice.

"Hey," Tyler returned, keeping his gaze averted. A strand of his longish black hair hung over one eye as he rang up her purchases.

"Gee, didn't I see you at the Scary-Licious Smorgasbord on Saturday?" Carly asked him, sticking her card into the electronic reader. "I remember, because you were dressed as a vampire!" She flashed what she hoped was an innocent smile. "It was a great costume, by the way. Best vampire I saw that day."

Tyler shrugged, but his cheeks were red with embarrassment. Her question had made him noticeably uneasy.

He handed her the receipt and muttered, "Yeah, I was there. Thank you for shopping at Quayle's. Have a nice day." *Don't let the door bump you on the bum on the way out.* His curt dismissal came through loud and clear.

"Yes, you too." Carly looked at the receipt and frowned. "Oh, darn." She sighed heavily. "I'll be working on my accounts this evening, and I need duplicate receipts for my accountant. I always keep the originals for my records. And wouldn't you know, my copier bit the dust this morning."

"What a shame," Tyler said, his monotone making it crystal clear he couldn't possibly care less.

"I don't suppose you could make a quick copy of this for me?" Quirking a smile, she held out her receipt. "I'd really appreciate it." She hoped he wouldn't suggest taking a picture of it with her phone, which would have been the logical solution.

Tyler's cheeks tightened and he sucked in a breath. He took the receipt from her, then disappeared around a corner. About a minute later, he returned and handed her a letter-sized sheet of paper along with her original receipt. "There you go." He went back behind the checkout, then craned his neck and glanced over Carly's shoulder, as if a customer was waiting in line.

Carly turned her head slightly, but no one was there. "Well, thanks. Believe me, this is a big help."

Tyler stared at her, stone-faced.

"You know," Carly gushed, "I can't wait till the *Balsam Dell Weekly* comes out this Thursday. I saw the editor at the event on Saturday, and he was taking all sorts of photos with his camera. Who knows? You might get your picture in the paper!"

With that, Tyler snapped. His brown eyes seemed to shrink as they darted over the store and then returned to drill holes through Carly. Through gritted teeth he hissed, "Lady, what do you want from me? I know who you are, and I know you and your boyfriend were dressed like vampires that day. BFD, okay?"

Carly lowered her voice, cutting to the chase. "Tyler, did the police talk to you about Ferris Menard?"

He swung his lank black hair away from his face. "Yeah. Not a pleasant memory."

"How well do you know his daughter? Someone mentioned that you and Holly have been friends for a while."

A hint of something flickered in Tyler's brown eyes. Fear?

"That's none of your business. And your *someone* fed you bogus intel, okay? Holly and I know each other, that's it. Have a good day, ma'am. Thank you for shopping at Quayle's."

Carly nodded. It was obvious she wasn't going to extract much more from Tyler.

Not today, anyway.

She also needed to get back to work before the eatery got busy again.

Carefully, she folded the sheet of paper her receipt had been printed on and slipped it into her tote. Hands gripping her cart, she wheeled her purchases out to her car and loaded them into the back.

If nothing else, she'd learned one important fact: Tyler Huling had easy access to a photocopier.

And Quayle's was barely a ten-minute walk from Balsam Dell's town green.

CHAPTER EIGHT

THE USUAL AFTER-SCHOOL CROWD HAD DESCENDED ON the eatery by the time Carly returned. Grant looked so relieved to see her that it made her stomach hurt.

"Just in time," he said, sliding a Farmhouse Cheddar Sleeps with the Fishes onto a plate. The tuna melt on ciabatta with a smidge of spicy mustard was another one of the eatery's favorite sandwiches. "Table four," he said. "Did you finish your errand?"

"Oh, you bet." Carly debated with herself whether or not she should share what she learned. Either way, it would have to wait until after the midafternoon hordes had been sated.

Several booths were already occupied, she noticed with satisfaction. Stan Henderson had claimed one of the booths near the back, his accordion file and study materials spread out before him. After checking to be sure everyone's orders had been taken, Carly went over to greet him. His gaze, always intense, followed her as she approached his table.

"Hey, Stan. Nice to see you. Did you order yet?"

"Not yet, but I'm not in any rush. How are you doing?" The compassion in his gently spoken words made Carly's eyes water.

"I'm okay. I'm sure you heard what happened to Ferris Menard," she said quietly.

He shook his head and set his pen down, his brow creased with dismay. "Unbelievable, isn't it? Could things get any crazier in this town?"

"I sure hope not."

"And what's the deal with Saturday's voting?" He snagged a few napkins out of the metal dispenser and set them down next to his notebook. "Does anyone know why they haven't named the winner yet?"

Carly thought about how to respond before saying, "I guess there was a glitch. I'm sure we'll have an answer soon."

Stan's eyes flared. "In my book you were the clear winner. In fact, I was hoping you'd be serving more of those grilled cheeses on pumpkin bread today."

"I was too, but after what happened on Saturday, I decided not to. Out of respect for the deceased," she added. "So, what can we get you?"

Stan rubbed the tips of his fingers over one eye. "Decisions. Decisions. I think I'll have a Party Havarti with a cola."

"Great. Instead of cola, would you like to try our apple cider today, fresh from the orchard?"

He grinned. "I would love to quaff a glass of your apple cider fresh from the orchard."

"You got it," Carly said, hoping *quaff* meant drink. She went off to give his order to Grant, then poured him a glass of the cider and delivered it to his table.

The remainder of the day was busy, but she and Grant managed to serve everyone without getting any complaints. By 6:55, they were ready to close, much to Carly's relief.

She'd nearly forgotten today was Halloween. Luckily, she'd planned for it in advance. She'd already delivered several bags of candy to Becca, who agreed to combine it with Joyce's and host trick-or-treat from their front porch. Despite the sad circumstances of Saturday's event, Carly had always loved seeing the kids in their Halloween getups. She hoped she might get home in time to catch a few latecomers.

Carly was locking up the front door when she remembered the slip of pink paper her mom had given her, which she'd tucked into her pocket. She pulled it out and read another one of Evelyn's lovely notes.

> So hearty are her sandwiches,
> Where bread and cheese make magic partners
> I can't imagine a finer lunch
> So hurry over to Carly's now and
> Send your taste buds to heaven

Grant came over to her. "Whatcha reading?"

When Carly showed him Evelyn's note, he read it and smiled. "She's such a nice woman, isn't she? And that note is so poetic. You can tell she really put thought into it. Hey, Carly, can I talk to you for a minute?"

Something in his voice made Carly's insides plummet. "Sure, Grant. Walk me to my car?"

After securing the back door, they went outside into the parking lot. It was a perfect Halloween evening—the kind Carly had always hoped for when she was a kid. Cool, but not so cold that she needed a jacket under her costume. The night sky was clear, the crescent moon hanging above the horizon like a silver sling for the stars.

They stood together next to Carly's green Corolla. Gina's

car was missing, which meant she was probably working late at the card shop.

Grant shoved his hands into his pockets. "Carly, my dad is having fits over me working here. Not because of you," he put in quickly. "My folks think you're terrific. It's this nightmare with Mr. Menard. I'm the one who turned him in to the Board of Health, and everything went south after that." His voice broke, and Carly felt her heart break with it.

"I understand his feelings, honestly I do," Carly said. "But what you did had nothing to do with Ferris's death." She paused. "Does your dad want you to quit temporarily, or..." She couldn't bring herself to add *quit for good*.

Grant lowered his eyes and leaned against the car. "He wants me to quit working altogether so I can start music classes at the college next semester. But right now, he wants me out of here, away from the publicity and gossip over Mr. Menard's death. He said if I stayed home, I could get a head start on my studies, assuming my application is accepted. But if it did get accepted—which is pretty much a given—I'd be eligible right away to join the string ensemble." His eyes lit up at the prospect.

Carly tilted her gaze upward at the darkened sky, struggling to staunch the onset of tears. She'd always known she'd have to face Grant leaving the job one day. He was only twenty and had his entire life, his entire career, ahead of him. Once he started culinary school, he'd probably be too busy to work even part time. But now she saw that he was truly torn between a career as a chef and one as a music professional.

"Grant," she finally said, turning to face him. "If I were your dad, I'd probably feel exactly the same, with one exception. I'd want you to follow your own dream. And right now, I'm not even sure what that is."

He squeezed his eyes shut and shook his head. "I'm not sure either, Carly. At one time I thought I saw a clear path to my career. I had it all planned! But now—"

He didn't need to complete the sentence.

Carly already knew.

~

In spite of the ups and downs of her day, Carly's short drive back to her apartment put a huge smile on her face. Though trick-or-treat had officially ended at 7:00 p.m., a few stragglers, mostly taller kids wearing fright masks, roamed the sidewalks.

It didn't seem all that long ago that she and Norah were prowling the sidewalks of Balsam Dell on Halloween. Their mom would be hovering like an umbrella over them— steering their little shoulders, cautioning them not to stray close to the road. Norah always dressed in a ball gown and tiara, while Carly's picks were usually characters from her favorite stories.

She was still reliving the memories when she pulled into her driveway. Becca and Joyce were sitting on the front porch—Becca on the wicker rocker and Joyce in her wheelchair, a multicolored shawl around her thin shoulders. Havarti, nestled in Joyce's lap, leaped to his feet and wagged his tail when he saw Carly climb out of her car.

Last evening, after everyone had left, Carly had gone downstairs to talk to the women about the events surrounding Menard's death. She knew they'd hear about it on the news, and she didn't want them to be blindsided—just in case Carly's name, or Ari's, came up.

Fortunately, it hadn't.

"You missed so many great costumes!" Becca laughed as Carly trotted up the porch steps. "We had a ton of kids tonight."

Shifting her tote, Carly bent to give Havarti kisses on his snout, along with a thorough head rub. The plastic pumpkin bowl sitting on the metal table between the women was empty save for a few candy bars at the bottom. "I hope you didn't run out of candy!"

"Nope," Joyce said. Carly's seventysomething landlady looked sparkly in her orange witch's hat with glittery spider webs fluttering from the headband. "There's another couple of bags in the house. And don't worry. I won't let 'em go to waste." She winked at Carly.

"I'm sure you won't." Carly hugged Joyce and Havarti at the same time, straightening when she heard her cell phone ring.

Excusing herself, she walked over to the far end of the porch. Earlier that afternoon, Ari had texted to let her know he'd be working late and promised to call when he got home. Which was fine, except that it wasn't like him to stay out of touch for an entire day, especially when he was out of town. Then again, the past few days had been far from normal.

Relief washed through Carly when she saw his smiling face on her screen. "Hey, stranger, you must've had a pretty long day." Why was her heart beating out of control?

"Oh, I sure did," he said, his voice laced with fatigue. "I worked ten hours with the construction crew putting in the electrical fixtures at the new medical building in Pownal.

I wish I could say we finished, but I'm headed back there tomorrow."

"Oh, I'm sorry to hear that, Ari." She almost added, "I missed you," but something in his tone made the words halt in their tracks. "Are you okay?"

"I'm fine. How was your day?"

"Kind of stressful." She gave him a brief recap of Suzanne showing up for work but having to leave, and the failed experiment of her mom trying her hand at being a fill-in server.

As he listened in total silence, which was so unlike Ari, a ball of anxiety wormed its way into Carly's chest. "I also learned a few bits of information I want to share with you, but I'll save them for when I see you. Have you heard anything from the police?"

"Not about Menard, but I did get a call from a patrolman friend of mine—a guy named Gavin Connor. His name might sound familiar." Something in his tone sent red flags popping up in her head.

Gavin Connor. The name rang a distant bell, but nothing she could pin down.

"Ari, is something wrong? You sound almost angry."

After a long pause he said, "Gavin is one of the officers who responded to your complaint last Thursday about a skull someone painted on your car."

Carly's stomach dropped with the force of a giant boulder. She'd never told him about it, because she didn't want him to worry. Almost certainly the creepy artwork had been the handiwork of a prankster. Aside from the nightmare over Saturday's competition, no one had bothered her since that night, which confirmed her theory.

"Ari, it wasn't a big deal, and I knew you'd worry

needlessly." She swallowed back the lump that was setting up a roadblock her throat. "Are you actually upset about that?"

He ignored her question. "Worrying is what people do when they care about each other, Carly. After what happened between you and Menard last week, didn't it occur to you that the vandalism to your car might be connected? That he might have been targeting you?" His voice was a mixture of frustration and disappointment. "I'm sorry. Maybe I shouldn't have brought it up over the phone, but it's been eating at me."

And now it's eating at me.

"For the record," she said, hating the rattle in her voice, "I don't think Officer Connor had the right to disclose the nature of my complaint to you."

"He only said it in passing, Carly. He knows you and I are...friends, and he wanted to be sure you were okay."

"Then he should have contacted me directly."

Ari released a long sigh. "God, I'm sorry, Carly. I shouldn't have done this over the phone."

Or at all, she wanted to blurt.

"I guess we need to talk," she said softly, "but tonight's not a good time." She'd planned to ask him about having dinner with her mom and Gary on Thursday, but that probably wasn't going to happen now.

After agreeing to see him the following day after the eatery closed, she disconnected. Tears pushed at her eyelids, but she pulled in a breath and blinked them back.

Maybe this is the first chink in the armor, she thought dismally.

The first checkmark in Ari's minus column.

CHAPTER NINE

On Tuesday morning, Carly kept her promise to Havarti and took him for a long stroll around the neighborhood. A layer of frost carpeted the ground. The sidewalks were coated in places with wet, decaying leaves. She tried to force a smile as she waved at her neighbors along her normal route, but her heart felt heavier than molten lead.

All night she'd tossed and turned, flipping over her pillow a hundred times, trying to squeeze her unresolved conversation with Ari out of her head.

But she couldn't.

Had she misjudged Ari from the beginning? Had she been so taken with his kindness, with his adorable ways, and—if she were totally honest—with his handsome features that she failed to notice a controlling streak in him? Her feelings were so jumbled that she wasn't sure what to believe anymore.

One thing was certain—they needed to have a serious talk.

After Havarti was settled in the apartment with all his creature comforts, Carly headed to the restaurant. It was reassuring to have Becca living downstairs, especially since the former army veteran adored the little pup. Several times a day, Becca checked on Havarti, making sure his water bowl was filled and doling out treats. She also took him outside for exercise—the fenced in backyard was a bonus. Carly had tried paying her for her pet-sitting services, but Becca had staunchly refused.

Inside the eatery, Carly performed her usual tasks. Once again this morning, she passed on having her usual cheesy, buttery breakfast biscuit. It would only make her feel worse by reminding her of all the mornings, before the restaurant opened, that she and Ari had enjoyed them together.

Coffee made, she sat at her pine desk in the kitchen, laptop open and mug of java in hand. The day before, with Suzanne out of commission, she and Grant had experienced periods of near frenzy. Carly had intended to check into temp agencies before she hit the sack the night before, but she'd been so preoccupied and out of sorts that it had slipped her mind.

In Google's search bar, she typed in "temporary employment" and "restaurant," along with the name of the town. A long line of links popped onto the screen, but only two looked like actual temp agencies. After writing down the contact info, Carly closed her laptop.

"Hey."

"Oh!" Carly jumped at the sound of Grant's voice. "I didn't hear you come in."

Grant hung his jacket in the narrow coat closet. Without preamble he said, "Carly, I made a decision. I told Dad there's no way I'm leaving you hanging with no one to help out this week."

Carly gulped back a knot of sheer relief, but she had a feeling there was a *but* coming. "Um, what did he say?"

"He wasn't exactly thrilled, but he agreed that my quitting now would be totally unfair to you." Grant's smile was genuine. "He has a ton of respect for you, Carly. But—"

Here it comes.

"He wants me to visit the college with him on Sunday so he can give me an in-depth tour. I've been there before, but I think this time he's hoping he can sway me into choosing a major in music."

"That's a fair request. I hope you said yes."

"Of course I did. Hey, we'd better get cracking if we're going to feed the masses again today." He rubbed his hands together, his brown eyes beaming over his determined smile.

"I agree, but what do you think about my getting a temp to fill in for Suzanne? Someone with experience would be ideal, but I might have to settle for training someone."

"Gosh, it's so weird that you said that." He pulled his phone from his pocket and tapped at it. "I'm going to propose something, and you'll probably say *no way*, but hear me out, okay?"

"Okaaay," Carly said warily. She drained her mug and rinsed it, then stuck it in the dishwasher.

Grant sucked in a breath. "I got a text last night from Holly Dalrymple, Mr. Menard's daughter. She wanted me to ask you something."

"Wait. Her name isn't Menard?"

"No." Grant swiped at his cell. "Her mom never married Mr. M. They were young, and Holly's mom was just out of high school when she got pregnant with her. Holly ended up taking her stepdad's name after her mom married. But anyway, how would you feel about hiring Holly to work here on a temporary basis?"

Carly felt her jaw drop. "You *are* joking, right? You know that I'm a possible suspect in her dad's death, right?" Her voice rose to a squawk. "Besides, isn't she in mourning? I wouldn't think she'd want to work so soon after...you know."

"I know." Grant held up his hands. "I hear everything you're saying. But Carly, she doesn't believe for a second that either you or Ari were involved in her dad's death."

"Did she tell the police that?"

"I'm not sure. I didn't ask." Grant shoved his phone in his pocket, then removed three large cans of tuna from one of the storage shelves. "She has a retail job lined up for after Thanksgiving, but right now she desperately needs a short-term position. She's had experience in fast food service, which'll be a big plus. I can testify she's a hard worker."

"But what about her dad's sub shop? Doesn't she want to keep it up and running?"

"The sub shop's fate is in limbo right now," Grant said. "After finding her dad the way she did Sunday morning, Holly's not keen on going in there any time soon. Besides, it'll need a major cleanup before it can open for business again."

Carly tapped a finger to her lips, her mind sorting through the possibilities.

First, she had to consider that Holly could have killed her dad. Not likely, and horrible to contemplate, but she couldn't ignore the possibility.

Second, Holly might have an ulterior motive. Was she hoping that by working at Carly's she could do some spying? Ask sneaky questions about Carly's—or Ari's—whereabouts at the time Ferris was attacked?

All too well, Carly understood the feeling of wanting to hunt down a killer. She'd done some serious snooping herself when her own server had been accused of murder. Maybe Holly figured that by wriggling her way into Carly's good graces, she'd be in a prime position to ask probing questions or do some poking around.

A third, even more disturbing thought crossed her mind. Despite Grant's assurances, what if Holly believed Carly *did* kill her dad—in which case, would Carly be putting her own life at risk by hiring her?

On the other hand, Carly reasoned, if Holly's only motive was to secure an interim job until Thanksgiving, she might be the perfect fit. Grant already vouched for her work ethic. Carly had only met her briefly, and not under the best of circumstances, but the young woman hadn't seemed like the "killer" type—if there was such a thing.

"Carly?" Grant waved a hand in front her.

"Sorry. My mind was jumping all over the place." Carly reached under the work counter for her new cutting board. "Why don't you ask Holly to come in this morning for an interview. If I feel comfortable with her, I'll take her on as a server—just until Suzanne can come back to work."

Grant looked more relieved than pleased. Carly suspected he was envisioning another workday without Suzanne and wasn't looking forward to it. "I'll text her now. I'm sure whatever hours you can offer her will be great." He dug out his phone out from his pocket again and thumbed a text message to Holly. It pinged within seconds. "Oh, cool. She can be here by ten. Can I tell her we'll leave the front door open till she gets here?"

"Sure." Carly removed a plastic container of tomatoes from the fridge and set it on the work counter. "It occurs to me," she said, feeling a tiny smile touch her lips, "that having Holly in our midst might give us an edge in learning more about her dad. I mean, I know *I* didn't kill Ferris, and I know Ari didn't. What we need to find out is…who had reason to want him gone?"

Grant removed a can opener from the drawer next to the sink. "I don't like the sound of that, Carly. It's too risky. You know from past experience that asking questions can be dangerous, even if they sound innocent to you. I don't want a repeat of your last escapade with a killer."

"I'll be very careful," Carly promised.

"As the saying goes," Grant replied with a shake of his head, "famous last words."

~

Holly arrived promptly at 10:00.

When Carly first met her on Saturday, the young woman had sported sausage curls and a Little Bo Peep jumper, in keeping with the character she was portraying. This morning she wore her blond hair tied into a neat ponytail, and her green jersey top and black jeans were wrinkle free.

Cups of coffee before them, they sat opposite each other in the rear booth. "Holly," Carly began, "I'm sure you realize, under the circumstances, that your wanting to work here seems a bit strange to me."

"I know." Holly met Carly's gaze without flinching. "But I really need a temporary job, just until Thanksgiving. I'm moving into an apartment with a roommate in January, and I have to come up with half the security deposit, like, really soon. Plus, I have to buy my own furniture."

Carly folded her hands on the table. "The thing is, my server will probably be back to work before then. If I give you the job, it might only be for a week, two at the most."

"That's okay, at least I'll be working." Holly hesitated, then her voice grew soft. "Ms. Hale, I know you and my dad weren't exactly friends. I also realize my dad wasn't the easiest dude to get along with. But Grant's talked a lot about you, and I know you'd never kill anyone—not even someone you *really* didn't like."

Wow. Talk about cutting to the chase.

"Well, you're right about that." Carly reached over and gently touched her hand. "Holly, I want to express how very sorry I am for your loss. Ferris was your dad, and you loved him. I'm sure this is all pretty hard on you."

Holly's expression shuttered. "It is, but I'm over the initial shock. I just want the police to do their job and arrest my dad's killer. The sooner the better," she added sharply.

"And I wish the same thing." Carly removed her hand. "Holly, forgive my being nosy, but you seem like a capable young woman. Do you have any specific career goals?"

Holly flushed slightly. "Actually, I want to stay working in the fast-food biz. Dad might've been a bear to work for, but I learned to love the business. The food industry is really fun for me." She patted her tummy self-consciously. "You can probably tell I love to eat."

"You look fine, Holly. So, you're planning to keep your dad's sub shop going?" Carly pushed aside her near-empty mug.

"Um, sort of. My stepmom and I are thinking about running it together, but bigger and better. Maybe open a few more shops in Vermont, if things work out. Portia is *sooo* great and so smart. I think we make a good team."

We make a good team.

From Holly's phrasing, Carly wondered if the plan to take over the sub shop had already been in the works.

"Eventually, we hope to franchise it," Holly said, and then

her cheeks turned bright pink. "I mean, obviously I want the police to find Dad's killer first. Portia and I both do. But after that…"

"I understand." Carly gave her a disarming smile.

After asking her several more questions, Carly's comfort level with Holly was complete. Unless she was a superb actor—or, heaven forbid, a sociopath—Holly appeared to genuinely need and want the job.

"I have one more question," Carly said. "When can you start?"

Holly's blue eyes widened. "Um, like, today! Are…you giving me the job?"

"I am." Carly supplied her with details about the hourly wage and anticipated tips. "We'll do all the paperwork later, when we get a break. In the meantime, welcome to Carly's Grilled Cheese Eatery."

CHAPTER TEN

HOLLY TURNED OUT TO BE A FAST LEARNER AND A HIGHLY competent server. She was quick on her feet, wrote down detailed orders, and had an easy rapport with Grant. Customers warmed up to her immediately, and a few of the regulars paid her compliments on learning the routine so quickly.

If anyone thought it was odd that Ferris Menard's daughter was working there, no one said a word. Carly suspected that many of her customers weren't even aware of the connection, which was definitely fine by her.

"This is working out great," Grant said quietly to Carly when she came over to wait on the counter customers.

"It is," Carly admitted. "Although I feel a little disloyal to Suzanne."

"Aw, come on. You know Suzanne wouldn't mind." He flipped over the two Vermont Classics that were sizzling on the grill. "It's only for a few weeks, anyway. Suzanne will be back before you know it."

Carly nodded. "You're right," she agreed and peeked into the tomato soup pot. "I'll bring out some more soup. Looks like you're getting low."

Once in the kitchen, Carly scooted over to her desk and plopped down on the chair. She'd been checking her messages repeatedly throughout the day, but so far she'd gotten nothing from Ari. She hated thinking it might be the end for the two of them over what was a simple matter.

But if it was, it meant their relationship hadn't been on solid footing to begin with. Either way, they needed to resolve the issue that had caused the rift.

Carly also remembered she hadn't talked to Gina since Saturday. They'd texted a lot on Sunday, but Gina was up to her eyeballs in a wedding invitation project and was struggling to meet a tight deadline.

Gina's description of the cards she was making had boggled Carly's mind—a bride and groom floating off in a heart-shaped hot air balloon, toasting each other with glasses of golden champagne as they rose toward the clouds. The betrothed couple had insisted Gina use the quilling technique she was known for, so intricate that each card took at least a few hours to complete. Carly couldn't imagine working with that much detail, but Gina assured her that she was being paid handsomely for the project.

Still, Carly thought with a sigh, she missed her almost-daily visits with Gina, even if they were usually short ones. Maybe she'd suggest making a plan for the weekend, depending on…well, so many things.

"Ms. Hale?" Holly poked her head into the kitchen.

Carly waved her over. "Please call me Carly, okay?"

"Um, sure." Holly wiped her hands over her apron and approached Carly. "Um, I just got a text from my dad's lawyer. He wants to see me in his office at ten tomorrow morning. If I'm a *tad* late, will it be okay? I tried to move it to nine, but he has a closing then. I guess he wants to go over some stuff with me. I hate doing this when I've only worked here one day."

"It's not a problem," Carly assured her. "Your family matters are more important, so don't ever hesitate to ask for personal time if you need it."

"Oh, phew. Thanks. I was afraid to ask you." A smile brightened Holly's face, and Carly realized it was quite a pretty one. Her blue eyes were a startling shade of azure, and her skin was creamy and smooth.

"By the way," Carly said, "my customers have been impressed with what a great job you're doing for your first day. I just want to say—I'm glad you're here."

Another broad smile widened Holly's lips. "Geez, um, Carly, thank you." She turned on one rubber sole and hurried back to the dining room.

After she was gone, Carly reached for her phone. She took in a deep breath and texted Ari.

We still need to talk. I should be home by 7:30. Can you stop by then?

She tapped the Send icon and then squeezed her eyes shut, as if the phone might suddenly explode.

No, the phone won't explode, Carly told herself soberly. *It's our relationship that might get blown to bits.*

~

For the remainder of the afternoon, things went as smoothly as melted brie.

As Carly passed by a booth packed with teenaged boys, she overheard them jabbering about Ferris's murder. Avoiding her gaze, they'd lowered their voices immediately, but she was sure they'd continued the thread of their conversation as soon as she was out of earshot.

Had Holly picked up on any of it? Carly wasn't sure, but if she had, she hadn't reacted. She was clearly a nose-to-the-grindstone kind of worker, a trait for which Carly was grateful.

Holly had agreed to work until closing time every day until Suzanne returned. She was accustomed to putting in long hours in the sub shop, she'd told Carly, and was happy for the chance to earn the extra money.

Carly couldn't help noticing that Holly had been getting some hefty cash tips. About half the eatery's customers paid with a debit or credit card—it was surprising how many of them preferred cash in these days of electronic everything. But even the ones who paid with cards often left a cash tip for the server.

"These tips are awesome," Holly had whispered to Carly at one point. "I never got tips like this at the sub shop."

"It's because the customers appreciate your attentiveness, Holly. It's a compliment!"

"I guess so." Holly had blushed and strode off to retrieve an order.

A tiny part of Carly, the part ruled by the suspicious troll tiptoeing around her brain, still wondered if Holly had an ulterior motive for working there. So far, the young woman hadn't shown any interest in spying, or even in asking questions. Nonetheless, Carly planned to keep an eye out for any fishy behavior.

Evelyn Fitch came in at her usual time, pink notepad at the ready. Carly waved to her from behind the counter, pleased when Holly went right over to the elderly woman and chatted kindly with her before taking her order.

The remainder of the day passed without any hiccups. By

7:00 p.m., the trio had done more than a day's work. Grant insisted on walking both women to their cars, his protective instincts kicking in big time.

Holly had parked her car on the opposite side of the town green, near Ferris's sub shop, so she and Grant accompanied Carly out to the parking lot behind the eatery first.

Shivering in her thin windbreaker, Holly hugged herself and rubbed her arms. "I think it's time I dragged my winter jacket out of the closet." Her eyes suddenly widened. "Oh my gosh, I nearly forgot." She reached into her pants pocket and pulled out a folded sheet of pink paper. "That nice lady with the white hair told me to give you this. I am *so* sorry I spaced on it."

Carly took it from her and slipped it into her own pocket. "Thanks. It's nothing to worry about. Evelyn writes me uplifting notes sometimes, that's all."

"Oh, thank heaven. I won't forget next time, I promise."

Carly gave her short timer a quick hug of appreciation. "Hey, thanks for helping out today, Holly. I'm glad you're on board with us, even if it's only for a few weeks."

"I am too." Holly said weakly. She looked as if she wanted to say something more, but instead she clamped her lips shut.

Grant scooped his keys from his jacket pocket. He waited for Carly to slide onto her driver's seat, then he closed her car door.

Carly locked her car and waved goodbye to the pair, then started her engine. As Grant and Holly strode off in the direction of the now-closed sub shop, she removed Evelyn's folded note from her pocket. In the light of the dashboard, she read the message.

Gone are the days of plain grilled cheese
On slices of rye she builds her beauties
Under the Gouda bacon teases
Dairy is the name of the game
Amid the bread delights

Carly smiled at the words, written with so much thought behind them. She was really beginning to enjoy receiving these darling notes. As for Evelyn, she was clearly enamored of the eatery's offerings to write so eloquently about grilled cheese sandwiches.

Maybe one day, to thank Evelyn for her thoughtfulness and loyalty, Carly would name a special sandwich after her.

CHAPTER ELEVEN

THE MOMENT CARLY PULLED INTO HER DRIVEWAY, SHE felt her heart leap into her throat. Ari's pickup was parked behind Becca's old Lincoln, and he was sitting on the top step of the porch, a pink box resting beside him.

With her stomach doing what felt like a triple cartwheel, Carly pulled into her own space and killed the engine. On wobbly legs she got out of her car and pushed her door shut.

Why am I so nervous? She forced her knees to stiffen and hoisted her tote onto her shoulder.

Ari hopped off the step and came over to greet her. In the beam of the porch light, his eyes looked heavy with weariness. Carly wondered if he'd gotten as little sleep as she had the night before.

"Hey, Carly," he said awkwardly. "I guess I'm early."

"That's okay." Carly's voice came out hoarse, and she cleared her throat. She noticed he didn't greet her with a light kiss, as he normally did. "Let's go inside. Havarti will be thrilled to see you."

They climbed the steps together, Ari grabbing the pink box on his way into the house. The second they entered Carly's apartment, Havarti launched himself at his favorite guy like a heat-seeking missile.

"Oh sure, ignore your mom," Carly teased. She eased the

pink box from Ari's grip as he lifted the dog into his arms and let him slobber all over his face. When she reached over and rubbed Havarti's head, her fingers brushed Ari's. That same *zing* of electricity she always felt at his touch zipped through her like a bolt of lightning.

Ari grinned at the dog. "It's only because he sees you more than he sees me. You're the sun that lights his sky." He set a wriggling Havarti on the floor and helped Carly remove her jacket. She noticed he left his on, as if wasn't sure he'd be invited to stay.

"Would you like something to drink?"

Ari nodded, and they went into the kitchen. Carly set the pink box on the table, fed Havarti and freshened his water, then poured them each a glass of apple cider.

"Ari, it's okay to take off your coat," Carly said. "Come on, let's talk in the living room."

Once they were settled on the sofa, Havarti's legs draped over Ari's thigh, Carly said, "You're so quiet."

Ari wove his fingers through the pup's silky fur. "I know. That's because I'm a big A-S-S who's sorrier than he can express. I'm not even sure how to begin apologizing."

"You're not an A…that word you said. Not even a little bit."

"But I was way out of line, Carly." His eyes crinkled, and he shook his head. "I thought about it all night, about what a jerk I was. I wasn't sure you'd even want to talk to me again."

Carly gave him a wry smile. "I had a terrible night's sleep too. I must've punched my pillow a thousand times." She took a sip of cider from her glass and set it down on the table beside her.

"I admit I was hurt," Ari said, "when I found out about

the vandalism to your car. It seemed like something you would have shared with me—for moral support, if nothing else. Plus, Gavin said you reported the culprit's car as having a loud muffler. That's the kind of thing I could've kept an ear out for."

That much was true, Carly acknowledged to herself. After the police left that night, she'd thought about texting Ari. But by the time she'd removed the painted skull from her car, she'd convinced herself it'd had been a Halloween prank, and nothing more. Becca had been more concerned than she had.

"Ari, I hear what you're saying—"

"No, let me finish…please?" His gaze was so remorseful that it pinched Carly's heart. She nodded.

"Carly, you're the poster girl for an independent woman. It's one of the zillion things I've loved about you from the beginning."

Zillion? Loved?

"I've never told you much about my family, but my sister and I grew up in kind of a sketchy neighborhood. There was a little girl living next door to us, a bit older than me. Her parents were never home. I swear I only saw them twice in my life. They didn't notice—or care—that she was getting *way* too much attention from boys." His eyes creased and he shook his head. "Almost every day, two or three boys would show up after school, trying to coax her into going into the backyard shed with them."

"That's awful," Carly choked out. "How old were you then?"

"I was eight. She was about eleven," he said quietly. "One day she came over after school and asked if she could hang out with my sister Susie and me. One of the boys had tried to get too 'friendly' with her."

Carly shook her head. *That poor child.*

"It became a regular thing—her staying with me and Susie after school. My folks worked, but Mom's job was at an all-night laundry, so she was home in the afternoon. Mom was wonderful—she gave this girl decent meals and washed her clothes." He ran his fingers over Havarti's furry neck. "One day, this girl was suddenly gone. Her parents had reneged on the rent and gotten themselves evicted. They left in the dead of night, so I never saw her again. I heard some years later that she'd gotten pregnant at fifteen and dropped out of school. All I could think of was—why hadn't I done something? Reported her parents to the police for never being home, or begged my mom to get help for her?"

Carly rubbed his shoulder. "Oh, Ari, you were a child. That wasn't on you. You and Susie and your mom gave her comfort and safety when she had none. To this day, I'm willing to bet she remembers that."

He shook his head. "She died of a drug overdose three years ago. I saw her obituary in the paper."

With that, Carly wrapped Ari in her arms and hugged him for a long time. When she finally sat back, she said, "This girl—what was her name?"

Ari swallowed. "April," he said. "She told us she was named for the month she was born because her parents couldn't think of a name. And Carly, I know that story has nothing to do with us. I was only trying to explain why I went off the charts when I heard what someone did to your car."

Carly laid a hand gently on his cheek. "You didn't go off the charts, Ari. And I'm sorry I got so…bristly over it."

One hand on Havarti, he squeezed her hand with his other one. "Carly, there's something else. Something I've kept from you too, and for the same reason—I didn't want you to worry. You have every right to be mad at me in return."

Carly frowned at him. "What is it?"

"Sunday morning," he said, "when the police ordered me to come in for an interview, I had somewhat of a glitch. I discovered my right rear tire was flat. I called to let Holloway know I'd be delayed, but they wanted me in there right away so they sent a patrol car to pick me up."

Carly's pulse pounded. "And the tire?"

"When I got back, I started to change the tire and saw that it had been sliced open. It had a deep gash in the side."

"Ari!" She covered her mouth with her fingers. "Did you report it?"

"Right away," he said. "Holloway himself came over. He told me not to touch anything till he got there. When we took off the tire, we saw the blade of a knife broken off inside."

Carly felt her head spin. No, her entire *world* spin.

"The blade—it was from a steak knife." Ari blew out a long, slow breath. "The handle was missing, but when Holloway saw that serrated blade, his face went stark white. He told me it looked exactly like the one that was found in Menard's chest."

~

With the air cleared between them, Carly's appetite returned. Ari's obviously had too, and within fifteen minutes, a bowl of leftover pasta and meatballs sat on the table, along with a hastily thrown-together green salad and a pitcher of spring water.

"Sorry we ate all the Parmesan rolls on Sunday," Carly said, after swallowing a cucumber round.

"That's okay." Ari's warm smile was back, along with that adorable twinkle in his dark brown eyes. "Leaves more room for spaghetti."

Her mouth full, Carly nodded as her thoughts trampolined in her head. Had the person who left the knife blade in Ari's tire intended for him to find it? Or did the blade break off as he—or she—was slitting open the tire and the culprit wasn't able to retrieve it? Were Ferris's killer and Ari's tire slasher one and the same?

As for the police, they had to know Ari wouldn't kill Ferris Menard and then slash his own tire with an identical knife. There wasn't an ounce of logic in that!

"I can almost see the wheels turning in that brilliant mind of yours," Ari said, rolling spaghetti around his fork.

"I'm far from brilliant, but I can't help being curious." *Curious* sounded better than *nosy*, she figured. She shared her thoughts about the knife blade. She also told him what Suzanne had revealed about the footprint on Menard's chest.

"This is the first I've heard about the footprint, but none of it makes sense to me either," Ari admitted. "If Menard's attacker wanted to implicate me, why slash my tire?"

"Killers don't always use logic," Carly said grimly. "That's why most of them get caught. One of the reasons, anyway." She took a sip of spring water from her glass.

Ari set down his fork and looked at her. "Carly, I'm getting worried. Regardless of everything we talked about tonight,

I'm scared you're going to stumble on the killer without even realizing it. Remember last time?"

"Oh, do I ever. I wish I could forget, but I can't." She reached over and touched his wrist. "Ari, listen, I don't see any harm in my asking a few questions here and there. I'll be more discreet than I was the last time. And I still have that pepper spray you gave me, remember?" She smiled, hoping to disarm his fears.

"Good. And don't hesitate to use it."

"Hey, I almost forgot." Carly reached for another bite of salad. "Mom and Gary want to treat us to dinner Thursday evening. Are you interested?"

"Hmmm, let me think." He rested his chin on his knuckles, then gave her a playful smile. "Of course, I'm interested! I wouldn't miss it."

"Great! I'll get back to you with the deets, once I have them," Carly promised. "Mom's going to be so happy."

His face relaxed and they went on enjoying their meal. Gazing across the table at him, it struck Carly that she still knew so little about Ari. The story from his childhood had given her a tiny glimpse into his past, but there was so much more she wanted to learn.

After they finished dinner, Ari cleared the table while Carly loaded the dishwasher.

"Did you finish that commercial job today?" Carly asked him, wiping her hands on a dish towel when they were through.

"Yes, finally," he said, closing the dishwasher. "Tomorrow I'll be working locally. In fact, I'm planning to have lunch at a charming little eatery in downtown Balsam Dell."

"And what eatery would that be?" Carly said coyly.

He glanced at the ceiling, pretending to think. "Hmmm, I'm pretty sure it's called Carly's Grilled Cheese Eatery."

"I've heard of that place." Carly slid her arms around his neck. "In fact, I think it's been getting rave reviews. But right now, I have a more immediate issue."

"Oh?" Ari grinned.

"I want to know what's in that pink box."

He laughed. "I knew you'd get around to that. Maybe you should open it and take a peek."

Carly moved the box over to the table and cut the string. When she pulled back the flaps, six large frosted sugar cookies shaped like Thanksgiving turkeys gaped up at her with their beady, candy-coated eyes. "Oh, these are wonderful!" She removed one and held it up.

"Are you sure you can squeeze one in after all that spaghetti?" Ari joked.

Carly leaned over and kissed him on the nose. "Gobble gobble."

CHAPTER TWELVE

ON WEDNESDAY MORNING, GRANT SHOWED UP EARLIER than usual. His mood had improved dramatically from two days earlier. It was almost as if Ferris Menard's murder had never happened.

For Carly's part, she was loving having him work full time. She didn't even want to think about the day he would give his notice to pursue his own dream. It was going to happen soon enough, but she'd worry about that when she had to.

Grant smiled as he poured himself a mug of coffee and freshened Carly's. "It worked out great having Holly here yesterday, didn't it?"

"It did. Even better than I imagined." Carly set her mug on the counter. "I admit I had reservations at first. But after yesterday, my gut instinct tells me she genuinely needs the job—and she enjoyed working here. She definitely loves the food biz."

"Breakfast biscuit?" Grant asked, bending to remove biscuits, butter, bacon, and cheddar from the fridge beneath the counter.

"Absolutely. Hey, Grant, if you don't mind my asking, do you think Holly liked working in her dad's sub shop?"

"I do. Holly was in her element there because she loves working with food. She's a little shy about meeting people, but she's getting better at that." He popped two biscuits into the microwave to thaw.

"Interesting." Carly tapped her fingers on her mug. "How did Ferris treat her when she worked there?"

Grant's expression tightened. "Most of the time, okay, but on a bad day he could get pretty nasty. One day, three or four weeks ago, she was carrying a big tray of subs that were fresh out of the oven. She was almost at the customers' table when someone bumped her arm, and two meatball subs slid onto the floor. Made a godawful mess."

Carly winced. "I can empathize. I've actually done worse."

The microwave beeped and Grant removed the biscuits. "Yeah, so have I, but Mr. M. went nuclear. His face got almost purple. He stormed over and started screaming at her. Called her a not-very-nice name too."

"I'm almost afraid to ask."

"And I hate even saying it, but…he called her a clumsy cow."

Carly's stared at him. "Grant, that's despicable," she said, feeling her blood simmer.

Grant layered bacon and cheddar slices onto the biscuit halves. "We cleaned up the mess quickly, but I thought Holly was going to burst into tears. You know what, though? She sucked in a couple of deep breaths, apologized to the customers, and kept on working. They left her a huge tip too. I think they were dying of embarrassment for her."

"If I'd been her, I'd have left." Carly had no use for bullies. On her mental list of things to shun, they were way above poisonous snakes. "Did you say anything to Ferris?"

"You bet I did." He buttered the biscuits and set them on

the grill. "When I got him alone, I told him accidents happen and that he owed Holly an apology."

"Did he do it?"

Grant chuckled. "My first thought was, *He's gonna send me packing.* Instead, he gave Holly a grudging apology. He had the nerve to deduct the cost of those subs from her paycheck, though. That really frosted me."

No wonder Holly didn't want Grant to quit. He was her emotional safety net.

"Not to change the subject, but did Tyler Huling go into the sub shop much? Don Frasco had the impression Holly was sweet on him. Do you know if they've been seeing each other?"

Grant shrugged. "Not that I noticed, but remember, I worked mostly morning hours." He held up his spatula. "Now that I think about it, I *did* see them together a few times, and one time they were holding hands. Gotta tell you, though, Tyler never struck me as the romantic type. He always has that deadpan expression like he couldn't care less about anything."

"Maybe he's just shy in public," Carly offered.

They ate their biscuits quickly and began preparing for the day. Holly came in a little after 11:00. Her face looked flustered and her eyes puffy. She apologized for being a few minutes late.

"I told you it was okay to be late, Holly," Carly said kindly. "Would you like some coffee?"

Holly shook her head, and her blue eyes brimmed with tears. Her meeting with the lawyer must have been an emotional one.

"Would you like to talk?" Carly offered. "You seem upset."

Swallowing back more tears, Holly nodded. "Okay."

Carly ushered her into the kitchen, and they sat at the pine desk.

"I don't know where to begin." Holly dug a crumpled pink tissue from her pocket and blotted her eyes. "A little over two weeks ago, my dad got an overnight envelope at the sub shop. I think he'd been expecting it because he was super anxious to open it." She pulled in a shaky breath. "When he read it, his face got really red, like whatever was in that envelope had made him mad."

"Did you see who it came from?" Carly asked her.

"I sneaked a look when he went into the freezer for something. It was from a...a company that does DNA testing." With that she broke down.

Carly leaned over and gave her an impulsive hug, then fetched a box of tissues for her. She waited until Holly had collected herself, then asked, "Did you sneak a peek at what was inside the envelope?"

Holly shook her head. "No. Dad locked it in his car before I had a chance. He obviously didn't want anyone to see it. The only reason I knew what the company did was because I googled the name on the envelope."

Carly pondered the possibilities. Had Ferris sought a DNA test for himself or for someone else? Or for himself *and* someone else? What kind of biological connection had he been anxious to learn about?

"Holly, do you have any clue why he'd have ordered a DNA test?" Carly was careful to sound neutral.

Holly dabbed her eyes again. "I...I think he was trying to find out if I was his real daughter. He'd been, like, acting really odd the last few weeks. He's never been a mellow guy, but he was way more jumpy than usual."

"Why would he think you weren't his real daughter?" Carly pushed the tissue box closer.

"Because my mom got pregnant with me when she was only eighteen. Ferris paid child support, I'll give him that, but he never wanted much to do with me. But when I was fifteen, I really wanted to get to know him. I mean, my stepdad is great and all, but he's not…blood, you know?"

That still didn't answer the question, but Carly nodded at her to go on.

"So, I showed up at Dad's sub shop one day. I was almost sixteen and I wanted to know him better! Was that so awful?"

"Not at all," Carly said. "I would have felt the same way. How did he react?"

"At first he was miffed that I'd show up like that out of the blue. Then I asked if I could help him out in the kitchen, and after that he seemed to welcome my visits." She wiped her eyes again. "Oh my gosh, I was so happy. All I wanted was to know him better and for him to know me."

"So you've been working there since you were sixteen?"

"Kind of, but only part time, and sporadically at that, until recently," Holly said. "Back then I still had school and homework to deal with. The other thing was, Mom and Da—I mean, my stepdad—were leery of my spending too much time at the sub shop. They thought I was being used for cheap labor."

They might have been right, Carly thought uncharitably.

"Did you call them both Dad? Ferris and your stepdad?"

"Eventually, yes. When I first reconnected with my real dad, I called him Ferris. After a while he told me to call him Dad, said that he was proud to have me for a daughter."

Which belied the way he treated her, according to the story Grant had related.

Carly glanced at the clock. She needed to learn more about Holly's relationship with Ferris, but the eatery was going to get busy very quickly. For now, she'd settle for the answer to one question. "Holly, what happened at the attorney's office today that upset you so much?"

Holly's voice broke. "I found out I'm the beneficiary of Dad's life insurance policy. It's twenty-five thousand dollars!" She started to cry again and snatched a tissue from the box.

Carly thought about what that meant. By today's standards, $25,000 in life insurance wasn't a huge figure. But to Holly, who was barely past twenty, it must have sounded like a fortune. So why the tears? Did she think the amount should have been larger? Or was the life insurance simply a grim reminder of her loss?

"I think I'm missing something," Carly said softly. "Were you surprised about the life insurance?"

"Yes, but that's not the problem." Holly leaned toward Carly, her blue eyes wide with fear. "The attorney told me that Dad had made an appointment to see him next week. Dad refused to discuss his issue over the phone with him. He said he'd only do it in person. And then..." She sniffled. "Well, obviously Dad never made it there."

Carly was starting to fit the pieces together, but she wanted Holly to voice it. "And you're worried because..."

"Don't you see, Carly?" Holly's voice trembled. "What if the DNA test was about me? He could've easily gotten my saliva sample from a glass I drank out of. If Dad found out I wasn't his biological daughter, he was probably going to change his beneficiary to cut me out."

Something still didn't make sense. "But why would Ferris question if you were his real daughter?"

"Because my mom admitted to him recently that she'd"—Holly swallowed—"you know, been with another man right before she got pregnant with me."

Carly closed her eyes and let that sink in. "I don't mean to sound critical, but after all this time, why would your mom tell him that?"

"Mom got furious when Dad docked my paycheck for something really dumb. She called and told him he was lucky to have me working there for the pittance he paid, and the only reason I turned out so good was that he probably wasn't my real father. That's when she told him about the other guy she slept with." Her eyes welled. "Afterward she regretted telling him that, but it was too late to take it back."

And she set off a firestorm that must have enraged Ferris.

"So now Dad's gone," Holly said bleakly, "and I'm the one who found him that morning, lying there like—" She shook her head. "It was so awful. His eyes were open, and there was part of a dirty footprint on his chest, like...like someone stood on him. His pills—they were lying right there on the floor, but out of his reach. And that steak knife..." More tears spilled from her cheeks. "The police told me not to tell anybody what I saw, but I don't care anymore. They're making zero progress, so the more people who know the better. Maybe it'll ring a bell in someone's head, and they'll come forward with a suspect."

Or the killer will destroy the shoes that made the footprint so they'll never be found, Carly thought soberly. She didn't reveal that Suzanne had already squealed about the footprint.

Holly covered her damp cheeks with her hands. "Oh, Carly, what if I'm not Dad's real daughter and the police find out? They might think I killed him before he could remove me as his beneficiary!"

Exactly what Carly had been thinking, but two big questions loomed: What had been in that overnight envelope, and where was the envelope now?

"Holly, is the envelope still in your dad's car?"

She shook her head. "I peeked inside his car, but I didn't see it. He probably locked it in his safe at home. And before you ask—no, I don't know the combination."

Something else struck Carly. "Holly, I'm not accusing you of anything, but do you have any shoes that could've made that footprint?"

"Not that I know of, but that doesn't matter. Don't you watch TV? The police could say I had an accomplice." Her eyes suddenly narrowed, and her blue gaze flickered.

She's holding something back, Carly thought. *Was there someone she didn't want Carly to know about, like maybe Tyler?*

"I don't mean to beat this up," Carly prodded, "but the footprint—how big did it look?"

Holly shrugged. "I couldn't tell. It was mostly a heel print. Kind of like, with zigzag lines across it?"

Voices drifted from the dining room, which meant customers were starting to come in. "One last thing," Carly pressed. "Aside from the life insurance, do you know if Ferris left a will?"

Holly's lips quivered, and her tear-stained face blanched. "That's the other thing, actually the big thing. There's not going to be a formal reading of the will. The lawyer said Dad cut out Portia entirely. He left everything to me, including the business assets."

Carly sat up straighter in her chair. She stared at the young woman whose distress now made perfect sense.

Holly had just admitted to having a perfect motive for murder.

~

After Holly freshened up her face in the bathroom, the day soon blossomed into one of the busiest ever.

Carly was behind the counter helping Grant prepare orders when Ari came in for lunch. Her heart did the usual flutter in her chest when she saw him take a seat at the counter.

"I missed you," he whispered as she leaned toward him.

"Me too," she said, feeling her cheeks grow hot. Grant looked over at them and grinned, and Carly waved him off with her hand.

"Hey, I've firmed up our plans for tomorrow," she told Ari. "Can you pick me up here a little after seven? Mom made reservations at the Balsam Dell Inn for seven thirty. I'll ask Becca to babysit Havarti."

Carly had gotten a text from her mom a bit earlier, confirming dinner reservations at the town's most well-known eating establishment. The rambling old mansion had been a mainstay of the town since before the Second World War. It remained a popular destination for diners who sought elegance, grace, and pricey but gourmet food.

Their date confirmed, Ari lingered over a Brie-ng on the Apples, Granny, and then headed back to work. He was doing a local job—an electrical upgrade for a new business that specialized in spices and seasonings.

Evelyn Fitch, her white hair slightly windblown and a green scarf tucked around her neck, came in around 2:00 for lunch. That made the third day this week, Carly reflected. She wondered if the elderly teacher was feeling especially lonely to be coming in so often.

"I loved yesterday's note," Carly told her, setting a glass of apple cider on her table. "And this is on me, because you've been enjoying the fresh cider so much."

"Oh, you're so kind." Evelyn smiled sweetly and took a sip from the glass. "I'm glad you like my writing, Carly. I try to keep my brain cells in good shape, and writing helps!"

Carly agreed, and told her Holly would be right over to take her order.

Stan Henderson came in earlier than usual and grabbed the empty booth behind Evelyn's. He looked distracted and sulky as he opened his accordion folder and spread his study materials over the table.

"Hey, Stan. Everything okay?" Carly asked him.

"Not really." He scowled. "I found out my job at the school might be in jeopardy. I guess guidance counselors aren't valued the way they used to be."

"They'd do that in the middle of the school year?" Carly asked him in surprise.

He looked irritated at the question. "They can do it any time they want. There's been a big push to trim the school budget before the calendar year ends. I mean, I don't know if they'd can me right away, but I've got to be prepared for the worst."

Carly felt for him. "When can you take the Realtor's exam?"

Stan removed a pen from his accordion folder. "Even after I pass the national and state exams and get my license, I still can't hang out my own shingle. I have to work with a licensed broker first. And my starting commissions will be like…birdseed. They aren't going to keep my rent paid." His tone was bitter. "It was supposed to be my side job until I could get established in the realty biz."

"I'm truly sorry to hear this, Stan," Carly said, feeling genuinely bad for his situation. "I know it's hard, but try to stay positive. Sometimes the things we fear most never happen."

His frown slowly softened into a grudging smile. "Thank you, Carly. You have a rare knack for making me feel better."

Startled by the odd compliment, she touched his shoulder lightly as Holly came over, her cell phone in her hand. The server tugged Carly's sleeve urgently. "Hey, Carly, I just got a message from one of the state police investigators. Remember I told you about the footprint they found on my dad's chest? Well, guess what? The police think they have a solid lead on who it belongs to!"

Stan's head jerked up. "Did you say footprint?"

"Yeah," Holly said. "Dad's attacker stood on his chest and left a partial footprint. This new lead might just be the key to finding the creep who murdered him." She crossed her fingers in front of her face. "Let's hope, right?"

Evelyn Fitch swung around in her booth and faced them, her already pallid face almost absent of color. "Are you… referring to Mr. Menard?" she asked Holly in a crackly voice.

"I am," Holly said. "He was my dad."

Evelyn looked stricken. "And…the killer left a footprint on his chest?" She pressed a white-knuckled hand to her lips.

Holly flicked her gaze around the dining room, then lowered her voice. "Yeah, but it was more like a heel print. The police think the killer stood on him so he couldn't reach his medication. That's their theory, anyway."

Evelyn turned and slid back down on her bench seat, her thin fingers pressed to her lips. Her eyes darted back and forth as her mind seemed to race.

"Holly, why don't you take Stan's order while I talk to Evelyn?" Carly said quietly.

Holly's face flushed a bright pink. "I'm so sorry. I didn't mean to upset anyone." She rushed over to Stan and took his order.

Carly turned and bent over the elderly teacher. "Are you okay, Evelyn?"

Evelyn pressed a hand to her throat. "I'm all right. I'm afraid I got a bit lightheaded by those awful details. My imagination is rather vivid, and I was picturing it in my head."

Carly squeezed Evelyn's shoulder. "Can I get you another cider?"

Evelyn's eyes creased. "No, I'm fine, dear. If it's okay with you, I'll stay here for a while and collect myself. I feel like a ninny for getting so rattled."

"You're not a ninny. Take all the time you need. And your lunch is on the house today. What would you like?"

"Thank you. Is it all right if I have just a half Vermont classic today? I'm not sure I can eat a whole one."

"You sure can. I'll put in your order right away. Will you need a ride home later?"

"Oh, you're so kind, but I always walk to the library and my daughter drives me home. I like to read the magazines while I'm waiting for her. I will use the restroom, though."

Carly moved aside to give Evelyn room to slide out of the booth, then went over and explained to Grant what Evelyn was having. Holly avoided eye contact with Carly as she took orders and delivered sandwich platters. As soon as things quieted down, Carly intended to have a talk with the young woman. If Holly didn't have the sense not to blurt murder details in front of customers, then her temporary stint as server would have to be cut short.

Stan beckoned Carly over and spoke in a worried tone. "Carly, I feel so bad for that poor elderly lady. My gosh, she didn't need to hear all those grisly details." Although he didn't put it into words, he shook his head in clear disapproval of Holly's conduct.

"I appreciate that, Stan, but don't worry. I'll be sure she's okay."

She returned to the kitchen. In spite of Holly's poor timing, her declaration about the foot/heel print had sent off an alarm bell in Carly's head.

She pulled her phone from her tote and texted Ari: Still miss you. I forgot to ask: Did you ever find your work boots? She added a double-heart icon to the message.

When he didn't respond right away, she set her phone on the pine desk. Ari was probably too busy on the job to check his cell. With any luck, he'd take an afternoon break and reply to her text.

Too jittery to take a break to gulp down a half sandwich, Carly made herself a few crackers with cheddar. Her thoughts drifted to Gina. Both women had been so busy—Gina with work, and Carly with work *and* murder. It was time to remedy the situation.

Her mouth stuffed with crackers and cheddar, she sent off a quick text to Gina: We need a girls' night! Lots to discuss. How's tonight?

Gina texted back right away. I'm in! Your place? 7:30? Pepperoni and mushroom calzone from Louie's?

Carly agreed to the time and to the calzone, Louie's being the best pizza joint in town and Gina the best friend on earth. She'd have to scramble to get home by then and squeeze in a bathroom break for Havarti, but it was definitely doable.

Voices hummed from the dining room. Carly slipped her phone into her pants pocket, then pushed her way out of the kitchen through the swinging door. Her gaze skimmed over the customers filling up the booths. Mostly high school kids, they chattered and joked and grabbed at menus, even though most of them knew it from memory.

Steve Perlman had also come in. It was his first visit this week. With the restaurant filling up, he quickly snagged Evelyn's booth as she was gathering her things to leave. He smiled and waved at Carly over Evelyn's head, a paperback book in his hand.

Carly's insides sank when she went over to check on Evelyn. The elderly woman's face was pinched, the usual sparkle in her eyes gone. She'd barely touched her half sandwich. Most of it still sat in her plate. She poked her head under the table and peered around as if she'd lost something, then shook her head. She spoke briefly to Steve, jamming her pink notepad and pencils into purse as she did so.

"Need any help?" Carly asked her. "Did you lose something?"

"No!" Evelyn shook her head. "No, I'm fine. Thank you for treating me to lunch today." Without another word, she padded toward the front door. Carly almost ran after her to be sure she was okay, but then stopped herself. No one appreciated a mother hen. Besides, once Evelyn got to the library, she'd have her daughter, Lydia, to look after her.

"How's it going, Carly?" Steve said, sounding genuinely concerned.

"Okay. A little hectic this week."

"Everyone's talking about Menard," he said, pushing his paperback to the side of the table. "Have the police talked to you?"

"Oh, you bet they have."

"They talked to me too," Steve said with a gusty sigh. "I'm sorry, Carly, but I had to tell them about the little altercation I witnessed last week."

"Steve, please don't worry about it. I told them about it too. My mom has a saying she always drilled into me as a kid: *To get to the truth you have to tell the truth.*"

"Can't argue with that, I guess." His brow furrowed when he noticed Holly delivering sandwich plates to a booth at the back. "Isn't that Menard's daughter? Where's Suzanne?"

Carly explained why Suzanne wasn't there and confirmed for him that her temporary replacement was, indeed, Ferris's daughter.

Steve shook off his obvious surprise and picked up his paperback, which looked to Carly like a sci-fi thriller. Instead of waiting for Holly to come over, Carly took his order and gave it to Grant. When she returned with Steve's drink, she said, "Steve, did you know Ferris? I mean, on a personal level?"

With a slow nod, he set down his paperback, and his jaw hardened. "Actually, we were in high school together. We both played on the basketball team, for a while anyway." Steve glanced around and frowned. "This isn't the best place to talk, Carly."

She sensed it was his way of dismissing her, which made her wonder if he knew something. "I'm sorry. You're right."

She'd made the same blunder Holly had—talking about murder within earshot of customers. Carly smiled at him. "Grant should have your order ready in a few minutes."

Carly went behind the counter and picked up a tray of dirty plates and glasses. She was bringing them into the kitchen when her cell phone rang in her pocket. She quickly set the tray on her desk and grabbed her phone. Ari's handsome face beamed at her from the screen.

"Hey, Ari."

After a long beat, he said, "Honey, listen, I have some bad news. After I left your place this afternoon, the police were waiting by my pickup. They served a warrant to search my house and my vehicle—and my downtown shop."

Carly felt a boulder of fear plop inside her stomach. She dropped onto her desk chair to keep her knees from buckling. "I don't understand. How—"

"They were looking for the shoe, or the boot, that made the footprint on Menard's chest. Turned out, they didn't have to look far. They found my work boots in a brown paper bag in the covered trash can behind my house."

No, no, no. This is all wrong.

"Wait a minute, Ari. Are you saying the police think those were the boots that Ferris's killer used to…" She covered her mouth, too horrified to finish the question.

"Right now, that's the theory," he said. "They're going to compare the dust and dirt remnants from my boots to the ones found at the crime scene. Oh, and guess what the work boots were wrapped in? My vampire cape, the one that went missing from my pickup."

Carly felt a cold chill wash over her. Someone went to a lot of trouble to make Ari look like a killer.

"Something's not adding up. Did you tell them you left your work boots at the job site on Friday?"

"I did, but they weren't satisfied with that. The truth is, I can't say with any certainty exactly when those work boots went missing. I'd have sworn I stuck them in the back of my pickup after I left the Pownal site Friday, but obviously I was wrong."

Unless you weren't wrong.

Carly pulled in a slow breath and released it. If she was going to figure this out and help Ari, her mind needed to be crystal clear. At the moment, her thoughts were so scrambled she could've whipped them into a cheese omelet.

"Ari, please help me wrap my head around this," she said, as calmly as she could. "What prompted the police to get a search warrant in the first place?"

He sighed into the phone. "The police have a dedicated number where people can leave anonymous tips about a crime. Someone called it this morning and claimed they had personal knowledge that the shoe, or shoes, that made the footprint on Menard's chest were in my possession."

A thousand scenarios flitted through Carly's brain, not one of them the slightest bit comforting. Then something occurred to her. "This tip line," she said. "Can't the police just trace the call and find out who left the tip?"

"It doesn't work that way, Carly." Ari sounded defeated. "Anonymity to callers on the tip line is strictly guaranteed. That avenue, I'm afraid, is a dead end."

Something was horribly wrong with this entire picture. How many people even knew about the footprint? Suzanne and her hubby had found out from a cop friend, but he'd told them about it in strict confidence. Had Holly spread the word so quickly that it was now common knowledge?

"Honey, the good thing is—the police didn't have enough to hold me, so for now I'm a free man. I'm meeting with my lawyer tonight at seven. His office is down on High Street, behind the insurance building."

A breath of relief burst out of her. "Do you want me to go with you?" She knew Gina would understand if their girls' night had to be postponed.

"I appreciate the offer, but I think it's better if I consult with him alone, at least until I have an idea what—" He broke off abruptly, sending Carly's mental antennae zinging out of control.

What kind of trouble you're in? Is that what you meant?

"Okay, I understand. But will you call me right after the meeting?" She told him about her plans with Gina but reiterated that she'd gladly postpone if he wanted her to accompany him to the appointment.

"Listen, I want you and Gina to enjoy your evening. Eat a hunk of calzone for me, okay?" He tried to sound cheerful, but Carly knew he was worried.

After extracting another promise from him to call her after his appointment, she wished him luck and disconnected. Her insides felt as if they'd been fed through a steam roller and hung out on a stake to dry.

A stake...like the one through Ferris's heart?

Was that the message the killer had intended to leave by plunging a *steak* knife into Ferris's chest?

CHAPTER THIRTEEN

BACK IN THE DINING ROOM, CARLY NOTICED THAT STEVE Perlman had already left. She thought about canceling Gina, but then changed her mind. Some quality time with her bestie this evening would be just the medicine she needed. Plus, Gina had a unique way of looking at things, and Carly valued her input. The calzone would be an added bonus, assuming Carly would be able to choke down a mouthful.

Grant signaled Carly over behind the counter. "Hey, do you mind if I take a break?"

"Gosh, I'm so sorry," Carly groaned, a blade of guilt piercing her. "I've been shirking my duties today, haven't I?"

He sighed. "I'm just really wiped right now." He tapped three order slips that hung above the grill. "I've already started these three sandwiches. You just have to flip 'em and plate 'em. If I can take fifteen or twenty minutes, that'll be great." He gave her a sheepish look. "Um, Holly could probably use a break too."

"Take a half hour or more," Carly told him, another wave of guilt crashing over her. "And don't worry. I'll talk to Holly."

He whipped off his apron and tucked it beneath the counter. "Be back in a jiff!"

Carly reviewed the orders—two Classics and a Sweddar Weather, all with extra chips. She set up three plates with a mountain of chips on each, then flipped over the sandwiches. As she waited for them to grill, she glanced over the counter into the dining room. A woman seated alone in one of the booths was deep in conversation with Holly, a mug filled with coffee in front of her. From their body language, Carly sensed that the two knew one another, and not just casually.

After plating the three orders, Carly delivered them to a booth at the rear part of the restaurant. Ensuring that all other customers had everything they needed, she ambled over to Holly, who jumped at her approach.

"Oh, um, Carly, this is Portia Fletcher, my stepmom. Portia, this is my new boss, Carly Hale." Holly twisted her fingers nervously.

Portia Fletcher, *not Menard?* Either way, this was a perfect opportunity for Carly to glean some info from Menard's ex.

Carly smiled at the woman. "I'm pleased to meet you, Portia. Welcome to Carly's Grilled Cheese Eatery."

"Hey, glad to be here," Portia said brightly. Her smile was wide with perfect white teeth, her gray eyes sharp with intelligence. "Holly told me how much she enjoys working here. Looking around, I can see why. You've created a warm and welcoming ambience."

"Thank you. My regular server is out for a few weeks, and we're pleased Holly was able to fill in." She lowered her voice to a reverent tone. "By the way, I'm terribly sorry for your loss."

For a second or two, Portia's expression froze. Then she blinked and said, "Thank you, but it was Holly's loss, not mine. Ferris and I were estranged, soon to be divorced."

Startled by her bluntness, Carly said, "Still, I'm sure it was a shock."

Carly stole a few seconds to study Holly's stepmom. Late thirties, forty at the most, her short auburn hair spiky and stylish, her tanned skin smooth and toned. Clad totally in a dazzling shade of pink, from her chunky earrings and silky scarf to the designer kitten heels that peeked out from under the table, she could probably be spotted from a block away.

Portia reached into the oversized pink satchel that rested beside her. She pulled out a plastic bag containing three glass bottles adorned with fancy labels. Her gray eyes sparkled when she held out the bag to Carly. "Carly, may I offer you a sample pack of the three salad dressings I've created? They range from mild to spicy, but all have the same avocado oil base. Scrumptious, if I do say so myself."

This woman doesn't waste time, Carly thought wryly.

"I'm teaming up with a start-up spice company based in our fair state," Portia went on. "In fact, they're opening a retail store across the green, near that charming card shop. The downtown gets so glutted with tourists during the high season, that they think it will do quite well there."

"I'm sure it will," Carly agreed, wondering what Portia considered the "high season." "Someone told me recently that your salad dressing recipes are based on the one Ferris Menard used in his sub shop."

Another blink, followed by a mild pursing of her pink-tinted lips. "Only in a cursory way," Portia was quick to point out. "Suffice it to say, I learned what *not* to do from his example. My dressings are far more complex and flavorful than the pedestrian blend Ferris served in the sub shop."

Holly's face flushed almost as pink as Portia's ensemble, but she kept her eyes lowered and said nothing.

The door opened, and two women came in. "Portia, I

need to attend to my customers," Carly apologized, "but it's been a pleasure meeting you. Thank you for the samples. I'm anxious to try them."

"It's been a joy meeting you as well, Carly. Please let me know your opinion of the dressings. My business card is in the bag with all my social media links. Commercial customers are going to be key to our growth, so I'll value your thoughts."

"I'll be sure to let you know. Holly, after you chat with Portia, why don't you grab yourself something to eat in the kitchen and rest your feet for a few, okay? You've been working almost non-stop all day."

"Are...are you sure?" Holly stammered. "Some customers just came in."

"No worries. I'll take their orders."

Holly looked relieved. "Thank you, Carly. Is...would it be okay if I sat with Portia instead?"

Carly paused for a beat. She wanted to learn more about Portia, but she had to serve customers first. "Sure. Go ahead."

She tucked Portia's sample dressing packet into the pocket of her apron, then took the women's orders, delivered their drinks, and went around the counter to the grill. In the short time she'd been distracted by her conversation with Portia, she'd put Ari out of her mind. His situation now came back at her full force, making her stomach flip-flop like a landed fish.

I've got to figure out how to prove his innocence, she thought fiercely. *He wouldn't be in this mess if I hadn't battled with Ferris Menard.*

Grant came in just then, his face looking a bit more relaxed than before he left. "Hey, want me to take over?"

Carly nodded and set down the spatula, her voice stuck in her throat.

Grant slipped on a pair of vinyl gloves and put on his apron. When he caught her expression he said, "What's wrong? Did something happen?"

She nodded again. "I'll tell you later, okay?" She turned and fled through the swinging door into the kitchen.

~

For the remainder of the workday, Carly went through the motions of scraping food into the compost bin and stuffing plates and mugs into the dishwasher. She debated how much to share with Grant, but with Holly there, she really couldn't talk openly with him, especially about Ari. She promised to update him the following morning, when they'd be alone getting the eatery ready for the day.

Holly was dropping her apron into the laundry bin when Carly went over to her. "Holly, I apologize if I sounded like an ogre today. I know you didn't mean to upset Evelyn. You were excited about the progress on your dad's case, and I totally get that."

"Yeah, but I should've told you privately, not in front of everyone else." Her eyes suddenly brightened. "Did you like Portia? She's great, isn't she?"

"She's lovely, and very accomplished from what I saw." Carly hesitated, then said, "I know your dad's death is still unresolved, but given what the attorney told you, are you at all interested in taking over his business?"

"Um…I might be, depending on Portia's plans. Like I said, I took a retail job for the holiday season, so I can't back out on it now. Whatever I decide to do, it'll be after the first of the year."

"What do mean by Portia's plans?" Carly removed her jacket from the closet.

Holly's face suddenly reddened, as if she'd revealed too much. "Um, you know, just that Portia might be interested in being, like, a silent partner. It's not definite, though."

"Even though she's partnering with the spice company?"

"Um, yeah. She's still going to do that. That's her baby." Holly's smile reflected her hero worship of her stepmom, but then it faded quickly. "Tell you the truth, I'm not sure how it's all going to work with the sub shop. I had no clue Dad would even consider leaving his business assets to me, so I'm still kind of in shock, you know? I mean, I sure as heck didn't expect him to die." Her eyes glazed over. "I'm sure he didn't expect it either." She shook her head, as if to dispel the grim thought. "One thing's for sure, nothing's going to happen until his killer is behind bars. I'm keeping the sub shop closed till that's resolved."

Carly decided not to press her anymore, not until she learned more about Portia. Her primary worry was Ari, who was going to end up wearing prison orange if the police succeeded in pinning the murder on him.

If those work boots turned out to be the ones used at the crime scene, then someone was setting up Ari to take the blame for Ferris's murder.

CHAPTER FOURTEEN

"Auntie Gina will be here any minute," Carly told Havarti, who was prancing around her feet as she set down his food dish.

Carly set the table with plates, glasses, and flatware, placing a trivet in the center. Although her stomach was gurgling with hunger, she wasn't sure how much of Louie's delicious calzone she'd be able to enjoy. Her mind was firmly stuck on Ari and the mess he'd found himself in through no fault of his own.

Gina arrived only a few minutes later, calzone in hand and flashing a harried smile. Her dark brown hair framed her face in fashionable waves, and a ring with a lavender gem sparkled on her left hand. "Whew! What a busy day. I got three new orders—two for shower invitations and one for a family reunion." She shed her jacket and tossed it on the sofa.

Carly pointed at the ring. "Um, Gina—"

"Don't look like you swallowed an egg. Yes, Zach gave it to me, and no, it's not *that* kind of ring. We're calling it a friendship ring, for now."

"If you say so." Carly squelched a smile.

In the kitchen, Carly set the calzone on the trivet and poured them each a glass of cola. It was their go-to drink whenever they ate anything in the pizza family.

"New business is great to have," Carly said, slicing the calzone into quarters and setting the two cups of dipping sauce on the table. "But at some point, won't you need more help?"

"I already do need more help." Gina speared a chunk of the spicy calzone with her fork and swirled it through the sauce. "The good thing is, I've been training my salesclerk on the quilling technique, and she's really getting the hang of it. Best part is, she's willing to work on special orders at home. Like most of us, she can use the extra *do-re-mi*."

Carly nodded, then took a small bite of her food. It went down hard, which did not escape Gina's attention.

"Something's wrong," Gina said, staring at Carly. "What is it?"

Carly swallowed a mouthful of her cola, and then the dam burst. She told Gina everything—about Ari being served with a warrant and his work boots being confiscated. About Holly's meeting with her dad's lawyer, and then Holly blabbing about the footprint and upsetting Evelyn. About Portia coming into the restaurant...

"Oh my gosh. You've had a wild day, haven't you?" Gina leaped off her chair and hugged her friend, then sat down again. "Unless I'm hearing this wrong, someone's trying to frame Ari. But who?"

"That's what we need to figure out," Carly said. "What do you know about Portia Fletcher, other than her supposedly stealing Ferris's salad dressing formula? Which she denies, by the way."

Gina chuckled. "Yeah, she would. I don't know much about her. She's not from these parts, as they say. As for the salad dressing formula, who knows the real truth? I never thought it was anything special, although it did improve over the last few years. Ferris hyped it so much that eventually people believed he'd conjured up some magic formula."

Smoke and mirrors, Carly thought. *Fool enough people and you've got yourself a recipe for success.*

Carly mulled that as she poked at a slice of pepperoni with her fork. "When did Ferris and Portia get married?"

Gina blew out a breath. "Oh gosh, I don't remember, exactly. Two, three years ago? It was a short-lived marriage, for sure. His business was floundering at the time, partially because of his charming personality." She quirked a crooked grin. "The way I heard it, Portia saw the possibilities and wanted to franchise the sub shop. You know, start locally and then open more stores throughout New England."

"Ferris didn't agree?"

"He hated the idea. He said quality control would be a big problem, and he didn't want to take the risk. Which was a joke, because he didn't maintain quality in his *own* shop. Last year, two customers claimed they got sick from mayonnaise he'd left out all day."

"I've heard stories from Grant, so that doesn't surprise me," Carly said. "Still, I'd have thought Ferris would leap at the chance to make money from franchising."

"Ferris was a weird guy, Carly. Suspicious of everyone, petty as all get-out, didn't even like his own daughter much until she started helping him in the sub shop." Gina took another bite of her calzone.

"When Holly started working for him, was he married to Portia?"

Gina swallowed her food, then tapped a finger to her lips. "I can't quite recall, but I don't think so. The way I heard it, Ferris manned up and started acting like a real father *after* he hooked up with Portia. Portia had no use for a man who didn't treat women with respect. Especially when it came to his own daughter."

Carly smiled. "I like that about her. Makes me wonder what she saw in him in the first place. What attracted her to him?"

"Beats me." Gina shrugged.

"Anyway, from what I saw today, Holly adores Portia. Maybe because Portia went to bat for her with her dad. More cola?"

Gina nodded, and Carly replenished their glasses.

"Let's get back to Ari," Carly said. "If those work boots turn out to be the ones the killer used, then someone framed him, and that someone was Ferris's killer. What do you think—should we add Portia and Holly to the suspect category?"

"Together or separately?" Gina mumbled over a mouthful of food.

"Either. Both."

"Motive?" Gina slugged back a mouthful of cola.

Carly sat back and thought a moment before she answered. "Okay, how's this? Take over the sub shop, run it their way, turn it into a franchise business?" She ticked off points on her fingers.

Gina looked doubtful. "I don't know, Carly. I'm not sure I can picture Holly plotting against her own dad. Not that I know her well, but she doesn't strike me as the type."

"What if Portia influenced her?" Carly offered.

"It's possible, but I'm not buying it." Gina stabbed another chunk of calzone. "Now Portia alone, she's a different story. You know what my aunt Lil calls her?"

Carly chuckled. "I'm afraid to ask."

"She told me once that Portia Fletcher is an enigma, wrapped in a puzzle, sauteed in a conundrum. Something like that, anyway."

Carly laughed. "I love your aunt Lil."

"Yeah. I do too. I'm just saying that no one really knows Portia very well."

For a while they ate in silence, Havarti resting his furry chin on the tip of Carly's shoe. Talking about possible suspects had boosted Carly's appetite, but she didn't polish off as much of the calzone as Gina had.

"I just remembered someone else I wanted to ask you about," Carly said. "Do you know the guy with the pale, pale skin who works for the compost company? His name's Chip Foster."

"Chip? Sure, I know who you mean," Gina said, nodding. "He helped Dad paint the inside of our house once. He never works outside because of his condition. It's some kind of skin disease that makes him allergic to sunlight."

Carly made a mental note to ask her mom's hubby, a retired dermatologist, about that. "Grant told me that Ferris referred to him one day as 'Drac.' Is that his nickname, or was that Ferris being cruel?"

Gina made a face. "The latter, I suspect. Leave it to someone like Ferris Menard to make fun of the poor man's affliction." She dabbed her lips with her napkin. "So, are we adding him to the suspect list because Ferris called him Drac?"

"We?" Carly smiled. It was great to have her best bud to confab with. Since the day she was born, Gina had never lived anywhere except in Balsam Dell. Her insight into the locals was endless. "I'd like to add him, but we need a motive. What else do you know about Chip?"

"I have to confess, not much." Gina finished her cola. "I'm pretty sure he's single. Not sure where he lives. Bit of a loner, I think. I've never once seen him smile, poor man."

"Maybe you can ask your dad?"

Gina's dad, a retired firefighter, had moved into assisted living over the summer. According to Gina, her dad was content there, except he'd regretted having to sell the only home Gina had ever known to pay the cost.

"I definitely will. In fact, I'll call him when I get home. Anyone else on your hit list?" Gina joked.

Carly batted her arm. "It's not a hit list. It's a suspect list. There is one other person, but I'm not sure if or how he fits in. Do you know Tyler at the hardware store?"

"Tyler? Oh sure, he's a pretty good kid. Well, he's probably in his twenties, but guys that age all look like kids to me. Why, is he a possible?"

Carly explained about him being the only other vampire at the competition, and how she'd learned from Don Frasco that he was friendly with Holly.

"Again, we need a motive. Being a friend of Holly's doesn't cut it, nor does dressing like a vampire."

"I know." Carly groaned. "I questioned him at the hardware store on Monday. Except for finding out that he has access to a photocopier, I didn't learn much. He claimed he knows Holly, period—end of story." She explained her theory about the fraudulent votes submitted in the competition.

Gina frowned. "I can't imagine the voting having anything to do with the murder, though." Her brown eyes creased with concern. "So, the cops are taking this vampire thing seriously, huh? I heard they found a Dracula figurine under Ferris's body, but to me that doesn't mean much. It could've gotten kicked around during the scuffle and he landed on it. But the cape and the work boots in Ari's trash can, that's different. That was someone's way of trying to pin the murder on him."

Carly pushed her plate aside, her last chunk of calzone now a cold lump. "Gina, this is bad." Her voice shook. "The killer was at Ari's house. The killer must have stalked him to find out where he'd be and when, so he could plant the evidence without being seen."

"He or she," Gina said thoughtfully. "I don't suppose Ari has a security camera?"

"No, he lives in a modest home on Methuen Street." Carly had been there only twice and was surprised at how spartan his décor was. Her own place was far cozier and homier.

"So, do we add Tyler to the list?" Gina asked.

"For now, yes." Carly carried their plates to the sink and brought over the sealed container with the turkey-shaped sugar cookies. "Ari brought these over last night."

"Ah. Thank you, Ari." Gina's eyes lit up as she nabbed one and bit off the turkey's head.

Carly grabbed one for herself and closed the container. She took a tiny bite, then set her cookie on a napkin.

"So," Gina said, wiping a crumb from her lips, "what's been happening in the restaurant this week, other than Holly working for you?"

Carly sneaked a peek at her cell. Nothing from Ari yet. "Busy," she said, with a weak smile. "It's actually a relief that Holly asked to sub for Suzanne, but I'm not totally sold on her innocence. If she has a hidden agenda, she's darn good at hiding it. But she's a good worker and the customers like her."

"And your faithful band of defenders?" Gina grinned.

"If you mean Grant, Mr. P., and Stan, they're all fine. Grant's dad wants him to quit, but so far he's still with me. Oh, and that sweet Evelyn Fitch has come in every day this week. I really think she's lonely."

"I bet you're right. Did she write you another note?"

"Two, actually." Carly broke off a corner of the turkey's feathers. "The poor woman. She got horribly rattled today after Holly blurted out the news about the police having a lead on the footprint on her dad's body. I think it was a little too graphic for Evelyn."

Thinking about it again made Carly squirm. Evelyn's demeanor had gone from sweet to distraught in so short a time, it was like someone had pulled a switch. Even more troubling was she'd been abrupt with Carly, which wasn't like her at all.

"Yeah, I can see why. Speaking of Stan Henderson," Gina said with a giggle, "do you remember what a huge crush he had on you in middle school?"

"He did not," Carly protested, feeling her cheeks flush.

"He totally did! Don't you remember the day he tried getting you to promise you'd marry him when you both grew up?" She broke off a chunk of frosted feathers and batted her lashes playfully at Carly. "It was right after one of our poetry classes with Mr. Slosek. The poetry must have made poor Stan feel romantic, because he pulled a cheap ring out of his pocket and tried to give it to you. You tactfully escaped betrothal by telling him your mom would have a double-duty fit."

Carly choked on a crumb. She *did* remember that. "Oh ugh, Gina. We were only twelve. *Romantic* wasn't even on my radar then."

Thinking back, the poor kid had seemed so earnest, as if a promise of marriage between two twelve-year-olds was the most natural thing in the world. To soothe his hurt feelings—plus he was rather cute—Carly had told him they could talk about it again when they were old enough to date. Fortunately, his family moved out of town shortly after that, so Stan ended up attending a different high school. Not that he would have taken the proposal seriously, but it was a relief not to have to see him every day in class.

"I think I actually blocked that from my memory," Carly said in amazement. "But now that you brought it up, I *do* remember. Funny how some things slip our brains."

Gina shrugged. "He had an odd family too. The dad was sort of a loose cannon, never kept a job long. That's gotta be hard on a kid."

Carly nodded absently. Reminiscing about Stan made her think of Mr. P., or Steve, as she now called him. "Speaking of school days, how much do you know about Steve Perlman?"

"Our old physics teacher?" Gina munched thoughtfully on a turkey foot. She swallowed and said, "Far as I know, he's unattached. I think he was engaged once but never made it to the altar. Why, are you interested in him?"

"I certainly am not," Carly scoffed. "But I asked him today if he knew Ferris Menard, and guess what? They played basketball together in high school."

"Huh," Gina said. "Doesn't really mean much, though."

"True, but when I tried to get more info out of him, he said it wasn't the best place to talk. That made me wonder if he *did* know something."

Gina sat up straighter. "Then if I were you, I'd *find* a place to talk, and soon."

"Believe me, I plan—" Carly's cell pinged with a text. She swept it off the table, her heart hammering when she saw Ari's face pop up. "Ari?" She nearly shrieked his name into the phone.

"Hi, honey." The weariness in his voice made Carly's heart turn over. "I just left my lawyer's office. He threw a lot of legal jargon at me, but the bottom line is, if my work boots get matched to the crime scene, it's possible I'll be arrested, or at the very least hauled in again for more questioning."

"Ari, I'm so sorry," Carly choked out. She pulled in a slow, shuddering breath. "Is your lawyer experienced in criminal defense?"

"Fortunately, he is. Carly, please don't worry. The truth has to come out eventually. We both know I had nothing to do with Menard's death. The police will know it too, once they find the real killer."

Unless they stop looking for the real killer.

"I have a job lined up for tomorrow, but my attorney advised me to postpone it. He told me to lie low until we see how the evidence shakes out."

Carly looked at Gina and shook her head. "Try to get some rest tonight, okay?"

"I will. You do the same," Ari said. "And Carly, I know you're going to want to start asking questions, but please remember—Menard's killer is a very dangerous person. And a bold one, to be sneaking onto my property and leaving false evidence in my trash can."

"I know." Carly swallowed. "I'll watch everything I say, I promise." *But I won't stop looking for the killer.*

They murmured their goodbyes and Carly disconnected, a little awkwardly with Gina staring at her as if she thought

Carly might spontaneously combust. Carly gave her friend a recap of Ari's meeting with his lawyer.

"I'm calling Dad as soon as I get home," Gina said adamantly. "I'm going to ask him about Chip Foster and see if he knows of anyone who had a beef with Ferris."

"Thanks, Gina." Carly glanced at the clock. It was almost quarter to nine. "Hey, do you want to take a short ride with me and Havarti?"

"A short ride? Sure, I'm game," Gina said. "Where're we headed?"

"To Evelyn's Fitch's house. She was so upset when she left the restaurant today. I want to be sure she's okay."

"What if she goes to bed early?" Gina asked.

"She stays up late reading sometimes, so I'm willing to chance it. If the house is dark, we won't bother her."

Carly rose and retrieved Havarti's leash, while Gina found Evelyn's address on her cell and programmed it into her map app.

"You're up for an adventure tonight, aren't you, baby?" Carly asked her dog, clipping on his leash.

Havarti gave a short yip and a leap into the air, and the trio was on their way.

CHAPTER FIFTEEN

LESS THAN TEN MINUTES LATER, THEY WERE PULLING into the narrow driveway of a gray and white bungalow, its front porch boasting two large tubs of colorful mums. To the right of the white-painted front door, a wicker chair with a padded seat rocked slightly, swayed by the same stiff breeze that rustled the trees.

The blinds on the front windows were closed, slivers of light peeking around the edges. The porch light was also on, making Carly wonder if Evelyn was expecting a visitor. Or did she always leave it on during evening hours?

"Well, the lights are on. That's a good sign," Gina said as they got out of the car.

Looping her fingers through Havarti's leash, Carly glanced around Evelyn's shallow front yard. The grass had been recently mown, and the few hedges that lined the front of the house were neatly trimmed.

Havarti strained at his leash as they climbed the wide front steps. "I know, you're anxious to meet a new friend," Carly said, smiling down at her sweet dog. She rang the doorbell, eliciting a *ding-dong* chiming sound from inside the house. After a silent minute or so, Gina pressed her ear to the front door. "I don't hear anything. Maybe she's in the bathroom?"

Carly rang the bell again and knocked on the door. Anxious to get inside, Havarti whined at her feet.

"Ms. Fitch?" Gina called through the door. After another minute or so, she looked at Carly and shrugged. "She could be out. I always leave a light on in my apartment when I'm not home."

"I guess," Carly said doubtfully, an odd feeling creeping over her. She jiggled the doorknob, and when the door opened a crack, her heart lurched. She exchanged worried glances with Gina. "Should we go in? I don't want to scare her if she's only resting."

"I don't hear a TV or anything," Gina said, biting down on her lip. She called Evelyn's name again, but again, there was no response. "Wait a minute." She gripped Carly's coat sleeve. "Did you hear something out back? It sounded like an animal or…" Leaving the thought to dangle, she lifted her chin and listened.

"Probably just a raccoon," Carly said uneasily.

Havarti's ears and tail suddenly stiffened. He thrust his nose into the slightly open doorway and whined to go inside.

"He acted like this once before," Carly said, "when a baby robin fell out of the tree in the backyard. Becca rescued the bird, but Havarti nearly went nuts until she did."

His agitation growing, Havarti barked at the door. "Hush, Havarti," Carly said, but the dog continued to bark.

"I have a feeling something's wrong," Gina said. "I think we should go inside."

Decision made, they entered the house, Havarti trotting ahead of Carly. Nose to the floor, he checked out all the smells, while Carly skimmed her gaze around the cheery room.

Evelyn's kitchen was orderly and spotless, its walls papered in pale blue with a yellow buttercup pattern. The sink was clean, save for one unwashed bowl filled to the rim with water.

"Evelyn? It's Carly," she called out, hearing the tremor in her own voice. Havarti barked and tugged at his leash.

"Looks like she was working on something," Gina said, noting the sheets of pink paper with writing on them scattered over the kitchen table.

"Havarti, be still," Carly urged, until she realized what he was straining toward. A door at the opposite corner of the kitchen was partway open. Weak yellow light spilled through the gap.

Carly didn't know why her heart was pummeling her ribs, only that something felt very wrong. She handed the leash to Gina. "Watch Havarti for a minute, okay?"

"Okay, but be careful."

Carly padded over to the partially open door and inched it open farther. She peered down the stairs and, in the next instant, sucked in a gasp. "Oh, no. Evelyn!"

She pounded down the stairs until she reached the small figure that was sprawled, face down, across the bottom two steps. Evelyn's head was on the concrete floor, one slippered foot hooked over the second stair from the bottom. She was clad in a quilted robe that had ridden up past her knees.

Gina rushed to the doorway and looked down. The leash slipped from her fingers, and Havarti immediately bounded down the stairs. "Oh good grief, Carly, is she breathing?"

Carly maneuvered herself around Evelyn's still form until she reached the cellar floor. Kneeling on the cold concrete, she pushed Evelyn's white hair gently off her face and pressed two fingers to her neck. "She's breathing, but it's faint. Gina, call 911. She needs an ambulance, ASAP."

Moments later, she heard Gina speaking urgently into her cell, while Havarti rested his furry form on the floor. He kept his brown-eyed gaze on Evelyn, as though guarding her from further injury.

Carly wanted to shift Evelyn to a more comfortable position, but she didn't dare move her. After plucking her cell from the pocket, she took off her coat and draped it gently over her elderly friend. The best thing they could do now was to wait for help.

As they waited, Carly used her cell to take a few quick photos of the area where she'd found Evelyn. On the wall directly opposite the stairs, barely a foot from the bottom step, a row of metal shelving stretched the length of the cellar. Large plastic storage boxes lined the shelves, most of them labeled with a different year. One box, Carly noticed, was protruding from the shelf, directly above where Evelyn lay. It looked close to toppling, so she pushed it back in place, then snapped a picture of it.

Relief flooded her when she heard the shrill drone of the ambulance outside. A police car followed. After that, everything happened quickly. Evelyn was gently but efficiently placed on a stretcher and shuttled into the waiting ambulance.

"I've got to call her daughter," Carly told one of the officers, after answering about a hundred questions.

"I was just going to ask if you had an emergency contact," the officer said.

"I do," Gina announced. "I found it on the chalkboard above Evelyn's kitchen phone. I took a picture with my cell."

Evelyn's so organized, Carly thought, a lump clogging her throat.

After the officer took Lydia's contact info, the police secured the house. The last official vehicle departed, leaving Carly, Gina, and Havarti shivering on the front porch.

A brisk wind whipped through the trees. The night air felt like icicles, tunneling beneath Carly's coat sleeves and freezing the tips of her ears.

"That's weird," Gina said, staring at the hedge underneath the front window.

Before Carly could question what she was talking about, Gina had pulled out her cell and was taking pictures of the mulch surrounding the shrubs.

"What is it?" Carly asked her, so tired she could barely think.

Gina held up her cell. "Unless I'm crazy, that's a footprint."

Clutching Havarti's leash, Carly clomped over to where Gina stood. She peered at her friend's phone. "You're not crazy. That is indeed a footprint. The question is," she said ominously, "who made the footprint, and when?"

CHAPTER SIXTEEN

THURSDAY MORNING WAS A WHIRLWIND OF PHONE CALLS and texts, many between Carly and Lydia, Evelyn's daughter, and a few between Carly and Gina. Gina had texted photos of the mystery footprint to the responding officer. He'd thanked her and said they'd look into it.

Evelyn had regained consciousness overnight, but was still very disoriented. She had no memory of how she ended up at the bottom of her cellar stairs. Fortunately, she hadn't suffered any broken bones—although her forehead now sported a massive purple bruise. Lydia couldn't stop expressing her gratitude to Carly. She berated herself for not having taken her mom's troubled demeanor more seriously the day before.

Grant came into the eatery early again. He immediately went behind the counter, where a fresh pot of coffee was waiting. "Hey," he said to Carly, who was sitting on the stool Ari usually claimed. A half-filled mug of coffee sat cooling in front of her.

"Hey yourself," she said, trying and utterly failing to inject a note of cheer into her voice.

"I can tell something's wrong. I mean, even more wrong than yesterday." He poured himself a mug of coffee and refilled Carly's.

Nodding her thanks, Carly choked back tears.

"Carly, what is it? Did something happen?"

Carly told him everything, beginning with finding Evelyn unconscious in her cellar, to Ari's horrible situation. "It sounds like Evelyn's going to recover. Lydia said if she improves enough today, they'll discharge her tomorrow and send her to a rehab facility. The one in town here is excellent. There's an entire unit devoted to the kind of care she'll need."

"Sounds awfully soon," Grant pointed out.

"I know, but Lydia said her mom has a horror of hospitals. She's been clamoring to get out of there since she woke up."

"Wow. She's one tough lady."

Carly took a long sip from her mug. "Getting back to Ari, I'm so terrified he's going to be arrested, Grant. I can't even imagine him in a jail cell."

"It would be a travesty, totally ridiculous." Grant's eyes blazed with outrage. "Ari's one of the best guys I ever met. Anyone who knows him will realize it's a bogus charge."

Her throat tightening, Carly nodded in agreement. "I've been racking my brain trying to think of who the murderer is. I almost hate to suggest this, but what do you think about Holly?" Carly asked him. "You know her far better than I do. Is there any way she could have, you know, done that to her dad?"

Grant's eyes flickered with doubt. "Man, I honestly don't see it. More than anything, Holly wanted his approval." He paused. "Although, I gotta say, there were a few times when I saw her manipulate her dad. She had a way of twisting facts so he'd see things her way."

That got Carly's attention. "Really? What kinds of things?"

"Well, one thing is, Mr. M. had a habit of giving deep discounts to some of his favorite customers. Like, the man who heads up the town's Select Board—Ralph Bairstow? The guy's super arrogant, swaggers into the sub shop like he owns the town. He and Mr. M. were good buddies, I guess. Anyway, Mr. M. would charge him only half price for his subs and throw in a lot of extras for free."

"Did anyone complain?"

"No, Mr. M. was careful about it, but it ticked off Holly something fierce. She told her dad some of their customers had gotten wind of his *cronyism*, as she called it, and were going to boycott his shop."

"Was that true?"

"Nope. Holly only said that because she couldn't stand Bairstow. He always looked down his nose at her, like she wasn't good enough to be in his presence."

"Sounds like a jerk. In a way I don't blame Holly, but she should have just told her dad the truth instead of making up a story. Did she do anything else?"

He hesitated. "Yeah, there was one thing that kind of bothered me, although I suspect Tyler Huling was behind this one. About four months ago, Mr. M. got a new car. Holly asked him if she could take it for a spin, and he reluctantly gave her the keys. I'd just left to come over here when I saw her tooling around in the car, except that *she* wasn't the one driving. Tyler was behind the wheel, and let me tell you, he was taking some of those corners practically on two wheels. Mr. M. would've thrown a fit if he'd seen them."

"Did Holly know you saw her?"

"I think so, but I didn't say anything. It wasn't my place to tattle."

That confirmed Carly's suspicion that Holly was crushing on Tyler. Did he reciprocate her feelings, or was he taking advantage of her? Maybe he'd prodded her to borrow her dad's car so he could take it for a spin himself.

Carly was beginning to view Holly in a whole different light—one that cast a harsh shadow on her harmless demeanor. Manipulation was a far cry from murder, sure, but didn't it demonstrate a willingness to fudge the truth? To lie to get what she wanted?

"Whoever killed Ferris," Carly said, "had to have planned it in advance. The killer somehow managed to steal Ari's work boots, and then his vampire cape. I might be overthinking it, but I can't help picturing him, or her, using the boots to stand on Ferris's chest so he couldn't reach his medication."

Grant looked troubled. "When you lay it out like that, it really is awful, isn't it? But Carly, Mr. M. would only have needed his medication if he had an angina attack. That's what his prescription was for. So how could the killer have planned that in advance?"

Carly stared at the aquamarine counter, one finger looped through her mug handle. "The killer wouldn't have had to plan it. He, or she, brought a *steak* knife with him, and it was found in Ferris's chest. By a twist of fate, it ended up not being the real murder weapon, like the killer intended. At least that's how I see it."

"So you're saying the killer planned all along to use the steak knife to kill Mr. M., and the angina attack was a bonus."

"Exactly."

Grant shook his head and after a long silence said, "Want a breakfast biscuit?" He stooped to collect the ingredients from the fridge.

"Not today, thanks. My stomach is in tangles." She pushed her mug toward the edge of the counter. "I'll take another java refill, though."

Grant obliged, then went about making his own cheesy biscuit. "Do you think that overnight envelope from the DNA testing lab had anything to do with the murder?"

"I don't have a clue," Carly said. "But here's the thing—hear me out on this. What if Holly knew, or even suspected, that she's not Ferris's biological daughter, *and* she knew she was the beneficiary on his life insurance? That would give her a motive for murder, wouldn't it? Eliminate Ferris before he had time to change his beneficiary?"

"Only if she were a sociopath, Carly." His expression pained, he said, "I just don't see it. I truly don't." He slathered butter on his stuffed biscuit and set it on the grill. "Besides, why would she have confided all that stuff in you if she really *did* off her dad? Wouldn't that be risky?"

"Maybe." Carly blinked. "Grant, what's that saying in sports? The best defense is a good offense? By telling me about it in advance, maybe she figured it would give her the illusion of innocence. Like, why would she tell me all that personal stuff if she had something to hide?"

Grant let out a long sigh. "Anything's possible, but again, I'm not seeing it. I'd be more suspicious of Portia Fletcher."

Carly twirled around on her stool and faced him. "Any particular reason?"

Grant shrugged. "Nothing I can pin down. It's just...well, Holly seems to have developed a kind of starry-eyed hero worship for her. I think Portia has a lot of influence over her." He removed his biscuit sandwich from the grill and set it on a plate.

"I thought that too," Carly said. "When I offered my condolences to Portia for her loss yesterday, she made it clear that the loss was Holly's, not hers."

Grant's eyebrows shot up. "See? Doesn't that tell you something? 'Course that doesn't make her a killer, but why didn't she just say, 'Thank you,' and leave it at that?"

Carly smiled. "People are strange." *And some people are murderers.*

Before she'd gone to bed the evening before, Carly had googled "Portia Fletcher." Unfortunately, nothing useful had jumped out at her. Portia had begun her career as an administrative assistant to a manufacturing mogul at a company outside of Boston. She stayed on the job eleven years. By the time she resigned, she was the top-earning sales executive for the company's northeast region. It wasn't clear why or when she moved to Vermont, but at some point she married Ferris Menard in a civil ceremony in Bennington. Like Carly, Portia had kept her own surname instead of taking her new husband's.

Grant polished off his biscuit and said, "Guess we'd better get to work. I'll do that floor this morning. There's enough soup in the freezer for another two days so I don't have to make another batch."

They went about their separate tasks. Carly was in the kitchen slicing Swiss cheese when Grant came in through the swinging door and held up a slip of paper. "I found this under one of the booths when I was cleaning. It was folded up so small I almost threw it away, but then I thought I'd better look at it first." He gave it to Carly.

"Looks like the paper Evelyn writes on!" Carly read the note, then read it again—aloud this time. "'Do not despair, dear Carly. Everything will turn out fine. Among the lies, the truth shines through. Think of the flamingo, oh flagrant bird. He stands out among the rest.'" Puzzled, she looked at Grant. "What the heck?"

"My thoughts exactly. She was obviously trying to tell you something, but what?"

What, indeed. Carly took a picture of the note, then shoved it into her pocket. After slicing and separating enough varieties of cheese to get them through the afternoon, she stored everything in the fridge and wiped her hands on a dish towel. She remembered that today was Thursday, the day Don Frasco delivered his *Balsam Dell Weekly* to the various newspaper boxes in town.

"Be right back," she called to Grant and scooted outside through the front door. She returned with two copies of the paper—one for each of them.

Carly sat down in one of the booths and spread out the paper. This particular edition was thicker than usual. The front cover, which boasted the headline LOCAL RESTAURATEUR FOUND DEAD, was followed by a surprisingly short account of the discovery of Ferris's body and a reference to the investigation. Carly wondered if Don had been warned by the police not to disclose too much information. Below that, a smaller headline read: FROM FARM TO FABULOUS—SOUTHERN VERMONT'S NEW OPERA HOUSE OPENS TO FULL HOUSE. Interesting, but not what Carly was looking for. Another, even smaller article was titled: VICTIM'S DEATH SPURS POLICE TO RAMP UP SEARCH FOR DRIVER IN HIT-AND-RUN.

Carly had read about the hit-and-run a few months before. A man had left a local pub late one night, using the back door to exit into the narrow alley that ran behind it. He'd been so intoxicated that he collapsed onto the pavement seconds before a car sped down the alley and ran over him. The victim had survived, but only barely. A few weeks ago, it was reported that he'd succumbed to his injuries. Without any witnesses to the incident, the police had almost nothing to go on.

So tragic for the poor man and for his family, Carly thought.

She turned to page two, where coverage of Saturday's event was featured. Don had taken some great photos, at least two dozen of which filled pages two and three. The article that accompanied them was titled: ANNUAL COMPETITION MARRED BY BALLOT STUFFING. The words alone made Carly's anger bubble up all over again. Her first year in the competition, and someone had tried to cheat. And for what purpose? Whoever the true winner was, Ferris Menard was dead.

Carly told herself to chill. In the scheme of things, the contest wasn't important. A local man had been murdered and his killer was unknown. That was the real news.

Perusing the various photos, she grinned at one that showed her and Grant handing out their Cheesy Jack-O-Lanterns. Grant looked positively dashing as he posed for the shot, but Carly looked so ghostly white she almost resembled a real vampire.

She glanced over the other photos and was about to turn the page when one of them caught her attention. In one of the shots Don had taken of the crowd, a woman with light, shoulder-length curls walked beside a tall, lanky man with longish dark hair. The man wore a cape, and the woman sported a Bo Peep–style jumper. The man's face was turned toward the woman, and her arm was linked through his. From their location, and with their backs to the camera, it seemed clear they were leaving the event.

There was no doubt. Don had inadvertently photographed Holly and Tyler Huling as they were walking away from the town green. Together.

CHAPTER SEVENTEEN

BY 10:30 A.M., GRANT HAD THE DINING ROOM SPARKLING.
Carly was in the kitchen preparing a bowl of tuna salad when
her cell rang on the pine desk. It was her mom, confirming
their dinner date that evening at the Balsam Dell Inn. Carly
hoped Ari would still be a free man by then, and not sitting
in a police holding cell or interrogation room.

After disconnecting from her mom, she dropped her
phone on the desk and took a moment to collect her thoughts.
Only a week earlier, she was eagerly planning for her first
Scary-Licious Smorgasbord competition. Now, her signifi-
cant other was a suspect in a murder, and one of her favorite
customers was lying in the hospital with a head injury.

There was a reason why Evelyn had written that last note
to Carly. Whatever it was, whatever the "flamingo" referred
to, it must've had something to do with Evelyn bolting out of
the restaurant the day before.

And if Carly was going to help her friend, she had to
figure out what it was.

CHAPTER EIGHTEEN

ON HER WAY INTO THE DINING ROOM, IT OCCURRED TO Carly that their compost delivery man, Chip Foster, hadn't come in yet. Since he normally showed up in the morning, she wondered if there'd been a change in the schedule. If the company didn't send someone by the end of the day, she'd give them a call.

Aside from Ari being a murder suspect, Carly couldn't get Evelyn off her mind. Did she fall down those cellar stairs, or was she pushed? Why was her door unlocked, and who left the footprint beneath her window? The timing bothered her too. Was it possible Ferris's murder and Evelyn's accident were connected?

Her mind scrolling backward, Carly replayed Evelyn's departure from the eatery the day before. Evelyn had gathered up her things rather abruptly and offered only a curt goodbye. Carly had chalked it up to her distress over Holly blurting out the news about the footprint. Steve Perlman had just come in as she was leaving, Carly remembered. He'd quickly nabbed her booth before someone else claimed it, although he'd greeted Evelyn politely.

A thought struck her. Steve and Ferris had been in high school together. They'd played on the basketball team. Had Evelyn been teaching at the time? Could she have been their

English teacher, maybe known something about them they didn't want revealed?

If Steve came in today, Carly was definitely going to pin him down. In fact, she had a number of things she wanted to ask him, and this time she wouldn't let him escape.

Holly arrived promptly at 11:00, looking much cheerier than she had the day before. Was it because the police had homed in on a suspect in her dad's death—namely Ari? Carly tried not to judge her, but it wasn't easy. Especially after Grant's stories of her manipulation of her dad.

After accepting a mug of coffee from Grant, Holly turned to Carly and said, "Portia was so happy to meet you yesterday. She really admires successful women in business. She believes networking with other women is the key to everyone growing their businesses."

Sounds like a line from a brochure, Carly thought wryly. Was Holly trying to set up Carly for something, like maybe an endorsement of Portia's specialty salad dressings?

Carly smiled and said carefully, "Well, I enjoyed meeting her too. And she's right—networking is important in any line of work."

One early customer came in just then, and Holly took his order with a smile. Carly waited until he'd finished his meal and left to show Holly the latest *Balsam Dell Weekly.*

"Aren't these pictures great?" Carly opened the paper and held it up to display the spread from Saturday's event.

"Yeah, cool." She blinked several times.

Holly started to turn away when Carly pointed to the page and said, "Gee, isn't that you with Tyler from the hardware store?"

Holly's face flushed. "Um, yeah, it looks like us." She

dropped her gaze and then lifted it again. "I'm probably risking my job saying this, but Tyler told me about you going over to where he works and asking him questions. I know you didn't mean to, but he felt kind of blindsided."

"I know the feeling," Carly said quietly. "Are you and Tyler dating?" It sounded old-fashioned, but she didn't know how else to phrase it.

"Kind of." Holly's shoulders dropped. "Okay, look, here's the deal. Tyler and I are going to be moving in together. There's a cute apartment in one of the older homes on Main Street. It's kind of like the house you live in, except it needs a little more work."

"You know where I live?"

A look of sheer panic froze Holly's expression, as if she'd realized her blunder. "I...I heard you lived in Joyce Katso's two-family home," she finally said.

Carly decided not to press it. Nearly everyone in town knew where her landlady lived. She was more interested in learning about Tyler. "Tell me more about the house."

Holly's face relaxed slightly. "It belongs to Tyler's uncle, and he's going to let us move in the first of January. Tyler's going to help him with the upkeep in exchange for a break in the rent."

"Holly, I can't help wondering—did your dad like Tyler?" Carly asked.

The question clearly threw Holly off kilter. "I...yeah, he thought Tyler was a pretty good guy."

"How did Tyler feel about him?"

Holly rubbed her neck, her pale eyebrows scrunching toward her nose. "That's the same thing the police asked me. Tell you truth, he was a little intimidated by him. My dad isn't…wasn't the easiest dude to get along with. You know that yourself."

Is she trying to get me to admit I had bad blood with Ferris? Carly thought warily.

"Holly," Carly said, "the only reason I questioned Tyler is because it seemed he was the only other vampire at the event on Saturday. I know it rattled him a bit, but that wasn't my intention."

"He said you asked him to copy the receipt he gave you." Holly's lower lip rolled into a pout.

"I did, and he was very helpful." Carly started moving in the direction of the kitchen, assuming Holly would follow.

Holly held up a finger. "Um, before it gets busy, I need to use the restroom." She hurried past Carly and went into the bathroom.

Carly waited for the click of the lock, then pretended to straighten up the booth opposite the restroom. Sure enough, the sound of soft murmurings filtered through the door.

Holly was calling Tyler. Carly would bet her entire bank account on it. Was she warning him that Carly was still asking questions about him?

More than ever, Carly felt certain that Holly was hiding something. Something that involved Tyler.

Something she was desperate to keep Carly from finding out.

CHAPTER NINETEEN

THE LUNCH RUSH WAS BUSIER THAN EVER. A CHILLY RAIN
had begun to fall, and the outside air felt damp and raw.
Customers came in rubbing the November cold from their
hands. They smiled as the warmth of the restaurant and the
comforting scents of grilled butter and cheese washed over
them like a cozy blanket.

Once again, Holly performed her job with grace, good
cheer, and efficiency. There wasn't a single thing Carly could
fault her for. Their regular customers were definitely warming
up to her, although most of them still inquired about Suzanne.

Still, there was a part of Carly that didn't trust the young
woman. A famous line from a classic old movie rolled
through her mind: *Keep your friends close and your enemies
closer.* If Holly *were* the enemy—and Carly hoped to holy
heaven she wasn't—then she couldn't get much closer than
working in the restaurant.

As for Evelyn's accident and injury, Carly decided to wait
to spring the news on Holly until she could fully gauge her
reaction.

Stan Henderson came in around his usual time, his accordion folder of study materials tucked under one arm. Carly
noticed that the elastic had broken, and the flap was hanging
open. Spotting a free booth, he slapped the folder onto the

table so forcefully that several papers and receipts slid out and onto the floor.

Stan cursed under his breath, his face flushing with irritation. Carly stooped and retrieved as many stray papers as she could, while Stan shuffled everything else off the floor. He snatched the ones Carly had retrieved out of her hand.

"I've got them, thanks," he said brusquely. He crammed everything back into the folder, which had torn along the side. He gave Carly an embarrassed smile and said, "Guess I need to replace this thing, huh?"

She gave him a disarming smile in return. "Looks that way. Stan, I'm guessing you didn't have a good day. Can I treat you to a cola?"

"Uh, sure. That would be great. And you're right. I had a crummy day. Even so, I'm sorry I got so testy."

"Not a problem. We all have our moments."

He didn't bring up his job situation and Carly didn't ask. She gave his order of a Party Havarti to Grant, then returned with his cola.

After that, Carly pushed through the swinging door and went into the kitchen. Something she'd seen when she was picking up Stan's spilled papers had stuck in her mind. It was a bank withdrawal slip for $5,000, dated about two weeks earlier.

Not that it meant anything. But Carly wondered why Stan would be taking money out of his account if he was worried about the school downsizing him out of a job. Unless he knew he wouldn't be working much longer and wanted cash on hand to buy essentials and pay bills.

If that was the case, Carly truly felt for the guy. She'd never had to worry about losing her job. It had to be a scary feeling.

She texted Becca, who said she'd be happy to check in on Havarti during the evening. The only hitch in the plan was that Carly's mom had made their dinner reservation for 7:30. That wouldn't leave Carly enough time to dash home, shower, and change into something appropriate for the elegance of the Inn.

Back in the dining room, Grant was flipping over two Vermont Classics when Carly went over to him. "Hey, what do you think about us closing at six tonight? We'll have to put out a sign, but I don't think any of our regulars will mind."

"That sounds good to me," Grant said. "There's a student string quartet playing at the high school tonight and I was planning to attend." He grinned. "Now I won't have to be late."

"Perfect. I'm sure none of our customers will object. It won't be a regular thing."

When Holly came around the counter with two more orders for the grill, Carly took her aside to let her know the plan.

"Sure, that's fine by me." Holly stuck her pencil behind her ear. "Do you want me to make a sign for the door?"

"Um, actually that would be great. There's some paper and felt-tip pens in the supply closet in the kitchen."

Holly's blue eyes brightened. She smiled and clipped her orders above the grill. "I'll do it on my break."

That settled, Carly took over the grill for Grant while he headed over to Gina's shop to buy a birthday card for his dad. The school kids were streaming in, their laughter and good-natured banter lifting Carly's spirits.

"Two Farmhouse Cheddars," Holly said, clipping two more slips above the grill. She flicked her gaze over the dining room, then leaned closer to Carly. "Um, Carly, there's something I need to tell you. Tomorrow morning, there's going to be a short prayer service for my dad at the church on South Mountain Street. I don't know what church you attend, but this one is non-denominational. It's not like a funeral or anything—his body hasn't been released—but Portia thought it would be appropriate for us to do something in his memory."

That's a twist, Carly thought wryly, remembering Portia's stone-faced denial that Ferris's death had been a loss to her.

As for Carly, she wasn't a member of any particular church. Though she tried to lead a spiritual life, she'd never felt comfortable subscribing to a specific religion.

"What time is the service?" Carly asked her, scooping tuna salad onto an oval slice of ciabatta.

"It's at nine, and it won't be very long. Portia told the pastor to keep it short and sweet." She gave Carly a sheepish look, then swallowed back a lump. "Anyway, you're welcome to attend, if you want to."

Carly looked at Holly, and a mixture of both sympathy and suspicion swept over her. "I will make it a point to be there," she promised quietly. "And thank you for wanting to include me." Holly started to grab two lunch plates that were ready when Carly said, "Wait. Can I ask you a quick question?"

Holly's eyes were suddenly wary. "Uh…sure."

"Are your dad's folks living? Does he have any siblings?" Carly layered sharp cheddar over two ciabatta slices.

Holly shook her head and lifted the two plates that were ready to be delivered. "Dad was an only child. His own dad died a long time ago, and his mom—my grandmother—is in

the Balsam Dell Long-Term Care place. She's, you know, not
all there mentally. She's also dying of cancer." Holly frowned.
"Actually, Dad told me a few weeks ago not to visit her again.
I'm not sure why. He was adamant about it too. Maybe he
thought I'd be upset if she didn't recognize me."

"I see," Carly said. "Well, thanks for telling me that. For
what it's worth, even if she doesn't recognize you, it might
give her comfort to see a caring face."

Holly nodded and went off with her sandwich plates.

Grant returned, happy that he'd found a unique birthday
card for his dad in Gina's shop.

"By the way," Grant told Carly, "Gina really needs to talk to
you. She said to give her a call when you get a few free minutes."

The remainder of the afternoon went without any
glitches. Steve Perlman never showed up—not that he was
obligated to. Carly had hoped to nab him for a brief confab,
but now she'd have to figure out another way to talk to him.

After things had quieted down, Carly went into the
kitchen. She plunked herself onto the desk chair and called
Gina.

"Hey, I was wondering when you'd call." Gina's normally
bubbly voice sounded anxious.

"It's been busy," Carly said, blowing out a tired breath.
"Did you find out anything?"

"I did, but Dad still has to do a little more digging. One
major thing is, he knows about Chip Foster's medical condition. Chip was born with a rare skin disease that makes him
extremely sensitive to sunlight. Dad couldn't remember what
it was called, but I googled it. It's xeroderma pigmentosum."

Carly grabbed a pad and pen from her desk drawer and
asked Gina to spell it.

Gina did, and then went on. "People who suffer from it need to seriously protect their skin from any exposure to ultraviolet light—which, mainly is the sun. If they go outdoors when it's daylight, they have to wear sunscreen and protective clothing. Plus, people who have it are at greater than normal risk for skin cancer."

Wow, now Carly felt bad for the man. Was his condition the reason he always seemed so gloomy when he came in?

"Dad said Chip is actually a nice guy, if not exactly sociable. He lives with his mom—how cliché is that?—and as far as Dad knows, never dated or went out with anyone. But there was something that happened like, eons ago, that Dad only got bits and pieces of—something about a schoolboy prank that went horribly wrong. Chip Foster was involved and had to be rescued by the fire department. He ended up in the hospital. Dad was off duty that day so he's fuzzy on the particulars, but he's going to check with one of his old buddies at the firehouse to see what he remembers. I'll let you know as soon as I hear back from him."

"Thanks, Gina. Ari and I are having dinner with Mom and Gary tonight at the Inn." *If Ari doesn't get arrested first.* "I'll ask Gary about this skin condition Chip has, see if he can fill in some details."

"Lucky you, having a dermatologist for a stepdad," Gina joked. "Speaking of Ari, any news on that front?"

Carly leaned her cheek on her free hand. "So far, he's still at home. But I'm getting nervous."

"I hate to say it, Carly, but I'd be nervous too," Gina said quietly. "Let's make it a point to catch up either tomorrow or before the week is out, okay? A whole posse of customers just came in, so I have to dash."

Carly circled the words *xeroderma pigmentosum* on her notepad, then tore off the page and set it on her desk as a reminder to take it with her to dinner.

Holly came in just then and asked if she could take a break.

"Sure," Carly said, "and I'll get you those pens and paper so you can make that sign."

"I'm always available to help," she said. "Anything you need."

"Thanks."

Once again, a flicker of suspicion skipped through Carly's mind. Sometimes Holly was almost too accommodating, too eager to ingratiate herself. Was she hoping Carly would keep her on permanently? Or was there another, more sinister reason she wanted Carly to let her guard down?

Carly retrieved the writing materials from the supply closet and left them on the desk. Then she pocketed her cell phone—just in case Holly was inclined to spy—and left her to make a snack for herself. "Let me know if you have any questions," she told Holly on her way back into the dining room.

Stan Henderson had already left, as had most of the high school kids. It was that time of the day when Carly felt she could breathe again, wind down after a hectic afternoon, and take stock of her restaurant. She was contemplating making herself a cup of pumpkin tea when Lydia called her.

"Hey, Carly, I know you're probably super busy." She sounded apologetic.

"Not too busy for you. Any word on your mom?"

"Physically she's better, but she still doesn't remember anything. Listen, can you pop over to see me at the library for a few minutes? I'm covering for someone, so I can't leave. I found some things at Mom's house I think might've been meant for you. They might not be important, but in case they are..."

"I'll be there in a jiffy."

Ten minutes later, Carly was pulling into the parking lot of the Balsam Dell Public Library. She hurried into the ancient brick building, the scent of old books wrapping around her with memories of simpler times. Moving past aisles of book-shelves, she peeked down each one until she spotted Lydia.

"Oh wow, you made great time."

They shared a brief hug, then Lydia steered her over to a table adjacent to the front desk. Carly waved to Agnes Merrill, the primly dressed woman checking out books behind the counter. Agnes graced her with a brief smile, then went back to helping a customer who was checking out a stack of hardcovers.

"My mom's not working today?" Carly asked quietly.

Avoiding eye contact, Lydia shrugged. "She took today off. Said she had to work on a project at home."

Strange, Carly thought. Her mom hadn't mentioned any-thing to her.

After retrieving a canvas bag from a nearby closet, Lydia sat down beside Carly. "If the line gets long, I'll have to jump up to help Agnes, but meanwhile I thought you should see these." She extracted a manila folder from the bag and opened it on the table, displaying several sheets of pink notepaper.

Carly's eyes widened. "Are these the papers that were on your mom's kitchen table last night?" She and Gina had noticed them, but once the ambulance and police arrived, they never had a free minute.

"Exactly. I thought they were just ramblings at first. Sometimes when Mom's reading a book, especially a mystery, she writes down what she thinks are the clues to the solution. She likes to see if she can guess the ending before the final reveal." Lydia smiled. "But then I saw your name on one of the sheets, so I knew that wasn't it. I'm hoping you'll be able to make some sense of it."

Carly examined each of the pink sheets—four in all. Odd phrases were scribbled here and there, with no apparent connection. Phrases such as *sheer tragedy befell,* and *secret from the world* had been written in haste. It was a phrase on the last sheet that made Carly's breath halt in her throat. "*Read the truth, Carly*" she read aloud.

"That's the one that got me," Lydia said soberly. "Do you have any idea why she'd write that?"

Stymied, Carly gave a helpless shrug. "Honestly, no. Do you mind if I take pictures of them?"

"Be my guest," Lydia said. "And before you ask, I showed them to Mom at the hospital this morning. She got so agitated I had to put them away. I got a firm reprimand from the doctor for upsetting her."

Carly took a quick photo of each sheet. "Lately, Evelyn's been leaving me sweet notes in the restaurant. They're complete notes, though, not—oh, gosh, wait a minute." She went back to the photos on her cell. She showed Lydia the copy of the most recent note.

Lydia took the phone from Carly and read it twice. "This is so strange. *Think of the flamingo, oh flagrant bird. He stands out among the rest.*" She sat back and tapped her fingers on the table. "Mom mentioned a flamingo to me once, but it was a long, long time ago—back when she was still teaching.

She used to tell stories from her classes. I'm not even sure why I remember that."

"It must have left an impression," Carly said pensively. "Lydia, did Evelyn usually leave her door unlocked?"

"No, but once in a while she forgets. Memory issues go with aging, I guess." She sighed, and her troubled eyes filled. "I'm not letting her stay alone anymore. Not after this."

"I don't blame you," Carly said. "This might sound like an odd question, but did your mom ever have an encounter with Ferris Menard?"

Lydia sucked in a sharp breath. "Ferris Menard? The man who was killed in the sub shop? Darn right she did," she continued before Carly could respond. "A few years before Mom retired, he was one of her students. I remember because he was a chronic troublemaker. One time, after she gave him a grade he didn't like, he left a dead squirrel in her car."

Carly gasped. "That's awful."

"Turned out it was a stuffed squirrel, but it nearly gave Mom a heart attack. She drove into one of those metal poles in the school parking lot." Lydia shook her head. "How that boy got away with all the stunts he pulled, I'll never know. But he always managed to avoid getting kicked out of school or even properly disciplined."

A horrible thought struck Carly. Could the kindly teacher have harbored a long-standing grudge against Ferris? Would she have gone to his sub shop late at night to exact revenge?

Not likely, but not impossible, Carly thought morbidly, then instantly discarded the notion. Evelyn surely didn't steal Ari's work boots or his cape from his pickup, or plant phony evidence in his trash can. The elderly woman didn't even drive, so she wouldn't have had the means.

"Lydia, do you think the school showed favoritism toward Ferris?"

"I absolutely do, but I could never figure out why." She folded her hands over the table. "Menard's dad was a long-distance trucker, and his mom was a grocery clerk. They didn't seem to have any 'political pull' with the school authorities."

"Maybe a family connection?" Carly suggested.

"Nope." Lydia crossed her arms. "At the time, I checked into that, but I came up empty. Nonetheless, I wanted the boy to own up to his actions and apologize to Mom. But he never did, and Mom told me to let it go." She waved a hand. "Oh, listen to me, dishing about it like it was yesterday. I need to focus on the present so I can help Mom. Carly, what happened yesterday at the restaurant? Why did Mom leave there so distressed?"

Carly gave Lydia a brief recap of Evelyn's agitation over the footprint on Menard's chest and her abrupt departure shortly after that.

"I don't even know what to make of all that," Lydia said helplessly.

Nor did Carly. She thought about the footprint Gina had spotted beneath Evelyn's front window. "Lydia, if something did happen yesterday to frighten your mom, do you think she'd have called the police?"

Lydia pushed out a breath. "No, no way. Mom, I'm afraid, has a bit of history with the police. They think of her as the woman who 'cried wolf' a few too many times."

"What do you mean?"

"She tends to misinterpret things, like the day she caught her new mailman peeking through her window. Poor fellow, he was new on the job and a bit too eager. He wanted to be sure she was okay because she hadn't taken in her mail the day before. He knocked loudly, and when she didn't answer, he got worried. He went from window to window, trying to see if she was okay. Poor Mom came out of the shower, saw his face in the bathroom window, and got hysterical. He was mortified when the police showed up and started questioning him. Once they realized it was a misunderstanding, they apologized and left."

"Oh my," Carly said. "Has she done that more than once?"

"Similar things, yes," Lydia admitted, "but she wasn't always like that. When I was young, I thought she was the bravest woman in the world. But as she got older, she grew more nervous about living alone." She glanced toward the checkout desk. The line had grown three deep with customers. "Agnes is giving me the stink eye," she whispered. "I'm afraid I have to dash."

"One quick question," Carly said. "What are all those plastic bins in your mom's cellar? One of them was almost falling off the shelf, so I pushed it back."

Lydia rose from her chair. "Thanks for catching that. The ones labeled with years are records from Mom's teaching days. She saved *everything*." She pushed in her chair. "Thanks again for coming over here, Carly. You're just as wonderful as your mom tells everyone."

"Believe me, she exaggerates," Carly said, both embarrassed and pleased by her mom's bragging.

Lydia touched her arm. "Once Mom's transferred to the rehab center, do you think you could spare some time to visit her?"

"I sure will," Carly promised, glancing at the wall clock.

When she saw how late it was, she went into a mild panic. She'd left Grant and Holly alone, and on a day they were planning to close early!

She sent a quick text to Grant, then hurried past several rows of books. She was almost at the exit when she spotted a familiar profile. Browsing in one of the fiction aisles, his nose buried in a paperback, was Steve Perlman.

Gotcha, she thought. She turned on her heel and headed straight toward him before he could get away.

CHAPTER TWENTY

CARLY PADDED OVER QUIETLY TO STEVE UNTIL SHE WAS standing beside him. "Fancy meeting you here," she said with a smile, trying to sound casual.

He snapped his head toward her, his eyes narrowing behind his spectacles. Clearly flustered, he shoved the paperback back on the shelf. "Yeah, same here. Shouldn't you be at your restaurant?" He squeezed out a smile, but it had all the warmth of an arctic storm.

"I had a meeting here. I was just heading back when I saw you browsing. Now that I've stumbled into you, though, can we chat for a few?"

His expression tightened, and for a moment he looked trapped. Then he graced her with a flat smile and said, "Sure. Let's find a place we can talk privately."

They located a free table near the periodical section. Steve pulled out her chair for her before dropping into an adjacent one.

"I know we're both busy, so I'll be quick," Carly began. "Tell me about you and Ferris in high school. You said you played basketball together."

Steve glanced around, then folded his arms over the table and spoke quietly. "Ferris was a punk, but he was a good basketball player, so he got away with a lot. One day he played a cruel, humiliating trick on a fellow player—a kid who was pretty good at sinking the ball. I'm sorry to say Ferris persuaded me to participate." His face reddened, and he averted his gaze. "When I realized what we'd done to that kid, I was physically ill. It was the most horrible thing I'd ever done, and that's no exaggeration. I wasn't raised to be a bully."

"So, why did you do it?"

He shook his head. "Back then I'd developed a kind of schoolboy hero worship for Ferris. He was funny, popular with a certain crowd. Your typical class clown, but with a nasty underbelly. He got away with stuff no one else ever did, for reasons nobody understood. At the time I was only fifteen, but that was no excuse. The look on my dad's face when I confessed my role in the prank made me want to throw up. His disappointment was way worse than any punishment he could've given me. Oddly enough, the school didn't see fit to issue any punishments, to anyone. They wanted the incident swept under the rug so our rival schools wouldn't find out about it. The school board treated it like a 'boys will be boys' sort of thing." He scowled. "They'd never get away with that today."

"No, they wouldn't," Carly agreed. She tried, and failed, to dredge up a pinch of sympathy for him. Even at fifteen, he had to have grasped the sheer wrongness of being sucked into a vicious prank.

"I won't ask what the prank was, but can you tell me who the victim was?" She was fairly certain she knew, but she wanted Steve to confirm it.

He shook his head. "Sorry, but that wouldn't be fair to him."

"Even if he was a killer?" she pressed quietly.

Steve sat back and gawked at her. "Are you kidding me? Is that what this is about?" His voice rose.

"I'm only trying to find out who might've had it in for Ferris," she said calmly. "The police are homing in on Ari as the killer, but the evidence was obviously planted."

"So now you're playing girl detective? Trying to flush out the killer yourself?"

Carly bristled. "I'm trying to help Ari, that's all," she said evenly.

"Okay, listen to me, Carly. Digging up ancient history won't help you, and you're playing a dangerous game. I seem to recall you being in the news a while back for tangling with a killer. You nearly got *yourself* killed. Are you looking for a repeat performance?"

His words hit her like a slap, and she shrank back. *Was that a threat or a warning?*

Steve hung his head and groaned. "I'm sorry. I shouldn't have snapped like that." His voice was softer now, and his face flushed. "But I'm begging you, please. Stick to what you do best and leave the police work to the police. Besides," he said with a hangdog look, "if something happened to you, where else would I get the best grilled cheese on the planet?"

It was his way of defusing the tension, Carly knew, but it was patronizing and it left her smarting.

"Thanks, Steve. As the saying goes, I'll take it under advisement." She rose from her chair, tossed him a wave, and went straight toward the exit.

CHAPTER TWENTY-ONE

THE MOMENT CARLY STEPPED INSIDE THE RESTAURANT she knew something was wrong.

"We have a situation," Grant murmured, meeting her at the back door. "I tried to calm him down, but he's fuming. He's threatening to file a lawsuit for harassment."

Unbuttoning her coat, she glanced around the dining room. Everything looked peaceful and calm. "Grant, what are you talking about? Who's fuming?"

"Chip Foster," Grant explained in a low voice. "He went into the kitchen to exchange the compost containers and saw that paper on your desk. What the heck, Carly? What did those words mean? When Chip saw them, he went ballistic."

Carly slapped her forehead. "Oh no! I forgot I left that there." Chip had obviously seen the paper on which she'd written *xeroderma pigmentosum*. "It's the medical term for the disorder he has. Gina googled it and spelled it for me so I wrote it down. Is he in the kitchen now?"

Grant nodded. "He is."

Carly turned and went into the kitchen, a baseball-sized lump filling her throat. One look at the man seated at her desk and her heart sank with dread. His pallid face was taut with anger, and his foot was jiggling furiously.

Chip flew off the chair and jabbed a skinny finger at her,

dwarfing her as he hovered inches above her face. "Who do you think you are, checking up on me? You think because I have a skin condition I can't handle your compost?"

Carly flinched. "Oh gosh, Chip, no! I never thought anything of the sort. I'm so sorry you saw that slip of paper, but that's not at all why I wrote it."

"Then why did you?" he hissed.

Carly scrambled for a plausible answer, but it was obvious nothing she said was going to pacify him. "My stepdad is a retired dermatologist, and I only wanted to ask him about it," she said meekly. "I honestly meant no disrespect to you."

Chip's gaze narrowed with suspicion. "Who's your stepdad?"

She told him and his lips twitched. "Gary Clark was my doctor, back when he was still practicing. He's a good man, a caring man. I'm only sorry he got saddled with a nosy witch like you for a stepdaughter."

Carly recoiled at the word *nosy*. Not that *witch* was very complimentary. "What do you mean?"

He grabbed the handle of his dolly and tilted it toward the door. "You think I don't know about you making secret calls, pumping people for information?"

Carly felt her face redden. Had he heard something, or was he guessing?

"In case you're wondering, I'm friends with some of the firemen. One of them tipped me off about you poking into my private business. And by the way, do you think Ferris Menard's the only jerk who ever called me Drac? I've been called that and worse ever since I started school. Drac is mild compared to some of the things people call me."

"I'm so sorry," Carly said earnestly. She decided to put

out a feeler. "It must have been terribly upsetting when you found out Ferris's sub shop was on your compost route."

"And why would you think that?" he said darkly.

And in that moment, Carly realized her mistake. She'd practically admitted knowing that Ferris had tormented him in high school. There was no way to cover her tracks now. Best to just stumble forward. "I, um, heard there might have been some, you know, difficulty with him back in your high school days."

Chip's face froze, and his eyes zeroed in on her like deadly lasers. "You're a piece of work, you know that? You'd better watch your step if you don't want to hear from my lawyer. In case you didn't know, slander is a crime." He paused and leveled another menacing glare at her. "If you're going to keep asking questions, I'd look a lot closer to home."

"Closer to whose home?"

He gave out an ugly cackle. "Figure it out yourself. And one last thing. If I hear you've been spreading stories about me, I'll sue you from here to the moon and back."

He banged through the door with his dolly and rolled it noisily through the rear exit.

Carly dropped onto the desk chair, guilt tearing at her like an iron claw. " I sure made a mess of that, didn't I?" she said in a shaky voice when Grant returned to the kitchen. "Right now, I feel like the worst person on earth."

Grant straddled the chair opposite her. "I heard most of it. And you're far from the worst person on earth. Did all this start because I told you about Mr. M. calling him 'Drac'?"

"Sort of. It got me thinking about the whole silly vampire thing." She explained what Gina had learned from her dad about Chip's condition. "I wrote the name of the disease down so I could ask my stepdad about it. I should have tucked it into my tote, but I foolishly left it on the desk."

Grant puffed out his cheeks and expelled a breath. "He thought you were spying on him, didn't he?"

"Yes, but he also thought I didn't want him in my kitchen because of his condition." She related the highlights of their conversation.

Grant looked visibly upset. "This is getting nuts, Carly. For argument's sake, what if Chip's the killer? He might decide you're a liability, and then what?"

Carly hated to admit it, but Grant was right. The level of anger Chip displayed had been a bit frightening. Still, she couldn't picture him conspiring to kill Ferris and framing Ari for his crime. He'd threatened Carly with a lawsuit, yes, but not with physical violence. His meltdown aside, she sensed deep down that Chip was a decent person stuck in a rotten situation.

"Grant, who do you think he meant by 'closer to home'?"

"It's anyone's guess, but I'd say the two women closest to Ferris—Holly and Portia. Now will you please stop all this murder talk?" Grant begged her.

Carly sighed. "Okay, no more murder talk. So, are you visiting the college with your dad this weekend?" She flashed him a tiny smile.

"Nice try, but don't change the subject. A more important question—are you going to the prayer service tomorrow?"

"I am."

"Yeah, I am too. Maybe we can go together? If I pick you up early, we can grab some coffee first."

Carly saw through that one. "I'll need my car afterward,

so I'll meet you there. It'll be interesting to see who attends, won't it?"

Grant nodded bleakly. "Yeah. For your sake, I just hope none of them is the killer."

CHAPTER TWENTY-TWO

THE 6:00 P.M. CLOSING TIME TURNED OUT TO BE THE BEST idea Carly'd had all day.

Holly had made a sign for the door that read: *Closing today at 6 due to family obligation. We apologize for any inconvenience.* She'd written the message in calligraphy style, with curlicues at the beginning and end of each word. In each corner of the sign, she'd sketched a tiny block of cheese.

"Great job," Carly had complimented her. "Thank you for taking care of that."

Holly flushed and beamed. "Thanks. I hope I'll see you tomorrow at the prayer service."

"I'm planning on it," Carly said.

Having closed the eatery early, Carly had just enough time to dash home, shower, and dress for an elegant dinner at the Balsam Dell Inn. With an extra hour to work with, she and Ari decided that he'd pick her up at her apartment instead of meeting at the restaurant.

As she attached a pair of gold earrings to her ears, it struck her how much was looking forward to the evening. Her mom and Gary were always great company, and the fact that they adored Ari was a bonus.

"You look fantastic," Ari breathed when Carly answered the door.

"As do you," she said, with her first genuine smile of the day. Ari looked handsome in a gray jacket and blue-striped tie, his hair and mustache neatly trimmed and a broad smile lighting up his features. Her pulse quickened at the sight of him, and he kissed her lightly on the cheek.

Carly had chosen to wear her one and only cocktail dress—it was either that or her boring navy pantsuit. The forest green sheath with its lacy, cream-colored overlay hugged her form lightly, brushing the tops of her knees and giving her a graceful yet mildly sexy look. Judging from Ari's expression, she'd made the right choice.

On the way to the Inn, Carly updated Ari on Evelyn Fitch's situation and on her embarrassing faux pas with Chip Foster.

When she was through, he reached over and squeezed her hand. "Sometimes things seem worse than they are. You didn't intentionally hurt Chip's feelings, so don't beat yourself up. As for Evelyn, you'll probably know more by tomorrow. Maybe you can even visit her on the weekend."

He squeezed her fingers again, sending a pleasing jolt through her. "Thanks, Ari." He always seemed to know exactly what to say to peel the layer of gloom from her heart.

The sight of the Inn as they drove into the parking lot made Carly's spirits lift. With its porticoed entrance and white pillars, it sat on an expanse of carefully tended lawn that stretched toward a forest of dense firs. Above the portico, tiny white lights glimmered along the railing of the balcony.

Carly's mom and stepdad were already seated in a cozy corner of the dining room. A thick white tablecloth covered their table, which was set with antique china and crystal wineglasses. In the center of the table, a candle glowed softly in a pewter holder.

Rhonda waved at Carly and Ari as if she hadn't seen either of them in a year. Hugs went all around, and Rhonda insisted Ari sit on the brocade-covered chair beside her.

"You both look wonderful," Gary said, winking at Ari. His kindly blue eyes beamed at them from behind a pair of gold-rimmed glasses.

Over a bottle of sauvignon blanc and a sampling of appetizers, they indulged in a few minutes of pleasant small talk. After that, Rhonda and Gary listened intently as Ari gave them a shortened version of his current situation.

"How ridiculous," Rhonda huffed, "to think a man would murder someone and then hide the evidence in his own trash can."

Gary looked incensed as he lifted his wineglass to his lips. "I suppose they have to follow the evidence, but it makes no sense to me either, dear." He took a small sip of his wine and pronounced it top notch.

"At my attorney's suggestion," Ari said, "I left a note on my front door explaining where I would be this evening. That way if the police show up, they can't claim I was trying to evade arrest." He said it lightly, but Rhonda gazed at him intently with a worried expression.

Carly shivered. What if the police *did* show up to arrest Ari while they were having dinner? She shuddered at the image of him being handcuffed at the table and led out of the dining room like a captured felon. While the idea horrified her, she couldn't discount the possibility.

When their salads arrived, Carly took the opportunity to ask Gary about the skin condition Chip Foster suffered from.

Gary nodded. "Xeroderma pigmentosum. In all my years of practice, I treated only two patients who suffered from the disease. Since it seems you already know, I can tell you that Chip Foster was one of them." He poked at a grape tomato with his fork. "The other one was during my residency in Boston, about a thousand years ago." He chuckled at his own joke. "The patient was a young woman barely out of her teens. Interesting case, of course, but a sad one."

Rhonda bestowed a "cut to the chase" smile on him. She knew he loved to elongate every tale he told. "Why don't you talk about the *first* patient, dear? The one Carly asked about."

Gary blinked behind his glasses, then looked from Carly to Ari. "Since you already know who it is, I'll give you an overview. Given that *particular* patient's condition, he's actually lived longer than many with the disease. What helped is that he was diagnosed at a young age and didn't present any neurological symptoms. Not then, anyway."

"Oh, for the love of Peter, Paul, and Mary," Rhonda bleated. "We all know who you're talking about. Just say his name."

Carly stifled a giggle, then grew serious. "Gary, is there any treatment for Chip's condition?"

"Unfortunately, there isn't a cure, but the symptoms can be managed. The crucial thing is to avoid exposure to the sun and all forms of UV light. The eyes, especially, need to be protected. Even with great care taken, however, skin cancers are always a looming possibility."

Carly took a sip of her wine. "Gary, this would be going *waaay* back, but do you recall Chip being hospitalized for his condition as a teenager?"

Gary's expression sobered. "Indeed, I do," he said somberly. "Terrible thing. The poor boy had fallen victim to an ugly prank and was trapped in a sun-filled atrium for far too long. By the time help arrived, he'd suffered severe sunburn." He dabbed at his lips with his napkin, then took a larger than usual gulp of wine.

And it was, no doubt, the prank orchestrated by Ferris Menard that Steve had told her about earlier.

At least she knew now what Chip Foster was dealing with. It made her feel even worse about him seeing that slip of paper on her desk.

"Can we please stop talking about diseases?" Rhonda said. "I feel for that poor man, I truly do, but that's not why we're here, is it?"

Gary flushed, and Carly apologized. Fortunately, their server came by at that moment and delivered their entrees. The aroma of herbs and butter wrapped around them as their plates were set before them. They'd all opted for the chef's special—maple cured pork tenderloin with creamy gravy and rosemary popover.

"This looks fantastic," Ari said as they dug in.

After they finished eating, they ordered coffees all around but declined dessert. Carly asked her mom if she'd heard from Norah since the day the chief dropped the bombshell about Ferris Menard.

"Once," Rhonda said tartly. "And it was a most unsatisfying conversation. Every time I talk to her lately, I get more and more frustrated. She won't tell me what her *boyfriend* does that he has to dress like a clown. She said she'll let us all know when the time is right. She's being very mysterious about it. I think she's enjoying teasing me."

Carly sipped her coffee. "When you talk to her, does she sound happy?"

Rhonda's lips pinched together. "That's the odd thing. She's been sounding more relaxed and more bubbly than I've ever heard her sound. I'm not getting that desperate 'I gotta have a man' vibe that she usually gives off."

Carly smiled inwardly. She and Norah were like night and day, but Norah was really the more fun one. Compared to her older sister, Carly sometimes felt like a stodgy old lady.

"Mom, give her a break, okay?" Carly suggested. "Have faith in her decisions, whatever they are. You know Norah. If she decides she made a bad boyfriend choice, she'll dump him faster than a boiled potato. And who knows? Maybe this one'll end being a keeper."

Gary nodded as if agreeing, but he kept his mouth shut.

Rhonda tapped her manicured fingernails against her china cup. "I'd go along with that, except for one thing. This *work* the boyfriend does where he dresses as a clown—he does it during the evening. Ergo, he can't be entertaining children, can he?" She threw up her arms.

"Sure he can," Carly said. "Lots of places have children's events in the evening."

"Maybe," her mom grumbled, "but even so, how can he make a living that way?"

Carly didn't have an answer for that one. She'd long believed Norah was seeking a partner as solid and dependable as their dad had been. If one boyfriend wasn't a good fit, she moved onto the next—without ever looking back.

Carly had been only seven when their dad died, but Norah was almost ten and had formed a much stronger bond with him. While Carly had only vague memories of Paul Hale,

Norah could describe him in detail, right down to the tiny scar over his left eye. She could hum every song he played on his harmonica; she could recite the trick he'd taught her to tie her shoes so she wouldn't trip over the laces. His death had left a much bigger hole in Norah's heart than it had in Carly's.

Rhonda suddenly sat up straighter in her chair, her eyes dancing with mischief. "By the way, Carly, have you noticed anything different about me?" She turned her head slowly back and forth, as if trying to land on the perfect pose for a head shot.

Carly studied her mom's face at every angle. If there was a noticeable change, she wasn't seeing it. "Sorry, Mom, I don't," she admitted.

"Good! Then they passed the test." With a sly wink at her husband, she reached up to her right ear and removed a tiny device.

Carly let out a squeak. "You finally…I mean you got hearing aids!"

"I caught the word *finally*, young lady," Rhonda said with mock offense. She grinned. "It's so wonderful, isn't it, Gary? I can hear everything! I don't have to give people that blank look anymore, pretending I knew what they said when I didn't have a clue."

"That is, indeed, a blessing," Gary said, gracing his wife with a loving smile. He winked at Ari, who hid his own smile in his napkin.

Getting her new hearing aids must have been her mom's secret mission the day before, Carly realized. That's why she wasn't at the library.

"It's amazing," Carly said. "They're totally invisible. I'm impressed, Mom."

When they'd all finished their coffee, Gary signaled their server for the bill. After he paid, they retrieved their coats from the coat check in the Inn's beautifully appointed foyer. Everyone hugged goodbye, but Rhonda lingered a moment with Carly.

"Now *he's* a keeper," Rhonda whispered in her daughter's ear, referring obviously to Ari.

Feeling a flush in her cheeks, Carly nodded and smiled. "Thanks for everything, Mom. I enjoyed every minute of the evening."

Rhonda moved over to Ari. She'd already hugged him once, but now she grasped him as if he were departing on an arctic expedition. "Remember, Gary and I are here for both of you. Whatever you need, whatever we can do."

"That's very comforting, thank you. And thank you both for the terrific dinner and the fine company." Ari smiled at Carly. "Next time it will be our treat."

Our treat. He said it as if he and Carly were a confirmed couple. A *permanent* couple.

There was a part of Carly that relished the feeling, that gave her a warm sense of belonging.

But there was another part of her that told her to cool her jets—not to mistake her feelings for something they weren't until she was absolutely sure.

CHAPTER TWENTY-THREE

Located on a winding country road, the South Mountain Church of the Valley was a plain white structure sitting adjacent to a dirt parking lot. Save for the wooden cross attached to the façade, it might easily have passed for a private residence.

Inside the church, a dark blue runner ran along a central aisle that led to a raised altar. A podium rested off to the left, its base surrounded by at least a half dozen vases filled with tall white lilies. *Were the flowers courtesy of Portia?* Carly wondered.

Carly had intentionally gotten there early. She wanted to sit as far from the front as possible—it would give her a better view of everyone who came in to pay their respects. Two of the cars in the parking area had looked suspiciously official. She suspected they belonged to plainclothes police investigators.

She slid into a wooden pew in the back row on the left. The church was warm, and she loosened her coat. She hadn't seen any sign of either Portia or Holly. Maybe they were in another section with the pastor? A dark-haired woman garbed in black was seated about halfway down the aisle on the opposite side. Her head was bowed, as if in prayer—but for all Carly knew she was reading her text messages. These days it seemed the more likely scenario.

People were starting to amble into the church. An elderly woman with tight gray curls and a generous coating of makeup toddled up alongside Carly's pew and pointed to where she was sitting. "Would you mind if I sit where you are?" she said in a reedy voice. "It's hard for me to slide over."

Carly glanced down the row of pews, wondering why the woman didn't just choose one of the empty ones in front of her. Nevertheless, and remembering where she was, she smiled and moved over so the woman could have her seat.

The woman gave out a slight groan as she dropped onto the wooden bench seat. "My hip's acting up something awful today. Were you a friend of Ferris's?"

"More of a business acquaintance," Carly said quietly.

The woman unsnapped her shiny clutch purse and dug out a lace hankie. "I barely knew Ferris, but I'm good friends with his mom, Irene," she said, latching her purse shut. "Poor thing. Her memory issues came on so quickly. She's getting good care in the facility, but she's failing more every day. It won't be long before…" She let the sentence dangle for Carly to fill in the rest.

"By the way, I'm Helen Fairchild," the woman said. "What's your name?"

"Pleased to meet you. I'm Carly." Had they been in a more social setting, Carly would have offered more than her given name. Attending a prayer service for Ferris Menard didn't seem like the appropriate place.

A low hum fell over the church as more people began coming in and murmuring to one another.

"What facility is Irene in?" Carly asked her.

"I'm sure you know it. It's the Balsam Dell Long-Term Care place. She has a lovely room, but her mind is a jumble."

She shook her head. "Shame on me, I haven't visited her in a while. But I'm determined to visit her today, even if it pains me to see her like that." She dabbed at her dry eyes with her hankie.

"I hope you have a good visit," Carly said.

"You know," Helen went on, "Irene doesn't know about Ferris's death. The doctor and nurses decided it would be kinder to keep her in the dark. She only has a few months left, so why upset her now? Besides, after she told her son about his father, he stopped visiting her."

Carly nodded absently, her attention drawn to a handsome, silver-haired man who'd slipped in through a side door on the opposite side of the church. He sat down in the rear pew, his back ramrod straight as he stared toward the altar. A few people nodded to him as they came down the aisle, but no one paused to greet him or speak to him.

Aware that she was gawking, Carly pulled her gaze away. Helen elbowed her, two pink spots sprouting on her powdered cheeks. "That's Lawrence Kendall, in case you're wondering. Started out as a used car salesman decades ago, until he married into the Jepson family. He's been living like a king ever since."

Jepson. The surname was familiar to Carly, but she didn't recall ever knowing any Jepsons. "I guess I don't know them."

"Oh my, the Jepsons own car dealerships all over the state! As you can see, Lawrence is still a looker, but in the old days he was movie star gorgeous. I almost had a shot at him once," she tittered with a waggle of her penciled-on eyebrows. "But he was more interested in Irene. Believe you me, those two were hot and heavy for a while." She shook her head in disgust. "Poor Irene. He dumped her like a bag of bugs when

that Pamela Jepson came along. Pamela was rather plain, but
the dollar signs won out, if you get my meaning." She rubbed
her fingers together in a gesture that signified having lots of
cash.

*Hot and heavy? Bag of bugs? Did this woman write soap
operas for a living?*

Helen fingered her wrinkled neck. "Oh, dear. I've said too
much, haven't it? Irene would be very upset with me." She
smacked her own hand as if to scold herself, but a telltale
smile formed on her lips.

Yeah, tell me another one, Carly wanted to say. It wouldn't
surprise her if Helen had a PhD in gossip-spreading.

More people were streaming in and seating themselves,
filling in the empty spaces in the pews. Carly wanted to question Helen further about Ferris's mom, but just then she saw
Steve Perlman come in. After the conversation they'd had at
the library the day before, she was surprised he'd even attend
Ferris's prayer service. If she could nab him after the service,
she'd ask him about that too.

And where the heck was Grant? He'd told Carly he
planned to get there early, but so far she hadn't seen any sign
of him.

Carly gulped when Chief Holloway strode in. She should
have known he'd attend the service—he was law enforce-
ment. Dressed in full uniform, he scanned the room for
several seconds. His eyebrows dipped toward his nose in a
frown when he spotted Carly. Without acknowledging her,
he sat down in the row in front of her.

He is not happy to see me, Carly thought. *He probably
assumes I'm spying.*

Which, of course, I am.

After all, killers had been known to attend their victims' funerals, hadn't they? Or was that just Hollywood hype?

Probably the latter, but Carly still wanted to take note of who showed up for the prayer service.

The pews were nearly filled to capacity, which surprised Carly. She hadn't imagined that so many people would want to pay their final respects to Ferris Menard, but then chided herself for having such an uncharitable thought. She honestly hadn't known the man well enough to judge his character. For all she knew, he was secretly a philanthropist who gave tons of money to the needy. Besides, mourners came mostly for the family, not for the deceased.

Carly was beginning to worry about Grant, though. Where was he? One thing about Grant—he was never late.

It was nearing 9:00 a.m. when a slight man carrying a prayer book emerged from a different side door and stepped up to the podium. Trailing him were Portia and Holly, huddled together as if in deep mourning. Walking arm in arm, they took a seat in the first row. Holly was garbed in a navy skirt and blazer with a white blouse, while Portia's stunning black pantsuit was accentuated by a bright pink scarf.

Carly was still fretting about Grant when the man in question slid into the pew beside her. "Hey," he said.

"Hey, yourself. Everything okay?"

His expression tightened. "Tell you later, when we get to the restaurant."

Uh oh.

"Good morning, friends," the pastor said in a well-modulated voice. He waited for everyone to quiet before reciting a short prayer. After that, and within a span of about ten minutes, he did an admirable job of highlighting the life and times of Ferris Menard. *Short and sweet,* Portia had instructed him, and he'd followed her wishes to the letter.

The pastor concluded with a final prayer and then added, "I want to thank you all for being here this morning to bid farewell to Ferris Menard and to wish him Godspeed, and also to pay your respects to his loving family." With that, he nodded and bowed, then ambled down to the front row to speak to Portia and Holly.

It struck Carly that she hadn't seen Tyler at the service. If he was going to be sharing an apartment with Holly, wouldn't he have wanted to make an appearance?

"Well, it's been lovely chatting with you." Helen hoisted herself up from the bench. "I'm heading over to see Irene now with a box of her favorite chocolate-covered cherries."

"Have a nice visit," Carly said.

With a wave of her hand, Helen was gone.

"You headed to the restaurant now?" Grant asked Carly.

"In a little while. I want to nab Steve Perlman if he's still here. He told me some stuff about Ferris that I want to follow up on. I also want to pay my respects to Holly and Portia, if I can find them."

"Okay, but please be careful, Carly, and keep your phone handy, okay?"

"You know I will. See you shortly."

Carly buttoned her coat and slipped out of the pew, then hurried toward the exit. There was no sign of either Portia or Holly. Didn't family members usually greet mourners and thank them for being there?

Not that anything about this particular service had been typical. Everything about it was strange, although the pastor had seemed like a kind man. Carly had never heard of anyone throwing together a rushed prayer service the way Portia had for Ferris. Did she have some ulterior reason? Had it been only for show?

Outside, people huddled against the November chill as they made their way to their cars. An occasional burst of laughter sliced the air.

Carly couldn't believe her luck when she spotted Steve Perlman. He was walking at a brisk tempo, weaving among parked cars—including her Corolla—apparently heading for his own.

"Steve," she called to him, hurrying to catch up.

He turned sharply, then halted in his tracks when he saw Carly waving to him. The friendly smile she'd grown accustomed to seeing was absent.

"Fancy meeting you here," he said sarcastically, mocking her greeting of the day before. "You're getting to be like my shadow. You're also about the last person I expected to see here."

"Actually, I'm surprised to see *you* here. Do you have a minute?"

"If it's anything like yesterday's minute, no. I'm already late for school."

"I'll be quick. Why did you come to Ferris's prayer service today? You made it clear yesterday there was no love lost between you."

His face relaxed slightly, and he shrugged. "I know it sounds weird, but it was a kind of closure for me. I took pleasure in knowing that somehow, some way, there was a force in the universe that gave that SOB exactly what he deserved. Now if you'll excuse me—"

"I totally get that," Carly said, although she didn't get it at all. "After that school prank you told me about, did you ever speak to Ferris again?"

"Only when I had to," he said tightly. "I quit basketball in the middle of the season. The kid who got pranked did too— although he never spoke to me *or* Ferris again. Both of us quitting ticked off the coach something fierce, but it gave me a wicked sense of satisfaction. I was the high scorer, and the team sucked without me. They didn't even come close to making the finals. Ferris was livid, but he didn't dare say a word to me."

The harsh gleam in his eye told Carly everything. Steve had enjoyed exacting that bit of revenge against Ferris. Quitting the team had given him a chance to do the right thing, even if it affected the other players and the school.

Was it possible Steve carried his hatred of Ferris into adulthood? Had he nursed it like a carefully tended plant, allowing it to grow and fester until it threatened to smother him?

Maybe his life mirrored one of his sci-fi books. *Mild-mannered teacher morphs into hideous monster when the wrong person pushes his buttons.*

No, that was crazy.

But still, something wasn't adding up. The cruel prank Steve got lured into by Ferris happened nearly thirty years ago. That was a long time to be waiting for the universe to exact revenge. She couldn't help thinking something more recent had happened between Steve and Ferris. Something that stoked Steve's loathing of Ferris Menard all over again.

Unfortunately, she couldn't think of a tactful way to broach the subject. Steve was no fool. He'd clam right up if he thought she was trying to squeeze some sort of pathetic, Perry Mason–like confession out of him.

"Steve, one last thing." Without going into detail, she told him about Evelyn Fitch being in the hospital.

"That's terrible. Poor Evelyn." He looked genuinely sad. "I hope she makes a full recovery."

"Her daughter said if all goes well, she'll be transferred to rehab today. Speaking of Evelyn, did you ever hear of Ferris harassing her?"

"Back in school, yeah. The punk left a fake dead squirrel in her car. Scared the poor woman half to death. Carly, I've really got to run."

"Sure, Steve. I wouldn't want you to end up being one of the school's budget cuts," she joked.

He looked confused. "Budget cuts? I haven't heard of any."

"Never mind. I probably heard wrong. Hey, if you stop in later, your grilled cheese is on me."

Steve glanced toward the church building, his gaze lingering for a moment. Was he looking for someone? "I'll take you up on that. See ya!" He sprinted off toward his car.

Hustling toward her own car, Carly pulled out her phone and checked the time. Yikes! She really needed to get to the restaurant. She'd have to scramble if they were going to be ready to open on time.

"Carly!"

At the sound of her name, Carly swerved around. Portia and Holly were hurrying along the sidewalk from the church. Waving as if they were afraid she'd escape, they moved swiftly in her direction across the dirt parking lot.

"Whew," Holly said, bending over to catch her breath. "I'm not used to running."

Portia reached over and wrapped Carly in a hug, the faint

scent of jasmine swirling around her. "Thank you so much for coming to the service today. It meant a lot to Holly, but also to me." She took a step backward and wrapped an arm around Holly's waist as if to emphasize the point.

"Yes, thank you," Holly said, beaming at her stepmom.

The intensity in Holly's eyes reminded Carly of what Steve had said. He'd referred to his youthful adoration of Ferris as *hero worship*. Is that how Holly thought of Portia, as her hero?

"It was heartwarming to see so many people show up," Holly went on. "I honestly didn't think Dad had that many friends."

Nor did Carly. "It was a good turnout," she said, then realized how odd that sounded.

"I'm going to follow Holly so she can drop off her car at her auto mechanic's shop," Portia explained. "After that I'll drive her to your restaurant."

"What's wrong with your car?" Carly asked Holly, unlocking her door.

Portia rolled her beautifully made-up eyes, which were tinged with pink shadow. "You should hear it. It sounds like a jet plane. She needs a new muffler."

Carly's mouth opened, her gaze going from Portia to Holly. A lump that felt like a jagged rock scraped her insides. She mumbled a hurried goodbye to the women and got into her car.

But Holly's deer-in-headlights expression had given her away.

It was Holly who painted the skull on the trunk of Carly's car.

CHAPTER TWENTY-FOUR

SHAKING WITH FURY, CARLY STARTED HER ENGINE. THE rumble of Holly's muffler as Portia followed her stepdaughter out of the parking lot echoed in her ears like thunder.

Initially, Carly had suspected Holly might have been behind the graffiti. But over the past week Holly had so ingratiated herself, working hard and earning the admiration of the eatery's customers, that she'd decided it could not have been her.

What an idiot I was. This ends today.

Carly started to shift into Drive when she noticed something tucked under her windshield wiper. Peering more closely at it, she saw that it was a tightly folded slip of paper. It looked like the notepaper Evelyn used, although she obviously wasn't the one who'd placed it there.

Carly unfolded the paper, smoothing out the wrinkles as best she could. With every word she read, she felt the knot inside her tighten.

> *Carly likes to play at spying*
> *Always asking questions*
> *Remember, though, it's not a game, and*
> *Later she will pay the price when*
> *Yesterday's spy ends up tomorrow's bad news*

Carly read the note again, then folded it carefully and slipped it into her coat pocket. Woven among the words was a subtle, or maybe not so subtle threat. She considered showing it to Chief Holloway, but she'd be letting herself in for the lecture of the century.

But who wrote it? Who left it on her windshield?

Steve Perlman was the obvious culprit. Only minutes before, he'd strode past her car. He'd had the perfect opportunity to stick a note under her wiper.

Grant's warnings about her asking too many questions began circling her brain. She decided not to share the note with him, not yet. She'd wait for the right time to show it to him.

By the time she got to the restaurant, her anger at Holly had receded to a simmering boil. Grant was alone in the kitchen, preparing another batch of his delicious tomato soup.

Carly hung her coat in the closet and went over to where he stood at the worktable, a bowl of tomatoes at his elbow. "You're making more soup?"

He nodded. "I want to stock the freezer in case we run low." He slammed a sharp knife into the center of a plum tomato. It burst open with a *splat*. "Dad and I had a blowup this morning. I mean a *big* blowup, like, majorly awful."

"Oh no. What happened?"

"I found out he filled out an application for me to attend spring semester at the college. Over next summer I can catch up on what I missed so far, but the powers that be"—he made air quotes with his fingers—"at the school are ready to welcome me with open arms. The application just needs my signature. Dad even filled out my musical preferences for me. Wasn't that swell of him?"

The bitter edge in Grant's voice surprised Carly. She'd

never seen him this angry before—especially at his dad, who he revered.

"Is there any chance of a compromise?"

"Compromise?" Grant threw up his arms. "Carly, this is my life, my career. I'm twenty years old. Why should I be compromising anything? And why should the decision be anyone's but mine?"

Carly knew that Grant's folks were eager to pay his full tuition—*if* he chose music as his major.

"To be honest, Grant, the last time we talked about this, I wasn't sure which career you were leaning toward either. You're an amazingly talented cellist. Is it possible your dad sees your dilemma and is trying to nudge you in that direction?"

"Yeah, so? It's still my decision!" His cell pinged from his pocket, and he looked at it. "It's Dad again. Is it okay if I take this outside?"

"Of course. Take all the time you need."

Watching Grant push through the swinging door, Carly realized she hadn't dropped her own little bombshell on him.

The moment Holly walked through the door, Carly was going to fire her.

~

It was shortly after 10:30 when Carly unlocked the front door for Holly. She'd asked Grant to do an outside errand for the restaurant so she could be alone when she confronted her soon-to-be-ex-employee.

Carly extended her arm toward the nearest booth, where a white envelope rested on the table. "Have a seat."

Her eyes puffy, Holly pulled her gaze away from Carly
and did as she instructed. She looked so downcast that Carly
felt genuinely sorry for her. In Carly's entire career, she'd
had to fire only one other person—an employee who'd been
stealing from the till at the historic inn where she'd worked.
It hadn't been a pleasant experience.

Carly sat down opposite Holly and pushed the envelope
toward her. "These are your wages for the week through the
end of today," she explained. "Now, do you want to tell me
why you painted a skull on my car last week?"

Staring at the table, Holly pressed a fist to her mouth. She
pulled in a breath and said, "Dad paid me and Tyler to do it.
Tyler can't draw at all, so he drove my car and waited while I
painted the skull. We were supposed to use Tyler's car, until
the fool noticed his gas gauge was on E. I should've known
my stupid muffler would give us away!" Her eyes filled, and
she blotted them with a napkin.

Carly folded her hands over the table. The curlicues on the
sign Holly had made the day before were nearly identical to
the ones on the grinning skull. It wasn't until Carly had looked
again at the photos of the graffiti that she saw the similarities.

"And yet you had no qualms about asking me for a temporary job. About coming in here and serving *my* customers
and accepting tips from people who support *my* business. I
can't help questioning your motives, Holly."

Holly snapped her head up. "I had no *motives*, Carly, other
than to make a few bucks," she said defensively.

Carly waited to see if Holly had more to add. When she
remained silent, Carly said evenly, "That day, when the
police called you to say they had a lead on the footprint, did
they name a suspect?"

The sudden change of topic seemed to throw her off kilter. Her blue eyes flickered. When she finally looked at Carly, she said, "No, they did not, and that's the truth. I still don't know who it is. They said they're not going to tell me until they make an arrest." She twisted her fingers around the napkin. "Are you going to turn me in to the police? I mean, about the skull?"

"No, but I need you to answer a more important question for me. Did you and Tyler make up the phony ballots at the competition on Saturday?"

Holly looked away, her eyes watering again. She nodded dismally. "Dad paid us to do that too. We used the copier at the hardware store. It only took a few minutes. Tyler's boss thought I was copying my resume."

Carly's ire flared. She was torn between fury at Holly and pity that the young woman felt compelled to cheat just to please her devious father.

"Honest, Carly, I never wanted to hurt you," Holly said tearfully. "Tyler was trying to get in Dad's good graces, so he jumped on the plan to screw up the voting. Dad blamed you for Grant quitting—he thought you engineered the whole thing. I knew he was carrying his vendetta too far, but between him and Tyler I felt pressured and I…I went along with it. I told Dad it wasn't going to fool anyone, that they'd know there were too many votes. He didn't care. He told us to do it anyway." She swallowed hard. "I'm sorry, Carly. It was a terrible thing to do. I apologize for causing you so much trouble."

"Holly, if nothing else I appreciate your honesty," Carly said, troubled by the revelation. "Tell me, how do you feel about Tyler now?"

Holly coiled her napkin around one finger. "I thought I loved him, but now…I'm really not sure. Portia never thought I should move in with him. She didn't see a lot of *potential* in him, is how she put it." Holly shrugged. "She's had more experience with men than I have—not that her and my dad were a great match. I think she married Dad on the rebound after her first engagement broke off. And before you ask, Portia knows nothing about what Tyler and I did, so please don't give me away, okay?" She gave Carly a pleading look.

Carly sighed. She wasn't out to cause trouble for Holly, but she wanted the young woman to accept responsibility for her actions. "No, I won't. But you need to speak to the organizers of the competition and admit what you and Tyler did. The committee volunteers spent a lot of unnecessary hours examining ballots to figure out what happened. You and Tyler made a lot of extra work for people who didn't deserve it."

Holly nodded. "I know, and you're right. I will do that today. I promise. I'll invite Tyler to come with me, but I suspect he'll find an excuse to get out of it."

Carly gave her what she hoped was an encouraging smile. "That alone might tell you something. Holly, you're a smart and competent young woman. You deserve someone who cares enough to respect and support your decisions. I have no right to offer you advice, but if I did, it would be not to rush into anything."

Holly blinked, her blue eyes damp. "You're being so understanding about this. No wonder Grant loves working here."

Was that a hint that Holly wanted to continue there as a temporary fill-in?

"The work is frantic sometimes," Carly said, "but having the right people as co-workers makes all the difference."

Which might not matter anymore if Grant quits.

"Well," Holly said, her voice thick with emotion, "you guys'll be opening soon, so I'll get out of your hair. I'm not going to accept any wages, not after what I did to you." She pushed the envelope back toward Carly. "Please tell Grant I said goodbye, okay? Tell him I really appreciated him vouching for me." She scooted out of the booth and started to leave.

Carly debated whether or not to insist Holly take the envelope. She'd worked hard and earned her pay. Then again, refusing her wages might be a form of self-imposed penance. Carly let it go.

"Wait," Carly said. Something Holly said stuck in her brain. "You said Portia married your dad on the rebound after her engagement broke off. Who was she engaged to?"

Holly paused and turned toward Carly. "It was that teacher who comes in here. You know the one. You said he used to be your physics teacher—Steve Perlman. According to Portia, they were one step from the altar when Dad swept her off her feet and stole her away."

CHAPTER TWENTY-FIVE

AFTER HOLLY LEFT, CARLY'S CONCENTRATION WENT down the drain. She couldn't perform even the smallest task with efficiency. An image of Portia and Steve, nestled together as lovers, kept hurtling through her brain.

Portia and Steve Perlman had been engaged.

All this time, a major piece of the puzzle had been dangling in Carly's face—agonizingly out of reach. Did the police investigators know? Did anyone else know?

Why hadn't Holly said something earlier? Didn't it occur to her that Steve might have been carrying his own vendetta against her dad?

It made sense, now, why Steve had secretly reveled in Ferris's death. Portia had chosen Ferris over him. End of story. Considering Steve's early history with Ferris, Portia's betrayal must have gnawed at him like a flesh-eating bacteria. Maybe his appearance at Ferris's prayer service hadn't been to gloat over his death, but to divert suspicion away from himself.

Meanwhile, Carly's head was swimming with more immediate troubles. If Grant's dad forced him to quit, she might as well close up shop until she could find another grill cook. Suzanne would be back soon, but even then, they couldn't run the eatery alone.

She sighed with relief when Grant returned carrying a large brown bag. It was almost time to open, and they needed to get moving if they were going to be ready for customers.

"You're a sight for sore eyes," Carly told him, wiping her hands on a dish towel.

Grant set the bag on the edge of the worktable. "Man, these breads Sara baked look fantastic. She researched the kinds of ingredients used by the early colonists. Breads were mostly made with maize. I can't wait to experiment with some of these loaves."

His eyes flashed with excitement at the thought of creating new menu items for the eatery. In his heart, he was a chef first, a musician second. Carly felt it in her bones.

"Leave out one of those loaves and we'll test it," Carly said. "We can freeze the rest until we decide how we're going to use them. You never told me, how did you leave things with your dad?"

Grant went over to the freezer. "I told him, once again, that I'm not going to leave you here without any help. I explained how much I love this job, but I promised to keep an open mind when we visit the college on Sunday." He began stashing plastic-bagged loaves in the freezer. "So, how did it go with Holly?"

"Better than expected," Carly told him. "We came to an understanding, even though I did have to let her go. She wanted you to know how much she appreciated your support."

"I can't help feeling bad for her, although I'm bummed by what she did. Um, Carly, why is there a container of sliced tomatoes in the freezer?"

Carly swung around. "What? Oh no. That shows you where my head was this morning."

With a tiny smile, he removed it and placed it in the fridge. "No harm done. So, what else happened?"

Carly explained that Holly and Tyler had been responsible for the phony votes.

He shook his head. "Wow, I'm disappointed to hear that. I'm surprised at Holly."

"But listen to this," Carly continued. "Holly also told me that her stepmom, Portia, was engaged to Steve Perlman before she married Ferris. Portia dumped Steve for Ferris!"

Grant's jaw dropped. "Whoa. Even I didn't know that, and I worked for Mr. M. It sheds a whole new light on his murder, doesn't it?"

"Yeah, but only if Steve is guilty. Being jilted for another man isn't exactly a solid motive for murder."

"It is for some people," Grant pointed out. "Don't you watch those crime shows on TV?"

Carly shuddered. No, she did not watch them, but Grant was right. Murdering for love gone wrong was an age-old story.

Once again, she thought about whether she should show Grant the note she found under her windshield wiper. He'd flip, for sure. Then again, maybe she should confide in someone she trusted. Just in case something happened to her...

Nothing's going to happen to me. Once I figure out the killer, I'll go directly to the chief.

Reluctantly, she dug the note from her coat pocket. "I found this under my windshield wiper after I left the church," she said, giving it to him. "I'm telling this only to you. I don't want the chief to know, or, heaven forbid, my mom."

With a quizzical look, he unfolded the note. After he read it, he said, "Carly, this is too serious to ignore. I promise not to tell your mom, but you've got to show Chief Holloway. And what about Ari?"

Carly dreaded telling Ari. He didn't need one more thing to worry about. But after their conversation a few days earlier, she wasn't going to keep him in the dark. "I'll let Ari know about it later, and I guess you're right about telling the chief. Unfortunately, we have a more immediate problem. It's only you and me today, so we'll be working our proverbial buns off."

Grant's head shot up. "Yikes! It's eleven-oh-one!" He raced out of the kitchen and went into the dining room to unlock the front door.

Carly puffed her cheeks and blew out a breath. She was tempted to call Suzanne to see if her ankle was better, but that would be laying a guilt trip on her. From her daily text messages, Carly got the impression that Suzanne would be out of commission for another five days, at least.

Between 11:00 and about 1:30, Carly and Grant barely got a break. They kept up a steady pace, working on autopilot to keep up with orders. Carly knew her legs would be aching by the end of the day. She told herself it was temporary, only until Suzanne got back.

When she finally had a chance to go into the kitchen to call Ari and check her messages, she noticed that Gina had left a voicemail. "Got stuff to tell you. Call me!"

His timing perfect, Grant came in with a half Farmhouse Cheddar Sleeps with the Fishes and a cup of tomato soup for her. "I'll eat the other half when you're done." He grinned and returned to the dining room.

Carly took a bite of her sandwich and then called Gina. "Is this a good time to talk?" she said over a mouthful of tuna.

"Didn't your mother teach you not to talk with your mouth full?"

Carly choked out a laugh and then swallowed. "Sorry. It's been that kind of day."

"I'm just yanking your chain. Hey, listen, I heard back from Dad a little while ago. He talked to that old buddy of his in the fire department."

Carly sneaked in a spoonful of tomato soup. "Before you start, I already know what you're going to tell me about Chip Foster."

Gina confirmed the facts Carly already knew, but with a few additional details. "The fire department got a 911 call that day to go to the high school, pronto. Chip had gotten trapped in that small atrium outside the gym and couldn't get back inside. The sun was bright, and the atrium glass made it like a greenhouse. Someone had tossed the poor kid's gym shoes out there, and when he ran out to retrieve them, he couldn't get back in. The door was locked, and the key had gone mysteriously missing. Chip was screaming his lungs out. All he had for protection was a gym towel."

Carly shook her head with disgust. "But there's another way out of that atrium, isn't there? I seem to remember a door facing the football field."

"There is, but he'd have had to run all the way around to the school's front entrance. The fire department ended up smashing a hole in the glass to get the inner door open. By then Chip was crying so hard he couldn't even tell them what happened. He'd huddled under one of the tables for protection."

Protection...not from the cold, but from the sun.

"He was only exposed to sunlight for about ten minutes, but for someone with his skin disorder that was like hours. Ferris Menard eventually admitted to staging the prank but claimed he knew nothing about Chip's condition—or if he did, he didn't know how serious it was."

Carly related Steve's version of the story to Gina.

"You mean...Mr. P. was in on that?" Gina squawked. "I'm really surprised and, frankly, kind of nauseated."

"He claimed he's felt sick about it ever since. He said it's one of the reasons he always held a grudge against Ferris. I also found out from Holly—who I fired today—that Steve was once engaged to Portia Fletcher. After she met Ferris, she dumped him."

"Wow! This gets curiouser and curiouser. Why didn't my aunt Lil ever tell me that? She must be losing her touch! And why did you fire Holly?"

Carly gave her a short recap of Holly and Tyler's offenses. "Anyway, I've gotta get back to work. Grant and I won't have much downtime today."

"Wait, I almost forgot! Dad said there was one other thing his buddy told him that was odd. About two weeks after the school incident, Chip's mom was tooling around town in a spiffy new car. Since she worked as a grocery clerk, everyone wondered how she paid for it."

Interesting, but probably not relevant, Carly thought. People do get car loans.

After making vague plans with Gina to get together either on Sunday or the following week, she bade her friend good-bye and disconnected. Carly next tried reaching Ari and was surprised to get his voicemail. He rarely went anywhere without his phone. She left him a brief message asking him to call her.

She was heading into the dining room when she remembered what that chatty woman, Helen, had said to her at the prayer service. She'd told Carly that the silver-haired man who'd sat on the opposite side of the church—Lawrence Kendall—had been "hot and heavy" with Ferris's mom, Irene. But before that she'd said something else.

After she told her son about his father, he stopped visiting her.

Darn, why hadn't she asked the woman what she meant? Even if it had nothing to do with his death, it might have been a piece of the puzzle that was Ferris Menard himself.

Carly was making herself crazy with all these thoughts crashing around in her head. With only her and Grant running the eatery today, she didn't have time to sort through them.

The high school kids invaded in a throng. Carly worried that she'd run out of seating. In a way, it was a good problem to have.

She was surprised when Steve Perlman came in. After their encounter in the church parking lot, she figured he'd try to avoid her for a while. Maybe Carly's promise of a free grilled cheese had won out.

Steve's normally genial smile seemed forced, as if he'd had to stitch it in place. He set his sci-fi paperback on the table. "I'll have my usual, thanks. On the house today, right?"

Carly smiled. "You betcha. A Vermont Classic with extra pickles, coming right up."

She scribbled on her pad and returned with his coffee. By then his nose was firmly planted in his book.

"By the way," Carly said, "after you drove off this morning,

I met up with Ferris's daughter and his soon-to-be-ex-wife, Portia. For a stepmom and stepdaughter, they sure have a great relationship. Have you ever met Portia? She's kind of an interesting woman. Sort of a go-getter type." *And I'm a babbler who doesn't know when to quit.*

Steve's face shuttered. "First of all, why do I care? And second, how would I have met Ferris's *whatever she is* if I never patronized the sub shop?"

Carly shrugged. "Oh, you know. Small town and all that. I figured you might've run into her at some point."

He stuck his bookmark into his paperback and set the book aside. He spoke quietly. "You know, Carly, you're about as subtle as a coronary. You obviously know I was engaged to Portia, so why don't you drop the act, okay?"

"I'm sorry. You're right, I did know. Holly told me this morning."

"And you've made it your business why?"

"Because I'm wondering if you told the police about it when they questioned you. I mean, it seems like something they'd want to know, don't you think?"

His left eyelid twitched. "It's ancient history, so no, I don't. Portia and I parted with no hard feelings, despite what you'd like to think."

I'd like to think you're not a murderer, but I'm struggling.

"Steve, did it occur to you that the police might find out anyway? If they do, they'll wonder why you didn't disclose it up front." She kept her voice calm, but her heart was doing a road race inside her chest.

A tic in his right cheek pulsed. "I want you to listen to me," he said in a low voice. "I had nothing to do with Menard's death. I watched a sci-fi marathon from Saturday evening straight through Sunday morning at 5:00 a.m. Not that it's any of your business, but that's the truth." He sat back and stared at her. "Why are you doing this, Carly? Why are you suddenly harassing me?"

"I'm not harassing you, Steve, but someone is trying to frame Ari Mitchell for the crime. I care about Ari, and I'm trying to help."

"Then let me give you a clue, in case my message didn't come through the first time. There's a building about two blocks from here, and it's filled with people who solve crimes. They're called the police. I suggest you let them do their job, and you stick to doing yours." He snatched up his book and slid out of the booth. "You can cancel my order. Permanently."

"Did you leave a note on my windshield at the church?" she blurted.

Steve froze, then shook his head at her. "You're insane. Leave me alone."

He turned and strode out, switching instantly into kindly, easygoing teacher persona. He smiled and waved at some of the high school kids as he left.

Carly went behind the counter, her hands shaking. She hoped none of her customers had overheard any of their exchange. She hadn't expected Steve to react with such vitriol.

What else did you expect? You practically accused him of murder.

Grant was piling chips next to three orders he'd plated. "That didn't look good."

"I'll tell you about it later. He wasn't exactly thrilled with some of my questions." She set all three plates on a tray, not trusting herself to carry them in her hands. She could feel Grant's eyes on her back as she delivered the sandwiches to one of the booths.

For the next hour or so, she wrote out orders and delivered food like an automaton. When business slowed down to only three or four customers in the dining room, she dashed into the kitchen to check her messages.

Nothing from Ari, but Lydia had called. Carly punched in Lydia's number, but got her voicemail.

"Hey, it's Carly. Please give me a call. Sorry I missed yours."

Grant came through the swinging door. His face looked weary. He straddled the desk chair opposite hers and faced her. "I don't want to leave the dining room for long, but what happened with Mr. Perlman?"

Carly gave him a rundown of their exchange.

"After what happened today, I don't understand why you're still questioning people."

"Grant, you know why. I know you're not crazy about me asking a lot of questions, but how else can I help Ari? Any minute he could be arrested. Once that happens, the police aren't going to be looking for the real killer."

Fatigue etched on his young face, Grant gave her a resigned look. "Then there's something I need to say."

Uh oh. Here it comes.

"I've been thinking about this all day. I know you won't like it, but just hear me out, okay? Maybe you should close the restaurant for the next few days. Tomorrow's Saturday, and I know it's a big tourist day—especially this close to the holidays. But if we shut down over the weekend and re-open on Monday, things might look different by then."

"You mean, the police might have made an arrest by then." Her voice rattled. "That's what you're saying, isn't it?"

"Partly, yes," he conceded. "But by Monday we'll also have a better idea of how Suzanne's doing. We're closed on Sunday anyway, so we'd really only be closing tomorrow."

Carly shook her head. "I...just can't do it, Grant. I hear what you're saying, but to me it would feel like giving up. And I can't even imagine what our customers would think. They'll either think *I* killed Ferris, or they'll think I couldn't make a go of the restaurant."

"No chance anyone will think either of those." He quirked a look at her. "Listen Carly, without Suzanne, and now without Holly, we've both been struggling to keep our heads above water. Even people who love their jobs can reach critical mass. And you have the added stress of being worried sick about Ari. And I have the added stress of worrying about you asking questions of the wrong people, knowing one of them might be the killer."

Carly couldn't help smiling at that. "I thought my mom was a mother hen, but I think you just took away her medal." She pinned an imaginary medal on him.

"Yeah, very funny," he said, but he looked secretly pleased. "Look at it this way. It would only be for a few days, and it would give us a chance to regroup. We could put up some seasonal decorations. We could work on grilled cheese recipes for the holidays. How about a sandwich called Gobble This with cranberry sauce and brie, grilled with a light coating of herb-seasoned mayo?"

"Mmm, that sounds scrumptious." Carly stared at him in admiration. "You've already been thinking about it, haven't you?"

He shrugged. "Actually, yeah. In my head, I never stop creating recipes. And now that we've got Sara's new breads to try out, the timing is perfect, right?" He gave her a hopeful wiggle of his eyebrows.

"I can't argue with anything you said," Carly told him. "But I can't close the restaurant—not even for a day. I'm sorry, but I just can't."

Grant's face went deadpan. With a slow nod, he said, "I had a feeling that would be your answer. And now, you leave me no choice."

Dread filled Carly. *He's going to quit. I'm toast.*

Using two fingers, Grant slid his phone out of his shirt pocket. With a cryptic smile at Carly, he punched in a saved number. "Okay, it looks like we're on for tomorrow. Yup. Okay, I'll see you later."

"I'm afraid to ask," Carly said, after he disconnected.

"Congratulations. Tomorrow you'll be showing the ropes to your new temporary employee. He has patience, experience, and he worked his way through college slinging hash in a New York diner." Grant grinned at her. "My dad, Alvin Robinson."

CHAPTER TWENTY-SIX

"*WHAT?*" CARLY'S JAW DROPPED. SHE STARED AT GRANT.

"Yup. Dad and I discussed it when he called me this morning. I stood my ground, Carly. I told him that, murder or no murder, I wasn't going to quit and leave you without a grill cook."

A giggle escaped Carly's lips. "I mean, I'm thrilled that you recruited some desperately needed help, but I'm also a little in awe that it's your dad. To be honest, I'm also a little terrified. Are you sure you didn't trick him into it?"

He waggled his hand back and forth. "Not...*trick*, exactly. But I told him that since I agreed to visit the college on Sunday—which includes an informal meeting with the dean, I found out—I asked him to at least do me the courtesy of doing my job with me for a day. It will help you, plus I want him to grasp the sheer pleasure it gives me to prepare meals people enjoy—even if it's only grilled cheese sandwiches."

"Hey, now," Carly teased with mock annoyance. She hopped off her chair and hugged him hard. "Sorry, that was unprofessional, but it had to be done."

"Meanwhile," Grant said, "um...customers?" He dashed out to the dining room.

With that, Carly began making plans for Saturday. Knowing the eatery would be properly staffed was a huge relief, although it didn't take away her nagging fears about Ari. But at least she could breathe again, and that was huge.

By closing time, Carly's legs felt as if they'd walked a thousand miles. Grant looked beat, but a tiny twinge of elation glimmered in his dark brown eyes. He was clearly psyched by the arrangements he'd made with his dad for the following day.

"Everything's going to work out," Grant assured her, as they were locking up. "No way is Ari taking the rap for Mr. M.'s death. The *police* will find the real killer."

"I know." Carly noted the way he emphasized the word *police*. She wished she believed it as much as he did. "So then, I'll see you and Professor Robinson tomorrow," she said brightly.

Grant laughed. "You got it, but I'll warn you now—he'll insist you call him Alvin. Come on, I'll walk you out to your car."

Outside, the sky was an inky blue, scattered with stars, with a near full moon hovering low over the horizon. Gina's car was gone. She was probably working late. A chill crept under the sleeves of Carly's coat, making her shiver.

Once inside her car, Carly locked it and started the engine. Grant waved at her and then sprinted off. She flicked on her headlights, and then a knock on her driver's side window made her shriek.

The man peeking into her driver's side window held up both hands. "Sorry, Carly. I didn't mean to scare you."

With a contrite smile, Steve Perlman made a gesture of rolling down her window. Meanwhile, Carly's heart felt like it was whipping her lungs into a soufflé.

Take deep breaths. Deep, calming breaths…

Instead of powering down her window, Carly inched her hand over to her tote and slipped it inside. Sheer relief flooded her when her fingers curled around her cell. She pulled it out slowly.

"I just want to apologize," Steve called through the window. "I would have texted you, but I didn't have your number."

"Apology accepted," she said woodenly. "I have to go home now, Steve."

Steve pointed toward Main Street. "Can you meet me at the donut shop? It's open till nine. I just want to explain a few things. About Portia."

Carly closed her eyes and opened them again. *Don't take the bait,* she warned herself. But there was another part of her telling her she was acting silly. How could her former physics teacher be a killer? Plus, she desperately wanted to hear what he had to say about Portia.

"Carly, please, you know me. I'm not going to hurt you," Steve pleaded. "You can park right in front of the building there. It's very well lit."

Carly blew out a breath and finally said, "Okay. I'll be there in a few."

Steve gave her a thumbs up sign. Carly immediately texted Ari to let him know who she was meeting and where. She promised to let him know the moment she got home.

Ten minutes later, she was sitting across from Steve in the town's favorite donut shop, a cup of coffee in front of her. Steve had unbuttoned his corduroy jacket. His face was drawn with worry lines, and he kept rubbing his fingers together nervously.

"I'm so sorry about the way I spoke to you today," he said

softly. "I got defensive because you're right—I never told the police about me and Portia. Since I have nothing to hide, I figured it would only muddy the waters."

Carly wasn't sure how to respond to that. Before she entered the donut shop, she'd made sure the mysterious note was in her coat pocket. Whether or not she'd show it to him was still up for debate.

"Carly, you know me," he said soberly. "I'm still the same nerd I always was. I met Portia at an all-day seminar one Saturday for future business owners of America."

Carly shot him a confused look. "But I thought you loved teaching. Why would you go to something like that?" She took a small sip of her coffee.

"Sure, I love teaching—for now. But kids today? Man, they're not easy. They know too much. Some of them know more than I do." He gave out a sheepish laugh. "Anyway, I've always had this idea that someday I'd open a combo sci-fi book/gift shop. I'd sell all the classics. You know, like H. G. Wells and Aldous Huxley. But I'd also sell mugs, T-shirts, vintage action toys, stuff like that. In my head, I'd pictured it a million times." His voice grew animated, and his eyes lit up.

Carly nodded, wanting him to get to the nitty-gritty. "Tell me about Portia."

Steve took a gulp from his coffee cup. "I was grabbing a sandwich at the buffet table when I saw this vision in pink reaching for a veggie wrap." He blushed fiercely. "She wasn't especially beautiful, but she had a bubbly energy about her that made her pretty as a picture to me. Our eyes locked, and I guess we sort of clicked."

"Did she tell you why she was there?" Carly asked him.

"She wanted to start a business, but she had no idea what

kind. She was there to 'collect ideas' as she put it. We had dinner the next day, and soon after that we were, you know, a couple. She was living in Bennington, but we talked about her moving into my condo."

"How long ago was that?"

"Before she hooked up with Ferris, obviously," he said sourly. "It was about four years ago. We didn't even last a year."

"Did you break it off?" Carly remembered Holly saying that Portia married her dad on the rebound.

"I did." His voice grew quiet. "Portia had already set her sights on Ferris. He had the manners of a warthog, but he owned a successful business. Me? At that point I'd only dreamed of a business. The part that hurt most was her accepting a diamond from me. We even agreed on a wedding date. But I knew something didn't feel right. Turned out she'd been stringing me along, waiting to see if things would materialize with Ferris. When they did, I knew it was over." His lip curled into a bitter scowl.

"I'm so sorry to hear that," Carly said, wondering if Portia was truly that cold and mercenary. *Every story had two sides,* she reminded herself.

"Don't be. It taught me a lesson." He leaned forward. "Carly, I know you want to help Ari, but I'm telling you, as God is my witness, I didn't kill Ferris. Portia was leaving him anyway, and even if she wanted me back, I'd never take her." He chuckled. "Frankly, if I never see the color pink again it'll be fine with me."

Carly smiled. Portia did seem to be overly enamored of all shades of pink. As for Steve, she sensed he was telling the truth. Nevertheless, she was keeping him on her suspect list until she was one hundred percent sure.

"I appreciate you being up front with me, but I have one more question. Why are you so positive Chip Foster couldn't have killed Ferris?"

Steve's face clouded with annoyance. "Because Chip's not that kind of person, that's why. I know that's not hard proof, but the guy's had enough trouble all his life without someone going around accusing him of murder. And by the way, you're the only one who considers him a suspect. As far as I know, the police haven't even talked to him."

"Maybe he hasn't landed on their radar yet," Carly suggested.

Steve narrowed his gaze at her. "And it's your job to put him there?"

"No, I never said that. But I can't help thinking he could've had a long-standing grudge against Ferris—a serious enough grudge to want him dead. I learned some additional details of that high school prank you told me about. I know it was pretty harrowing."

Steve blew out a frustrated breath. "It was, but it didn't make him a killer. You're barking up the wrong tree, Carly."

They'd reached an impasse. Carly gathered up her tote. "I'm glad we talked. If nothing else, it's given me some clarity. I really have to go now."

"Yeah, me too, I have tests to grade. Thanks for hearing me out, Carly." Steve drained his coffee cup. "So why did you ask me if I left a note on your car?"

For a moment Carly hesitated. She'd been mulling whether or not to show it to him, but he'd just given her an opening. "Someone left this under my windshield wiper when I was at the prayer service this morning." She pulled the folded paper out of her coat pocket, unfolded it carefully, and gave it to him. She watched his face to gauge his reaction, but all she saw was curiosity.

> Carly likes to play at spying
> Always asking questions
> Remember, though, it's not a game, and
> Later she will pay the price when
> Yesterday's spy ends up tomorrow's bad news

As he read the words, his brow furrowed. "I can see why you're concerned. I gotta say, it reads almost like a threat. Do you have any idea who wrote this?"

She shook her head. "Not a clue." *Except that it was written on the same pink paper Evelyn Fitch uses.*

But it couldn't have been Evelyn. She was still recovering from the fall she'd taken down her cellar stairs Wednesday night. Besides, Evelyn was fond of Carly. All her other notes had been glowing and complimentary.

She held out her hand for the note, but Steve was still staring at it. "Carly, whoever wrote this used your name to spell out the first letter in each line. It's called acrostic poetry. Back in the day, Ms. Fitch—Evelyn—taught it to her classes. Here, look."

Carly took the paper and studied the words again. She gasped when she realized he was right.

"She taught it to help students build self-esteem," he explained. "We had to print our names in a vertical line and write a poem that highlighted our individual qualities. I swear, every kid in that class developed the same precise printing style Ms. Fitch had. She drilled it into us like an army colonel."

Carly could easily imagine the kindly Evelyn teaching that to her students. As luck would have it, Evelyn had already retired by the time Carly took seventh grade English. Her replacement, Mr. Slosek, never taught that style of poetry.

"You know a lot about it," she commented.

"I didn't write this, Carly, and this is the last time I'm going to defend myself. Not to be an alarmist, but if I were you, I'd show it to Chief Holloway." He dropped it on the table in front of her.

"I think I will. Thanks for your input, Steve. I really have to go now."

As they left the donut shop together, Carly winced at the irony.

One of her suspects in Ferris's murder was walking her to her car.

CHAPTER TWENTY-SEVEN

ONCE INSIDE HER APARTMENT, CARLY FED HAVARTI AND then led him into the backyard for a bathroom break. The nip in the air was a reminder that winter was rapidly approaching. She wouldn't be surprised to see a few flakes fall before long. She'd been meaning to buy a warm coat for Havarti but hadn't had a chance to check out the pet supply store. It was one more item on her long list of errands that needed her attention.

She tried reaching Ari again, and this time he answered. "Hey, you're a tough guy to get a hold of," she teased.

"Carly, I'm so sorry. My phone dropped out of my jacket pocket when I was raking leaves in the yard, and I've been going nuts trying to find it. I just saw your text a few minutes ago. Did things go okay with Perlman?"

"They did, pretty much." She related the highlights of their conversation, then told him about the note on her windshield.

"Shoot, Carly, I don't like that," Ari said, after she read it to him. "Did you show it to Chief Holloway?"

"Not yet, but I will tomorrow. Right now, I'm trying to keep it in perspective. I'm home and I'm safe. Becca is right downstairs, and she'd be up here in a heartbeat if I had a problem." She gave a tiny laugh, hoping to allay his fears.

"Are you sure I shouldn't sleep on your sofa tonight?"

"Not necessary," she said, although a big part of her wanted him to do just that. "Havarti and I will be fine."

With a promise to keep her apartment locked up tight and her cell phone at her fingertips, Carly ended the call. She threw together a salad and ate it with a slice of buttered bread. After that she dropped onto her sofa, a deep weariness settling into her bones. Havarti snugged into the curve of her hip, and she rubbed his silky head. The moment she rested her head back and closed her eyes, the events of the past week scrolled through her mind like scenes from a bad movie.

It started with Ferris's meltdown in her restaurant and then Suzanne injuring her ankle. From there, things had gotten progressively worse. Between the voting debacle and Ferris's murder, the competition on Saturday had gone straight to a hot place. Add all that to Ari being framed, and it had been one grueling week.

Was she burning out? The thought that it might be true disturbed her deeply. Running her own grilled cheese restaurant had been her dream for so long. Was it possible she was already fried from the long hours and the stress?

Even people who love their jobs can reach critical mass.

Grant's words of only a few short hours ago clattered through her head.

No, she refused to accept that. Sure, Suzanne's ankle injury had been a setback, and Ferris's murder definitely hadn't helped. But once Suzanne was back to work and Ferris's killer was in custody, they'd be in full swing again.

Wouldn't they?

Her cell rang, jerking her out of her ramblings.

"Carly, I'm glad I reached you," Lydia breathed into the

phone. "I've been at the rehab place with Mom since early this afternoon. I'm totally wiped." She gave a tiny laugh.

Carly sat up. "So, they did transfer her to rehab. That's good news. I've been thinking about her all day."

"Her head injury, thank heaven, turned out not to be a severe one, but of course her age works against her. Her speech is labored and a bit jumbled. The facility assigned a therapist to work with her, but they cautioned that progress is likely to be slow. The frustrating part is that she has no idea what happened to her that night. The neurologist at the hospital said that in a case like this, short-term memory loss isn't uncommon."

Carly mulled over everything Lydia had told her. "Is there anything I can do? I still feel terrible about seeing her leave the restaurant so distraught that day."

"As I mentioned before, I think Mom would love a visit from you. You seem to be one of her favorite people these days. Even a short visit would cheer her up, if you could manage it."

"I sure will try." Carly wondered how she could squeeze one more thing into her schedule. "Tomorrow's a workday for me, and Saturdays can get pretty crazy. What are the visiting hours there?"

"Actually, you can visit until nine at night on Saturday. But if you can get there during the day, she might be more alert. I'm going to look for some of her old scrapbooks tomorrow. The therapist suggested it might trigger some memories if she went through them, although her long-term memory seems intact."

Memories...

"Lydia, remember I told you that one of the plastic bins in

your mom's cellar was hanging halfway off the shelf the night Gina and I found her on the stairs?"

"You did mention that," Lydia said. "Do you think it's important?"

"I'm not sure, but I can't help wondering if Evelyn was reaching for it when she fell."

"Do you remember the year on the label?" Lydia asked.

"No, but I took a photo. Let me check." Carly switched to her cell's photo app and found the one in question. Using her thumb and forefinger, she enlarged the picture. "Yes, I can see it clearly. 1996."

"Huh," Lydia said. "Doesn't ring a bell as being a standout year, but I'll grab it and check out the contents. If Mom was looking for something in particular, maybe looking through the stuff will jolt her memory."

"Maybe," Carly mused. Unless she was sending Lydia on the proverbial wild-goose chase. "What did she put in her scrapbooks?"

"Oh, you know, notes of appreciation from students, poems they'd written, things like that. They all made her feel she was making a difference. Lots of class photos too. Mom was big on those."

"I'll definitely try to get there tomorrow, Lydia. I have some temporary help at the restaurant, so I'll see how things go. Does your mom like flowers?"

"She sure does. A small bouquet of mums would delight her."

"Got it. Lydia, do you know anything about acrostic poetry? Someone told me your mom used to teach it in her English classes."

Lydia sounded surprised at the question, and a tad annoyed. "Um, a little. Why would you bring that up out now?"

"Sorry. I should have explained first. Someone stuck a note under my windshield this morning. It was written on the same pink notepaper your mom uses, but it obviously wasn't from her. The poem was kind of unsettling. I showed it to someone, and he recognized it as acrostic poetry."

"Isn't that strange?" Lydia sounded puzzled. "To answer your question, yes, Mom used to teach that in her classes. She thought it helped spark creativity. What do you mean by unsettling?"

Carly didn't want to alarm Lydia. "It pretty much implied that I'm nosy, that's all. Which, of course, I am." She gave a laugh she hoped Lydia would interpret as *no biggie*.

She was anxious, now, to compare the note with the ones Evelyn had written. Where had she put Evelyn's other notes? She was sure she hadn't thrown them away. She would never toss out keepsakes from a favorite customer.

Then she remembered. That night at Gina's apartment, when she showed Gina the first note, she'd dropped it into her tote. The others she'd tossed into the cookie jar in her kitchen where she kept odds and ends.

She promised to make every effort to visit Evelyn on Saturday, and using the excuse that she needed to take Havarti outside for his nightly bathroom break, she said a quick goodbye to Lydia.

She collected all the notes Evelyn had written and spread them out on the kitchen table. Next to those she set down the one she'd found under her windshield wiper. She wanted to compare them all, side by side.

The first one from Evelyn had been neatly printed in large, straight letters with a blue ballpoint pen. Although she'd written it as a single paragraph, viewed as an acrostic poem it read:

> Carly's food is tempting and tasty
> Always stuffed with melted cheese
> Remnants of cheddar sizzle and brown
> Leaving a flavor so unimaginably fine
> You'll return again for more.

And there it was, just as Steve had pointed out. The first letters of each line spelled out the name *Carly*.

The next one, which began, "So hearty are her sandwiches," spelled out the word *Swiss*. Again, the poem was written as a single paragraph, so the first letter of each line wasn't obvious until you viewed it as a poem.

The third note from Evelyn was Carly's favorite: "Gone are the days of plain grilled cheese…" Line by line, the poem spelled out the vertical word *Gouda*.

Studying the printed notes more closely, Carly noticed something else. The first letter of each line was much larger than the others. Evelyn had probably been testing Carly's powers of observation to see if she'd pick up on it. *What a clever and darling woman,* Carly thought. That she'd written the poems to praise Carly's eatery made them all the more special.

But it was Evelyn's most recent poem that had thrown her.

> Do not despair, dear Carly
> Everything will turn out fine
> Among the lies, the truth shines through
> Think of the flamingo, oh flagrant bird
> He stands out among the rest

Carly's breath halted in her throat. Viewed as an acrostic poem, the first letter of each line spelled the word *Death*.

She was sure, now, that Evelyn had been trying to tell her something. But why was she so cryptic? And why mention a flamingo?

Using her cell, she googled "flamingo." A myriad of images came up. A bright pink bird with a curved neck, it had a black beak that looked sharp enough to tear flesh. Several of the photos showed a flamingo in a graceful pose, one long leg held aloft as if ready to perform a ballet.

Flamingoes were pink. Portia Fletcher adored the color pink.

Could it be that simple? Did Evelyn even know Portia?

Carly recalled Gina saying that Portia wasn't from "these parts," which meant she wouldn't have been one of Evelyn's students.

I'm missing something.

Something that should be obvious was stuck like a jagged thorn in the back of her mind. She needed to pluck it out so she could figure out what it meant.

"Okay, I'm officially driving myself nuts," she said aloud, smiling at the little dog gazing up at her with liquid brown eyes. She bent and rubbed Havarti's furry head. "Don't worry, sweet boy, I'm not *officially* crazy. Not yet."

Carly rose from her chair, stretched her back muscles, poured herself a glass of cider, and then sat down at the table again. This time, she looked at the poem with a more analytical eye.

A flamingo was an elegant, bright pink bird. So why would Evelyn describe it as flagrant? Did flamingoes like to strut around and show off their pink finery?

Even more important, what did Evelyn mean by, *He stands out among the rest.*

Wait. Evelyn had used the male pronoun, not the female, to describe the flamingo. If she'd been implying the flamingo was the killer, then she couldn't have meant Portia.

I've got killers on the brain, Carly chided herself. *It probably wasn't about a killer at all. It was probably a bit of whimsy by a woman who loved the English language.*

Except that it wasn't like Evelyn to write about death. Her other notes—poems—had been whimsical and light, a tribute to Carly's eatery and the joys of grilled cheese.

Carly smoothed out the final note, the one she'd found under her windshield wiper. The printed letters looked similar to Evelyn's, but they'd been written in black ink and with a far heavier hand.

A shudder crept up Carly's spine. Had someone been watching her? Much as she hated to admit it, the tone of the poem was ominous, as if someone was trying to scare her.

What baffled her most was the pink paper. It was identical to the notepaper Evelyn used. Had the person who penned the poem bought a pad like Evelyn's? Or had someone torn off sheets from her pad when she wasn't looking?

Before Evelyn left the restaurant that day, Carly remembered seeing her searching under her table. Whatever she was looking for, she hadn't found it.

It'd had been busy that afternoon, especially with all the high school kids jamming the booths. Anyone strolling by Evelyn's table on their way to the restroom could easily have torn off a handful of blank pages when she wasn't looking. The more Carly thought about it, the more she was convinced that was what happened.

Her cell phone rang. Her mom's bright smile beamed up at her.

"Hey, Mom." Carly tried to sound upbeat.

"Hey, yourself. Listen," Rhonda gushed, "Gary and I had the most *wonderful* time last night with you and Ari. Gary said we need to do that way more often, maybe once every few weeks? We can try out some of the new restaurants in the area. What do you think?"

Carly chuckled to herself. Her mom's adoration for Ari was so blatant it's a wonder she didn't put an announcement in the *Balsam Dell Weekly*.

"I'm sure we'd both enjoy that, but right now Ari's…situation is up in the air. Before we make another dinner date, maybe we should see how things pan out. I'm doing everything I can to—" She stopped herself before blurting the rest.

"You're investigating again, aren't you?" Rhonda squawked. "Remember what happened last time?"

No, Mom, being trapped with a desperate killer totally slipped my mind.

"Mom, I'm not investigating." It was only a little fib. "I'm just acting as sort of a…a sounding board, in case anyone has something they want to confide in me."

"A sounding board? Sounds more like a confessional if you ask me!" She went on to lecture Carly for the next few minutes, her voice rising and falling with each dire warning. Carly closed her eyes and shook her head, waiting for the tirade to fizzle.

"Honestly, Mom, nothing bad's going to happen," Carly finally cut in. "I wish you wouldn't worry so much."

"After your last escapade, how can I *not* worry?" Rhonda grunted and then let out a gusty sigh. "Okay, I'll stop ranting now. Before you hang up, I did call for another reason. Your sister's invited all of us to meet her new…clown guy on Sunday." Her clipped tone held a touch of sarcasm. "She seems to delight in tormenting me over his occupation by keeping it a national secret."

"Mom, that's the best news I've heard all day!" Carly squealed. "We're finally going to meet Norah's mystery man! Just give me the deets and I'll be there."

"Norah's working out the logistics now, but I'll let you know when we finalize things. Meanwhile, young lady, you keep your doors locked, your eyes open, and your mother on speed dial."

"You're always on my speed dial," Carly soothed, thanking her lucky stars for a caring, if occasionally annoying, mom like Rhonda Hale Clark.

Rhonda's voice grew uncharacteristically soft. "Listen, honey, I know you're concerned about Ari. But you've got to let the police do their jobs. That's what we pay them for, remember? I just feel in these old bones of mine that everything's going to turn out fine. Only a nincompoop would think Ari Mitchell killed Ferris Menard."

"I agree, and your bones aren't old. They're aged to perfection." Carly giggled into the phone.

"Oh, you," Rhonda said with mock offense. "Okay, I'll catch you tomorrow, honey. Love you."

Carly signed off with a sigh of relief, a lump filling her throat. It hurt to think she'd been causing her mom so much worry. Unfortunately, she could think of only one cure for it.

She had to figure out who killed Ferris Menard.

CHAPTER TWENTY-EIGHT

EARLY SATURDAY MORNING, CARLY STOPPED AT TELLY'S Market for an arrangement of mums in a ceramic planter and a box of chocolate-covered cherries. At the restaurant, she found Grant and his dad in the kitchen, chopping and slicing in preparation for the Saturday lunch crowd. Seeing father and son working together like two longtime pals brought a huge smile to her face.

"Mr. Robinson," Carly said, removing her coat. "It is an honor to have you here today. Thank you for offering to help."

Alvin Robinson wore a rust-colored knit shirt with a tiny violin embroidered on the pocket, and a pair of crisp beige chinos. He'd just finished slicing a plump tomato into rounds and was sliding them into a plastic container. "First of all, Carly, the pleasure is mine. And second, none of that Mr. Robinson nonsense. It's either Al or Alvin, your choice." His smile was wide beneath his slender mustache.

"I like Alvin." Carly hung her coat in the closet. "You guys sure got here early!"

"Are you kidding?" Grant snorted. "Dad was on his treadmill at five fifteen this morning blasting Mozart's Violin Concerto no. 3."

"I have to say," Alvin said, "I'm really enjoying myself

here. Brings back my college days, when I manned the grill at a busy all-night diner in upstate New York. I had to work fast and furious to keep those customers happy," he joked. "Patience was not on their agenda."

"No, I'm sure it wasn't. Did you get some coffee?"

"We both had our coffee and a breakfast biscuit," Grant said, removing a block of cheddar from the fridge. "I also did the bathroom. Later I'm going to show Dad a few of my fancy moves on the grill"—he made a few mock karate chops—"and then let him take over for a while, if that's okay."

"It's more than okay," Carly told him. "I'm impressed by how much you've both done already."

By 11:00 a.m., they were ready for customers. Alvin had come up with an idea that required panko crumbs, and Carly agreed to let him try it—but as a test only. He'd dashed off to the store and returned minutes later with a box of the crispy crumbs.

With Grant at the grill, Carly acting as server, and Alvin helping out on both ends, the lunch crunch passed without a hiccup. At one point Alvin had disappeared into the kitchen and returned with a plastic container. Carly was tempted to ask him what was inside, but then decided to trust him. It probably had something to do with the recipe he wanted to test.

Carly was delivering orders to a family of four when she saw Chief Holloway come in. She'd texted him early that morning and asked if she could talk to him.

Twirling his hat in his hands, he nodded at Grant and Alvin and then waited for Carly to finish with her table.

"You wished to speak to me?" he said, when she finally beckoned him into the kitchen. His expression was stern, but the twinkle in his eye broadcasted his curiosity. Carly offered him coffee, but he refused.

They sat at the pine desk. "I've been wanting to speak to you for a few days, but things have been so chaotic..." She let him use his imagination to fill in the rest.

"This is obviously about Ari," he said, looking uncomfortable.

"Partly, yes, because I don't believe the police are looking for Ferris's killer."

She saw the chief resist an eye roll, but his mouth twitched slightly. "Carly, you know the state police take the lead on a murder investigation."

"But you know this town, Chief. More importantly, you know Ari."

"Yes, I do," he said, his patience already sounding strained. "And I'm having as much trouble as you are believing that Ari killed Ferris Menard. But someone called in an anonymous tip, and that tip led the police to finding items in his trash barrel that tie him to the crime scene. That's not something we can ignore."

Carly groaned in frustration. "Items Ari had reported were taken from his pickup!" She waved a hand. "Sorry. I didn't mean to snap."

She described what she'd learned about Chip Foster and Steve Perlman, and their reasons for despising Ferris. "After talking to Steve, I feel *pretty* sure he had nothing to do with killing Ferris. But Chip Foster is a different story. His history with Ferris goes way back."

The chief sighed. "Carly, that old story about Chip Foster has been circulating since I was a young patrolman. It's been embellished so much no one really knows what happened that day."

Carly was at a loss. All this time, he'd known about Chip?

"While I'm here," Holloway went on. "What were you doing at Menard's prayer service yesterday? You and he weren't exactly chums."

"You're right, we weren't. I went to pay my final respects to a fellow restaurateur, and also to his daughter. Holly helped us out here for a few days—Suzanne twisted her ankle—and she asked if we'd like to attend."

"Who did you talk to?"

The question irked Carly. He was turning the tables on her and doing it quite cunningly. "I talked to Holly and her stepmom briefly after the service. I also talked to a woman who seemed to know the family, a Helen something."

"Helen Fairchild. Biggest gossip this side of the Hudson River."

Carly nodded. "That was her. Actually, I wasn't able to linger after the service. I had a restaurant to run, and I needed to get to work."

"But you lingered long enough to chat with Steve Perlman in the parking lot."

Carly pressed her hands to the table. "Okay, that I did. Chief, were you spying on me?"

Holloway laughed. "Oh, that's rich, Carly. How—"

He was interrupted by a tap at the swinging door, followed by Alvin Robinson dashing over to them with two plates and a pile of napkins. "Try these. Gotta run." He flew back into the dining room.

Carly and the chief exchanged puzzled looks. They each picked up one half of a plump grilled cheese and tomato sandwich and bit off a corner. After Carly swallowed hers, her eyes widened. "Good berries on a beanstalk! He coated the tomato slices in panko and grilled them first."

The chief nodded, totally absorbed in enjoying his sandwich. "That was delicious," he said after chowing down his half. "I'll have to thank Alvin on my way out." He wiped his lips with a napkin. "While I'm here, there's been some resolution on Saturday's voting. One of the cheaters came forward and confessed to adding phony votes to the legit ones. Ms. Gray is going to contact you later today."

Carly sagged in her chair. "I know all about it, Chief, and frankly I don't care anymore. I just want Ferris's murderer caught." She sighed and said, "The other reason I asked you to come by is to show you what someone left under my windshield wiper. I noticed it as I was leaving the prayer service yesterday." She pulled up the picture of the poem on her cell phone and handed it over to him.

He took the phone, his eyebrows dipping farther into a V with each line he read. He texted it to someone, probably himself, then gave her back the phone. "Where's the original?"

"I left it at home. I didn't want it to get misplaced, so I put it in a safe place."

"The poem was written on pink paper," the chief pointed out, slinging an arm around the back of his chair. "That suggests to me that a woman wrote it."

"Not necessarily, and isn't that rather sexist?"

"Merely an observation," the chief muttered.

Carly explained her theory about someone ripping off a portion of Evelyn Fitch's notepad.

Holloway leaned forward and folded his arms on the table. "Carly, all of this adds up to one clear fact. You've been playing Miss Nosy Spy again, and someone doesn't like it. And the person who *really* doesn't like it is me." He gave her a stern look.

"I understand how you feel. Honestly, I do," she said evenly. "But if the police keep trying to prove Ari is the killer, it means they're not making serious progress. Chief, in your heart of hearts, do you really believe Ari was responsible for Ferris's death?"

He stared at her for a long moment. "First of all, Carly, you're not giving the police nearly enough credit. And second, I'm going to tell you something that is for your ears only, and I'm dead serious when I say that." Holloway lowered his voice. "The homicide detectives are looking closely at another suspect, someone who had both motive and opportunity—and mostly likely the means."

Carly's pulse raced. "Who—"

"No questions." He held up a hand.

"But how can I protect myself if you won't give me the name?" she pressed him.

"Nice try," Holloway said, "but I know you too well. If I give you the name, the first thing you'll do is start asking them questions. Not only would that put you at risk, but it would tip our hand."

"Does her name begin with P?"

The chief sucked in a breath, and his face flushed.

Nailed it.

Holloway slapped his hand on the desk. "What you need to do now, Carly, is to pack a suitcase, collect your dog, and move in with your mom and Dr. Clark until this is resolved."

So…the rock has met a hard place.

Carly respected the chief. She always had. And though she didn't want to admit it, the notion that Ferris's killer had left her the ominous note was never far from her mind.

Nevertheless, she had to stand her ground until the killer

was in custody. Moving in with her mom, even for a few days, would be a monumental hassle.

"Chief, that's just not going to happen," she said quietly. "That would scare my mother to death. Besides, I'm very safe with Becca and Joyce living downstairs from me. I also have Havarti."

"That pipsqueak of a dog?" Holloway gave her an incredulous look.

"He's fierce when he wants to be," Carly defended.

"Fair enough," the chief relented. "I can't force you. I can only strongly advise that you cease and desist and leave the questions to the police." He rose and slapped his hat on his head. "I'll be in touch. And put that poem in a bag. I'll send an officer over to your apartment this evening to pick it up." He paused when his cell phone pinged with a text. After reading the message, he heaved a guttural sigh. "Great. The wife and son of that hit-and-run victim want to meet in my office in an hour. Just what I need to round out my day."

His sharp retort surprised Carly. "They must be devastated over their loss, Chief."

"If so, they're the only ones. I don't know another soul on earth who had a nice word to say about the man. Without going into detail, he was well known to the police."

"You still don't have any leads on the driver?" Carly asked him.

"Unfortunately, no. I have to go, Carly. Just remember what I said."

You said a lot of things, she wanted to remark, but wisely kept it to herself. She watched him push through the swinging door, her nerves jangling like cowbells. *He is reeeally not happy with me.*

But he'd given her a sliver of hope. If the police were looking at a different suspect, it meant they were focusing on someone other than Ari.

She returned to the dining room to find Holloway still there. He was chatting with Grant's dad. She waited until the chief left to thank Alvin for the sandwich.

Alvin's smile was a mile wide. "So glad you liked that little twist," he said, a touch of pride in his voice. "It's obvious why Grant enjoys working here so much. You're big on letting him express his creative side."

"With Grant, that's easy," Carly said, meaning it. She wanted to add, *He'll make a great chef one day*, but it was too sore a subject—plus it wasn't any of her business. Grant and his dad would work it out eventually, and without any input from Carly.

By around 3:30, there was a lull in customers. Carly was anxious to visit Evelyn, but she was nervous about leaving Grant and Alvin alone. And while she'd been thrilled to have Alvin help out for the day, it wouldn't be fair to keep him there any longer.

"Hey, Carly," Grant said, as if he'd read her mind. "I know you want to visit Ms. Fitch in the rehab place. Why don't you go now while we hold down the fort? Dad thinks you should too."

She glanced at Alvin, who nodded and smiled. "You guys are the best, you know it?" she said. "Alvin, as soon as I get back, you should go along home."

He laughed. "You won't have to twist my arm. I'm just glad I could be here to help." He clasped his son's shoulder.

Half expecting to find another "gift" under her windshield wiper, Carly walked cautiously to her car. She breathed out a sigh of relief when it was all clear.

On the way to see Evelyn, she mulled over the new tidbit the chief had dropped in her lap. He'd practically admitted the police were looking more closely at Portia. But Portia was already divorcing Ferris, so what did she stand to gain? A financial settlement would already have been in the works, but maybe she had loftier goals.

She'd been keen on franchising the sub shop—something Ferris had strongly objected to. Had she envisioned herself as the Sub-a-Dub-Sub mogul, the woman who would bring national fame to a mostly forgettable sandwich joint? According to Steve, she'd long dreamed of owning a business, but had nothing specific in mind. Had her marriage to Ferris been the stepping stone she'd been seeking, only to find him unwilling to cooperate with her franchising idea?

Then there was Ferris's "famous" dressing recipe, the one he'd accused Portia of stealing. Sure, Portia could fight it out with him in court and probably win. But killing him would be far more expedient. Besides, with Ferris out of the way, Holly would be a much more pliable business partner.

The real wild card was Holly.

Carly thought back to that fateful Sunday morning. The chief had called Carly's mom before 7:00 a.m., so Ferris's body had to have been discovered well before that. She recalled Holloway's words when he delivered the bad news.

His daughter found him this morning in the restaurant...

So why had Holly gone into the sub shop so early on a Sunday? It would still have been dark outside, and Ferris didn't open until 11:00. Had she gone in early to help him do prep work? Or did she have a more devious reason?

Maybe Holly was tired of being treated like a servant, sick of being underappreciated. It wouldn't have been hard to figure Ari's truck would be in Carly's driveway. She could easily have stolen the cape, although the shoes were problematic. Ari had never been able to pinpoint exactly when his work boots went missing.

But why frame Ari? That's what Carly couldn't wrap her head around.

Or had Holly been influenced by Portia, the stepmom she'd developed such a deep admiration for? Maybe Holly figured that with her dad out of the picture, she could hitch her star to Portia's ambitious wagon and carve out a shining future for herself.

By the time Carly spotted the turnoff to the facility where Evelyn was, her head was whirling with theories. And that's just what they were—theories. She had no proof of anything, nothing she could hand over to the police with a smug, "Here's your killer!"

The place to begin, she decided, was with Holly. The problem was, how would she approach her? She'd just fired the young woman. And though she'd told Holly she wouldn't report her graffiti caper to the police, maybe she could use that as a bargaining chip.

First things first.

She'd visit Evelyn, then come up with a plausible reason to have a confab with Holly.

CHAPTER TWENTY-NINE

THE SKY WAS ALREADY DARKENING BY THE TIME CARLY pulled into the parking lot. Balsam Dell Long-Term Care was a one-story brick building flanked by neatly trimmed shrubs. Illuminated on all sides by tall overhead lamps, the lot was surprisingly packed with cars. Carly lucked out and found a space in the second row.

Flower arrangement in hand, the chocolates tucked into her tote, she entered the lobby. Although the furnishings were plain, the green/blue color scheme was soothing to the eye. A sixtyish couple sat on a sage green sofa beside an elderly gent in a wheelchair.

Beyond that, at the circular reception desk, Carly was greeted by a young woman with lilac-tinted hair. Carly asked for Evelyn, and after signing in, was directed down one of two long corridors. "There's a nurse's desk at the end," the receptionist explained. "Press the buzzer if no one's there."

Carly thanked her and made her way down the corridor. The scent of air freshener was strong, but not unpleasant. As she strode along the tiled hallway, she peeked into the rooms. Most of the doors were open, but a few were closed. She was hoping she might find Evelyn's room without having to bother the nurse.

When she reached the nurse's desk, she was greeted by a

broad-shouldered man with kind brown eyes and a genuine smile. His name tag read: *Elliott G, RN*. He looked up from the sheaf of papers he was reading. "Good afternoon, may I help you?"

"Good afternoon. I'd like to visit Evelyn Fitch, but I don't have her room number."

He craned his neck and peeked over at the closed door to one of the rooms. "Oh, I'm sorry. Her therapist is still working with her. Their session just started, so they'll be a while. Can you come back a bit later?"

Disappointed, Carly pondered whether or not she should wait. Every minute she was away from her restaurant racked up her guilt a notch. "I'm not sure I can," she said. "Do you know how Evelyn's doing?"

He tapped his fingers over a keyboard and peered at a screen. "I can't give out medical information, but she seems to be holding her own. Is she expecting you?"

"Yes, in a way. She asked her daughter if I would pay her a visit."

"Oh! Her daughter was here earlier, but she went home to get some things."

If Carly waited around for the therapist to finish, she'd have to hurry through her visit. But if she returned the following day, she wouldn't have to rush. She could spend some quality time with Evelyn and give her some cheer. And, depending on Evelyn's state of mind, learn more about the mysterious poem—although Lydia had already warned her that her mom's short-term memory had been compromised.

"I'm afraid I'll have to leave," Carly told the nurse. "Would you please give Evelyn these flowers? Tell her they're from Carly, and that I'll see her tomorrow."

"You bet I will," Elliott said, taking the mums from Carly.

Carly thanked him and then remembered her other mission. "By any chance is Irene Menard in this wing? A friend of hers told me she was here. I was hoping I might see her for a few minutes."

The nurse's smile faded. "She is, but there's been a tragedy in her family. She's unaware of it, and her doctor wants it to remain that way. Upsetting her at this stage would be cruel."

"Oh, I understand," Carly said solemnly. "Whatever it was, I would never say anything. Is it okay if I bring her some chocolates?" She removed the gold box from her tote and showed it to the nurse.

Elliott studied the cellophane-wrapped box for a moment, and then his smile returned. "Well, I don't see any harm in that. Irene doesn't have any dietary restrictions. I'm sure she'll be pleased. Do keep your visit short, though. Her mind tires easily, plus she's usually a little loopy from morphine, although that's more than I should have revealed." He made a *zip your lip* motion over his mouth, and Carly nodded that she understood. "Oh, and be prepared," the nurse added with a chuckle, "Irene will probably be watching one of her shoot-'em-up cowboy shows when you go in there. You'll find her in 129."

Carly thanked him and proceeded to Irene's room. She needed to make the visit short so she could get back to the restaurant.

The door to Irene's dimly lit room was open enough for Carly to peek inside. Save for the hospital bed, the furnishings looked as if they belonged in a little girl's room. The white pine bureau and nightstand were stenciled with faded flowers. Plush animals nestled on the bureau next to clusters of framed photos. A large, flat-screen TV hung on the wall opposite the bed. Two cowboys with six-shooters were firing at each other while horses' hooves thundered in the background.

Carly knocked lightly and then stepped into the room. "Irene?"

A diminutive woman wearing a flannel nightie was huddled in the bed. Her white hair, threaded with blond strands, framed a tiny face. Vestiges of the beauty she must have been at one time still lingered, but her frame was shriveled from illness. Her gaze fixed on the cowboys, she startled at the sound of her name. "Yes? Do I know you?"

Carly walked softly over to the bed. "No, but my name is Carly. I recently met a friend of yours. She told me you love chocolate-covered cherries."

Irene stared at Carly, and her pale eyebrows knitted together. If she wondered who the friend was, she didn't inquire. Her blue eyes snapped wide at the sight of the gold box, then dimmed again with confusion. "I'll take them," she said and snatched the box from Carly's hand.

Carly smiled at her. "Shall I open it for you?"

"No, these are all for me," Irene said, hugging the candies to her chest. In the next moment, her attention shifted. She gawked up at the TV and pointed. "See that man in the black hat? He's the spitting image of my Larry. Why, a handsomer rascal you never saw!" She covered her mouth and giggled, rocking forward in the bed.

Carly looked at the cowboy in question. Sculptured features, tanned face, wavy, coal black hair. A typical western hero from 1960s television.

"He is very handsome," Carly agreed. "Is…Larry your husband?"

Irene giggled again, then her smile morphed into a child-like pout. "He was supposed to be. Then he met someone else." She gave a haughty lift of her chin. "She wasn't pretty like me, but her daddy was rich."

Carly's pulse throbbed. She felt sure, now, that Larry was the silver-haired man—Lawrence Kendall—Helen had pointed out in church.

"I still love him," Irene prattled on, her eyes growing misty. "Even though he left me in a family way and married that prissy Pamela Jepson."

A family way. Pregnant with Ferris?

"Did he know you were…in a family way?" Carly asked gently.

Irene's gaze sharpened. "Of course he knew. I told him. But that didn't stop him from marrying that plain wrapper of a woman." Spittle formed on her lips.

"I'm so sorry. But you married someone after that, right?"

Irene sagged back in the bed, and her eyelids fluttered. "Ben Menard knew about…me," she said in a papery voice, "but he didn't care. He thought I was too pretty to pass up. We eloped, and that was that. He wasn't handsome or fun like my Larry, but he took decent care of my boy—when he was around, that is. Told everyone Ferris was his son."

"I'm sure that was hard," Carly said softly. "But it sounds like Ben loved you."

She smiled and nodded, then her eyes watered. "Ferris is mad at me. He won't come to see me anymore."

Carly reached out and touched Irene's thin wrist. "Maybe he'll change his mind. Give him time, okay?"

It was a terrible distortion of the truth, but Irene seemed to take comfort from it. She nodded and her eyelids lowered. The chocolate box slipped from her grasp onto the blanket. Carly removed it and set it on her bedside table.

On her way out, she glanced over the photos on the bureau. Most were of Irene and Ferris in their younger days. A stout man with a thick beard appeared in only a few of them. Ben Menard, Carly assumed, but that was only a guess.

Carly hurried out to her car, intent on one thing. She needed to talk to Holly.

If Larry Kendall was Ferris's biological dad, then Holly had a grandfather she was completely unaware of.

CHAPTER THIRTY

At the restaurant, everything had gone smoothly in Carly's absence.

Alvin looked tired, and she urged him to go home and relax. She thanked him profusely for his help but wanted to do more. She knew he'd be insulted if she offered him wages, so she'd have to be more creative. Maybe with Grant's help she could come up with an idea.

Before he left, Alvin asked to speak privately to Carly. They went into the kitchen.

"Carly, I will get directly to the point."

Uh oh. Was he going to launch into a speech about Grant's music career?

"This entire day has been an education for me," he continued. "Watching my son work at what he loves best was a real eye-opener. I'm sure you know the proverb, 'There are none so blind as those who will not see.' Well, up until now I've had blinders on. They officially come off—today."

Carly's heart soared. Was he saying what she hoped he was saying? She started to speak, but Alvin held up a hand.

"Let me finish," he said quietly. "My son is a gifted cellist, and he has much to offer to the world of classical music. More than anything, I want his happiness. But today the truth smacked me square in the head: What makes Grant happiest is to feed others. If I'd been paying attention, I'd have realized it long ago. He's been feeding his mom and me since he was a kid." Alvin's smile was humble. "If my son is still determined to have a career as a chef, then his mother and I will support him. And we'll help with tuition."

A lump clogged Carly's throat. "I'm so happy to hear that, Alvin. Have you told him yet?"

"That's on tap for this evening." Alvin smiled broadly.

"That's great." Carly hesitated, then, "So are you still going to tour the college tomorrow?"

"We absolutely are. I want Grant to be armed with all the ammo he needs to make an informed decision about his future. I would ask one thing of you, though," he cautioned.

"What is it?"

"If Grant *should* choose a career in music, that you'll be supportive and encouraging."

Carly stuck out her hand. "I will, and that's a promise. I can't think of a more deserving person than Grant."

Alvin shook her hand, and then he hugged her. "Mrs. R. is picking me out front, so I'll go out that way. One last thing, Carly. *Please* be careful out there."

She agreed to that and saw him to the door. Only a few customers lingered in the dining room.

"You guys looked pretty chummy," Grant said after his dad left. He began putting away condiments in the fridge beneath the counter.

"I was just thanking your dad for all his help today," Carly said innocently.

"Yeah, it was cool having him here," Grant said, looking thoughtful. "You were okay with it, right?"

"More than okay. I thought the three of us made a great

team." She glanced around. "I thought we'd be busier about now. It's pretty quiet."

"Yeah, the high school had an away football game this afternoon, so most of the usual kids are out of town."

"Ah. Then is it okay if I take care of one more thing in the kitchen?"

He smiled. "You're the boss."

Carly immediately went to her cell phone. She had one message from her mom, which she somehow missed. She'd call her mom back shortly, but first she wanted to see if she could reach Lydia.

She tapped Lydia's number and was relieved when she answered.

"Hey, I heard you tried to visit Mom today," Lydia said, a smile in her voice. "She was so sorry you missed her."

"I was too," Carly said, "but I'm planning another visit tomorrow. Any idea what time would be good?"

"How about early afternoon?" Lydia suggested. "In fact, I want to meet you there. I went through that bin labeled 1996. It was crammed with letters and photos, too many for me to fish through. I thought you might want to take them home with you so you can peruse them at your leisure."

"That would be great, Lydia. Thank you."

"Of course that bin might have jogged loose on its own," Lydia cautioned. "It's possible Mom wasn't reaching for it at all."

Carly had thought of that too. "I know, I won't get my hopes up, but I would like to go through it. And I thought of something else. Remember I told you about the unsettling poem I got?"

"I do. Some nasty little worm trying to upset you, no doubt." Her tone was caustic.

"Probably, but something occurred to me. Since it was an acrostic poem, I'm betting the culprit who wrote it had been in one of your mom's English classes. By the time I took English in school, your mom was retired. As far as I know, none of the other teachers taught that."

Lydia issued a sigh into the phone. "You could be right, Carly, but that's still a needle in a haystack. Mom had oodles of students over the years. Plus, school wasn't the only place she taught acrostic poetry."

"It wasn't?"

"Nope. She used to volunteer summers to help younger kids who'd had problems during the school year. The program was called Summer Helpers, and parents had to sign their kids up for it. If she saved anything from the program in 1996, it should be with the stuff I'm bringing you to look through."

Carly's heartbeat sped up. "Thanks, now I'm more anxious than ever to see what's in there." They agreed to meet at 1:00 p.m. the following day in the reception area of the rehab place.

Next she made a fast call to her mom, who confirmed their plans for Sunday. Everyone, Ari included, was to congregate at Norah's townhouse no later than 2:30 sharp. Norah had something special planned and had instructed them all to "wear something nice."

Then she texted Gina. The weekend got away from me. How are things?

Gina texted back: Busy. Zach's mom made surprise visit. Treating us to BBQ tonight. Gulp. First time meeting her. Wish me luck. U and I still have to catch up!

Carly promised a "catch up" evening early in the week.

At closing time, Grant once again walked Carly out to her car. A light rain was falling, enhancing the scent of decaying leaves as it glazed the ground. She thanked him again for recruiting his dad as a helper and expressed how much she had enjoyed working with Alvin.

"I think he enjoyed it too. Man, he was like a little kid with a new toy when you let him experiment with the panko."

"Oh, that was a super idea." Carly smiled, and a thought struck her—a way that she could thank Alvin. "I definitely want to add it to the menu, but we need a good name for it. Something that will honor your dad."

"I'll brainstorm it," Grant promised. "Dad'll love it. You know, while you were gone today, he got a little weird."

Carly glanced at her windshield wiper. A blossom of relief went through her when she saw that it was untouched. She unlocked her car door. "Weird...in a bad way?"

"No, the opposite. Come to think of it," Grant said glumly, "he's probably just psyched that I agreed to visit the college with him tomorrow. I'm afraid he's going to get his hopes up, and I'll have to break his heart."

Carly turned and faced him. "Grant, I want to you listen to me. Your dad loves you fiercely. You will never break his heart by choosing what you know is right for you."

He gave her an odd look. "You really believe that?"

"I really believe that. Now go home and have a great day tomorrow. I'll see you Monday."

Grant waited until Carly was in her car with the doors locked, then trotted off toward his own. She was starting her engine when her cell rang.

Holly.

Excellent timing, Carly thought. She'd planned to get in

touch with her when she got home, so maybe the call was serendipitous.

Was it Holly the police were focused on now, and not Portia? Chief Holloway had been tight-lipped about it, but Holly would be the logical choice—especially since she was the one who discovered her dad's body. In Carly's opinion, however, Portia was the stronger suspect.

"Hi, Holly," she said, tapping into the call.

"Hey." Holly's voice quivered. "I figured you'd be leaving work about now. Um, look, I know what I did to you was terrible, but is there some place we can talk? I...I have some news."

Taking a page from Steve's playbook, Carly asked Holly if she could meet her at the donut shop in ten minutes. It was well lighted, and she'd be safe there. If she sensed anything awry, she'd stay in her car and drive directly to the police station.

The best laid plans...

The phrase swept through her mind, but she shoved it aside. Besides, she definitely wanted to learn Holly's news—and wanted to deliver a bit of news of her own.

She texted Ari her plan and then headed for the donut shop. On her way, she couldn't help wondering.

Was she meeting a sad young woman who'd just lost her dad in the most horrible way?

Or was she meeting his cold-blooded killer?

CHAPTER THIRTY-ONE

"I ORDERED YOU A COFFEE," HOLLY SAID, a flush in her cheeks. Her eyes were shiny, her lids puffy.

Carly wrapped her hands around the warm mug in front of her. The low chatter from the donut shop's few customers and the occasional clink of a spoon were a comforting backdrop. "Thanks. My fingers needed that." She added a touch of creamer.

"I won't keep you long," Holly promised. "Yesterday afternoon, I met with the recreation manager, Ms. Gray. She was crisp and to the point. She let me know how distressed and disappointed she was at what Tyler and I did. She thanked me, though, for coming forward and admitting it."

"Did Tyler go with you to the meeting?" Carly already guessed the answer.

"No. I knew he wouldn't. He's in for some trouble at work, I'm afraid. By Monday he'll probably be out of a job."

Carly tried to dredge up an ounce of sympathy for him. She couldn't.

"As for both of us," Holly went on, "Ms. Gray is going to consult with the town manager to see if they want to press charges. If they do, she's going to suggest some kind of community service for me and Tyler." Her eyes leaked. "I feel like such a…lowlife. I can't even imagine what people will think of me."

A part of Carly felt sorry for Holly. But a larger part wondered if she was guilty of something much worse than tampering with Saturday's event. "Holly, this is probably a touchy subject, but are you still going to move in with Tyler?" She took a sip from her mug.

Holly's expression one of sheer misery, she shook her head. "I've already decided to renege on that. I can't see us as a couple anymore." She sniffled.

"I think that's a wise choice," Carly said.

"Thank you. The other thing I wanted to tell you is that Dad's attorney wants to see me in his office Monday morning. I'm so scared, Carly. I found out he had that overnight envelope all along! Why didn't he tell me before?" she cried. "I've been agonizing over it."

Carly shrugged. She couldn't even guess why. "If I were you, I'd press to meet with him tomorrow, even if it is Sunday."

"I tried, but he'll be out of town tomorrow. Carly, if it turns out I'm not my dad's real daughter, then I am toast. The cops will probably accuse me of murder, and I won't be able to prove otherwise." Tears flowed again, this time in a stream.

Carly waited out the crying session, then said, "Holly, I might have an idea of what's in that envelope." She told her about her chat with the gossipy woman at church, and then about visiting Irene, who didn't know her son was deceased.

"Wow. You're really good at finding out stuff." Holly's shocked expression turned thoughtful as she started connecting the dots. "What you're saying is, you think the DNA test wasn't about me at all, but about Dad's own real father?"

"It's only a guess, but yes, that's what I believe. Your

grandmother pretty much said that someone other than Ben Menard was Ferris's true dad. She said Ferris stopped speaking to her after she told him."

Holly's eyes darted back and forth, and then she lifted her gaze to meet Carly's. "That would explain why Dad told me not to visit her anymore. He had a vindictive streak, you know."

No kidding.

Holly bit down on her bottom lip. "You know what's weird? About a month ago, a nice-looking older man came in the sub shop. I had the feeling Dad was expecting him, but he never said that. Anyway, he asked for Dad and they spoke privately, but after that Dad got unusually quiet. He gave the man a can of soda and a sandwich, but he wouldn't let me clean the table after. He insisted on doing it himself." She pressed her fingers to her cheeks, and then her mouth opened as reality dawned. "Oh my gosh, he was collecting DNA, wasn't he? He was trying to figure out if that guy was his father."

"That would be my guess," Carly said.

"It would mean…I have a different family. A living grandfather I've never known."

Carly nodded. She wanted to question her about Portia, but without making it sound as if she suspected her of murder. "Are you going to the attorney's office alone?"

Holly nodded. "Portia offered to go with me for moral support, but I told her I'd be okay going alone." She shrugged uncertainly. "She seemed annoyed when I said that, but it's just…lately I've been wondering if she's got some hidden agenda, you know? Oh gosh, I hate myself for even saying that. She's been so good to me!" She dropped her head in her hands.

After a long pause, Carly said, "Holly, deep inside, you know what's right for you. The same way you knew it was right to go to Ms. Gray and come clean about the votes."

"It was a huge load off my chest, that's for sure." She blew out a noisy breath. "It felt like a boulder was lifted."

"Then trust yourself. If you're more comfortable meeting with your attorney alone, then do it. Don't feel you're doing a disservice to anyone else."

"Okay. I will." Her face brightened. "By the way, I decided to tell Portia about what Tyler and I did. I didn't want her to find out from someone else."

"How did she take it?"

"She was ticked, but then she waved it off. She told me to forget about it and move on."

The same way she moved on after Steve Perlman.

Carly decided not to push the Portia issue any further, at least not with Holly. But there was one other matter she did want to push.

"Holly, I told you I wasn't going to report the skull you painted on my car, and I'm not. But I do have one simple request. There's a sweet, elderly woman who I'm sure would love to spend some time with her granddaughter while she still has time left."

Holly swiped at her face with her fingers. "Nana Irene?"

"She's the one." Carly smiled and drained her mug. "I have to go now. And in spite of everything that's happened between us, I hope you'll keep in touch."

"I will," Holly promised, pushing back her chair. She looked as if she wanted to hug Carly, but then she rose hurriedly and left the donut shop.

Carly sat for a few moments, staring through the front

window. She watched Holly pull out of the parking lot, this time without the grumble of a dying muffler. Finally, she collected her empty mug and set it in the bin designated for dirty dishes. She tossed her napkin in the trash barrel and hurried out to her car.

At the back of the parking lot, a car sat in the farthest corner. Its lights were off, but it sounded as if the engine was running. Had the car been there when she arrived? She was almost sure it hadn't been. A shadow suddenly flitted across the car's windshield, igniting every nerve in her body.

A sliver of dread slithered down her spine. A scenario she hadn't considered wriggled into her mind and took hold.

What if she'd been looking at the suspects all wrong? What if Ferris was murdered by Holly and Tyler together, working as a team? Holly's claim that they'd split up might simply have been a ruse, designed to throw Carly a curveball.

They had the perfect motive, didn't they? Eliminate Ferris from the picture, take control of the sub shop, and run it like a "mom and pop" sandwich place. They wouldn't need Portia. They could toss her under the bus and wave goodbye from the window.

Holly wasn't above lying to her father. Grant had witnessed that himself. Maybe she'd spied a way to secure a boyfriend *and* an established food business all at the same time. It wasn't only clever. It was diabolical.

Carly jumped into her Corolla, locked the doors, and swerved out of the lot. When she finally summoned the courage to glance at her rearview mirror, she saw a pair of headlights following behind her, a bit too close for comfort. She couldn't be sure it was the same car she'd seen at the donut place, but the twinge at the pit of her stomach told her it was.

The lights followed her through the downtown section, hovering in her mirror all along the main drag until she reached her apartment house. When she pulled into her driveway, the car sped off. By then her heart was flogging her ribs so hard she thought her chest would collapse. It didn't stop pounding until she was inside her apartment with the door locked.

After she hugged and fed her dog, she poured herself a glass of cider and grabbed a pudding cup from the fridge. It was far from an adequate supper, but it was all she could force down.

She didn't want to call Ari or her mom. They'd know from her voice something was wrong. She collapsed on her sofa with her meager meal and snapped on the television. She tried to focus on a mindless sitcom, but the silliness only annoyed her.

When her limbs finally relaxed and heartbeat slowed, she began to wonder if she was paranoid. The person in the car at the donut shop could've been a total stranger. People sat in parked cars all the time, didn't they? Making phone calls, waiting for a friend, paying bills online.

Even when it appeared the car had followed her out of the lot, she might have been mistaken. It was probably a completely different car. Plus, she lived on a main road, a frequently traveled road. It would have been strange if someone *hadn't* been driving behind her.

The parked car had made her jumpy, that's all. It had led her imagination to a dark place, a place where menace lurked at every turn.

A knock at her door startled her, until she remembered that the chief was sending an officer over to retrieve the poem she found on her windshield. To Carly's relief it was a woman, although she still made her flash her badge through the peephole before she would open the door.

After the officer left, Carly made sure all her blinds were closed and everything was locked up tight. Before she went to bed, she peeked outside her window. A car was cruising slowly by the house, almost as if the driver was lost.

Carly shuddered and dropped the blind back in place.

She picked up Havarti and squished him to her chest, rubbing his furry head. "I don't suppose you could shape-shift into a Doberman for the night?" she suggested, then kissed him on the snout.

He gave her a puzzled look, then licked her chin. Carly suddenly wished Ari were there with her.

CHAPTER THIRTY-TWO

THE NEXT MORNING, EVERYTHING LOOKED BRIGHTER. Carly's fears had dissipated, and she was looking forward to the get-together Norah had planned. She was finally going to meet Norah's beau, praise the heavens. She'd learned that his name was Nate, but everything else about him remained a mystery.

Not for long, she thought, giggling to herself.

Since she'd agreed to meet Lydia at 1:00 at the rehab facility, she'd asked Ari—who was excited about being invited—to meet her at Norah's no later than 2:30. Norah's townhouse was only a short distance from where Evelyn was, and that way they wouldn't risk the wrath of Norah by being late. Carly passed along the instructions to "dress nice," although she wasn't yet sure what she herself was going to wear.

By noon, she'd showered and dressed in her shimmery gold tunic sweater and black wool pants, her neckline boasting the chunky turquoise necklace she'd bought from an online crafter. She dug her rarely used curling iron out from the bathroom closet, and by the time she'd pinched her short hair into soft waves, she looked pretty darn nice, if she did say so herself. At least good enough to satisfy Norah's marching orders. As a final touch, she gave her coif a spritz from her travel-sized hairspray canister to hold it in place. With cold, windy weather in today's forecast, she wanted to be prepared.

Right on time, Lydia was waiting for her in the lobby of the rehab facility.

"Oh, what a lovely coat that is." Lydia rose from her wing-back chair to give Carly a firm hug. "And I love what you did with your hair. It's curlier, isn't it?"

"It is, thanks," Carly said, loosening her scarf. "When I saw how chilly it was this morning, I knew it was time to drag out my winter duds." Her olive-green quilted coat with its thick knitted collar and cuffs was her favorite. It kept her toasty when the weather turned bitter, and yet it was light-weight and washable. "After I leave here, I'm meeting my family at my sister's place. I'll be meeting Norah's new beau for the first time, so I'm kind of excited."

"Oh, you must be." Lydia smiled and held out a hand to indicate the chair diagonally from her own. On the floor beside her was a plastic shopping bag. Inside were oversized volumes that appeared to be photo albums or scrapbooks.

Unbuttoning her coat, Carly glanced around. The reception area looked brighter than it had the day before. Sunlight streamed through the tall windows onto the gleaming tiled floor. The spicy aroma of cloves and cinnamon wafted from a bowl of potpourri on the reception desk. Despite the overnight drop in temperature, the place felt warm and comfy.

Lydia smiled again, and then her expression sobered. "Carly, before we visit Mom, I want to warn you—she still doesn't remember anything about falling down her cellar stairs. She remembers making herself a bowl of cereal for supper, and the next thing she knew she was waking up in the hospital, wondering how she got there."

"Do the doctors think her memory will return?"

"In time, yes, but they can't say how soon or whether everything will come back."

"I don't mean to question the doctors," Carly said, "but didn't the hospital discharge your mom awfully fast? I'd expected them to keep her at least a few more days."

Lydia's lips pursed. "You don't know Mom. She was adamant that she be discharged, and she did so against medical advice. Her brother died of a raging infection he contracted in a hospital, and she's hated hospitals ever since. I tried talking sense into her, but she wouldn't listen. She was fine with having rehab, as long as it wasn't in a hospital. Bottom line, they did all the paperwork and transferred her here."

That is one determined woman, Carly thought. And while she wished Evelyn had listened to the doctors, she had to admire her spunk.

Lydia bit down on her bottom lip. "I brought along everything that was in that plastic bin. I'm afraid it's kind of a jumble, but you can go through everything. As the label said, everything is from 1996."

"Seems like an eternity ago," Carly said. "I would've been about seven then."

Lydia chuckled. "Mom thinks of that period as her heyday. By then she was a seasoned teacher, loving her job, and spending her summers helping younger kids. She always said to me, 'Lydia, I don't just want to teach. I want to make a difference.'"

"And I know she did," Carly said warmly.

"But first I have to tell you about the flamingo." Lydia pressed her palms together.

The flamingo! Carly's heart jolted in her chest.

"After racking my brain and getting nowhere," Lydia continued, "I finally called my sister last night. Up until a few years ago, she lived with Mom. I had a feeling she might remember what was escaping me. As soon as I said the word *flamingo*, it all came back to her.

"Back when Mom was volunteering for Summer Helpers, a little boy in her class got into a fight with another boy in the schoolyard. The instigator was a boy who had behavior problems, although he was very bright. At one point, this... instigator—Mom never told us his name—pummeled the other boy to the ground. Mom rushed to intervene, but before she could pull the boy off the other kid, he stood on the boy's chest with one leg and yelled, 'Mrs. Fitch, look at me! I'm a flamingo!'"

Carly felt her jaw almost hit the floor.

Look at me. I'm a flamingo...

Was that the memory jolted loose from Evelyn's mind when Holly blurted that detail about the crime scene?

It had to be. All this time, Carly had been focusing on the flamingo's pink coloring. She should have remembered the graceful bird's ability to balance on one leg.

The way Ferris's killer had done.

"The boy on the ground was crying his eyes out," Lydia was saying. "After Mom finally pulled the bully off the poor child, she explained, quite firmly, why that behavior was unacceptable." Lydia pressed a hand to her chest. "And—this is the part that gets me—Mom said the bully was absolutely devastated. He'd expected her to *praise* him, not scold him, for triumphing over the poor kid he beat up. He'd said he'd thought she'd be proud of him for being so strong and brave."

The story made Carly feel queasy. "I can't help thinking

the boy might've had a messed-up home life. But I think you may have stumbled onto something about the flamingo. Is that little boy in one of those scrapbooks?"

"I'm sure he is," Lydia said ruefully, "but I don't have a clue what his name is or how to find him. I brought them in case you wanted to look through them."

A needle in a haystack for sure, Carly thought.

"Before we go in to visit Mom," Lydia said, "I have something else to give you. Her purse was in the hallway closet, where she always keeps it. I decided to bring it to her. I'm hoping some of the contents might trigger a memory from the day she fell. I found this inside." She reached into the bag and pulled out a pink envelope. The flap was sealed with a flowery pink sticker. The name "Carly" was printed on the front in bold letters.

Mystified, Carly accepted the envelope from her. "Did you look inside?"

"No way. If Mom sealed it with your name on it, then it's for your eyes only. I'm only sorry I didn't think to check her purse before." She gave Carly a regretful look. "Mom was probably going to give it to you the next time she saw you."

Carly stared at the envelope. "But...I don't understand. When would Evelyn have written this?"

"Obviously before she fell," Lydia said with a shrug. "Probably after I dropped her off that day. Again, I'm sorry I didn't see it sooner."

Carly tore the seal carefully and lifted the flap. Inside the envelope was a sheet of Evelyn's familiar pink paper. She removed it and unfolded it, revealing another one of Evelyn's poems. She cleared her throat and began reading to Lydia. "'Sheer tragedy befell the man, that fate so cruelly took his breath...'"

Her hand froze on the poem. She stared at the words, almost in disbelief, as an icy chill skittered down her arms. Her lower legs tingled, and her fingers felt numb.

Lydia jiggled Carly's arm. "Carly, what's wrong? You look like you've seen a ghost."

No, not a ghost. Maybe a monster...

Carly shoved the poem into her pocket and began buttoning her coat. "Lydia, I have to go. Please tell Evelyn I got her message and that I'll see her tomorrow."

"But...wait a minute. Don't you even want the stuff from the bin?" Lydia gave her a flabbergasted look.

"I don't need them anymore. I'm sorry, but I really have to leave. I'll call you later!"

Still buttoning her coat, Carly flew out the door, using her free hand to dig out her cell phone. She'd parked her car near the back of the lot, adjacent to a grassy area where ornate benches were set out along a stand of sugar maples.

She fumbled with her cell as she scurried toward her car. Her fingers feeling like icicles, she punched in the speed dial for her mom's cell. "Mom? I'm leaving the rehab center now. I'll be at Norah's as soon as I can, but something urgent came up. I'm on my way to see Chief Hol—"

"You won't be needing that."

From behind her, two powerful hands tore her phone out of her grasp and pulled her tote off her shoulder. Carly shrieked and swiveled around.

Standing there, his eyes blazing with victory as he tossed her cell onto the grass, was Stan Henderson.

CHAPTER THIRTY-THREE

"Stan, wh...what are you doing here?" Carly's words came out like broken glass, and she stumbled backward a step.

"Following you, what else?" His lips twisted into a smirk. "I've gotten pretty good at it too, although a careful driver like you is easy to tail. Truth be told"—he flicked his head at the building—"I came here to pay a little visit to Ms. Fitch. Imagine my surprise when I saw your cute little Corolla turn into this place. What's that saying? Two birds with one stone?"

The truth hit her like a shovel to the head. *It was Stan, not Tyler, who'd followed her the night before.*

Carly shot a quick glance around the parking lot. A black SUV was parked a few feet behind her, but no one was inside. And now her phone was on the grass, out of reach.

Stan tossed her tote on the ground and moved closer. He withdrew a knife—a steak knife, Carly noticed—from the pocket of his jacket and held it up to her face.

Carly tried not to flinch, but her reaction was involuntary. Her fingers beginning to freeze, she tucked her hands inside the sleeves of her coat to keep them warm. "That was you in the parking lot at the donut shop last night, wasn't it?"

"Congratulations, you figured it out. But you've always

been a smart girl, haven't you? I thought you were going to hightail it to your boyfriend's house, but instead you went home and stayed there like a good girl. I was proud of you, Carly. It's too bad you're so nosy. With Ari out of the picture, you and I could've had a really good thing."

Not in this lifetime.

But something in his tone made her stomach curdle. "You killed Ferris and tried to frame Ari for it, didn't you? Why?"

His mouth turned down into a hard frown. "I had to kill Ferris. He left me no choice. He was draining me, milking me for everything I had. After I gave him my last five grand, he turned me into his errand boy. Raking his leaves, cleaning his gutters, doing every other crappy chore he didn't want to pay for. He had no right to do that! It was an *accident*, Carly. I never saw that guy until it was too late."

An accident.

And suddenly the missing pieces tumbled into place.

"You're the hit-and-run driver," Carly said. "Ferris must've seen you that night. He was blackmailing you, wasn't he?"

"He was going home after leaving the sub shop that night, and he saw me drive out of that alley. My luck, he was the only other driver on the road. I was going way too fast—I had to, to get away."

"But you didn't get away, did you?"

Stan swiped at his nose, which was pink and runny from the cold. "I thought I did, until a couple days later. I found a note on my car after school let out. It said, 'I saw what you did. Call this number, or I go to the cops.'" His eyes filled with misery. "It wasn't my fault, Carly. That drunk…he dropped right in front of me!"

"How did Ferris know it was you he saw? Did he get your plate number?"

"Only the first three numbers. But he spotted the parking sticker for the high school on my back window. He waited till school was in session, then searched the lot till he found a match."

"Why didn't you turn yourself in? Wouldn't that have been the logical thing?"

"No way. That would've meant jail time. My career, my whole life would've been ruined." He gave her a pleading look. "Try to understand, Carly. I was trapped."

"You were driving too fast, weren't you?" Carly kept her voice even, but inside she was shaking. "That's why you couldn't stop when you ran over that man."

"First off, that *man* was a known lowlife," he spat out. "And yes, I was driving too fast. I was angry. When I was in the pub, I'd tried to buy a drink for a woman who was sitting alone at a table. She looked at me like I was scum and told me to get lost. It freakin' ticked me off. After that I drank too many beers. I left there pretty buzzed."

"Why were you parked in the alley?" Carly asked him.

"That pub's kind of a dive, at least by Balsam Dell standards. In case one of my *illustrious* co-workers drove by, I didn't want them recognizing my car. I already had enough problems at school. The alley's more private."

"You stole Ari's work shoes and vampire cape so you could frame him, didn't you?" she accused.

He laughed. "Your boyfriend's sloppiness came in pretty handy. Leaving that stuff in his pickup where anyone could grab them was so dumb, especially those pricey work boots. But Ari's one of those types who probably trusts people, right? Who sees the good in everyone?" His lip curled with disgust. "I can't imagine what you ever saw in him."

Carly shivered. *I saw kindness, and honesty, and decency. Everything you lack.*

Stan's eyes took on a murky haze. "You don't get it, do you, Carly? With Ari out of our hair, you and I could have had something beautiful. Something lasting." He shook his head. "But you were a fool, and now you have to pay the price."

The thought of even touching Stan Henderson made Carly feel covered with bugs. "You're forgetting one thing, Stan. Ari had no motive. For that reason alone, he'll never be arrested."

Stan laughed. "You're wrong, Carly He did have motive. He witnessed Ferris verbally attacking you more than once. In the law's eyes, that's reason enough."

Carly stared at the man she'd known since grade school. The man who'd eaten at her restaurant so many times, shared his goals, praised her food. He'd seemed so normal, so congenial. Was there some clue she should have picked up on? Some subtle inkling that he would plot a man's death just to save his own skin?

"What about Evelyn Fitch, Stan? Did you push her down her cellar stairs?"

He gawked at her. "No! When Menard's daughter blabbed about the footprint on her father's chest that day, I saw the look on the old lady's face. Right then I knew—she remembered something I did as a kid and put two and two together. I figured she'd go to the cops, so I went over to her house to try to frighten her. I swear, I did *not* touch her! She was definitely afraid of something, though. She kept lifting the blind and looking out her window. I took advantage and popped my face up right in front of her. She screamed and I made a slashing motion across my throat. It was a warning, just in case she had any ideas about going to the cops."

But she didn't go to the police. She was afraid they wouldn't believe her. Instead, she counted on me to interpret her poems.

"After I heard about her accident, I worried for a while. But the cops never showed up to question me, so I figured I was home free. I'm hoping she doesn't even remember me scaring her that night, but that's what I'm here to find out. If she does remember…" He held up the knife and twisted it slowly. "I won't use the knife, though. I'll use a pillow. It'll look like she passed on quietly to her final reward."

The coldness in his eyes enraged Carly, and her gut churned with loathing. "Why did you start harassing me, Stan? What did I ever do to you? I thought we were… friends." She nearly choked on the word.

"You're too smart, Carly. That day my folder fell apart and you picked up that stupid withdrawal slip, I knew you'd eventually put it together. Especially since you were so buddy-buddy with old lady Fitch. How much did she tell you about me?" He fingered the knife absently.

Carly pictured a little boy, standing on a child's chest, crowing over his imagined conquest. *Look at me. I'm a flamingo…*

"Did you enjoy reverting to your childhood bullying days, Stan? Taunting Ferris by putting his pills just out of reach while you stood on his chest?"

His eyes glimmered. "Yeah, actually, I did. I also enjoyed slashing your boyfriend's tire. Just to add more stress to his day."

Loathing coursed through her. "You stole some of Evelyn's stationery, didn't you? You used it to write me a threatening note."

"A threatening poem," he corrected, then barked out a hollow laugh. "Yeah, when the old lady went to the can, I had the perfect opportunity. I tore a section right off her pink pad. Were you impressed with my poetry? It was Ms. Fitch who taught me the style."

"No, I wasn't," Carly ground out. "I'm not impressed by threats, or by cowardice."

"I have never been a coward," he hissed at her.

"Really? In my book only a coward runs over a man and then flees the scene."

Carly realized she'd pushed a dangerous button. She needed to dial it back, give herself time to figure a way out of this.

Slowly, she removed her hands from her coat sleeves and hugged her arms instead. The cold was beginning to numb her, but her brain was in overdrive. She glanced around, but there was still no sign of anyone within helping range. Two cars were driving slowly into the opposite end of the parking lot, but they didn't seem to be in a hurry.

"Don't bother looking for help, Carly. No one's around to save you. Your shining knight isn't going to rush in on his steed and rescue you. And if you utter one sound, this knife goes into your throat, so don't even try screaming for help."

"Okay," she whispered, feigning defeat. "I won't. Um, can…I have my phone back? I want to say goodbye to my mom."

"Yeah, you must think I'm stupid."

"No, Stan. You're far from stupid." *Evil, but not stupid.*

"And I'm getting really chilled. Can't we go into the building and talk about it? Maybe we can work out a compromise." *Like me turning you in and you going to prison.*

"Stop jabbering and let's get moving," Stan ordered. "My car, this time. I'm parked at the end of a row. You and I are going to walk there together, arm in arm like we're lovers." His eyes glittered at the thought.

Carly stifled a gag. "Stan, can't we talk first?"

"Sorry, Carly. Now that you figured out about Ferris, I'm afraid you'll have to follow in his footsteps." He laughed. "Hey, that was clever, wasn't it? *Footsteps.*" He held up the knife.

Carly put up both palms in a pleading gesture. "Stan, wait a minute. I want to show you the last poem Evelyn wrote. It's in my pocket and it's about you. It's actually kind of complimentary," she fibbed.

His eyelids flickered with suspicion. "She wrote a poem about me?"

"She did." Carly slid her left hand into her coat pocket. She tried to hide her triumph when her fingers curled around a slim metal tube.

And then, from across the parking lot, the powerful notes of a stunning tenor voice traveled through the air. Stan swiveled his head toward the sound, which seemed to be coming closer. "What the—is that someone's radio?"

The momentary distraction gave Carly the precious seconds she needed. Palming the canister, she removed her hand from her pocket. In the next instant, a towering clown with a vividly painted red and white face jogged out from between two parked cars and quickstepped toward Stan.

Stan's eyes widened in pure terror. He jabbed his knife

wildly at the clown, who continued singing at the top of his lungs as he closed the distance between them.

"Stan, look!" Carly screamed. When he jerked his head toward her, she sprayed the contents of the canister in his eyes.

Stan shrieked in pain. He dropped the knife, and it skittered under the SUV.

The clown grabbed him around the waist, swung him around, and tossed him to the pavement. Stan squirmed like a pinned bug, clawing at his own eyes and rolling around, his heels slapping the ground.

An army of helpers raced toward them, but one led the pack. Rhonda Hale Clark, wielding a golf club like a baseball bat, stomped toward Stan. "You touch my daughter and I'll pummel you into dust balls," she told him.

She was about to take a practice swing when the club was deftly removed from her grasp. "We'll take it from here Rhonda," Chief Holloway ordered. "Nice try, though."

Carly was too stunned, and too baffled, to speak. The clown, who looked six and a half feet tall, was helping the police subdue Stan.

"What did you squirt him with?" the chief asked her. "We're taking him to the hospital now."

Still reeling with shock, Carly gave him the canister. "Hair spray. I hardly ever use the stuff, but I dropped it in my pocket at the last minute in case I needed a touch-up. How did you know I was here?" Carly asked them, still bewildered by the chaos unfolding around her.

"You obviously took my advice and put me on speed dial," Rhonda gloated, after nearly squishing the insides out of her daughter. "When you called me, I knew immediately something was wrong."

"That call went through?" Carly was aghast. "You didn't say anything, so I wasn't sure."

"It certainly did. I turned up my hearing aids and you came through loud and clear. I knew where you were, but when I heard you say you were on your way to see the chief, and then a man's voice interrupted, I realized right away you were in trouble. I called out the cavalry, and...voilà!" She waved her manicured hand at the faces surrounding her. Two uniformed officers had joined the fray, as had Norah and Gary. The only person who wasn't a happy camper was the handcuffed man writhing on the ground. Stan spouted a cacophony of curses at the police as they escorted him to a patrol car.

With a light chuckle, Gary pressed his hand to the side of his mouth and in a faux whisper said, "She told me on the way over what she was going to do to the guy once she got her hands on him, but I can't repeat those words in polite company."

Carly laughed, and then she cried for the senseless loss of a life. Norah strode over to her on five-inch heels, squeezed her ferociously, and then shook her sister's shoulders. "What the heck's the matter with you, always cavorting with murderers?" She hugged her again, then took her hand and dragged her over to the clown, who wrapped his puffy-sleeved arm around Norah.

The clown was actually Nathaniel Carpenter, aka Norah's beau, Nate. He was, indeed, about six and half feet tall, with long-lashed amber eyes and a wide smile—although some of that might have been makeup.

"Let me guess," Carly said. "You're a professional opera singer, and you're starring in that famous opera that has a clown in it, the name of which I totally don't know."

"*I Pagliacci*," Nate supplied in lilting Italian, offering a white-gloved hand for her to shake. "I'm so happy to finally meet you, Carly, although I didn't expect all this high drama."

"Thank you for what you did today, Nate. Your timing couldn't have better." She glanced at Norah, who was beaming up at Nate as if he'd single-handedly strung the constellations.

"Nate hails from a long line of opera professionals," Norah said proudly. "His family bought that dilapidated old Flinthead farm near the highway. They restored it to pristine condition and made over the barn into a gorgeous opera house. Nate will be starring in *I Pagliacci* through the holiday season."

Carly snapped her fingers. "I saw an article about it in the weekly paper." Don Frasco had written about it in last week's edition, but she hadn't paid much attention to it. She'd been too focused on Ferris's murder and on the competition fiasco.

Norah looked at her phone and frowned. "Nate, honey, we're supposed to be there by four—you go on stage at five. What if the police hold us?"

"We'll be okay, sweetie," Nate soothed. "I'll have a word with the chief of police."

A few minutes later, they were allowed to leave, but not before Carly endured an excruciating lecture from Chief Holloway. "Be at the station first thing tomorrow morning," he finished, then he squeezed her shoulder. "Seriously, are you okay?"

"I think so, but you need to see this. Evelyn wrote it that night, before she fell down the stairs. Her daughter found it in her purse this morning, in a sealed envelope addressed to me." She removed the poem and the envelope from her pocket. "Check out the first letter of each line."

> Sheer tragedy befell the man
> That fate so cruelly took his breath
> Among the lies, the truth shines through
> No longer a secret from the world
> Listen to these words and read the truth, and
> Everything will turn out fine
> You carry the answer within you

Holloway looked stunned. "I still don't understand. How did she know Stan Henderson was the killer?"

"I don't think she knew for sure, but she made an educated guess." Carly explained what Lydia had told her about Stan's behavior as a child and how Evelyn had put the pieces together.

The chief blew out a frustrated breath. "I wouldn't exactly call that a smoking gun. Why didn't she just share her suspicions with the police?"

"With her history, she was probably afraid you wouldn't believe her. For what it's worth, Stan swore to me that he never went into her house the night she fell. He claims he only scared her through the window."

The chief folded the poem and stuck it in the envelope. "Go and enjoy the rest of your afternoon. You've done enough crime fighting for today. Thanks to you, I just scored four seats to the opera next Sunday. But if you ever go after a killer again, I'll lock you *and* the killer in adjoining cells. Permanently."

"I'll keep that in mind."

The chief lifted his gaze across the parking lot. "A black pickup just pulled in at the speed of sound. I'm tempted to give that driver a ticket for reckless driving."

"A pickup?"

A door slammed, and footsteps pounded toward them. Seconds later, in a whirlwind of motion, Ari swept Carly into his arms. "Thank heaven you're okay! I kept texting you, but you didn't answer. I finally reached Rhonda and she told me you were here!"

Carly squeezed him as tightly as she could, an overpowering warmth spreading through her. Ari kissed her long and hard. "I love you, Carly Hale."

"And I love you, Ari Mitchell."

Rhonda stared, open-mouthed, while Chief Holloway shot them a quick wave and trotted off. "Did I just hear what I thought I heard?" she warbled.

Carly didn't respond.

The only sound she heard was the beating of a heart that was totally, irrevocably in love.

CHAPTER THIRTY-FOUR

CARLY'S EVENING AT THE OPERA WAS A WELCOME AND wonderful change after the tumultuous aftermath of Ferris's murder. Nate portrayed Canio, the clown, brilliantly. After it ended, the audience clapped and cheered for several minutes before finally trickling out of the opera house.

Backstage, a spread worthy of a queen awaited them. The cast members remained garbed in their exquisite costumes, making Carly feel as if she'd been part of the performance herself.

Nate introduced everyone to his dad and his sister, both of whom had taken part in the performance. They dined on specialty cheeses, salads, meats, and wine—with a selection of pastries that looked as if they'd been flown in from Paris.

Norah looked radiant. Her face glowed with a deep contentment Carly had never seen in her sister before. And if the stars in Nate's eyes when he gazed at Norah were any indication, then each of them had truly found their soul mate.

Rhonda made the rounds. She sampled everything on the table as she rubbed elbows with the cast members. As she embarked on her second glass of wine, she regaled everyone with stories of Norah and Carly in their younger days. Her laughter and the twinkle in her eyes said it all—her daughters had each hit the jackpot.

That night, Ari drove Carly home. In the morning, he made sure she arrived at the police station without a trail of reporters hounding her.

Carly's interview on Monday with the state police was grueling, but it brought closure to all involved. The killer was in custody, and Ari was free from suspicion. In the end, it was a relief to have it over.

The restaurant was busier than ever, word having traveled through the local grapevine about Carly's role in catching a killer. Best of all, Suzanne was back to work. Her ankle was wrapped in an elastic bandage, but at least the clunky boot was gone. She hugged Carly and Grant and then declared, "I'm ready to roll. Start grilling those sandwiches!"

After the lunch rush dwindled, a face she hadn't seen in over a week strolled in. It was Don Frasco, his eyes and nose red and his face droopy.

"I wondered where you've been," she said, giving him a bottle of root beer from the cooler.

"I had the flu," he said sourly, twisting off the cap. He took a long swig of root beer. "Don't I still look sick?"

If he was looking for sympathy, Carly wasn't buying it. "You don't look like yourself, that's for sure, but probably not as bad as you think."

"The doctor said I'm not contagious anymore," Don admitted. "Did you see last week's spread?" His face brightened.

Carly smiled. "I sure did. I loved the photos, by the way. One of them gave me a clue as to how the voting got skewed last week. How did you manage to get the paper out on Thursday if you were sick?"

"It wasn't easy. My landlady's son helped me. I couldn't

pay him much, but he's only fourteen so he was happy with what he got. Anyway, wait till you see this week's paper," he said eagerly, his eyes dancing a bit. "Between Henderson's arrest and the new opera house, it's gonna be a bonus issue. I interviewed Teresa Gray this morning about how the votes got messed up, so that'll be in there too—although she's keeping mum about the culprits. I've actually surmised who they are, but I'm a reputable reporter. I would never print anything I couldn't confirm."

In Carly's view, it was a wise decision on Ms. Gray's part, and on the town's, not to reveal the wrongdoers' names. Tyler was facing dismissal by his boss, and rightfully so. Maybe that was punishment enough. As for Holly, Carly wasn't sure of her fate. She hoped Holly had learned something from getting caught up in her dad's deception. In the end, no one had gained a thing—Holly had only hurt herself.

Teresa Gray had stopped in to see Carly right after the restaurant opened. She had a bit of good news. After the valid votes were recounted, the competition ended in a tie between Carly's Grilled Cheese Eatery and Dot's Diggity Dogs. Each restaurant would be awarded half the prize money. Both Carly and the owner of Dot's had already decided to donate their share to the local food bank.

"Hey, Carly, how about an interview for this week's issue?" Don asked her.

Carly held up a hand. "I don't think so, but thanks—"

"Before you say no," he interrupted, "think about it! Once again, you were in the thick of things with a crazed killer." Don ran his hand in the air over an imaginary headline. "Second Time's the Charm for Local Restaurateur Turned Crime Fighter."

"That implies the first time wasn't the charm," she pointed out.

He shrugged. "Okay, so I'll come up with a different headline. How about I interview you right now?"

"How about this, instead," Carly suggested. "Since this week's issue is already a bonus issue, why don't we plan the interview for next week's, but without the dramatic introduction?"

Don cocked a finger at her. "I'll agree to that."

Grant came from behind the counter. With a big smile, he handed Don a brown paper bag. "Steamy hot tomato soup, on me. It'll cure what's left of your flu."

Carly's heart melted. Over the weekend, Grant had made the decision to attend culinary school next fall. To his folks' joy, he was also going to mentor music students at the college, in between working at Carly's. He was going to be one busy—and happy—young man.

"Hey, thanks, man," Don said. He gave Grant a fist bump on his shoulder.

After Don left, Carly thanked Grant and went into the kitchen. She and Suzanne shared their newest menu offering—Alvin's Panko Perfection. Grant's dad had been delighted at having a grilled cheese named in his honor, and Carly was officially adding it to the menu.

While they ate, Carly gave Suzanne a recap of the past week's trials and tribulations.

"I wish I could've been here to help," Suzanne groaned. "Maybe that stuff with poor Ms. Fitch wouldn't have happened." She popped a pickle chip into her mouth.

"Maybe. But in a way it helped lead us to the killer, so I'm not sure Evelyn would agree."

According to Chief Holloway, Stan's lawyer was already trying to finagle a plea deal. They'd learned that Stan had been fired from his job as guidance counselor—and not because the school's budget was being trimmed. His work had been substandard for quite some time, and parents had filed complaints.

"Did you ever get a chance to visit Ms. Fitch?" Suzanne asked.

Carly swallowed a bite of her sandwich. "Not yet, but Gina and I are going to pay her a visit some night later in the week. Her daughter told me her memory is starting to come back, and that she's very anxious to talk to me."

Suzanne swallowed her last bite and wiped her fingers with her napkin. "I officially predict that Alvin's Panko Perfection is going to be a customer favorite. Now, back to work. We have customers to serve!"

Carly felt her heart overflow with gratitude. Grant and Suzanne were the best co-workers she could ever imagine. When Thanksgiving week rolled around, she was going to give each of them as big a bonus as she could afford.

She was scooting back into the dining room when she heard her cell ping. She was surprised to see that it was from Holly.

I'm outside by your car. Can you spare a minute?

Carly slipped on her coat, signaled to Suzanne she'd be back in a minute, and scurried out through the back door. Holly was standing next to her Corolla.

"Hey," Holly said, flashing a tentative smile. Her wool jacket, which looked new, matched her lovely blue eyes.

"Hey yourself. How are things going?" Carly asked her.

"I'm okay. Listen, I wanted to let you know I met with my lawyer this morning. Alone," she emphasized.

"How did it go?"

"Actually, good. You were right about the DNA test. My biological grandfather is a man named Lawrence Kendall. Evidently, he's been watching out for Dad over the years—secretly of course. He'd bailed him out of trouble a bunch of times, especially when Dad was a teenager. It must've been hard knowing his only son couldn't be part of his life."

That explained a lot, Carly thought, remembering Lydia's complaint that Ferris had gotten away with a lot in high school. She suspected it was Lawrence Kendall who gave Chip Foster's mom a new car after the cruel prank Ferris played on her son.

"The best part is, Dad's lawyer already contacted him and he wants to meet me." Holly's cheeks flushed. "I hope he likes me. I mean, you know, after what I did. I gotta tell you, I'm a little scared."

"Holly, you made a mistake and you learned from it," Carly soothed. "Don't be so hard on yourself. Are you going to keep the sub shop?"

"I am, but I've decided to give it a total makeover. My dad's life insurance money will help." She laughed slightly, and her eyes lit up. "By the time I'm through, it'll be a whole new sandwich place. I might even change the name. Portia wants to partner with me, but since she's big on franchising, I think I'm going to decline. Don't get me wrong, she's a super person. I just don't think we'd be good business partners."

"I have faith in whatever choice you make," Carly said.

"After I left the lawyer's office today, I visited my grand-mother. Oh Carly, she was *sooo* happy to see me. Instead of doing a quickie visit, I stayed and chatted with her for quite a while. Sometimes her mind floats into the past, but that's okay. I know her days are numbered, so I want to spend as much time with her as I can."

"Gosh, that makes my day," Carly said sincerely.

Holly's voice softened. "Um, I also wanna thank you for what you did yesterday. It makes me sick to know that all this time, that Stanley Henderson guy was Dad's killer." She shuddered. "And to think I served him grilled cheese like he was a normal person."

Most killers seem normal, Carly thought. *Until they don't.*

"Thank you, but I'm just grateful it's over. I do have a question, though. That Sunday morning, when you found your dad, why did you go into the sub shop so early?"

Holly sighed. "I wanted to surprise him by getting most of the prep work done early. But I'd also planned to confront him when he came in about the way he treated me. I was going to tell him how wrong it was for him to use me and Tyler the way he did. I mean, yeah, we went along with it like idiots, but Dad shouldn't have put us in that position. Just because I was his daughter didn't mean I should have to prove my loyalty by doing his dirty work. I was essentially going to declare my independence." She lifted her chin slightly.

In that moment, Carly knew Holly was going to be okay. She was moving in the right direction and taking charge of her future.

"Thanks for explaining that," Carly said. "And before we both freeze out here, I'm going to let you go. Going forward, I wish you every good thing, Holly. I mean that."

Holly hugged her. "And *that* means a lot to me. Tootles for now. Let's keep in touch!"

CHAPTER THIRTY-FIVE

FIVE DAYS LATER, CARLY AND GINA WERE GATHERED with Lydia around Evelyn's bed at the rehab facility. Havarti was nestled in Evelyn's lap, his eyes closed in sheer ecstasy as his new friend stroked his fur.

Evelyn had regained most of her memory from that traumatic day, but parts were still a bit fuzzy. She'd also gained most of her color back, and the purplish bruise on her forehead was fading.

According to Lydia she was eating well. She was also anxious to return home, but her doctor at the facility wanted her to remain there a few more days as a precaution.

"That awful day in your restaurant," Evelyn told Carly shakily, "when I found out about the footprint on Ferris Menard's chest, I just knew...I *knew* it was Stanley. But how could I convince the police of that? They never believed me in the past." She gave her visitors a wry smile, then reached over and clasped her daughter's hand.

Lydia squeezed her mom's thin fingers. "Don't fret over it anymore, Mom. We can't change the past."

"When I think of that poor little Stanley as a child," Evelyn went on sadly, "it just squeezes my heart. He was so bright, and yet so determined to prove he was stronger, tougher than other boys. Even though I was only a summer volunteer, I filed an incident report the day he beat up that other child. In my mind I can still see him—standing on that boy's chest like he'd just conquered the world." She held out her thin arms as if to demonstrate.

Gina pressed a hand to her own chest and winced. "Even picturing that in my head hurts."

"The school district replied with a letter," Evelyn continued, "thanking me for my involvement. They'd planned to set up a meeting with Stanley's parents, but that was the last I ever heard from the school." She shook her head. "Truth be told, I don't think the parents were cooperative."

Carly mulled over Evelyn's story, trying to piece it together. "Is that what you were looking for the night you fell? The letter from the school?"

"Exactly," Evelyn said, "along with a copy of my incident report. I knew it was in that plastic storage box. I foolishly tried to use the second stair from the bottom as a step stool, and…well, the rest, as they say, is history."

"Were you going to show it to the police?" Gina asked her.

"I was, although I knew they'd probably dismiss it as coincidence. Circumstantial, is that what they call it?"

Carly nodded. "Sadly, that's probably what they'd have said. Especially since it happened so long ago."

"Almost twenty-five years," Evelyn confirmed, her eyes sparkling. "But that's why I wrote that poem to you, Carly. I had faith you'd figure it out, even if the police didn't believe me. You have a clever way of fitting the clues together. I was going to give it to you the next day at your restaurant, but I never made it there."

"Those papers we found on your kitchen table," Gina asked, "were those your practice notes?"

"Exactly," Evelyn said, "I always write out my thoughts before I complete a poem. I meant to throw them away, but I never got the chance."

"So, Evelyn," Carly said, "Stanley was telling me the truth when he said he never touched you?"

"That's right." Evelyn pulled her lavender cardigan more tightly around her. "But he did scare me half to death with that...that awful throat-slashing motion. I'll never forget his face in the window that night. It was...*manic* is the only word I can think of."

Gina looked at Carly with pain in her eyes, then reached over and gave her an impulsive hug. "He almost killed you."

"I know, but it's over and I'm safe." She didn't want her friend to know how terrified she'd been that day.

"Isn't it strange," Evelyn said to Carly. "All those days Stanley Henderson sat in your restaurant in the booth next to mine, he never acknowledged he remembered me."

"But you knew him, right, Mom?" Lydia asked her.

She let out a sigh and nodded. "And I didn't acknowledge him either. I think now that was a mistake. Maybe if I'd shown him some kindness, he might have gone to the police and confessed to the hit-and-run when it happened. Then he wouldn't have felt compelled to kill Ferris Menard to keep his secret safe."

"I doubt that, Mom, but let's not dwell on it," Lydia said. Her face brightened, and she smiled at Carly and Gina. "We haven't told you our good news. Mom's going to sell the house and move in with me."

Carly and Gina both squealed, "Yay!" at the same time.

Evelyn clasped her hands with delight. Havarti joined

in the celebration by licking her fingers. "Lydia is going to transform her den into a cozy room for me. My writing desk will go right under the window, where I can gaze out over the fields and the forest beyond."

"I'm so happy for you, Evelyn." Carly beamed at her.

"I should have done it long ago," Evelyn admitted. "I was clinging to my last shred of independence, but I know now that was my foolish ego talking. Now I'll have my own private space, and I won't be alone at night. With the money I get from selling my house, I can do some serious decorating." She winked at the women, and they all laughed.

"I can't wait till you come back to my restaurant, Evelyn. I'm going to make you the best grilled cheese you ever had."

"Oh, I'll look forward to that," Evelyn gushed.

"Hey, Carly, aren't you forgetting?" Gina tapped her friend's arm and pointed to her tote.

"Oh! I brought you a gift." Carly removed a wrapped package with a card attached and gave it to Evelyn. "Gina special ordered it for me and put a rush on it."

Evelyn's face glowed. She read the card, then opened the wrapping. Inside was a set of gorgeous pink stationery, complete with a fancy pen.

"Oh, the poems and letters I can write on this! Thank you so much, Carly. What a dear friend you are—both of you." She reached over and squeezed each of their hands.

Evelyn was also never going to pay for a grilled cheese again, but Carly would let her know that little secret when the time came.

Over the past week, Carly had made some other decisions. The eatery was thriving enough now that she needed extra help—someone who could step in and manage things in her absence. It would also allow her to spend more time with Ari, something they'd both been wanting to do.

Carly had already offered Grant the assistant manager position, but he'd graciously declined, as she knew he would. Suzanne had also turned her down. Although she loved her job, being Carly's part-time server suited Suzanne nicely. It allowed her to spend quality time with her husband and son and still contribute to her household.

So, the hunt was on for an assistant manager. Carly wasn't sure where to begin, but she was keeping her fingers crossed that she'd find the ideal candidate.

As for Portia's "sample pack" of salad dressings, she and Grant had tested them and found them wanting. But it had given Carly an idea. The eatery was now going to offer a side salad with fresh greens, blended with an herb dressing Grant was currently perfecting.

At Carly's request, Chip Foster had stopped in the day before. After graciously accepting her apology, he'd celebrated his new job as an inventory clerk for a local chain store with a "plain grilled cheese," courtesy of Carly. His days of hauling compost bins in and out of restaurants were over.

A young aide came by wheeling a cart. "Would anyone like juice?" she said sweetly. "We have cranberry, orange, grape—"

"Yes!" Evelyn cried. "Let's all have grape juice and pretend it's wine. We can drink to all the good things awaiting us in the future!"

The giggling aide poured them each a glass, and the women held them up in a toast.

"Here's to the best friends I could ever imagine," Evelyn said, her eyes growing moist. "May our futures be filled with sunshine, and may love blossom and grow." She smiled, rubbed Havarti's furry head, and with a sly wink at Carly and Gina took a sip of her "wine."

Gina's full cheeks flushed, while Carly slugged back a mouthful of grape juice.

A face flashed in Carly's mind.

Dark-brown eyes, an adorable mustache, a whoppingly sexy smile…

Carly lifted her glass again in another toast, this time a silent one. As if reading her thoughts, Havarti perked his ears. He gazed into her face with his doggy version of a grin.

Carly knew exactly what he was thinking.

Right on, Mom! I heartily agree.

Read on for a look at
Linda Reilly's next cheesy mystery

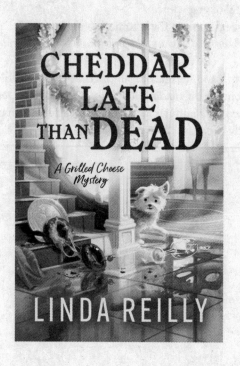

CHEDDAR
LATE
THAN DEAD

A Grilled Cheese Mystery

LINDA REILLY

CHAPTER ONE

THE DOOR TO CARLY'S GRILLED CHEESE EATERY OPENED on a *whoosh* of frigid air. Two women entered, and after shoving the door closed against the January cold, they stomped their boots on the mat.

Carly Hale, owner of the eatery, flipped over the Sweddar Weather she was preparing and peeked over the grill at the pair. The women, both around her own age, looked familiar. Had they graduated from high school with her? She thought they had, but after sixteen years, their names were eluding her.

"Oh gosh, it's adorable in here!" the shorter woman chirped, sweeping her gaze over the pale, exposed brick walls and the cozy booths upholstered in aquamarine vinyl. Wearing fuzzy white earmuffs that matched her ski jacket, she turned to her companion with a pout. "Dawn," she said in a girlish whine, "why didn't we come in here sooner?"

Dawn, who topped her friend's height by at least half a foot, shoved back the hood of her puffy, purple coat. "Because you've been on a diet for almost a year, remember?" she said, a touch of tartness in her tone. "You told me not to let you near this place until *after* your wedding. I was only following orders."

Dawn. Yes! Now Carly remembered them—Dawn Chapin and Klarissa Taddeo. In high school they'd been an inseparable pair. Klarissa the bubbly one with sparkling blue eyes and loose, titian-colored curls. Dawn, the quieter and more serious of the two, with hazel eyes and sculpted cheekbones, her straight brunette hair barely brushing the tops of her thin shoulders.

Carly handed over her spatula to her new assistant manager, Valerie Wells. "I want to say hello to these gals. Take over for me?"

Valerie smiled. "You betcha!"

Carly had barely made it around to the other side of the counter when Klarissa let out a squeal. "Carly Hale, is that you?" She rushed toward her and threw her arms around her, mindless of the remnants of snow she was pressing into Carly's green knit sweater.

Carly hugged her in return. "Klarissa, you look great. I haven't seen you in so long!"

"I know. It's been like, *forever*, hasn't it?"

"Hey, Carly." Dawn leaned in for a brief hug, then brushed wet flakes from her coat sleeves. "Sorry about the snow."

"Oh heck, this is Vermont," Carly said with a smile. "We expect snow to sneak in with our guests. Can I seat you in the booth at the back? It's close to the heat register so it's nice and cozy."

"We'll take it!" Klarissa pulled off her earmuffs and slid into the booth. Shiny auburn curls spilled around her face and onto her shoulder.

Dawn settled in opposite her friend, then shrugged off her coat and set her gloves down on the bench seat. Carly gave them menus. After taking their orders and delivering their hot chocolates, she went back behind the grill.

"Old friends of yours?" Valerie asked. Her brunette

topknot bounced slightly when she worked, which always seemed to be at warp speed. She slid a grilled cheese onto a plate next to a cup of tomato soup and a pickle.

Carly tucked her friends' orders on the strip above the grill. "Yup. I went to high school with them, although I haven't laid eyes on them since graduation." Carly delivered the sandwich plate to the elderly man seated at the counter. "Thank you kindly," he said.

Carly had lucked out the day she interviewed Valerie for the assistant manager position. She'd been looking for a responsible helper, someone who could take over the reins for her when she was out of the restaurant, and also feel comfortable in the role. In less than five weeks on the job, the fortysomething Valerie had already proven herself. It was obvious to Carly that a gem had landed in her lap.

Suzanne Rivers, Carly's part time server, came through the swinging door from the kitchen. In her hands was a covered, stainless-steel bowl. The mom of a boy in grade school, Suzanne had been with Carly from opening day, nearly a year ago. Another lucky find.

"More tuna," Suzanne announced, shoving the bowl into the mini fridge under the counter. "Seems like everyone's on a protein kick today."

"Must be the cold," Carly said, laughing. Her Farmhouse Cheddar Sleeps with the Fishes, the eatery's version of a tuna melt, had gained a sudden popularity.

When Klarissa's and Dawn's lunches were ready, Carly delivered them to their table. Klarissa had removed her gloves, displaying the colossal marquis diamond glittering on her left ring finger. Her gold-toned cell phone sat in front of her.

Carly set down their plates—a Vermont Classic for Dawn and a Smoky Steals the Bacon for Klarissa. "Beautiful ring," she commented to Klarissa. "Did I hear someone say you have a wedding in your future?"

Klarissa sat up straighter and wiggled her hand under the lights. A girlish flush colored her porcelain cheeks. "I do, in five weeks. I'm a very lucky woman, Carly."

"Congratulations," Carly said. "I wish you all the best."

Klarissa's glossy pink lips curved into a frown. "My shower is supposed to be a week from Saturday, if that idiot at the Balsam Dell Inn ever confirms it. You can't imagine the problems we've had with that place, Carly." She picked up a sandwich half and shoved a corner into her mouth. Her blue eyes lit up like tree bulbs. "This is what I've been missing," she said, after she'd barely swallowed. "I can't wait till I'm officially Mrs. Tony Manous so I can start eating normal food again!"

Dawn glanced over at her friend but said nothing. She took a dainty bite of her sandwich.

"I'll let you gals enjoy your lunches," Carly said, mulling over the name. Tony Manous. She'd heard it before, but where?

Carly went through the swinging door into the kitchen. The familiar aroma of tomatoes and basil and—something else?—swirled around her. Grant Robinson, her other grill cook and a budding chef, was preparing another batch of his hearty tomato soup.

He grinned at her, his dark brown eyes twinkling. He'd been growing out his short dreads, and, in Carly's opinion, was getting handsomer every day. "You detected a new herb, didn't you? I can see it on your face." He gently stirred the large pot that was simmering on the stove.

Carly closed her eyes and inhaled. "It's...darn, I can't put my finger on it." She pinned him with a look. "Come on, don't keep me in suspense."

"It's thyme," he said. "Just enough to tantalize the senses but not overpower the soup."

"Mmm. I can't wait to taste it."

From the dining room, the musical ringtone from a cell phone filtered through the swinging door. It was the 'Wedding March'.

"Someone's getting married," Grant commented.

"Two old acquaintances of mine from high school came in for lunch," Carly explained. "One of them is engaged. You should see the rock she's wearing."

Grant shrugged. "Won't be long, you'll be wearing one of those." He gave the pot another stir.

Carly felt a flush creep up her neck. "It's way too soon for that," she said firmly. "Ari and I are taking our time, as every couple should." She wasn't sure she believed that, but it sounded good. It was her current mantra, anyway.

Truth be told, she'd been spending most of her free time lately with Ari Mitchell, the electrician who'd installed the pendant lighting in her eatery. Their relationship had blossomed over the summer and deepened during the holiday season. On New Year's Eve they'd celebrated as a committed couple, much to the delight of Carly's mom, Rhonda Hale Clark. Rhonda was currently on vacay in Florida with her hubby, Gary, but she was itching for Carly to start sporting a diamond.

But that day, if it came, was in the distant future.

Retrieving a container of grated cheddar from the commercial fridge, she was picturing Ari Mitchell's adorable face when an angry voice erupted from the dining room. Carly set the container on the worktable and hurried out.

As she'd guessed, the commotion was coming from Klarissa's table. Klarissa's face had gone raspberry red, and she was shrieking into her cell. "Then you'd just better find a way to accommodate me," she threatened. "Otherwise, no one in the Taddeo family will ever patronize your moldy old inn again!"

Dawn reached over and touched her friend's arm in a calming motion. "Take it easy, and stop overreacting," she pleaded quietly. "Let me talk to her, okay?" She wiggled her fingers in a *give me the phone* motion.

Klarissa slammed her cell phone into Dawn's palm. "This is all your fault, so you'd better make it right," she ordered, and then took another massive bite of her sandwich.

Doing her best to appear she wasn't eavesdropping, Carly busied herself clearing the table behind theirs. A few patrons sitting in the front booths had turned their heads to see what was happening. Rather than looking annoyed, they appeared to be enjoying the verbal tussle.

Carly listened as Dawn spoke calmly into the phone.

"I'm sorry, I know we didn't bring the check over on time," Dawn said patiently, "but your assistant led us to believe you would hold the date for us. And remember, it was she who did the booking." She listened for a moment, and then her eyes closed. "All right, thank you. I can see we're not getting anywhere." She disconnected the call and set the phone on the table. She shook her head. "They won't budge, Klar. I told you we needed to get that check over there by the first, didn't I?"

Klarissa's fist closed on the table. "How. Dare. You.

Blaming me for *your* sloppiness. You're the wedding planner, and you're my maid of honor. This is all your fault."

Concerned over the mounting tension, Carly sidled over to their table. She spoke quietly. "Ladies, I couldn't help overhearing. Is there anything I can do to help?" She didn't seriously think there was, but she hoped her offer might calm Klarissa and get them to stop yelling in her eatery.

"I'm afraid not," Dawn said dismally, "unless you have connections at the Balsam Dell Inn. They doubled booked the date of Klarissa's shower, and now we're fresh out of luck." She looked apologetically at her friend. "You're right, Klarissa," she said meekly. "This is my fault. But now we have less than two weeks, and I have no idea how to fix my mistake."

For several scary moments, Klarissa went silent. Then a sudden gleam shone in her blue eyes, and her lips curved into a smile. "I do. We'll have my shower at your mother's house. It'll be perfect!"

Dawn's mouth opened in surprise. "What? Klar, that's crazy. Thirty women will be attending the shower. Where will they all go?"

"In that vast drawing room, of course," Klarissa said airily. "Oh, Dawn, it'll be perfect. You'll have to arrange for table and chair rentals, of course, and someone will need to decorate."

"But...but we'd need a caterer," Dawn said, getting rattled now. "There's no way we can find one at this short notice. It's literally like, twelve days away."

Klarissa sat back against the booth, an impish smile on her lips. "Well, I can think of the perfect caterer. Carly, didn't you just offer to help?"

Carly nearly choked. She hadn't meant *that* kind of help.

"Klarissa, I'm...honored that you would consider me," Carly told her. "The thing is, I'm not a caterer. I run a small restaurant with a particular specialty. I wouldn't have a clue how to cater a shower."

Actually, that was a fib. She *did* have a clue, sort of.

Half a lifetime ago, or at least that's how it felt, Carly was working as restaurant manager at a historic inn in northern Vermont. One of her favorite employees had gotten engaged, and Carly had eagerly offered to host the bridal shower. From the sumptuous array of food to the decadent champagne cake, the shower had been a huge success—and a total blast.

Hard to believe that was only five years ago. Three years later, Carly would lose her husband, Daniel, to a tragic accident. It was months before she got her life back on track. She sold their small home and returned to southern Vermont, to her beloved hometown of Balsam Dell.

"You have an odd look on your face," Klarissa said, waving her beringed hand in front of Carly.

Carly shook off her memories. "Sorry, my brain went off on a tangent. Klarissa, I'd love to help, but like I said, I've never done any catering." That much, at least, was true.

Ignoring Carly's protests, Klarissa pointed a manicured finger at her maid of honor. "Donuts. Remember? They'd be perfect. I'll bet no one's ever served them at a wedding shower before!"

Dawn groaned and gave up a weak smile. "Grilled cheese donuts. Leave it to you to remember." She looked at Carly and explained. "We saw grilled cheese donuts at a diner in Maine last summer. Klar was already in high diet mode—determined to squeeze into a size eight wedding gown—so instead of trying one, she plunked them onto her bucket list. Her *post-wedding* bucket list."

Grilled cheese donuts.

Carly had heard of them, but she'd never made one. She had to admit, the idea held a certain appeal. They weren't for everyone, but for sure they'd have some takers.

"It's an interesting idea," Carly said. "I hope you find someone who can cater for you, Klarissa. With my schedule, I can't possibly plan a menu for thirty plus people in such a short time."

As if Carly had turned suddenly invisible, Klarissa aimed a forefinger at Dawn. "It's your fault we lost the Inn, Dawn, so call your mom right now and firm it up with her. I came up with the solution. Now it's your job to make it work."

Dawn's expression hardened, and her slim nostrils flared. She dug out her cell phone from the pocket of her puffy coat and began tapping away.

Klarissa swerved her legs around in the booth and jumped up to squeeze Carly in a hug. "I just knew you'd save the day, Carly. And think what a feather in your cap this is going to be!"

"Wait a minute," Carly pleaded. "I'm not a caterer. You need to find someone who—" She halted midsentence, stilled by the look of desperation on Dawn's thin face.

Over Klarissa's shoulder, Dawn held up her hands in a praying motion. *Please*, she mouthed silently.

I guess I'll be catering a wedding shower, Carly thought wryly. *And with grilled cheese donuts, no less.*

CHAPTER TWO

CARLY WAS SURPRISED AT HOW LITTLE SHE'D HAD TO negotiate with Dawn on the pricing. In truth, she'd felt bad for her, but she still had to charge for her time, the supplies, and for recruiting Grant to help with creating grilled cheese donut recipes. Even after adding a surcharge for the short notice, Dawn had readily agreed to her quote. As for the double-booking mess, Dawn had hinted to Carly that there was more to that story, but hadn't explained any further.

One thing Carly had insisted on was a tour of the area where she'd been doing the food prep. Sissy's Bakery, a favorite of Carly's, had agreed to supply the donuts for the grilled cheese sandwiches. Since they'd also be preparing the massive cake—a delectable raspberry concoction that was Klarissa's favorite—everything would be delivered on the morning of the shower.

On Sundays Carly's restaurant was closed, leaving her one day a week for personal chores and relaxation, whatever that might entail. Today she'd be spending her Sunday after-noon visiting the Chapin home and consulting with Dawn on the shower details. Not exactly the relaxation she'd hoped for.

Her thoughts drifting, Carly wondered how her mom was faring back at her old stomping grounds, as Rhonda referred to her former Vero Beach neighborhood. Rhonda and Gary had moved to Florida shortly after they were married, but one too many stray alligators and a particularly bad bug season had sent Rhonda almost virtually screaming into the night. She told Gary they were moving back to southern Vermont, and that was the end of their Florida experiment. A yearly visit to the friends they'd made there was enough for her.

Meanwhile, Carly had Klarissa's shower to plan for. Dawn had agreed to give her a tour of both the kitchen and the drawing room ahead of the event. She'd even emailed Carly a preliminary sketch of how the tables would be arranged and asked if she had any suggestions. Impressed with the precision and detail of the sketch, Carly had nothing to add.

After three days of on and off snowfall, the roads of Balsam Dell were finally plowed clean. Sunlight glittered off the piled-high snowbanks, making the town center resemble a winter wonderland.

The ride to the Chapin home was a short one. Perched on a gentle hill overlooking a vast, snow-coated field, the mansion was impressive even from a distance. The private road leading to the house had been meticulously plowed and sanded, allowing for easy navigation by Carly's aging Corolla.

As Carly drew closer, her eyes widened. The house was stunning.

Surrounded by wraparound porches swept clean of snow, its five brick chimneys jutted out from the expansive roof, puffing out wisps of whitish smoke. The house itself was white, the shutters black. The mansion seemed to sprawl the length of a football field, but that might have been an illusion. At one end, an octagon-shaped porch rested beneath a second porch that extended out from one of the upper rooms. The master bedroom, Carly guessed.

She was maneuvering her car around the circular drive when Dawn emerged from the front door and onto the wide porch. Dawn motioned her to a cleared area off to the side where she could park.

"Hey," Carly said with a smile, treading carefully up the steps. "It's great to see you. I'm looking forward to my tour."

"I am too." Dawn's thin face looked drawn and pasty, her hazel eyes underscored with dark pouches. Carly could only imagine the kind of stress she was under.

Dawn led her through the front entrance and into the marbled foyer. On the left, at the back, was an elegant, half-turn staircase with an elaborately carved handrail. It reminded Carly of something out of a fairy tale.

"You can leave your boots right here," she said, waving an arm at the floor. "Astrid will take your outerwear."

As if by magic, a short, stocky woman with straw-like hair appeared, her smile wide and her arms outstretched. She wore a long-sleeved fleece shirt over navy slacks and a pair of flat, rubber-soled shoes. "I'll hang these in the coatroom," she said in a sweet voice. "They'll be nice and toasty when you leave."

"Thank you," Carly said, handing over her coat and gloves.

The woman nodded and shuttled off, disappearing through a doorway on the right side of the foyer.

Carly was glad she'd thought to bring along a pair of loafers. It wouldn't do to tromp around this gorgeous mansion in her clunky rubber boots.

After slipping on her shoes, she followed Dawn into

a cheery dining room. Slanted rays of sunlight streamed through the tall windows, casting tiny parallelograms on one papered, cream-colored wall. An oak table surrounded by eight curved chairs sat beneath a chandelier crafted from blue and white porcelain. In the center of the table, a cut crystal vase boasted a cluster of pale-blue hydrangeas, artfully arranged with what looked to Carly like sprigs of baby's breath. A mild floral scent permeated the room, a blend of lilac and vanilla. The decor was simple, yet elegant—not as fussy as Carly had expected.

"Your home is absolutely beautiful, Dawn," Carly said. "And that flower arrangement is gorgeous."

Dawn smiled. "Thanks, but it's my mother's home, not mine. As for the flowers, Klar's Auntie Meggs takes care of all our floral displays. It's kind of a side gig of hers. She and my mother have been friends since they were kids."

"So, your family and Klar's go back a long way?"

"You could say that."

Carly noticed an open doorway leading to another room, adjacent to where she was standing. Too nosy to resist, she stepped toward the entryway and sneaked a peek.

Unlike the airy dining room, this room was defined by dark paneling, Persian carpets, and heavy leather chairs. Brocade curtains hung from the soaring windows, blocking out most of the natural light. Two tall vases, ornately painted, bracketed a massive stone fireplace. In the center of the mantel, a large crystal vase held a cluster of red roses. Framed photos of sleek aircraft covered nearly one entire wall.

"That vase on the mantel is gorgeous," Carly commented. "Even from here I can see that it's engraved, but I can't make out what the engravings are."

Dawn smiled. "That crystal vase is one-of-a-kind. It was commissioned by my granddad from a glassmaker in France who created utterly unique pieces. Those lovely engravings you noticed are swallows. For him, swallows represented the freedom he felt when he was flying his jet planes. And per his strict instructions, that vase never leaves this room." She turned to Carly, the adoration in her eyes almost palpable. "He had an exact duplicate made for my grandmother, only hers was a perfume bottle."

"That sounds beautiful. Was your dad a pilot, too?"

"No, only my granddad was. But Dad loves that room. It's his haven when he's around, which is almost never," Dawn added tartly. "Technically my folks are divorced, but Dad has visiting rights. When he's here, he purposely smokes cigars in there to irritate my mother. We've taken to calling it the smoking room." Her lips twisted in a mild smirk. "Come on, I'll show you the kitchen."

Carly followed Dawn along another hallway. "Is your mom home?"

"She's around somewhere," Dawn said flatly. "She wasn't exactly thrilled about hosting the shower, but, as they say, duty calls."

Interesting comment, Carly thought. Did that mean Mrs. Chapin felt obligated in some way to Klarissa? Or did Dawn herself feel duty-bound to fix the mess created when the Balsam Dell Inn date fell through? She was mulling the question when suddenly they were standing in the most fabulous kitchen Carly had ever seen.

Stainless-steel appliances dominated, from the gargantuan refrigerator to the eight-burner Wolf stove, complete with double ovens and a griddle. A sink occupied one end of the granite island, the lower half of which was stacked with oversized pots. The wall behind the stove was white brick, a display of vintage blue Delft plates resting on the soffit along the top. If Carly had a kitchen like this, she'd want to live in it forever.

"My gosh, this kitchen is like something out of a dream. Is this where I'll be working?"

For the first time since Carly had arrived, Dawn actually looked pleased. Her smile was genuine, and her eyes bright. "It is. I had a feeling you'd approve." She aimed a hand at the stove. "The griddle is large enough to grill at least ten sandwiches at a time. We have two massive warming trays, which we'll set up in the drawing room, where the guests will be eating. Astrid will help you with anything you need, plus she'll do all the cleanup afterward."

"That's very nice of her, but I don't mind cleaning up after myself." She laughed. "I'm used to it."

Dawn waved a dismissive hand. "That's okay. She's looking forward to it. Will any of your helpers be with you?"

Carly shook her head. "No, I can't spare anyone, especially on a Saturday. Luckily, I have a terrific assistant manager. She'll handle everything at the eatery in my absence."

"Okay, then. Why don't you have a look around the kitchen, be sure it has everything you need?"

Carly did so, and after a few minutes was completely satisfied. "I can't think of anything I'll need to bring, except any food that's not being delivered."

"Excellent," Dawn said. "Would you like to see the drawing room now?"

Once again, Carly trailed in Dawn's wake. They passed through a small room that appeared to be a breakfast nook.

A microwave, a toaster, and a set of flowered canisters rested on a counter opposite the table. Even without a window to the world, it was cozy and inviting. Beyond that was a pantry, where painted white shelves were jam-packed with foodstuffs and enough bottled water to last till the next millennium.

They made their way along a series of short hallways. If Carly lived here, it would probably take her a month to learn the layout. When they finally reached the drawing room, she had to stifle a gasp.

The walls were painted a dark teal, the wood trim a rich gold. A brick fireplace dominated one wall, its mantel adorned with two large porcelain vases, one at each end. Between the vases was an ornate, gold-leaf mirror.

"These chairs and side tables are being removed temporarily," Dawn explained, indicating the gorgeously upholstered wing-back chairs and cherrywood end tables. "Our RSVPs are all in, and the final head count is twenty-eight." She explained the seating, and where the food and beverages would be set up.

"I'm…in awe," Carly said, gazing around with a grin. "No wonder Klarissa wanted her shower here."

They left the room through a different doorway. Carly realized they'd made a circle that had landed them back in the foyer.

Dawn's lips pursed, and she moved closer to Carly. "Carly, can I ask you something? In confidence?"

"Sure, you can."

"You remember what Klar was like in high school, right? She was outgoing and fun, but always kind to everyone."

"She was," Carly agreed, sensing a "but" coming. "We were never close, but I always liked her."

Dawn crossed her arms over her chest. "Ever since she met Tony Manous, she's become a different person. And not in a good way, either."

"What do you mean?" Carly asked.

"She's gotten snappy, impatient. Like she's better than everyone else, you know? You heard the way she sniped at me in your restaurant. Like I was her...*servant*. I was mortified."

Carly had been, too, but she'd chalked it up as a temporary aberration.

"Maybe it's just bridezilla syndrome," Carly suggested. "I've heard it happens to the most mild-mannered of brides-to-be."

"I only wish that was the case." Dawn sniffled and her eyes misted. "Don't mind me. I'm a mess these days."

"Oh Dawn, I'm so sorry," Carly said gently. "I didn't realize any of this was happening. Tony's name sounds familiar. Is he a local guy?"

"A local *jerk*," Dawn said. "He's head of the town's Grounds and Recreation Department. Loves to show off his muscular bod in his official green polo shirt and tight khaki pants." She rolled her eyes in disgust.

Carly remembered, now, where she'd seen his name—in the town's most recent annual report.

"Have you shared your feelings with Klarissa?" Carly asked her. "Not about Tony, but about the way she treats you?"

"I tried to, once, but she laughed it off. She said that one day, when I'm in love with a wonderful man like Tony, I'll understand how she feels." Dawn swallowed, a deep sadness filling her eyes. "It doesn't matter anymore. After she and Tony move to North Carolina, I'll probably never see her again. At one time the thought crushed me, but now…I'm actually glad she'll be out of my life."

"They're moving?" Carly was surprised.

"Tony landed a job as head greenskeeper at one of the big country clubs down there. *Very* prestigious, according to him. I guess a big salary goes with it. The club where he'll be working is on the PGA tour, so a lot of the pros play there. If there's anything Tony loves, it's rubbing elbows with the stars," she said gratingly. "He and Klarissa already rented a condo near the golf club."

"But what about Klarissa's job?" Carly said, then realized she had no idea where Klarissa worked.

"She's an aesthetician at the spa that opened in Bennington a few years ago," Dawn explained. "According to her, getting another job in that field will be a breeze."

"Wow. That's a lot of change in a short time. How do Klarissa's folks feel about her moving?"

Dawn blotted her eyes with her fingertips. "Her dad's remarried and lives in Toronto, so he rarely sees her anyway. Her mom's disappointed, but it's her aunt Meg who's really bummed. Klarissa and Auntie Meggs are like this." She held up two fingers and overlapped them.

Carly squeezed Dawn's arm. "I'm so sorry you have to go through all this. I can see you're struggling."

"Don't be sorry." Dawn gave up a tepid smile. "You're the one who saved my bacon, so to speak. I'll never forget what you did to rescue this shower for me."

"I'm glad I could help," Carly said, although she was beginning to wonder what she'd gotten herself into.

"If Klar had let me book the date at the Inn weeks ago like I told her," Dawn said through clenched teeth, "we wouldn't be here right now. I'm a wedding planner, for glory's sake! I know how these things work. But *nooo*. She loves to wait until the last minute, then expects everyone to do her bidding. It's like a control thing, you know? Only this time she got fooled, and I took the heat for it."

Carly nodded. She knew the type. Except that she'd have never guessed Klarissa Taddeo was one of them.

"To be totally honest, I *am* going to miss her," Dawn admitted. "We've been BFFs since we were kids. I guess now we'll have to drop the *forever* part, won't we?" With that, she burst into tears.

Feeling helpless and more than a little awkward, Carly hugged her and patted her back. "You'll feel different after the wedding," she soothed. "Once they settle into their new digs, I bet you'll be flying down to visit her."

Dawn pulled away. "No, I won't," she said bitterly, her face streaked with tears. "I won't even be invited." She lifted her gaze to meet Carly's, her eyes filled with pain. "I want my old friend back, Carly. And that's never going to happen as long as Tony Manous is in the picture."

RECIPES

AFTER NINE MONTHS IN BUSINESS, CARLY IS UP TO HER elbows in cheese! She and Grant have created some scrumptious new sandwich recipes—one of which is the brainchild of Grant's dad.

Carly's original eatery recipes remain customer favorites, but as she always advises—make your grilled cheese your way. Don't hesitate to combine cheese varieties or select unusual breads. Great sandwiches are made from inspired combinations. Your taste buds will thank you!

ALVIN'S PANKO PERFECTION

Carly was surprised and delighted when Alvin Robinson wanted to try his hand at creating his own grilled cheese recipe. Using panko crumbs to coat the tomato slices was creative and fun, and the result was a sandwich so delicious that Carly added it to her menu. Alvin used sharp cheddar, but as Carly always says—use whatever cheese tickles your palate! Havarti, Gouda, and Swiss all make fabulous substitutions.

This recipe is for one sandwich, so simply multiply the ingredients by the number of people you're serving.

Ingredients
Depending on the size of your bread, 4 to 6 thickly

sliced rounds (about ½ inch wide) of a firm, ripe
Roma or plum tomato
Salt
1 egg, beaten + 1 teaspoon water
About ¼ cup all-purpose flour
About ½ cup panko crumbs (Carly uses plain, but you
can also use seasoned panko)
About ¼ cup grated Parmesan cheese
Vegetable or canola oil
Salted butter, softened
2 large slices of coarse white bread
Sharp cheddar cheese—4 thick slices

Directions

1. Place the tomato slices on a plate, and then lightly salt
   both sides.

2. Place the beaten egg/water mixture and the flour in
   separate bowls.

3. Mix the panko crumbs and Parmesan cheese in a shallow dish.

4. Dip each tomato slice into the flour, coating both sides
   and shaking off any excess, then dip into the beaten
   egg mixture. Dredge each slice through the panko/
   Parmesan mixture until each side is thoroughly coated.

5. Fry the coated slices in a skillet with about ½ inch of
   very hot oil for about 2 minutes or until the bottom
   side forms a golden crust. Flip them *carefully* and do

the other side. When done, they should be golden and crispy. Blot them lightly on a paper towel.

6. To prepare your sandwich, butter one side of each slice of bread. On the unbuttered side of one slice, stack half the cheddar, then add the coated tomato slices side by side so that they cover the entire sandwich. Add the remaining cheddar and top with the remaining slice of bread, butter side up.

7. Grill over medium heat for about 3 minutes. As you grill, press lightly with a spatula or grill press, and then flip over and grill the other side for about approximately 3 minutes. Grilling slowly will ensure that the cheese is thoroughly melted and the bread is golden brown.

8. Slice in half and serve with chips, pickles, tomato soup, or whatever else gladdens your taste buds. For tomato lovers, this is a dream come true!

CARLY'S TIPS:

- After experimenting, Carly found that a skillet or frying pan works a bit better than grilling for frying the tomato slices.

- To avoid accidental burns, always be super careful when frying in hot oil. Kids and pets should be kept a safe distance away from the stove to avoid injury.

FARMHOUSE CHEDDAR SLEEPS WITH THE FISHES

The classic tuna melt has always been a favorite at Carly's eatery. For the bread, Carly uses ciabatta, an Italian artisan bread with a crisp crust and elongated shape. At the eatery, Carly prepares her tuna salad in large batches, but you can make enough for two sandwiches using the following ingredients.

Ingredients

- 1 (6-ounce) can of solid white albacore tuna packed in water, drained and flaked
- 1 tablespoon minced celery
- 1 tablespoon minced onion (Carly uses sweet onion)
- 2 tablespoons of mayonnaise
- ½ teaspoon spicy brown mustard (Omit this if you're not a fan of mustard!)
- A few sprinkles of black pepper, to taste
- 4 slices ciabatta bread
- ½ cup sharp cheddar cheese, shredded
- Salted butter, softened

Directions

1. In a bowl, thoroughly blend the first six ingredients, using a fork to break up the tuna flakes.

2. Lay out two slices of ciabatta, then divide the tuna mixture evenly over the slices.

3. Top each slice with half the shredded cheddar.

4. Butter one side of each of the remaining two slices, then place them, butter side up, over the grated cheddar.

5. Heat a large griddle or skillet to medium. Using a spatula, carefully turn each sandwich and place it butter side down in the skillet. Butter the top of each slice.

6. Grill over medium heat for about 3 minutes. As you grill, press lightly with the spatula or grill press and then flip over and grill the other side for about approximately 3 minutes. Grilling slowly will ensure that the cheese is thoroughly melted and the bread is golden brown.

7. Slice in half diagonally and serve with chips, pickles, tomato soup, or whatever else floats your tuna boat!

CARLY'S TIP:

- To save time, or if you don't enjoy making your own tuna salad, head to your favorite deli or market and buy it already prepared!

ACKNOWLEDGMENTS

Once again, I am overwhelmed with gratitude for the fabulous folks at Sourcebooks—from my superhero editor, Margaret Johnston, to the copy editors, to the marketing team, and so many more. Every one of you is a rock star in my book.

To my agent, Jessica Faust, who has been a guiding light all the way, thank you for never letting me lose the dream.

To Judy Jones, on whom I can always count for an honest and insightful critique, thank you for being there every step of the journey. To my fellow authors on the Cozy Mystery Crew, blessings for all your support and encouragement.

And to all those professionals who give dedicated care to my husband every day, I owe you a world of thanks.

ABOUT THE AUTHOR

© Amelia Koziol

As a child, author Linda Reilly practically existed on grilled cheese sandwiches, and today, they remain her comfort food of choice. Raised in a sleepy town in the Berkshires of Massachusetts, she retired from the world of real estate closings and title examinations to spend more time writing mysteries. A member of Sisters in Crime, Mystery Writers of America, and the Cat Writers' Association, Linda lives in southern New Hampshire with her husband and her cats. When she's not pounding away at her keyboard, she can usually be found prowling the shelves of a local bookstore or library, hunting for a new adventure. Visit her on the web at lindasreilly.com or on Facebook at facebook.com/Lindasreillyauthor. She loves hearing from readers!